PRAISE FOR MARIANA COSTA

"A tender, charming debut which entertains while masterfully delving into complex themes of regret, grief, friendship, and sacrifice, Shoestring Theory *gripped me by the heart and didn't let me go. Costa weaves a magical spell around readers with a tale of what it means to love someone enough to finally see the truth of them – and let them show you the truth of yourself in return."*
Laura R. Samotin, author of *The Sins On Their Bones*

"A surprising and clever gem of a novel, Shoestring Theory *sparkles with banter between scorned lovers and lost friends alike. Equal parts wittily irreverent and stirringly poignant, Costa has crafted a heartfelt story about second chances, never giving up on the people we love, and one very good cat."*
S. A. MacLean, author of *The Phoenix Keeper*

"Shoestring Theory *has a classic RPG feel woven into its diverse and queernorm world, and at its heart is a resounding message of found family and self-love. Come for the twists, but stay for Cyril."*
Al Hess, author of *World Running Down* and *Key Lime Sky*

Mariana Costa

SHOESTRING THEORY

ANGRY
ROBOT

ANGRY ROBOT
An imprint of Watkins Media Ltd

Unit 11, Shepperton House
89 Shepperton Road
London N1 3DF
UK

angryrobotbooks.com
twitter.com/angryrobotbooks
A time travel cat-astrophe

An Angry Robot paperback original, 2024

Cover by Alice Claire Coleman
Edited by Eleanor Teasdale
Set in Meridien

ISBN 978 1 91599 819 4
Ebook ISBN 978 1 91599 820 0

Printed and bound in the United Kingdom by CPI Group (UK) Ltd, Croydon CR0 4YY.

9 8 7 6 5 4 3 2 1

To second chances.

ONE

Rolling rust-red clouds blanketed the horizon underneath a lightless, lifeless sky. Stepping outside felt as oppressive as experiencing a heatwave, even though it was always tundra-frigid. There was the looming threat of frostbite with every doomed venture outside.

It had been like this for years, enough that the memory of *normalcy* – weather, food, friendship – was a bittersweet sting in the back of Cyril's mind.

Most days, he kept to himself. There was little to do in a world so thoroughly destroyed other than sit, be quiet and wait. These things considered, he'd found himself a nice little spot to wait out the imminent end of days. A small cottage by the ocean where a once grassy knoll met sand and sea. Before, when things weren't quite so bad, he'd thought he might like to retire here. Leave everything behind and plant his bare feet firmly in the damp ocean sand, letting the waves wash away his lingering guilt.

Cyril thought he could pretend there was still some hope to be had in the world, but that was before the sky went black.

Admittedly, it was very hard to ignore the sky going black.

Were he a younger man, he might have called himself plucky. Stubborn as a weed in a rose garden, he'd carved out his own slice of tranquillity in his quaint little cottage. With the little magic he could still force himself to manipulate, he cultivated a vegetable patch which grew the saddest, skinniest tomatoes ever known to man.

When the cold wasn't so dreadful, he ventured out into the ocean in hiked-up trousers and rolled-up sleeves and spent an hour or two trying to spear whatever wildlife was still resilient enough to make their home in the water. Honestly, he'd gotten quite good at it.

Before, when he went on these little fishing expeditions, he'd need to catch three or four fish, because his familiar, Shoestring, a huge, scraggly, Abyssinian cat who could be mistaken for a malnourished lynx, had, as most real cats do, very particular tastes.

It gave Cyril a sense of purpose, providing for something other than himself. It had made him feel useful for the first time in years. But spending hours wading around in the frigid ocean, dredging it up for any fish that didn't look *too* nasty, using up his magic to keep himself from freezing solid while Shoestring watched with his Cheshire-grin of 'Oh, what shall *I* do? I'm just a little kitty cat,' was perhaps the *second* biggest pain in the arse of his current living situation.

It was a stroke of luck, really, when, in an act of uncharacteristic thoughtfulness, Shoestring crawled underneath an old, underused writing desk and died.

Cyril found out two things that day: the first was that it was possible for the very manifestation of a mages' soul to *crawl under a desk and die* with zero physical consequences to the mage themselves.

The second was that he was no longer able to cry.

That was a whole month ago, though. Since then, Cyril had discovered a new sense of purpose brewing somewhere deep in his gut (couldn't be his chest. Not anymore). For a whole week he prepared, digging up ancient wisdom he thought he'd long since forgotten. He even dusted off that writing desk, finally using it for its intended purpose as opposed to a flat surface to take his meals.

By the end of the week, he had a whole diagram drawn up on the floor in chalk and, when that had quickly run out, a congealed mixture of spit and blood. He had positioned Shoestring's carefully embalmed body somewhere it could always be looking over his work, judging his method just like in the old days. He spoke to himself as he worked, incarnating the cat as best as he could in the absence of the real thing, muttering quips and corrections to himself, doubting his calculations.

It was a very good thing he seemed to be losing his mind, Cyril thought, because then this would all be quite easy.

He needed to be very precise about this whole business, if there was any chance it would end up in anything but a mess on his hardwood floors. Every time he triple-, quadruple-checked his sigils, he darted his eyes to Shoestring, willing the cat to form some posthumous opinion that would reassure him he was on the right track.

Familiars couldn't speak, of course. At best, Shoestring used to mewl and purr in variations of dis or assent, but Cyril realised he'd come to rely on those infuriating noises like a guiding beacon.

Even after everything, the years he spent in the cottage had never been *truly* lonely until that stupid, useless cat's death.

He found himself working faster, eager to get it over with. And if the spell failed, he thought, would that truly be the worst outcome?

Maybe once, a lifetime ago, he could have passed for a powerful mage, the king's favourite courtier (a gross understatement). But even a powerful mage wouldn't have been able to undo just how bleak things had gotten. Maybe divine intervention could bring back the blue sky, and the pure weather, and do away with the shadows gathering all around the kingdom, but Cyril had never been particularly devout, and he wasn't sure any god worth their salt would give him the time of day.

Best case scenario, the gods were eager to rebuild the world from scratch, like a spoiled little lady with her brand-new dollhouse.

Maybe they found this all a positive riot. Sure, the rot-spread so far seemed confined to familiar territory, but who could say it wouldn't seep and fester and poison the entire continent if nothing were done?

No. There was no way to save the world. No way to fix what had been done, when it had gotten this bad.

So Cyril was going to stop it from ever having happened in the first place.

First, though, he was going to die.

Maybe he should've felt slightly ashamed of how excited he was by the prospect. It baffled him that he hadn't thought of it sooner. Not the *ritual*, of course, that was an act of desperation. A last-ditch effort only a madman could come up with. Cyril was excited for *death*.

Maybe Shoestring had been tethering him all along. If he died, the cat died with him, and he wasn't an *animal killer*. But for years now, Shoestring had been floating through the days, glaze-eyed and sleepy. The fact that Shoestring had had enough and went and found a place to die by himself should've been enough of a clue to Cyril that he was doing absolutely no one any favours by staying alive.

But, as he fingered a brassy gold ring looped into a string around his neck, he realised he was scared what might happen if he tried.

Cyril didn't know how, but he was sure, he was *so* sure, that as soon as the life left his body, he'd awaken a day later, carefully tucked into a lavish little comforter in a lavish little room, with someone sat on the edge of the bed waiting to greet him.

This would be the outcome no matter how he did it. He might find a way to be drawn and quartered and the pieces would be lovingly stitched together like a favourite stuffed doll. He could drown and new life would be breathed into his lungs just as quickly. He would burn, and... he didn't want to think about what kind of half-life he'd live after *that*.

But this was different because Cyril wasn't throwing his life away. He wasn't giving up. He was going to right a wrong. And, as he tucked the ring back into his shirt, he felt certain no one could follow him all the way to where he intended to go.

Finally, his sigils were complete. He was satisfied enough with the draftsmanship that there was no need to fiddle with them anymore. His knees creaked from exertion when he stood up to look for a small paring knife from somewhere in his makeshift kitchen.

Cyril was going to die like a sacrificial animal. A long time ago, someone somewhere decided that was how it was meant to be. He was going to be exsanguinated, bleed himself dry until he lost too much to possibly stay upright.

Methodically, he cut diagonals up his arms, starting on his wrists. He was a bit of a coward like that. If he'd gone for the throat, maybe this would all be over much sooner.

As it was, he got to watch the blood pool into the sigils, filling it out and covering it up entirely as the steady stream of red drained from his forearms.

Soon, the blood had slicked the floor so completely he could see his reflection, distorted and ruddied as it was, in the pool. Cyril flinched.

He was under no delusions that he was a *handsome* man, not even in his youth, but the years of solitude and starvation hadn't been particularly kind to him. Sharp lines cut and chiselled his face at grim, unhealthy angles. He had always had a somewhat thin frame, but now he was surprised he was still alive at all.

The deep set of his eyes was so dark he could barely see the whites within, especially in dim candlelight, and especially when framed by overgrown, wheat-flaxen fringe obscuring his vision even more.

Cyril scoffed, looking down at his bird-bone wrists. At the end of the day, everything about him was meagre, from his build, to his familiar, to his resolve, all the way down to the tomatoes growing outside his house.

He didn't think he deserved a sacrificial beast's death. It seemed too noble. Though his crimes had been overwhelmingly of inaction and neglect, it was difficult to sit and watch someone become a monster without sharing some of that burden. And here, under the gloam of a black sky and a single candle, Cyril looked very much a monster too. A reedy creature from the bowels of the earth, come to snatch children from their beds and grind their bones into fine meal.

Exsanguination, he thought, was a death ill-befitting of Cyril Laverre, disgraced courtier of the king's inner circle and familiar-less mage.

It was just his luck, then, that his true cause of death was asphyxiation. He drowned gracelessly in his own blood as soon as he fainted face first into the pool he'd been staring at so intently.

TWO

The first thing Cyril wondered when he woke up again was if the ritual would still work.

He was certainly *somewhere* new. The synapses in his brain were firing erratically. He could *feel* things. The grass – grass? – under his hand and pricking the nape of his neck, the mystery weight on his chest, the texture of fabric on his limbs far breezier than what he'd become used to in the past several years

Cyril didn't dare open his eyes out of lingering anxiety. That and, from the way the inside of his eyelids glowed a bright, searing red, if he looked up too fast he would be blinded by a light he'd become unaccustomed to.

There was a *chance* – not an insignificant one – that he had died, and this was *hell*. It was certainly *hot* out, and maybe the bright warmth he could feel from far above was a twisted vision of a forge. A place he'd be forced to labour in until the end of his natural afterlife. Cyril was never the type for manual labour. Even working in his sad little garden made him break into a sweat despite the biting cold outside. He thought if he lay very, very still, he might be able to sink into the earth instead. Buried, scattered, a part of the soil. No one would ever find him and put him to work – or torture him into a second wave of madness – no matter how much he deserved it.

Maybe whatever god ruled the underworld wouldn't even mind losing one soul that much. Being buried alive for eternity

13

is its own kind of torture after all, and how significant could *Cyril's* life possibly be after what he'd become in his rundown cottage by the cold, deserted beach?

Try as he might to will it away though, the light behind his eyelids never got any dimmer, and the grass underneath never seemed to part and burrow the way he wanted. When he felt a sandpapery texture brush against his cheek, he knew he was done for. The servants of the Undertaker had come to get him. He should try and explain to them that he *really did* try to make things right at the end there, see if that would get him a lighter sentence.

And then he heard a mewl.

Cyril's eyes flew open so quickly that he had to blink back tears as his vision got used to a sunlight he could barely remember.

Mercifully, Shoestring, who even now was much too grown and big to be perching on top of Cyril's chest, was blocking out the brunt of the light. He stared down with his large, clever eyes and cast a stark shadow over Cyril's brow, impatiently waiting for his master to wake up.

Cyril sat up with a sudden, desperate headache. He rubbed it away from his temples as best he could, until a feline interloper wedged his head firmly underneath his palm, looking for his dose of affection.

He stroked Shoestring gently, afraid if he pushed too hard or believed in his own success too promptly, the cat would unravel in his fingers just like his name. And slowly, fat, globby droplets pricked the edges of his eyes, rolling shamelessly down his cheeks and onto the powder-blue fabric of his shirt. Shaking with relief, he hugged Shoestring to his chest and received a paw to the chin as a warning not to push his luck.

Shoestring stepped away from him, having accomplished his sworn duty of never letting his master indulge in a full, proper nap for as long as he lived. And that left Cyril alone to inspect his surroundings.

It *had* worked.

Blinking rapidly, still unaccustomed to how much daylight was freely available, he realised he knew very well *where* he was. The real, more pressing question was *when*.

Behind the royal palace, still within its grounds, there was a forest the servants and nearby farmers used for foraging. It was huge and ancient, a true marvel, and since it was so easy to get lost among its elderly trees and rich foliage, it was ill advised to wander inside it unaccompanied.

But Cyril had grown up here. He'd lived by these woods his whole life, so he knew that if you went deep enough into the forest, unerring in your path, eventually you'd come across a river (a brook, really) shallow enough to cross on foot. And if instead you walked along its shore, you'd find a bridge, naturally formed by three smoothed boulders, one after the other, that you could cross with four short hops. And then, a few metres more still, you would find a sunlit clearing and an unkempt field of weeds and fresh wildflowers, with grass soft enough to sleep in, especially if you were trying to avoid going to lectures, or meetings, or formal events.

Cyril revelled in the feel of grass under his fingers, gripping and tugging at the weeds just to smell that waft of fresh grass. He lay on his back and rolled his whole body on the ground like a madman or a child, eliciting a startled yeowl from Shoestring, who was watching him carefully from a shady spot under one of the few trees the clearing had to offer. Cyril didn't care. He rolled until his powder-blue shirt and his fine silks were stained with green. And then he picked himself up and hurled himself bodily into the soft grass once more.

"Shoestring!" he cried. His voice felt foreign, even to himself. The last time he'd spoken, hours ago in that cottage by the beach, it had been raspy. It felt like a lifetime ago. Then, he had needed to coax the words out of his throat, gritting them out like the croak of an old toad. Now, he nearly spooked himself. His voice was loud and clear, healthy. A young man's register. He had never been much of a chatterbox, but now he wanted to talk forever.

"Shoestring, I think it worked!"

It hurt to smile for too long, when it was a reflex he seemed to have lost the use for years ago. Fortunately, he didn't need to keep the grin on his face for too long. Cyril's expression was wiped clean when he realised Shoestring was staring at him with a curious, cocked expression. As if he were watching some strange street performance.

Shoestring had never been the most expressive familiar around, but he was still Cyril's familiar. Their emotions were one. Hell, their *souls* were one. That was the *point*. He didn't expect the cat to jump for joy at his master's success, but he expected... *something*. An approving purr, or a languid condemnation of his recklessness. Maybe even a thank you for saving his life, if he was feeling generous.

But had he? Cyril sat up on his knees and, carefully, crawled his way to Shoestring. He held his hand out with his palm down and outstretched, like he had done so many times before for the instant comfort of a soulmate connection. But when Shoestring touched his head to his fingertips, Cyril felt nothing but the fuzzy, gaunt ears of an overgrown house cat.

"Shoestring?" he murmured.

The cat purred.

There had been a part of him, a *very* strong part of him, that, upon realising his hare-brained scheme had *actually* worked, wanted to quit while he was ahead. Knowing what he knew now, about the future, about the horrors awaiting him, and feeling the grass under his feet and the warm breeze in his hair, he wondered why *he* had to be the one to bother fixing a fractured kingdom. Maybe he could run away before anything happened at all. He never actually wandered very far from the palace. The cottage, the ocean, the knoll, they were all still firmly within the kingdom's borders. There was some kind of unspoken oath that if his land died, he was meant to perish with it.

Cyril thought about the brassy ring around his neck. Maybe not as unspoken as he would've liked.

By the time he had finished rolling around in the dirt and grass, Cyril had damn near made up his mind that his new plan was going to be to scoop Shoestring under his arms. Then, he'd march the pair of them out the palace gates and into town and with whatever funds jingled in his pocket he was going to take the first ship out of the city and sail far, far away.

But staring deep into those slitted eyes, he realised with a growing sense of nausea that no matter what stood in front of him, nuzzling his hand with his wet nose, his familiar had died a month ago. He wasn't quite sure who this Shoestring was, other than a big, needy, stupid cat.

Cyril's heart sank in his chest. He tried searching for any sign that Shoestring knew what was happening. The plan, the blood, the circle. The desperate attempt to put his own life – *their* lives – back together. but there was nothing but the wide, innocent eyes of a domesticated animal trying to read his master's turmoil of emotions.

It was instantly sobering. He could still run. Him and his newfound youth and agility and his ill-gotten freedom and his phantom cat, but it felt wrong, sickening, to go through all that just to be alone again. To allow his beloved home to be destroyed anew when he'd gone through all that trouble in an attempt to salvage it.

Slowly, he sat up to a kneeling position, pulling his hand away from Shoestring's curious snout.

He'd done this to himself, he decided. He'd gone through all this trouble. He might as well go through with it, for better or worse.

Cyril looked down at his clothes again, searching for more clues hidden in the styling of the fabric. With some relief, he quickly ruled out the possibility of being uniformed. This was good. He was young, he could feel it in his bones and his joints and the ease with which he moved in his own body, but he wasn't a *youth*. He wasn't a fledgling initiate to magic, unaccustomed to his own sage-grey student's robes.

The fact that he wasn't wearing any kind of formal attire was a clue in and of itself. There was a chance it was an off day, but the cut of the fabric and the style of the clothes themselves lent to a casually put-together ensemble. A ruffled shirt, with the sleeves cut into festive triangular strips at the end, paired with an open vest and matching, violet-and-green striped trousers.

Then he noticed when he rubbed at his eyes again, still in a losing battle against daylight, thick black ink flaking on his knuckles. The same ink seemed to have seeped into the blue of his shirt, where he'd first cried.

Kohl. It'd been so long he'd almost forgotten how he had woken up every morning to painstakingly paint his face in front of a cracked mirror that Shoestring had knocked a vase into. If he could find somewhere to look at his own face, he might be able to pinpoint his age by the black lines contouring his eyes.

Long ago, he painted his face in the style of court mages, just as he was taught. A mix of a courtier and a circus act. Exaggerated lashes, tightlined eyes, thick contour waterlines, reds, blues and oranges under the brow, beauty marks of all different shapes.

Cyril himself liked to trace the outline of his eye with a hand so heavy he looked like a harlequin, or an etching of an ancient owl, extending his bottom lashes comically far down his under eye. From what he managed to wipe away with his hand, he pinpointed his age anywhere from nineteen to five and twenty. Which wasn't much, but it was a start. He shivered slightly, almost cautiously, at the smooth curve of his skin, boyish, fresh and unwrinkled. It would take getting used to, but all the same it brought him a fizzy, hopeful feeling.

Another clue, this time sprinkled all around the parts of the lawn he *hadn't* crushed under his own weight in a fit of mania, were the wildflowers. Dandelions that were just beginning to sprout. Combined with the pleasant breeze blowing through his hair, it heralded a lazy, flowering spring.

If he had to make an educated guess, he'd put himself in April. Early May, perhaps. When he looked back at the early days of adulthood, all those springs blended together. Always nice, warm, languid. He couldn't recall a bad spring.

Especially not after it became his first anniversary.

Cyril had been married on a day just like this, and the memory felt like a thick sludge down his throat, foreign and difficult to swallow. A perfect April wedding with all the fixings of one of the happiest days of his life. He'd worn his finest whites and flowers in his pinned-back hair, and at the time he really did believe there was nothing in the world that could go wrong anymore.

He had been in love. Truly and desperately, frenzied with a madness that reckless warriors go on death-quests to experience. He was far from perfect, but in retrospect it was the most devastating mistake he'd ever made.

Cyril stood up from the comfortable blanket of grass to make his way back to the palace grounds. Shoestring trailed a few feet after him, stopping every so often to paw at an anthill, or chase after a creature just out of human sight.

He only managed to take a few solid steps before paranoia overtook him, burning an acrid hole in his gut every time the cat left his field of vision.

While the Shoestring he knew had been fiercely independent, disappearing into cubbies or alcoves for hours on end to preen or feast on a hapless rodent, he always came back. A familiar *always* had to come back, no matter what. But for whatever reason, the bond between them had been severed. When Cyril looked into those mirthless eyes, he could no longer see a reflection of himself, the twin shine in their eyes that had bound them together since he was barely out of play-clothes.

Instead, he had a cat. Volatile and flighty, prone to his own whims and wants whenever he so wished. Cyril knew somewhere in the back of his mind that, familiar or not, if anything happened to this stupid cat, he would be so overcome by grief he might lose himself in the thick of the woods.

So, with the care of handling a newborn, Cyril took Shoestring into his arms and carried the Abyssinian all the way back with him, ignoring the pinpricks of claw at his hands, and the outraged, protesting mewls. He was so determined not to lose his one ally in this dreamy landscape of the distant past, that he paid no mind when the skin on his knuckles bloomed a bright red with his own blood after gruelling minutes of being scratched and nipped.

Cyril didn't let go. In fact, he held on faster, shoulders shaking with the weight of the overgrown creature. When he was halfway out the woods, Shoestring finally slacked within his grasp and Cyril let out a grateful sigh.

"I'm going to get you a harness," he said.

He wasn't sure if, deep down, his familiar was still in there or if the cat simply had always had a naturally obedient nature Cyril was just learning about. But at least for the moment, Shoestring didn't dare try to stray anywhere his master couldn't see him.

It was frustrating how many times he got lost navigating the forest. Nothing serious, no fatal wrong turns that would career him headfirst into a ditch, he was too smart for *that*, but Cyril took enough wrong turns the pink on his knuckles from carrying such a heavy load began to match the flush on his cheeks. This wasn't supposed to pose a significant challenge for him. Not the forest he loved, in the kingdom he grew up in. But he had to admit to himself that for the better part of a decade, his excursions had consisted of shuffling to and from the cottage and the sea, the sea and the cottage. Most days, as soon as he woke up, he screwed his eyes shut and went straight back to sleep, willing time to move faster.

This was a lot of adventure all at once for someone so unaccustomed to it.

Finally, he spotted the ruddy peak of the spires poking out through the mess of trees, red contrasting green and the blue of the sky so strongly it felt like a beacon just for him.

He quickened his step, then, stumbling over his own feet, which seemed to have become too sluggish from traipsing through the woods to move as quickly as his brain willed them to. By the time he reached the wrought-iron gates separating the palace grounds from the thick of forest, his calves ached – but not his lower back, he noted with almost tearful gratitude, as it had been plaguing him since his mid-thirties – and he *had* to put Shoestring down.

Cyril gave the cat a warning glance not to stray and, squaring his own shoulders, marched purposefully inside a place he only just realised he never thought he'd see again.

It was normal, expected even, for none of the staff to pay him any mind as he sauntered into the palace halls through the servant's entrance, cutting a path from the kitchen up to the main halls. The most attention he got were the curious looks from younger serving maids and the occasional valet, who weren't yet masters of the art of minding their own business, and he realised quite quickly it was because he looked a fright.

A polished brass shield mounted on a wall reflected a dishevelled, dirty young man, with kohl running down his eyes from his uncontrollable sobbing earlier, smudges of green staining every inch of his clothes and raw knuckles like he'd gotten himself into a tavern brawl.

Cyril flushed and quickly looked away from the shield. He clicked his tongue to will Shoestring to match his pace as he began a casual jog to his own chambers before anyone *important* saw him and started asking questions.

The family he had grown up with kept a particular tradition. Since recorded history began centuries ago, the royalty governing the kingdom had insisted upon relying on the power of mages to aid their rule. The current ruling family, the Margraves, valued their mages so fondly that they made sure to give them a permanent home in the palace. Thus, the palace had a peculiarity.

Still within its walls, towards the back centre of the palace, a king long ago had left ample room for a wide, open courtyard adorned with carefully manicured hanging-gardens. In its very middle, there was a tower that climbed seven storeys high, the tallest one in the entire kingdom. It had a red tiled roof the same colour as the rest of the spires flanking the palace walls.

It was a home within the palace, both separate from and attached to the main building, marking the mages of Farsala as both family and distinguished servants. Cyril had lived on the third floor of the tower with his aunt Heléne, the high-court witch for the current royal family, since he had first shown magical aptitude at the age of five.

In a sense, the Laverres had their own lineage that ran parallel to that of the de facto monarchs. He had lived the charmed life of a dukeling under his aunt's tutelage, and the Margraves treated him like one of their own.

Aside from his years at the Academy for Arcane Arts from ages twelve to eighteen, the tower had been his home well into adulthood. Despite how foreign it felt to enter it now, no one batted an eye when he began the short ascent to his chambers, Shoestring following close behind.

He *did* still live on the third floor of the tower, which meant arthritic aunt Heléne was still clinging tooth and nail to her seat in court. He could hardly begrudge her: the kind of sway that came with having the ear of the most powerful people in all the land was at times intoxicating.

Nostalgia hit him like a brick to the head as soon as he opened the door to his living quarters. It painted such a clear portrait of a spoiled young man revelling in a luxury he never had need to earn that it made Cyril's teeth hurt. Aunt Heléne had installed a series of complicated patterns and magic triggers when Cyril had initially moved in and she couldn't be fussed to call a maidservant over every little childhood mess. Despite that, it still had the confused quality of being lived in by a youth who still hadn't learned to be judicious with his keepsakes. He hadn't properly gotten into his room yet – just the study where he liked to read and take his meals – but already paraphernalia clearly too important to be let go of was in every corner. Rolled up scrolls and maps of places he'd like to visit propped against the wall, clothes he'd shucked off and left on the sofa or on the chair or even on his writing desk, a frankly *ridiculous* assortments of pens and quills, two different stacks of notebooks, one filled to bursting with annotations and another with lofty plans to be penned in at a later date (half of which would be thrown out brand new the first time Cyril would try his hand at decluttering), souvenirs from distant lands, glorified paperweights or doorstops, vials of potions, scattered plates containing cherry pits or pistachio shells, stacked mugs of cold tea, three musical instruments he'd tried to learn and given up on just as quickly, scrying runes, a kaleidoscope (broken), a telescope (repaired), letters from his parents, from his school friends and from professors, a vanity permanently stained in pressed pigments and kohl, a cat tower fit for royalty and, for some reason, a tricycle.

You could put a knife to his throat and Cyril wouldn't be able to make sense of what he was thinking when he hung a paper lantern off the leaf of a *fern*. After living so long in the ascetic seaside cottage, two steps into the third floor of the mage tower sent him into fits of mild claustrophobia.

And yet, part of him was indescribably comforted by it.

Had he been recounting the tale himself, of his intrepid escapade into the past in order to prevent a doomed future, Cyril would've remarked on his single-minded sense of purpose. After all, he *did* have a plan in mind. It wasn't particularly complex, but he was sure it would destroy the root cause of all his suffering in one fell swoop. And once he did a bit of research into exactly where in time he was and acquired a few things he might need that he couldn't immediately find in his own room, there would be nothing stopping him from setting his plan into motion.

Cyril had always been the meandering type, and he was *tired* in a way that had nothing to do with age and everything to do with the weary sense of dread that prey gets from being hunted. For eight-to-ten years (he'd lost count), he had lived in squalor, weaving salt out of seawater and picking meat out of gritty, bony fish. Even if in his current state he found himself in the body of a well-fed, pampered young mage, there was still an entrenched memory of the grime of that cottage permeating the roots of his hair and the undersides of his fingernails.

Not to mention the *actual* grime and fresh stains on his clothes.

So he drew himself a bath, and while he waited for the tub to fill and for the salts and oils to fully perfume the water, he rang up a maid to bring him what he now realised was an early afternoon meal. He still felt full from the lunch he'd presumably partaken in before his body had unceremoniously been taken over by a suicidal old man, but he was determined to eat himself into nausea.

As he began taking off his earth-soiled clothes, any thoughts of lofty idealism in his mind had been replaced by the memory of jam-filled pastries and salted cuts of meat. Then, a sudden *clink* against a button on his shirt drew Cyril's attention to his chest.

He stood in the middle of his washroom, half naked in front of a floor-length mirror, staring at the familiar brassy golden ring hanging from a dirty string around his neck.

Cyril blinked, hoping against all odds that by resetting his vision the strange apparition would clear away. But the ring remained steadfast where it lay, burrowing a hole into his chest.

He wasn't supposed to have this. Not *yet* and, in this reality, not *ever*. Carefully, Cyril willed his pulse to slow and wrapped his hand around the band to tug it off himself. It was looped through such a threadbare string; it should have been pulled off easy.

But the ring wouldn't budge. It stubbornly clung to the string around his neck regardless of how hard he yanked and attempted to prise it free from his neck. And upon realising he had brought the keepsake with him, a bubble of panic swelled in his gut as he considered the implications.

Aside from his last little foray with sacrificial magic in that gelid seaside cottage, Cyril had only ever performed one other spell potent enough to carry itself through entire *realities*. He didn't expect it to bite him in the ass so completely as it seemed to be doing now.

Cyril thumbed the ring on his chest as he finally gave up trying to take it off and dunked himself into the bath. He hoped that against all odds, the hot water would corrode through the loop strung around it.

On his wedding day, he made an oath upon the band, binding himself and his betrothed for eternity in something greater and more powerful than any church-sanctioned vow of matrimony. He thought he was being romantic. And, to his credit, he *was*. It was plenty romantic, regardless of the repercussions. He had truly believed he would be in love for all eternity.

Honestly, it served him right being married at *fucking* twenty-three, after a mere two months of courtship.

He decided that, until proven otherwise, he was dealing with a best-case scenario, because he couldn't afford the migraine that a worse situation would beset him. The ring marked him as a spoken-for man, regardless of time or space or logic, and in some insidious way, it would prevent him from straying. Not that Cyril had *flirtation* on the mind much these days, not at his advanced age.

He soaked in the magically heated tub, alone with his thoughts long enough that the olive undertone of his skin took on a scalded-red hue. He only rose up from his parboil when he heard the tell-tale bell of food being placed upon his desk.

He dressed, applied some healing bandages around his knuckles to assuage the better part of Shoestring's damage (the cat had settled nicely inside a cubby much too small for him), and finally got to work.

In retrospect, this all might've been easier if he'd still been a student. Sure, he'd need to make an excuse to leave the Academy and sneak back into the palace, but as a student, he was forced to keep a daily log of every class and lecture he attended, with detail so precise he could triangulate an exact date just by looking at a few timetables. The habit, unfortunately, didn't stick with Cyril into adulthood. By the time he had finished flipping his pile of logs and notebooks inside-out-upside-down, he found that the last time he bothered scribbling *anything* of substance down at all was on February 12th.

One look outside the window confirmed he was *long* past that.

At least he had a year to pinpoint. The Cyril he'd usurped was in the beginning of his twenty-second cycle (he was a January baby, if it mattered) and, if his meagre journal entries were anything to go by, there was yet to be a single exciting event to have happened that year. He flipped through the book over bites of cream petit-fours and found the last event he'd bothered writing down was a shopping list of things he needed from town that his aunt had made him commit to ink.

He was going to need a more hands-on approach to situating himself. It struck him as odd, that he couldn't remember anything important happening a year before his own *wedding*, but he chalked it up to old age. Honestly, if pressed, he wouldn't have been able to name the precise date of his anniversary save for a sheepish "mid-April?"

Either way, he couldn't put it off any longer. Cyril clicked his tongue in the direction Shoestring was hiding in to get him to follow.

"I'll lock you in the bathroom until I get back if you don't come with me," he said for good measure.

The threat was met with a hiss, but it was enough for the cat to poke his head out of the discarded box of tomes he'd been hiding in and follow Cyril out the door. They made their way down the steps of the tower, back into the main building of the palace.

Cyril felt as though he was forgetting something tremendously important as he wandered the halls, looking for a recent newspaper or an idle serving maid or butler to casually ask the date. "Cyril!"

Cyril turned and his heart instantly dropped.

"I was *just* headed to the tower!" She bounded towards him without a care in the world and clapped both hands on his shoulders like greeting an old friend. "Thanks for saving me the trip."

Tigris Margrave was the best, most charming and most beautiful girl he'd ever known. They had met when he was at the tender age of five, and Cyril had been instantly drawn by her full head of black hair, so dark it shone blue under the light, that perfectly dewy brown skin, stippled with delicate birthmarks only adding to her natural appeal, and that intoxicating grin so contagious Cyril was making a concentrated effort not to mirror her expression like a starstruck buffoon.

"I..." He nodded mechanically, suddenly unsure of what to do with himself. "Tigris," he added, stupidly.

Tigris cocked her head to the side and gave him a fond smirk. "Cyril, I've been gone for a *month*. Is it the hair? I've been wearing it loose, do you not like it?"

He shook his head, seeming to go into some kind of self-preservatory autopilot. "No! Of course not, I..." He racked his brain for any context clues that would allow him to smoothly continue the conversation and settled on a non-committal choke of, "Only... only a month, huh?"

It was ridiculous the way she looked at him, like a concerned older sister fussing over a particularly fragile baby sibling. Especially when Cyril felt old enough to be this woman's father.

"Well, Atticus finally let go of the leash long enough to let me come back and visit."

Cyril nodded along, putting together the most high-stakes mental jigsaw puzzle he'd ever had to assemble.

Her Royal Highness, Crown Princess Tigris Margrave of Farsala, had been engaged to Atticus Wulfsbane, King of Cretea, just after her twenty-sixth birthday. Since the betrothal, the newly engaged couple had spent more and more time together, meaning Tigris's trips to Cretea would increase in time and frequency. It had been a marriage of convenience, uniting two small kingdoms into a mutually beneficial political front, but from what Cyril could recall, Tigris was making the most of it. She seemed to think her fiancé genuinely handsome if nothing else.

"How's Cretea?" he asked after much too long a pause. Tigris didn't seem to notice.

"Oh, wonderful this time of year. You should visit, it's not like Auntie gives you anything *important* to do."

The "ey!" that left his lips was almost a reflex.

She rolled her eyes. "I'm right, aren't I? Well, when I'm queen, I'll give her the retirement she desperately needs, and you and I can run this place."

"Ostensibly, the grand mage isn't meant to have political power."

"Yes, but I'm *stupid* about all this *magic* stuff and I need your *help*," she whined.

Cyril wouldn't go as far as "stupid", not for *Tigris* who, at age fourteen, had managed to wrap all the high nobility around her little finger with her natural graces. Still, academic knowledge and magical comprehension weren't exactly the Princess' forte.

"Don't let your fiancé hear you say that, he'll start firing up for a coup."

Tigris giggled and wrapped an arm around his shoulder, serving as a reminder of how, in general, the Margraves had always towered over the Laverres. "He wouldn't do that before the wedding."

"You're *very* confident in His Majesty."

She recoiled like he'd vomited on her new shoes. "Don't *call* him that, ugh. We're practically *family*!"

"We're *not* family, princess." He mock bowed. "I am your humble servant."

"Gross!" She pushed him away, still laughing to herself. "Don't let Eufie catch you talking like that, you'll break his heart."

And just like that, Cyril was violently jerked back into the reality of his situation. The jovial grin he'd been sporting a second ago went slack on his face as Tigris, bless her heart, carried on.

"Oh, wait! That's why I was going to the tower. He's been asking for you."

There wasn't a spell on earth that could carry him normally through the rest of this conversation, so he decided he'd nod and nod and nod until Tigris decided she'd had enough of hearing her own voice and left to chatter somewhere else.

"Eufie, I mean. Not Atticus. Do you even know Atticus? Well, anyway–"

Cyril was nodding.

"I met him on his way back from a hunt this morning, and he was looking for you."

"Uh huh."

"But when *isn't* he looking for you?" Here, she waggled her thick eyebrows in a meaningful serpentine.

"Right?"

"So I said, 'Have you checked the tower?' but *he* said you weren't at the tower all morning! So I think you must've just missed each other."

He realised he had to put a stop to this before she realised there was something wrong with him aside from typical youthful ennui, so he blurted out, "I'll find him."

And then, after clearing his throat, "I'm sure he'll be at the dinner table, at least. It's… good. I needed to speak to him as well."

He extricated himself from the conversation with the social graces of a new-born foal, but in truth he felt as though if he spent one more second looking at Tigris, hearing Tigris speak to him about her *brother*, he was going to burst a major artery.

And truth be told, he was more than a little ashamed of himself for being so surprised to see her, to do something so *normal* as have a casual conversation with her. It just wasn't something he'd prepared himself to do, had *expected* to do.

Because Tigris Margrave had been dead for over twenty years.

Of *course* he hadn't forgotten about her. What kind of horrible, callous man would he be if he'd erased one of his best friends growing up entirely from his mind? But she had passed *so* long ago and reminiscing about it provided him with nothing but *more* grief than he already had.

How stupid of him. He had been so caught up in the simple joy of seeing her alive that he forgot to be concerned about her death.

As soon as she retreated from his line of sight, it was like a bolt of electricity shot through Cyril's whole body. He scooped up Shoestring, who had been languidly cleaning himself throughout their conversation and provided absolutely zero support for what was likely one of many traumatic situations his master was going to have to live through for the foreseeable future. Then, paying no mind to the frustrated mewls and howls, he darted down the stairs of the palace underground, to the armoury.

Cyril had had a full month to think about this when he was preparing his last spell as a wizened old hermit, and he'd concluded he was going to rule out magic. It was entirely too incriminating, considering the only mages in court were himself and Auntie Heléne, who would sooner throw herself off her spire than conspire against the Margraves. To be completely honest it was a fragile, hackneyed plan, as thin as spider silk and just as easy to spoil. Doubtless, sooner or later he would get caught.

It was also the only plan he had, now he realised how precious little time there was left.

Tigris Margrave, strong as an ox and hale as a well-kept housecat, died of a wasting sickness the summer of Cyril's twenty-second year. It was theorised that she had been stung by an insect or been contaminated by a rot that festered in the heat (long before the uninhabitable days to come, as though she were some grim portent), but whatever the case made no difference when he had to sit for days on end in vigil, watching the heir apparent to the throne of Farsala wither into a brittle, sallow husk before his very eyes.

He was not a fool, or a child, or *simple*. Obviously, they investigated into foul play. Cyril could only do one thing, but he did it very well. He spent tireless nights checking the strings around Tigris's body for any kind of manipulation. Once, he even opened up the pattern around her itself, despite his misgivings against doing something so invasive to the magic. The Guard conducted thorough searches of the kitchens, the greenhouse, the woods. Anywhere poison could be found or disposed of. He saw Atticus Wulfsbane, a *king*, laid low. Red-eyed and haggard as he submitted to every line of questioning directed at him, allowed Farsalan knights to turn his palace inside-out for signs of treason. He remembered the taste of retch on his tongue when he tried (and failed) to stay for the autopsy.

And Eufrates–

Eufrates.

Cyril clutched Shoestring tight to his chest and bounded down the spiral staircase leading to the armoury two steps at a time. He only let the poor cat down to throw the door open and begin his search.

If he had more time, he would have gone into town for this. If he was smart, he *should* have gone into town for this. But it was already such a *remarkably* ill-advised idea and he doubted this would be the drop that made the cup run over.

Shoestring stayed by the door, rubbing himself up against a box of spare armour parts as though he was on the verge of climbing inside, and Cyril didn't even *entertain* thinking about what would happen if some keen-eyed guard found the tell-tale tufts of Abyssinian peppered through their equipment.

He realised he'd never actually had to come down here before in this life *or* the previous. A mage who fought with *weapons* – not even enchanted ones at that, Heléne had always told him – was barely a mage at all. He would sooner pluck at the pattern around a sword until its grip melted in the wielder's hand than attempt to use one himself.

He considered the kitchen first, naturally. It would've been easy to abscond with a chef's knife or a meat cleaver.

It would've been just as easy to be seen. He could picture it now, a kitchen that never had fewer than five people in it at once, stopping their chopping and dicing and boiling in unison to watch as a comically misplaced little courtier plucked a knife off a countertop with a sheepish smile.

It was why he was in the armoury in the first place. For all the chaos and clutter in his quarters, there wasn't a single thing in any of the rooms that could be considered dangerous, save for a decorative letter opener that sat gathering dust on his writing desk. And a paring knife originally meant for mangoes and persimmons that was so dull he often used it to scoop hummus directly into his mouth.

Cyril needed something with a bit more *substance*.

No. He was already being reckless enough without self-sabotage.

It took him upwards of half an hour to scour the armoury for something even Cyril Laverre, notorious featherweight, felt confident he could use. A dagger, more decorative than functional, tucked away with the rest of what Cyril decided was a section of the room named "small sharp objects" (not to be confused with "long sharp objects" or "big sharp objects").

He found it inside a trunk containing everything baby's first assassin might need to perform a hit, so covered in dust and spiderwebs it was a wonder it hadn't blended in with the wall and sent him into a hacking fit upon opening.

Cyril grimaced. He supposed political subterfuge became more in vogue *after* Tigris's successor took up the mantle.

Before he left, he made sure to manipulate the pattern so everything looked exactly as it had when he found it, undisturbed. If another mage looked into it, they would see through the deception, but to the untrained eye, the trunk was as untouched as it had ever been.

Cyril wove a pocket on the inside of his vest with magic and tucked the dagger inside. As soon as he felt the metal press against his chest, his heart thrummed a war-drum tune. The reality of the situation finally sunk into his gut. It felt like he'd just swallowed a handful of wet sand, and yet the worst was still to come.

THREE

Fifteen minutes later, he was pacing outside opulent double doors, running a hand through his unruly hair, rehearsing.

It was difficult to concentrate when every time a busybody servant passed him in the hall, they tittered, thinking themselves oh-so demure, hiding the maddening noise behind a polite hand over their mouth.

Gods. He couldn't possibly have been this embarrassing in his youth. Or this *obtuse*.

Still rife with anxiety, Cyril wiped his hands on the bottom of his tunic and closed his left into a fist. Then, he made to knock.

Not to be outdone, at the same time Shoestring bumped his head against the door and yowled.

He heard seven quick steps, then the door his knuckles were poised to strike swung open.

"Cyril!"

Gods take him to the underworld. Bury him in the filthiest sandpit of hell and char the soil to glass. He wished the spell had failed. He wished he'd just slit his wrists open for the simple pleasure of taking his own life and never having to live through a scenario like this, because he *could. Not. Do. This.*

Shoestring mewled again and, for only a second, he thought he had his familiar back. But when he darted his eyes to the cat's, they were the same hollow he'd seen in that field. He would've groaned if he could. He *had* to do this.

"I heard… you were looking for me," he said slowly, testing the tone and timbre of his voice on his tongue.

He was a *little* surprised. He thought it would be harder to pretend. For all his face paint, farcical dressing and flourish, Cyril had never been a particularly gifted actor.

But as it turned out, it was easy to play the lovesick fool when he was staring at the most handsome man he'd ever seen.

The handsome man smiled so wide and with so much gentleness that Cyril would swear he could hear his own heart split open.

"I was! Did Tig tell you?"

Weakly, Cyril nodded.

"I thought I might see you at supper, actually. Though, sometimes you take meals with Auntie?" It wasn't a question, not really, but it was the kind of tone Cyril remembered so well from him. Uncertainty and kindness. A man who was loath to tell others what to do.

A man he had once fallen deeply in love with.

Eufrates Margrave, standing before him now, was the spit of his older sister. The same rich, healthy brown skin and midnight hair, his kept short with clean edges save for a stubborn curlicue down the middle of his forehead that Cyril had spent collected hours twirling around his forefinger, equal parts fondness and tease. He was growing out a trim, sculpted beard that was fashionable for the time (which Cyril had hated) and he often wore breezy, casual dress shirts that plunged at the neckline (which Cyril had loved).

Suddenly, the string around his neck felt like a hot noose.

He shook his head, regaining composure. "Not tonight. Not with Tig back in the palace."

"Well." Eufrates smiled and shifted his weight to one side, inviting him into his quarters. "Why wait till the evening? Please, come in."

Cyril peeked into the immaculately furnished bedchambers of the prince of Farsala, a place he had spent so much time in, even before any kind of blossoming romance, he could navigate the room with his eyes shut. Just over Eufrates's shoulder, he spied a timeworn lute, sitting atop a dark wood desk. Next to it, a hunting crossbow, misplaced next to an oak chair as though recently used. Even more tell-tale was the heavy outdoor cloak hanging lazily from the seat. Tigris *did* mention her brother had come from a hunt in the morning.

He balled his hand into a fist over his chest and stepped backwards, shaking his head. He could not do this in his room.

"Actually. I was hoping you'd join me out of doors, if you're not too tired from this morning."

Eufrates cocked a brow, but then he barked into laughter so fond it made Cyril's chest ache. "Tired! We gave chase to a hare thinking it a wolf, and Sir Tybalt shot a tree shaped like the horns of a deer. I wish you would have seen it."

Cyril couldn't help his own grin, infected by the good-natured cheer. "Invite me on your next hunt, then."

"Cy. My dear friend. I've received a king's ransom in rejections to know I'll be doing no such thing."

"Shoestring spooks easily. The crossbows frighten him."

Eufrates shot the offending cat a glance as he shut the door to his chambers and paced next to them down the halls. "If only we mere mortals had familiars to pin our excuses on."

Shoestring mewled.

It was easy, dangerously so, to fall back into this old routine. All the way up the steps of the palace, to the prince's quarters tucked away in the easternmost wing that faced the gardens (and his tower), Cyril had broken into a cold, damp sweat wondering how he was going to fool Eufrates into thinking he was the same youth he had grown up with and not an old, withered facsimile. Turns out, all he had to do was *talk* to him to feel as though all was right in the world.

* * *

When Cyril had been sent to live with his aunt in the Mage's Tower at age five, a nine year-old Tigris had immediately embraced him as the additional sibling she had always wanted. She had done this by, exactly one week after he'd settled into his rooms, shoving him off a metal swing built near the palace grounds so hard that he broke his arm in three places.

He couldn't begrudge her, not even as a sobbing, wounded child, lying in a pile of sand and woodchips waiting for a caretaker to come rescue him. Tigris had always been given to roughhousing, and it was how she treated her own brother. She hadn't expected this snivelling, flaxen-haired addition to the royal life to be quite so precious.

Tigris had never hurt him again, a fact he was very grateful for, but she still spent the better part of her carefree youth pushing and shoving and dragging him into danger like she was moulding him into her retinue. And of course, alongside Tigris was always her brother.

If the sister embraced Cyril like a sibling from the moment she had laid eyes on him, the brother cradled him like an injured baby bird he'd found beneath a broken branch of a tree. In those early days, Cyril wondered whether he was actually a friend to Eufrates or a beloved toy.

Only a year apart, the Margraves were inseparable in all aspects *but* Cyril. Often, Tigris and he would have to *beg* Eufrates to let Cyril join in on their excursions, the prince insisting he was much too young. And he had a point. Taking a six-and-a-half year-old boy spelunking into abandoned tunnels by the lake had not been Tigris's brightest moment, but the prince did not need to *baby* him so.

Years later, not too long after they had said their vows in front of what seemed like the whole of Farsala, Cyril saw something that made it click.

Out on an excursion into town, he spotted a gaggle of schoolchildren, in their uniforms and summer hats, playing their recess away in the square. He had spied a boy of no more than seven lay his shirt – his *shirt* – down on the dusty cobblestones so a girl in twin braids who had been shadowing him could take her meal undisturbed by the filth of the city. Mesmerised, Cyril kept watch, observing as that same boy fussed over keeping his companion's hat safe from the breeze, and plopped himself down a neat foot away from her, on the hard ground itself despite her protests. He asked if she was comfortable, if she had enough to eat, if she was getting too hot. When she grew bored and asked if he wished to play at something, he shot up like a rocket and returned with a small bag of iridescent marbles, eager to show her his treasures.

By the time Shoestring had bumped against Cyril's leg to break him out of his stupor, the restaurant he'd intended on visiting had already closed for daytime service.

Though he feared daring to flatter himself so wildly, Eufrates had spent his childhood behaving the same as that boy, fussing and fawning over Cyril like a lovebird. Treating him as gently as a piece of seafoam that would scatter if he turned away.

As a child, Cyril found this confusing. He had craved Eufrates's acceptance like a starving beggar. Somehow, he had convinced himself their bond would not be forged in the fires of friendship if the prince didn't *also* grievously injure him in some escapade, like his sister had. So he had been both clingy to a fault and standoffishly cool, hoping *something* would spark feelings in the prince that made him regard Cyril as an equal.

It turned out what they both needed to break out of that awkward impasse had been time and, crucially, *distance*. Eufrates's overbearing nature had cooled by the time Cyril enrolled into the Academy for Arcane Arts, urged by the king and queen and (less enthusiastically) by his aunt Heléne to mingle with other mages his age instead of listening in on old magically gifted courtiers who would spare him the time of day. The Academy was tucked in a valley three cities and one kingdom away, so Eufrates only looked a *little* sour when he and his sister saw him off to the boarding school. They wrote to each other at length, and it seemed the prince had a better way with words when committed to paper, at least in adolescence, because it felt like taking on a mystery correspondent.

Eufrates was witty and charming, regaling him with tales of how his own schooling was going from deep within the confines of the Margrave home. He wrote pages as though he were using Cyril as a diary, not leaving out a single detail no matter how mundane, but the exchanges were far from one-sided. In fact, if Cyril neglected to mention even a scrap of gossip from the Academy, or if he glossed over a detail too quickly, he'd be sure to receive back heated demands that he be more open in his letters.

The irony that it had taken *letters* to form a friendship between them was not lost on Cyril, not even as a youth, but he would not complain about it. In fact, it was the happiest he'd been. One day, when they were fourteen and seventeen, Eufrates had begun a page with 'Dear Cy' as opposed to the usual 'To Cyril Laverre' and it had made his heart thunder in his chest. He had slept with that letter under his pillow for months before Shoestring accidentally pawed down its middle finding a comfortable place in his bed, and Cyril had kept it under lock and key in his trunk instead. With the wisdom of retrospect, Cyril could pinpoint that day as the moment he'd fallen in love.

"Cy."

Cyril snapped out of his stupor just in time to realise he'd been staring wistfully at Eufrates's hands, unfortunately clothed in riding gloves. He would have liked to see the ink stains blotted on the tips of his nails and the writing callous on his left middle finger he'd felt so many times when twining their hands together. He darted his gaze up, to the prince's eyes. They were scrunched in concern.

"You seem troubled, friend."

A gross understatement, if he'd ever heard one, but Cyril shook his head. By now, they'd reached the edge of the back foyer leading outside in companionable silence.

"It's nothing. Auntie has been giving me grief over a new spell." The lie flowed easily, a trivial concern for a trivial courtier.

"Nothing you will struggle with too long, I hope?"

He smiled. "Am I not the best wizard in the kingdom?"

Eufrates tilted his head. "Your aunt–"

"Is a *witch*."

"They're the same."

"Oh, let me have this one, Eufie."

A scowl formed on Eufrates's perfect face. Eufie was a nickname reserved for Tigris, the king and queen, and Cyril, but *only* when he was being antagonistic. Normally he would keep needling, but now he tried to defuse the situation.

"You must be happy to see your sister again."

The scowl melted off as if under a hot August sun, and Eufrates looked light as air itself. "I am. Tig torments me for the excess sentiment."

Cyril raised a brow. "Gods, man, it's been a month. You've developed a complex."

Then, Eufrates regarded his friend as if seeing straight through him. Eyes inscrutable under the shade of the orange tree they'd just walked past. But the moment passed in a flash and once again he smiled.

"Perhaps. Perhaps I will be cured if I have to hear about the Cretian king for another second."

"Is she very enamoured, then?"

"I couldn't say. But she finds him exotic."

Cyril let out a huff of air through his nose. "*Exotic*?"

Atticus Wulfsbane, with his warm golden hair and freckled complexion, seemed a perfectly ordinary man of great beauty.

"She says he enjoys the snow overmuch and keeps an iron grill in his quarters to sear his own game."

"I should like to see a king engrossed in cookery."

"I don't believe my father has ever set foot in the kitchens."

"I should *love* to see *King Margrave* fry an *egg*!" Cyril said.

They looked at each other and, after a moment, both burst into laughter.

By the time they reached a shaded spot in the woods ideal for repose, they were arm in arm. Eufrates regaled him with a more detailed account of the hunt. Turns out, while it had only been a hare they chased down, it was one of the biggest hares he'd ever seen, and so fast not even a hound could give chase. Cyril laughed along their wild goose chase, teasing Eufrates for his ill-luck.

All the while, his stomach hurt like he'd eaten a pile of rocks.

He had planned this all out, as paltry a plan as it has been, but Cyril was not vicious, or brave, or anything of the sort. His insides were twisted up in knots as the reality of what he needed to do sunk in.

He was going to have to kill his husband.

His *future* husband, but that was exactly what made it so difficult. Prince Eufrates, who had settled on a rock by a babbling stream and patted the empty space beside him for Cyril to join, was innocent. He was a charming young man of five-and-twenty, with a soft heart and a love of poetry and fine arts. Killing him here would not make him a hero bound for the history books. It would make him a common cutthroat.

But it was what he *needed* to do. Eufrates could not be allowed to ascend to power, even if it meant his life must be cut tragically short. He pictured *King* Eufrates Margrave in his mind's eye, and it bolstered him with courage. The dagger in his vest seemed to thrum against his chest.

Cyril would take the opportunity while Eufrates had his back turned and kill him quickly. He could tamper with the pattern around the corpse, feigning accident, but Heléne would be able to see right through it. So instead, he would move the body outside the palace walls and hope the murder be deemed a vicious attack from bandits.

There was still a chance he would be caught. Cyril thought of his cottage by the sea, lonely and hopeless, and his shoulders sagged. He hoped they at least brought him something other than poorly-skinned fish in the dungeons.

With a wave of new determination, Cyril made to reach inside his vest.

"You hesitate, my love. Should I be flattered?"

Cyril's body frosted over. His fingers paused on his lapel.

"...Pardon?" he said.

Eufrates was still looking down at the stream, pretending to count the fish that swam by, but his posture had changed. The way he held himself shifted into a predatory hunch. He brought a hand to his chin and stroked his beard.

"I mean, if your plan is to lure me out far enough to slit my throat, you are taking your sweet time. The anticipation is maddening."

"I..." Cyril's voice was much too small for his liking. "I had actually meant to stab you in the back."

Finally, Eufrates turned to look at him, with a grimace so familiar it made his head spin. "Of course you did."

"Why are you *here*?" he blurted.

Cyril may not have been much of an actor, but he'd unfortunately forgotten that his husband was as much a practitioner of the arts as he was a patron. The man was a *bard*, weaving honeyed words with the same expertise Cyril wove his magic. He wrote, he acted, he told stories, he played. The only thing he couldn't do was carry a tune, which was a talent peculiarly wasted on Cyril himself.

All this to say, Eufrates had him utterly fooled.

"I asked myself the same thing. One moment I was in my chambers, taking care of state matters–"

"Is *that* what you're calling it?"

Eufrates ignored the interruption. "And the next I was among my old hunting party, listening to Lady Oriana describe a beast she'd seen in the woods yesternight that we *must* track down."

Cyril stood gobsmacked before taking a cautious step back. "You were not *meant* to be here, I assure you."

"Alas." Eufrates pushed himself off the rock and to his feet, stalking closer as though approaching a frightened animal. "I am here. I gather it's to do with the *curse* you've laid upon the both of us."

He tugged off his right riding glove and immediately Cyril saw the glowing golden band upon his ring finger, weathered by time. An accessory Eufrates was not meant to have in this life *or* the next.

Cyril wanted to scream. Apparently, this had been the best, most potent, most revolutionary and magnificent spell he'd ever woven in his life. He'd done it at *three-and-twenty* years old, and it was *wasted* on making Eufrates Margrave a permanent rock in his shoe.

The wording had been unfortunately vague, more lyrical romance than anything descriptively firm. *May we never be parted, may our bond be eternal. May we share our joys and griefs and let not even the hand of the Undertaker split our paths.* A silly, desperate weave borne of first love and dire circumstances. Cyril did not realise the repercussions would be so wide-reaching.

"A curse you *begged* me for," he spat.

Eufrates rolled his eyes dismissively. "The follies of youth."

He reached into his vest and Eufrates was upon him immediately, gripping his bird bone wrist so hard he could snap it in twain with the right amount of pressure. Cyril could see Eufrates spy the dagger tucked in his vest through his long, dark lashes.

Eufrates let out a huff of derision. "What did you think? That you'd be able to overwhelm me by force? It is not like in your adventure novels. It takes more than a single stab in the back to kill a man, my love."

If he called Cyril that again, his head was going to split.

Cyril winced from the pressure on his wrist, but he squared

his shoulders, forcing himself not to shrink back against the solid mass of the prince.

"Truly? I thought you would have let me." He dared to let a smile play upon his lips. "You were besotted. I think you would have gladly died by my hand."

He knew he'd pushed too far when a growl escaped Eufrates's throat and he was shoved against the bark of a tree, hard enough to knock the breath from his lungs.

The duality of man meant even as a youth prince, Margrave was a gentle, poetic soul *and* a beast in combat. The unfairness of it stung in a very real way now.

"So that was your brilliant plan? Nip me in the bud?" Eufrates said. "What about preventing me from taking the crown to begin with? What about preventing my sister's *death*?"

"I thought you'd relished in that." The words tumbled out of Cyril's lips before he could stop himself.

Eufrates gave him an acrid and, if Cyril didn't know better, heartbroken stare. He regarded him for a long while before clapping a large hand on the bone of his shoulder.

"I've misjudged you. Your devotion to us must be strong indeed if you'd choose to lie in the bed of a regicide, my love."

Cyril glared up, defensive. "It was not an *immediate* conclusion."

"Oh, no, no." Eufrates clicked his tongue. "You must have conjured it up in that seaside hovel while plotting how to kill me."

His eyes widened, throat cotton dry. "...You knew where I was."

"Of *course* I knew where you were!" There was a glint of madness in Eufrates's eye. He looked on the verge of shaking with laughter. Suddenly, his hand darted from Cyril's shoulder up to his throat, simultaneously cupping it dearly and holding him in place against that tree like quarry. "My love, we are *bonded*. You have *given* yourself to me, you are *mine*." His other hand snaked inside Cyril's shirt until it finally grasped at the ring hidden within. "There isn't a single corner of the universe you could hide in where I would not find you."

He was, at once, jocular and dead-serious. Cyril recognized the musicality of the speech, an improvised soliloquy. When the words hit his ears, they were sharp as blades, mocking their betrothal as a sham that ended in discord.

But at the same time Cyril's blood chilled in his veins. The best a playwright can do is romanticise what they know. He was no longer Eufrates's love, but it did not mean that, in the eyes of the prince, he was not Eufrates's property.

Eufrates rolled his eyes. "Besides, it is not as though you ran very far. You could have at *least* made it to Cretea."

"I *did*," Cyril tried his best not to swallow, worried Eufrates would feel it in his grip. He felt his throat bob against the gloved fist around his neck when he spoke.

"Oh, yes! The annex. It was so long ago, forgive an old man's memory."

The prince regarded him a while longer, smoothing his thumb against the underside of his cheek. He pursed his lips in rapt contemplation.

"It truly is a shame. I had held hope that perhaps I'd been sent back in time on the whims of a trickster god. I should have liked to meet you as you were again, sweet and soft. Ripe."

He narrowed his eyes into slits, refusing to cower. "What gave it away?"

Eufrates finally let go of his throat to trace a semicircle under his eyes, so tender it almost had Cyril fooled. He leaned in close enough; for a moment all Cyril could smell was sandalwood and musk. And then Eufrates's lips split into a mocking smile.

"Your eyeliner is crooked."

"You're *obsessed* with me."

"You are *mine*," Eufrates repeated, so low it rumbled in Cyril's ears like the growl of a monster. His fist closed around the ring and tugged the string taut around Cyril's neck, drawing him closer.

Cyril wondered what would happen if the Mage's Ward died by the prince's hand. Perhaps Eufrates would receive a hard slap on the wrist. But Eufrates was clever enough not to implicate himself. He'd play the grieving, lovestruck innocent so well that Cyril almost longed to see it.

A ruffle in the grass snapped them both out of their standstill. Eufrates took half a step back, but he did not let go of Cyril's wrist, by now bloodless in its lack of circulation.

Moments later, a young guard burst running in through the trees, windswept and breathless. Cyril had watched her train before. She was younger than him by a year and her name was Marta. She had a scar on her cheek from a hazardous drill.

She looked at the pair of them, wrapped up in apparent intimacy, but did not balk or look at all ashamed. A desperate glint in her eye hinted that whatever it was she'd run into the woods for superseded any need for propriety.

"His Highness needs to come with me. It is urgent," she gasped, and flicked the sweat off her slicked brow to look at Eufrates.

Everything about this seemed awfully familiar to Cyril in a way he couldn't quite put a finger on.

Until he did.

As Eufrates fully let go of him to turn to Marta, looking the picture of curiously concerned, Cyril tasted the cloying bile making its way up his throat.

"What is the matter?" he said evenly.

"It's – Your Highness, I can't–" Marta covered her mouth with one hand as though it was information she was unworthy of delivering. Cyril realised she was.

"It's *today*?" he whispered to himself, so low and so small no one could have possibly heard him.

But Eufrates did.

He glanced quickly at Cyril before nodding his head towards Marta. "Go on, sir. I will be right behind you."

"But–"

"I swear it."

Once the young guard was out of sight, returning to them their privacy, Eufrates turned and looked at Cyril as if he were considering whether to squash a bug under his shoe.

"I had *hoped* near half a century alive would have sharpened your wit." His voice was sour, dripping with contempt. "You did not even bother to ask for the date, then?"

Cyril looked steadfast at the ground. He was so stupid. He was *so* stupid. He shook his head.

"Ah. Well, my love. It is the sixth of April." Eufrates's words were clipped and slow, like talking to a child. He clapped a hand on Cyril's shoulder and drew close to his ear. "I will see you at the wake."

With this, he turned and left. Cyril did not see him go, because he was preoccupied vacating the excess contents of his stomach onto the grass.

It had been like a wall of dominoes, one after the other. That was the most apt description of the events following his twenty-second year.

The first tragedy had actually been the king and queen.

Because of how close and how *real* Tigris Margrave's death had been to him, Cyril was ashamed to admit the exact timing of the rulers of Farsala's deaths had slipped his mind. It had been so, *so* long ago, he forgot that they had been so close together.

On April fifth of that year, Rohan and Micaela Margrave died on a ship headed to a standard diplomatic enterprise, alongside a retinue of other foreign dignitaries sharing the same voyage. The news reached their surviving heirs and, subsequently, everyone else in the palace, merely a day later.

After a few months, it was Tigris's turn. She had not even begun to don the lavenders and slate greys of late mourning when disease overcame her, quickly after her rushed, ascetic wedding. The people needed *some* good tidings, after all.

Cyril truly believed Queen Tigris, despite her temper and her flaws, would have been one of Farsala's golden rulers, ushering it into a new age of prosperity. Remembering how she looked on her sickbed, a steadfast refusal to even entertain the idea of death by *disease* of all things, did nothing to prove him wrong.

The final death of the year, natural amidst a wave of inexorable tragedies, was no easier to swallow. In November, a serving maid found Aunt Hel – *Grand Mage* Heléne – dead in her bed, peaceful. A physician said the toll of misfortune had been too much for such an elderly heart to bear. On her chest was a spotted, moulting old crow, more salt and pepper than black by this point. His aunt's familiar.

Cyril saw to it that they were interred in the same casket.

And then it was just the two of them. Cyril and Eufrates, alone, together, surrounded by servants and courtiers and guards and knights and nobles and lords and cutthroats and peasants. Each and every one wanting something from their new king and his positively *juvenile* new grand mage.

It had felt like drowning, and while he wished to say the new king and he were each other's life rafts, it was more like they were taking turns pushing each other under so, one at a time, they could draw a gasp of air. There was no malice in the exchange. They were boys, and they were desperate, and Cyril remembered gladly ducking his head underwater so Eufrates had time to breathe.

All the while, they danced around each other. Simultaneously falling asleep in the same bed after long nights of statecraft and jolting away from each other in the halls if a single pinky brushed against the back of a hand. It was agony. To cool his heart, he read the letters Eufrates had sent him during school, over and over, obsessively, but it did little to quell the ache.

The alliance with Atticus, a kind and understanding man near a decade older than the two of them, was strong, and

Cretea vowed its help in whatever matters possible. But soon Cyril could overhear the whispers in Eufrates's ear urging him to choose a spouse. To form new bonds. To assure the kingdom an heir.

Cyril had shut himself in his tower after that. Dedicating himself to alchemy and sorcery and potions and poultices, pouring over his aunt's notes because they were the only sense of purpose he had now. Like a scorned child, he refused to leave, sending his reports by either carrier pigeon or in the hands of the more competent valets who brought up his meals. If there was a knock at the door, he dismissed it. His chambers became a whirlwind of disarray. He was quite sure at some point his hair had grown so unruly were he not gifted with magic he would have had to shave it off completely.

Then, one day, the king himself knocked at his door.

Well. Cyril was being gracious. Eufrates burst the lock on his door open with the back of a sword and kicked his way into his apartments. He found Cyril lying in a nest of blankets a foot away from his bed, which he had fallen from due to feverish night terrors and been too lazy to get back up into several hours before.

"Cy," Eufrates had declared as he scooped him by his arms off the floor. It was like Cyril was weightless in his embrace. "I've decided to marry."

Cyril blinked slowly, wondering why such a true friend would willingly choose to torment him so horribly. "Oh," he said.

"You are my dearest friend and most trusted companion." It was unlike Eufrates to speak so quickly, so awkwardly. "There is no one else I would have beside me upon that altar. Upon – upon that *throne*. No one else has my ear, my hand, my entire being."

So, Cyril thought, *the king needed a best man*. Perhaps he would need to do something about his hair after all. He nodded and cracked a facsimile of a smile. "So, is it Baroness Marguerite?

I think it would be cute. Marguerite Margrave." He rolled the alliteration on his tongue. "And she is a very nice woman. Very decent." Cyril wondered if his late aunt had left any liquor in her rooms.

Eufrates had looked truly, *deeply* wounded, which wasn't fair, because the only person who had the right to be hurt right now was Cyril himself. Out of the corner of his eye he saw Shoestring, whose expressive eyes seemed to be *expressing* that he was a fool.

Yes, I know that, stupid cat.

Cautiously, Eufrates's hands had roamed from Cyril's limp shoulders to his chest. He gripped him by the lapels of his nightshirt (the only thing he'd worn during those days) and looked deep into Cyril's eyes with a touch of madness that almost made him flinch.

He opened and closed his mouth, as if to speak. Then, thinking better of it, he had drawn Cyril up the few inches it would take to close the gap between their disparate heights, and kissed him thoroughly on the lips.

FOUR

Once the news about the king and queen broke more widely, a pall descended upon Margrave House and its court. Cyril was not there to witness the initial spread.

After he was done retching, he crawled to the stream Eufrates had sat by what felt like hours ago and rinsed his mouth with the cool, fresh water. Not finding this enough, he fully dunked his head in and held his breath to the point of light-headedness.

Shoestring, who had kept his distance for the entirety of Cyril's embarrassing little spat with his *ex*, sauntered over a few moments later to drink his fill, observing his master's pathetic state with empty disinterest. Cyril pulled the cat into his lap as though he were still a newly weaned kitten. He gently stroked Shoestring's back, burying his face in his side. His shoulders shook.

He had failed.

He was fool enough to come back to the past, to his youth, to *hope,* with only *one* shoddy plan and it had utterly and completely *failed*. He was not here to right some kind of terrible wrong. He was being punished. He was about to witness tragedy strike twice, only this time, he'd be lucky if he lived past Eufrates's coronation.

Cyril reached for the ring pressed against his chest, thumbing it curiously. He wondered if Eufrates *could* kill him. If they were bonded in more than just the plane of the living.

They were ghosts to each other now. Apparitions of the past, steadfast in getting in each other's way. Given their track record, Cyril was bound to lose.

It was late in the evening when he picked himself up off the ground and snuck back into the palace, a thief in the night. He was not in the right state of mind to play-act a reaction to a tragedy he'd mourned all too well, and he was not interested in hearing condolences.

Cyril's own parents, after dropping him off with his aunt on his fifth birthday, had died unceremoniously one after the next over the most trifling of misfortunes. While they kept a cool distance from their strange ward, Rohan and Micaela treated him kindly, with a certain fondness, and he was very grateful. He did not understand the cruelty of living through the same death twice until this moment and it made his heart ache terribly.

He would not be comforted over the death of the king and queen. He did not deserve it.

He crept up the steps to his quarters with Shoestring wrapped tightly in his arms, more out of habit than anything at this point, and contemplated what he was meant to do with the rest of his short life.

Perhaps Eufrates would spare him. He needed a mage to keep up appearances, after all. But he could just as well find a non-Laverre. Pluck an eager graduate from the Academy, perhaps even break tradition entirely and hire a team of specialists instead of one lone grand mage and replace Cyril completely.

Running away was starting to sound quite enticing.

Cyril paused in front of his door. He remembered this night, vaguely. Exhausted, he had gone to bed early. Grief-stricken and young, he had thought of no one but himself.

He opened the door to usher Shoestring in, but then shut it behind him, trapping the cat inside. He got little resistance save for a confused mewl.

Then, he began to climb farther up than his third floor of the tower.

Floors four to seven belonged to the grand mage, with the very tallest among them being Heléne's opulent apartments. Five and six were grandiose studies he had been eager to inherit, and four was a modest kitchen, more for potions than for cookery.

Cyril bypassed the kitchen and the studies until he stood in front of the great wooden door leading to the grand mage's private rooms.

He knocked. He received no answer, so he pushed the door open and walked inside.

"Tantie," he tried.

He did not expect a response, so he pressed onwards into the bedroom.

When Cyril was a child, his aunt's quarters were sacrosanct. He was not to enter without being invited in, and even the thought of it felt wrong in his gut. Heléne Laverre had not been famously good with children, having never had any of her own. So she'd kept her new ward at arm's length those early days.

Not that it wasn't obvious upon a glance, but Aunt Heléne was not *actually* Cyril's aunt. They were related by blood, of course, but his father had only had brothers. She was an older cousin of Cyril's grandmother, herself already a woman of some years. The well of magic in the Laverres seemed to have run quite dry until Cyril manifested his gifts out of the blue one day.

Cyril would never dare ask how old his mentor was, but he could make an educated guess that she was in the higher eighties. Perhaps even older, considering the revitalising properties of magical blood. It meant when he blundered into her life, snot-nosed and ruddy-faced, barely out of toddlerhood, she did her best with the very little she knew. But for the most part, she had palmed him off to nurses and tutors the Margraves were already employing.

They had formed a bond regardless, especially once Cyril really dedicated himself to the patterns. He had always guessed she held a fondness for teaching, if only to be able to show off.

"Tantie…" he called for her again and rapped on her door. It was only when he gently pushed it open that he heard a sob.

He had never seen her like this, and if he could guess, he would blame it on a mixture of her never *letting* him see her like this and him not *wanting* it.

Heléne Laverre was hunched over in her oversized plush bed, an embroidered blanket wrapped around her like a frightened child's comforter. She rocked herself back and forth. Her crow, whose name was Ganache, cooed and cawed at her in concern.

"I saw that boy be born…" She shook as she spoke. "I was at his delivery. I was never meant to outlive him."

It took Cyril a moment to realise she was talking about the late king. Rohan Margrave had perhaps been in his mid-fifties at the time of his death. He knew somewhere in his mind that his aunt *must* have watched him grow up, but to suddenly see him through her eyes, a young man in his prime taken before his time, wrecked him.

In that moment, Cyril realised that perhaps his entire life he had never regarded his aunt as a person. A witch, a crone, a menace, perhaps. A guiding hand, a strong presence, but he could not imagine her *young* or aging. He could not imagine her cradling the king when he was born, seeing him grow up, loving him and his future wife in deep friendship. To Cyril, she had always been Aunt Heléne Laverre, Grand Mage of Farsala, the Witch Upon the Tower.

"Tantie, it's me…" he whispered, doing his level best to soothe. "It's Cyril."

She looked up at him and her rheumy eyes were swollen with tears. He was sure that if she did not want him there, he would be woven to his rooms in the blink of an eye and tied to his bed till late next morrow. She did no such thing.

"Duckling." She reached out to him. They had the same bony limbs. "What are you doing up here?"

Gods. He had not heard *that* name in years.

He was not fool enough to insult her, to point out her weakness, so he sat next to her on the bed instead.

"I could not sleep."

"No…" She shook her head. "Neither can I."

"…I'm sorry," he murmured after a grave pause.

Heléne tilted her head up to finally look in his eyes. "What are you sorry for, child? You've done nothing wrong."

She had no idea. Cyril shifted, uncomfortable in his seat. "It's what you're supposed to say… after a death, I mean."

Sorrow welled up in her eyes again and she looked down at her fists clenched around a hunk of embroidered fabric. Her long, silver hair cascaded over her face just enough she was spared the humiliation of tearing up in front of a "child".

"It was not their time. They were too, too young, and now that *girl*." Tigris. "The weight on her shoulders. She's barely out of the tutoring room."

In a different time, Cyril would have balked. Protested, even. Tigris Margrave was to be wed soon. She was reaching her latter twenties. But being this elder in the shell of a youth, he nodded. People should only have responsibilities thrust upon them well into their forties.

This was going horrendously. He had crept up here to try and offer some solace and yet he was letting Heléne twist herself up in knots, carving away at the fresh wounds the more she spoke.

When he was a boy and the pressures of his station got to be too much, he would have crying breakdowns, sweaty night terrors and breathless anxiety attacks. He thought he hid them well, ensconced in his rooms with Shoestring's head against his chest, but sometimes his aunt would notice the change. Perhaps out of a dormant instinct for parenthood, she would then call him up to her own chambers and let him lay his head

on her shoulder as he sobbed, babying him until he finally
tired himself out and fell asleep.

With this vision in mind, Cyril clumsily scooted up on the
bed until he could make the old woman comfortable. Gentle
as a feather he tugged her towards him, resting her head upon
his chest.

She felt very frail, then. So frail that Cyril was scared to
touch her, but eventually he began to stroke her hair.

"You can cry if you'd like, Tantie."

Heléne seemed to be recovering from the initial shock of the
tenderness at first to do anything at all, but eventually she did.

She wept. She wept for the man she'd regarded at once a
surrogate son and a treasured friend, she wept for his wife who
she'd come to love just as dearly, she wept for their orphan
children and finally, she wept for Cyril. A lonely boy she now
wasn't even strong enough to comfort herself. And just like
Cyril all those years ago, she wept so long and hard she fell
asleep in his arms.

Cyril kept vigil until the sand in his eyes weighed much too
heavy, and then he had to retire himself. He did not leave the
room, however. The bed was large enough he could sleep at
one end of it without disturbing her, and he did not wish to
leave her alone.

It was, mercifully, one of the first untroubled sleeps he'd
had in years.

She was still fast asleep a few hours later when he awoke.
He lay in bed waiting for the sun to rise before restlessness
overtook him and he decided to make himself useful.

Cyril descended the tower to the kitchen floor, which was
empty of any servants at this early hour. Unlike the palace
kitchens, they did not use it to prepare meals, but occasionally
they flitted in and out of the room to replace and restore
produce.

He was no chef, and he was not about to begin trying. So instead, he found a large platter and piled it high with fresh, ripe fruit, biscuits, bread, small tins of butter and jam. Then, he brewed a kettle of rich, fragrant tea and balanced all this on a tray all the way up to the top of the tower, where Aunt Heléne was already rubbing the sleep from her eyes.

"Good morning, Tantie."

He cleared room on a table by clumsily shoving papers and trinkets out of the way and deposited their scavenged breakfast. Heléne, who had clearly regained her composure since the evening, regarded the offering with suspicion.

She sauntered over to the table and took a seat. Cyril poured her a cup of tea, spooned sugar and poured cream into the liquid.

Heléne looked at him with an arched brow. "Who taught you to serve tea?"

He felt almost embarrassed that this was unusual knowledge for him as he poured his own cup, more sugar than liquid in the end.

"It's hot water and leaves, Tantie. No need to underestimate me."

"Bah." She crunched into a biscuit and her familiar began pecking at the crumbs (Cyril would have to remember to fetch something for Shoestring later). "You've always been a milksop, boy. I can't imagine where you would have learned this." She took a sip. "It is quite adequate."

Cyril sighed. It seemed Grand Mage Laverre was back in fighting form. "Thank you, madam."

She paused in front of her cup. "Thank you, Cyril."

They sat in a companionable silence that was not meant to last, because eventually his aunt broke it with:

"You should have brought raisins from the pantry. They are Ganache's favourite."

Cyril stifled a laugh. It was very like her to make demands of a kindness.

He looked at the old crow. "Forgive me, Ganache. I will cut up some fruit for you instead."

Ganache preened, seemingly unperturbed by the lack of raisins on the table when she could peck at sweet biscuits and cream to her heart's content.

"Where is that cat of yours, Duckling? Still asleep?"

Cyril tensed. If there was anyone in the palace who could suss out the true nature of his familiar, it was his aunt. So he nodded. "Shoestring does love his naps. And you know how independent he is."

"Yes… a perfect complement for such a needy child." She smiled through a bite of an orange wedge.

His ears reddened and he slumped back in his chair with a defiant little pout. He could argue with her on this, of course, but he had a feeling she would win.

He stared at Ganache as she pecked her way through a halved papaya, crunching the black seeds in her beak without a care in the world, before he cleared his throat.

"Tantie…" he said.

She did not look up from her meal. "Yes, child?"

"Have you ever…?" He gripped the end of his tunic, as if wringing water from it. "Has there ever been a mage who's lost a familiar?"

She raised a brow at him. "Familiars die with their mages."

"Yes… yes, I know that, but…"

"Is something wrong with Shoestring?"

Yes. Desperately.

"Oh, no." He waved his dismissal. "I just get worried about him sometimes. He wanders about so often, I fear I might find him crushed under the wheel of a carriage."

Heléne snorted. "Well, worry no longer, child. Familiars cannot die before their time. They're beings borne of magic, the essence of a mage's soul. I do not believe your *essence* could be run over by a *vehicle*."

"No, perhaps not, but... you are so very..." He paused. "Experienced. Has there really never been a familiar death in your time?"

To Ganache, she grumbled, "The nerve of this child, coming up here to call me old." But before Cyril could raise his voice in protest, she pondered his question seriously. "I suppose... I have met mages who've lost their familiar. It would be hard to forget something like that. But Duckling, I could count their numbers on one hand."

Cyril leaned in in breathless rapture. He *had* to know. "What happened to them?"

"Oh, well, it is not a difficult deduction. If the very essence of a mage has passed on without them–"

"They no longer have an essence at all," Cyril finished in a very small, dry-throated voice.

"Precisely." Heléne did not seem to notice her ward's internal crisis. She rattled on as though giving a lecture, "Horrible creatures, those mages I met. They were living half a life, almost in defiance of the Undertaker. It was like the soul had given up, but the body was clinging."

"...Do you have any idea why?"

She shrugged. "Cowardice, most likely. A primal fear of death."

"Not unfinished business?"

She laughed at this. "They were not *poltergeists*, child. But perhaps. I've not met nearly enough to paint a clear picture. And I should loathe to encounter another mage so careless with their own essence that they would let a familiar die."

Cyril's blood ran cold. Regardless of being a ghost or not, he certainly *felt* like one now he was roaming aimless in an afterlife he had trapped himself within.

It was mid-morning when he descended to his own floor of the tower. As soon as he opened the door, Shoestring tumbled out, mewling for food and attention. The tell-tale scratches on the wood an indication he'd neglected his phantom a bit too long.

"I don't even know who you *are*," he murmured as he rustled up some leftovers from the morning's feast for the cat to eat, along with a bowl of clean water. Familiars had no particular dietary restrictions, but he did not know if whoever *this* was did.

This Shoestring seemed to behave like a normal cat, but if he looked closely, Cyril could see in his pattern that he was not of flesh and earth. He also held a vacant, empty look in his eyes, and no shine reflected off them.

Like Cyril, this was some kind of facsimile of life. A creature that had no right to exist.

If anything, they were twin flames.

Out of nowhere, he felt a bubble of laughter escape his lips, contained at first, but then hysterical.

Between bites of salted meat, Shoestring tilted his head at him and yowled.

"Oh, you would find it funny if you could grasp it, stupid cat." He sighed and steadied himself against a table to cool his outburst.

He truly had nothing to lose now. And if he had come to this place – this *time* – with a purpose then, well, he ought to fulfil it.

He examined the empty vessel of a creature prowling in his room and a new plan began to blossom in his mind. One perhaps even more foolish than before. As the gears turned in his head, a grin split his lips and he knelt down to pet Shoestring on the soft spot between his eyes.

"What have we to fear?" he said. "I'm living on borrowed time, and you aren't real!"

FIVE

It turned out the timeframe for Cyril's new-born scheme presented itself almost immediately. Tigris Margrave announced to palace and people that she would have her wedding dinner (not to be mistaken for an actual wedding) a fortnight after the wake of the late king and queen.

The poor girl barely had time to grieve before courtesans doubtlessly pressed her on her nuptials, begging the future queen to single-handedly lift the fog of mourning that had spread throughout the palace. Cyril would have liked to help, but he was busy keeping a profile so low it was beginning to crack its way into the earth's core.

He did not think he could evade Eufrates for very long, but he was going to give the man the chase of a lifetime.

Normally it was vulgar, even crude, to use magic frivolously. Messing with the pattern was meant to be reserved for dire, sacred, important circumstances. An over-reliance on weaving cheapened the art, debased it to a mere parlour trick for the amusement of a crowd. The grand mages in Farsala already toed the line between utility and entertainment, with their flamboyant dress and painted faces.

But decorum was the last of Cyril's concerns. Decorum had, in fact, flown out the tallest window of the tallest tower of the palace as soon as he stuffed a dagger in his breast pocket and clumsily tried to assassinate the prince.

So every time he heard the aforementioned prince's heavy,

61

distinctive footfall down a hall or up a flight of stairs, every time he heard the squeak of those leather gloves push open a door, Cyril played the weave like a harpsichord, manipulating the air around him so he became completely invisible. One week after Cyril's grand spell had been cast, they were thoroughly engaged in a game of cat and mouse, if the mouse was able to appear and disappear at will.

The only time they had been *forced* to interact had been, as promised, at the wake. They were not able to recover the king's and queen's bodies from the open ocean, so the funeral was symbolic. Two empty caskets were interred in ancestral ground, in a plot of land between the woods and the palace where all other royals had been buried. Cyril couldn't help but keep darting his eyes towards an empty spot near the fresh tombs, which would serve as Tigris's resting place only months later. He was surprised how affected he was by it.

Eufrates approached him once everyone else had left. He had stood beside his sister the whole day; the pair of them in their darkest blacks and kohl smudged over their eyes looked like twin Undertakers. Once thick droplets of rain started to hit headpieces and scalps, the procession moved inside. Cyril saw the prince say something to his sister and she followed the line of courtiers making their way to the dry warmth of the palace. Eufrates, though, made his way towards him.

"So, darling. What is your plan now?"

Cyril snapped his head up to look him in the eye. If Eufrates Margrave had anything in excess, it was *nerve*.

"We are *at* a *funeral*," he hissed.

"I'm surprised it bothers you. You were eager enough to see it *twice*."

It hit him then that, intentional or not, he had forced *Eufrates* to live through his parents' funeral a second time. He despised the man, but he did not wish to be cruel. He examined Eufrates's eyes for any kind of great sorrow, but before he could pierce through the stony dark brown gaze, the prince decided he had gone too long without an answer.

"Do you still intend to kill me? You will have to catch me unawares. And without me *or* Tig, who would rule Farsala? Perhaps they'll find a distant cousin in the court." He eyed Cyril up and down. "Perhaps the promising young mage, conveniently raised with the royals."

"What? I – what are you *saying*?" Eufrates was accusing *him* of being power hungry. The world might have spun against its axis.

"You're right." Eufrates stepped forward and Cyril hated the gooseflesh he triggered on his skin, even after all this time. "You'd rather work in the shadows. But I won't let you out of my sight."

"I thought you'd just kill me and get it over with. Are you waiting to be crowned?"

A flash of something inscrutable lit up his eyes and it was gone in an instant. Eufrates sneered, "Oh, no, my love. I am not a wasteful king. There is use for you yet, at my side."

Cyril frowned. "You will not be king."

Eufrates's brows raised, and for a moment he seemed to want to say something more, but movement caught the corner of his eye, and he pushed past Cyril.

"What are you doing?! I told you to get inside!"

Cyril turned and Tigris was several metres away, standing on a hill cresting the path back to the palace. Her dress, as well as Cyril's and Eufrates's clothes by this point, was soaked in rainwater.

She smiled and, whether or not it was feigned levity, she was doing an incredible job at holding herself together. "I thought I might see something nice if I played the spy," she yelled from her hill.

Eufrates, usually ever indulgent, did not smile back. He stomped his way up to her and withdrew his jacket to cover her head.

"You'll catch a chill, halfwit," Cyril heard him say with a flare of genuine frustration in his voice.

He watched them go until he felt the rain soak into his own bones. He sneezed against his sleeve before running into the foyer of the palace to join the rest of the mourning party.

Cyril did not know if Eufrates made good on the promise to not let him out of his sight, because for the next few days, he did his best to avoid him like the black plague. He had become a consummate expert at being a mouse, and all the while, preparations for his new plan were going better than expected.

Back in the cottage, Cyril had limited resources to work with. Half a stick of chalk and some blood. Spit to wet it when the mixture congealed too quickly from the cold. For a month, he was on his knees on a hard rock floor drawing and redrawing patterns until he got it *just* right. He neglected his fishing duties, so he relied on leftover scraps, barely bitefuls, picking at bones. He slept when necessary, when his body truly couldn't keep up with his brain any longer, and he drank just enough to stay alive.

But here in his tower, he was a king among wizards. He had all the charting chalk at his disposal, servants brought him fine foods with the ring of a bell, and he could use one of many cushions to prop himself up on the floor so his knees weren't scraped and raw from the ordeal. *And* he had the advantage of a spry, twenty-*nothing* young body to work with. He could hold himself up for hours at a time, picking away at the circles on the ground with barely a crick in his neck. Cyril vowed to himself that, if he managed to live to see Tigris's successful coronation, he would exercise more. Do the daily stretches he was taught and quickly eschewed at the Academy.

The only thing that remained the same was the heart-thundering anxiety that he had somehow gotten something wrong.

He'd been alone in the cottage by default, but here it was by choice. He couldn't have anyone coming in and *checking his work*. Aunt Heléne would know *exactly* what he was trying to do and question him endlessly with 'who's?' and the 'why's?' and a 'what rock did you hit your head against, child?'.

Once his draftsmanship was complete, he hid the sigil underneath a heavy ornate rug he found rolled up in one of the lower floors of the tower meant for storage. He also procured a medium-sized cage from a welder in town – just to be safe – which he kept inconspicuously under his desk for when the time was right.

Now all that was left to do was get dressed for Tigris's fancy little dinner, and hope nobody would notice the hummingbird beat of his heart against his chest.

Formal events were always an ordeal to prepare for, but Cyril would be lying if he didn't admit that he somewhat relished in the pageantry. Frugality did not agree with him, as had been proven by those many years wasting away on the shores of that beach, in a life so grim that it had quite literally taken his soul from him.

He allowed a trio of valets to dress him, and he noticed he was becoming perhaps concerningly used to being called 'Young Master Cyril'. In his mind, he knew he was a man of presumably fifty, but the youthfulness of the body and the way he was perceived distorted his own sense of self in a way he didn't expect. If he didn't keep himself in check, soon enough he'd truly buy into being a carefree twenty-two year-old again.

There was, among most of the continent that was known to him and especially in the south, a time-honoured tradition for mages to dress as bright, bejewelled creatures. Exotic birds in a menagerie. Even common folk upheld the unspoken rule of, frankly, costume dressing. The mages of Farsala were usually the most flamboyant of them all. He knew that upstairs, his aunt would be donning a mask of a painted face, opulent dress, beads and feathered headdress. For Cyril's part, he chose his usual fare. Brightly coloured silks, diamond and striped patterns. A chemise light as air, with bouffant sleeves layered under a cropped vest. Pointed-toe shoes that made him resemble an elf in a child's picture book, and a collar of stiff crinoline forming a halo around his head.

He dismissed the attendants for the face paint. He revelled in doing it himself. Cyril was not *vain* necessarily, but he doubted there was anyone in the world who did not have their ego bolstered by seeing their eyes, their lips, their cheekbones elevated in a way that was *just* right. He traced patterns with kohl under his waterline, making sure to get them perfect this time. The two weeks he'd spent back in court had done wonders for steadying his hands.

He would not be accused of sloppy application again.

A butler introduced him when he entered the foyer leading to the main hall and he realised he'd not seen it this full in eons. The funeral had been a private affair, upon the surviving Margraves' insistence. There were those who had wished to make it into a public day of mourning, with parades down the city streets, but not even the most hot-blooded courtier in Farsala had the nerve to suggest it to a pair of grieving siblings.

He saw all familiar faces. After all, he had been at this exact wedding dinner however many years ago. Some he was happy to see. A baroness he'd made friends with at one of the more boring functions, a lord who had a talent for playing cards, a couple of old classmates from the Academy who had not decided to dedicate themselves to magic having that much wealth at their disposal, instead conjuring up little spells for entertainment, centred on the simpler disciplines like illusion or animation.

Many, however, he could have done without. Cyril had gained a bit of a reputation in court within a few years of his arrival. The Margrave *Pet*. Not an insignificant faction of nobles in that room thought him coddled and spoiled, a dancing monkey with funny little tricks to amuse the royal family. By name alone, he was *dubiously* part of the peerage, and he clearly had not yet earned the respect Heléne Laverre had worked years to cultivate.

It became much worse after his wedding. He was, after all, the king's concubine, useless but to keep a bed warm and legs spread. And he did not even have the decency to be able to deliver an heir.

Cyril had been fairly sure, at the time, that these rumours never reached Eufrates's ears. He would have been outraged if they did. But thinking back on it, there would be no outrage if it were all true.

He stalked directly to the refreshments table, past a gaggle of nobles already eyeing him for courtly humiliation, and poured himself a glass of wine nearly to the rim. It was going to be a long night. Perhaps he should have considered all this before he chose violets and golds as his colour palette for the evening. The youthfulness his body provided was beginning to be quickly overtaken with the pressing notion that he was far too old for this.

Now that he found his place in one of the more secluded corners of the room, he scanned the crowd again, sipping at his wine. The woman of the hour was not here yet, which was of no concern. No host would ever show up to a party before everyone else, especially not when there were countless staff to take care of the guests.

Just as he was about to thank his lucky stars that *Eufrates* was also late, the prince's name was announced, sonorous and clear, right at the top of the double stairs leading from the bedrooms and the royal quarters.

Cyril shrunk into himself, which did nothing as he was spotted immediately. He could hear a maid with a platter of candied fruit titter a few feet away when Eufrates made an immediate beeline to him.

He was, infuriatingly, still the most beautiful man Cyril had ever seen. And of course, he was all smiles.

"May I have this dance, Cyril? Or are you otherwise engaged?" Eufrates made a show of looking from one side to the other, both scaring away any pretenders to Cyril's hand and making sure there *were* none.

Cyril bit his lip. What else could he possibly say? "Not at all. Of course, Your Highness."

Immediately, Eufrates swept him to the very centre of the ballroom, where they were the object of everyone's attention, but still not a soul in the room would hear their conversation. Cyril found it quite unfair, really, that his waltz was competently rusty at best, but Eufrates danced like he'd never stopped.

And of course, it wasn't even a question of whose hand was around whose waist, and who was following along. It made Cyril's heart tighten, being pushed and pulled at the whims of his partner.

Eufrates, for his part, leaned closer than propriety allowed to talk quietly in his ear, "You've been avoiding me."

"Aha. You've noticed."

"I *said* I wouldn't let you out of my sight."

"And yet I haven't laid eyes on you in nearly two weeks. Seems the bard prince is all pretty words."

Eufrates's hand snaked around his waist and tightened above his hip so hard Cyril was sure it would bruise. He bit down on his lip so he did not make a sound. The mortification would have been too much.

"I know exactly where you've *been*, dearest. I know how you spend your time, who you see, which servants attend to you."

"So much trouble to go through for a simple ward."

Eufrates snarled and spun him just a bit too hard, pulling him to his chest. "I would never make the mistake of underestimating you."

"Do you think I aim to kill you again, then?"

"No. You are not that daft. But–"

Cyril did not like this line of questioning. He was being interrogated, and Eufrates and his saccharine words had always been a particular weakness of his.

"Do you intend to wed me again?" he said bluntly.

That caught the prince off guard. Eufrates blinked, wondering if he'd misheard.

"Do I...?"

"Well, Your Highness." Cyril shrugged his shoulders. "You have been taking many liberties, and now you shower me with attention in the middle of your sister's wedding dinner. People will talk."

"*What* are you–?"

"Though, of course, I am not a suitable match for you. I'm sure no noble around us thinks of *marriage*. A fling, maybe. The prince's experimental phase with a plain-faced little courtier."

The grip on his waist tightened like a corset, and Eufrates drew him close enough to be *indecent*.

"Do *not* play the fool."

Cyril cringed but he said nothing. It was wishful thinking that such obvious taunts would divert him from his questioning. The next thing Eufrates said, though, had his head swimming.

"You act as though you are not the most stunning creature to grace any room you walk into."

Cyril paled, then coloured. *Gods.* He could not be *serious.*

"You've come with a mean streak, Your Highness," he said in a voice weaker than he meant it to be.

"Shut up. Even if we do not wed, we are bound. You made sure of it yourself. So I've nothing to worry about." He seemed to have regained his cool. Which was unfair, because Cyril still felt like the bottom had dropped out from underneath him. "You're a flighty, empty-headed fool, and the bane of my existence, but I intend to keep you at my side even if I have to fasten a chain around your neck."

"I'm afraid I'm getting mixed messages–"

Eufrates spun him a bit too hard, and Cyril was sent crashing against him, pressed against the solid warmth of his chest. Eufrates did not make to move away.

"*What* are you planning?"

Like at the funeral, his expression was inscrutable again. If Cyril was half the poet his counterpart was, he would try to describe it. Troubled, stormy, dark. All those adjectives came to mind, but it was impossible to gauge what Eufrates was truly thinking. In fact, he was beginning to think he wasn't the only one who had gone mad towards the end of his life.

Cyril opened his mouth to speak, hoping he could say something clever enough to buy himself some precious time and excuse himself from the dance floor, but just as he was about to intone the first syllable of his improvisation, another voice drowned him out.

"Excuse me. May I cut in?"

Both Cyril and Eufrates turned in unison to find they had been so absorbed in their conversation (if it could even be called that), that they neglected to hear the announcement of Tigris's arrival.

And with her, of course, was her future husband, King Atticus Wulfsbane, who now stood mere inches from Cyril with his hand outstretched and a pleasant smile etched onto that handsome, freckled face.

Just as Eufrates was about to tell him 'no', Cyril practically pried himself from his dance partner and offered the king a genial bow.

"Your Majesty. Of course."

For a moment, he was afraid Eufrates would not release him from the vice grip he still held on his waist (surely it would bruise), but he finally acquiesced to Atticus with a polite nod of his head.

Atticus, for his part, walked Cyril to a more secluded section of the room, without so many prying eyes. He also let him choose which position he would like in the minuet that was about to begin, which amused Cyril endlessly. He gave Atticus a cavalier shrug and guided his hand to his waist.

"It was very kind of you to ask me to dance," Cyril said.

Atticus glanced past Cyril's shoulder, where Eufrates had stalked up to the drinks table. "You seemed to be having trouble."

"Ah. Tig put you up to it."

Tigris, for her part, was holding herself up in a very dignified manner for someone who he knew was bouncing off the walls, ready to go interrogate her brother on his little display in her ballroom. She had always been a horrible gossip.

"Actually, she begged me not to intervene. She was convinced you would work it out on your own in a most, er... *public* way."

Cyril grimaced. That did sound like Tig. "So you went against the wishes of your wife."

"My *fiancée*. I will make it up to her later, but you truly did look like a fox caught in a net."

"A pity dance. How flattered I am." He regretted the sarcasm as soon as it escaped his tongue. Here was a gentleman doing him a favour and he might as well have spat at his feet.

But Atticus merely broke into a chuckle, which he stifled with one hand over his mouth (the hand holding Cyril's, he noticed. It could be mistaken for a kiss). "Tigris was right. You are *quite* fun."

"Tig has a habit of *making* things fun. Don't give *me* too much credit, Your Majesty."

"Please. Atticus is fine. From what Tigris has told me, we are to be practically family."

Cyril cringed inwardly. He almost felt bad, then, that he was about to delay this man's nuptials indefinitely.

For what seemed like the first time, Cyril took the measure of him. It was not as though he had never spoken to the King of Cretea before. In fact, he had often been trapped in long, tedious council meetings with him, where he spent the better part of his time feeling thoroughly out of place. But he had been so enthralled with his spouse, he barely paid attention to anyone else in the room.

From what he recalled, Atticus did not speak so prettily as Eufrates, but he had a way with words that was almost soothing. Solid and trustworthy. At the time he regarded him as a wise older figure, though looking back on it, one-and-thirty was hardly the pinnacle of experience.

Atticus was also perfectly good-looking. He had an innocent, boyish charm, like the statue of an old fairy tale hero, thrust into greatness against his will. His hair was a ruddy blonde and he kept it short and neatly styled, parted to one side. His eyes were a pale sage and the skin on each side was beginning to crinkle like layer pastry, a symptom of smiling too freely and too often.

He was pale, as most northerners were, and the famous freckles dotting his face almost complimented a tint of rosacea not even layers of fine creams could soothe. It made him look younger, but not in an unappealing way.

As Cyril studied the king's features, he noticed he was being regarded in kind. Atticus's eyes held a glint of barely contained mirth as they darted across his face and his hair and his clothes.

Was he *laughing* at him?

Cyril's lips thinned into a pout. "What is it?"

At once, Atticus blinked, refocusing his vision on Cyril's eyes. "Ah. Forgive me, you've caught me staring."

"And now you owe me an explanation."

"A more polite dance partner would have let it go."

"I will make sure you are paired with our most genteel courtier for the next song."

Atticus stifled a laugh that brought Cyril's hands close to his lips again. His cheeks tinted.

"Alright. It was my fault for being so obvious. It's your way of dress."

"Elaborate," he deadpanned.

"Gods, you *are* fun." Atticus led him in a twirl across the ballroom that made heads turn. Cyril would hear about this in the morrow. "The ruffles, the patterns, the *makeup*. They dress you up like a little Pierrot, Laverre. I am sure I had a poppet who looked just like you as a child."

If there was colour in his face before, now it must have been positively aflame. Cyril turned his face away from Atticus and sniffed, affronted, "It's tradition. Surely even in Cretea, mages distinguish themselves. How does your court dress *its* mages?"

"Oh, I would not know. What my people do and how they choose to dress, magically inclined or not, is out of my jurisdiction, but in court, well… we do not make a habit of keeping pet mages in Cretea."

"*Pet*– very well. How *do* you treat your mages, Your Majesty?"

"Well, we for certain do not groom one especially for court. But if we did, I'm sure we would not parade him around in silly clothes."

"I happen to *like* my silly clothes."

"Of course. Again, forgive me. Chalk it up to a cultural disparity."

"You know, I have quite the sway with Tig. I could have her call off the wedding."

Atticus raised a brow. "How curious. Tigris told me you were a *good* friend."

Again, Cyril flushed and looked down at his feet to recover some semblance of decorum. He did not remember Atticus being this quick-witted. He had been thoroughly bested with a *genuine compliment*.

"…Tell me more about your court's mages, then, if you'll indulge me."

Atticus's eyes lit up. "Indulging such a dear friend of my fiancée's is my greatest wish. When we need a mage, we outsource. If there is a dearth of potions, we call upon an alchemist. If there is need for a specific spell, we find a skilled weaver."

Cyril nodded. "Sounds… sensible."

"Being a jack of all trades must be a great burden on such slim shoulders."

He laughed through his nose. "Ha. You should see my aunt."

Suddenly, Atticus leaned in conspiratorially, lowering his voice. "You know, even the royal family is trained in basic magecraft."

Cyril's brows shot up. "Truly?"

He grinned. "Tigris told me that would get your attention. It's nothing to write home about, but I've learned to read the pattern here and there."

Cyril narrowed his eyes at him. "…You are trying to charm me."

The grin split into a wider smile, seemingly pleased to have been caught in his schemes. "Has it worked?"

"…Perhaps."

He did not remember this side of Atticus. In truth, he did not remember ever having this sort of conversation with him, which could be chalked up to the simple fact that he never had.

At Tigris's wedding dinner and every function that followed, Cyril had spent his time utterly besotted by Eufrates, not letting go of him for a single second, dancing the night away. His chest tightened when he remembered how the prince would sing to him in his brooding gravel, charmingly off-key, making up words to go with whatever waltz they were stepping to. He had been *obnoxiously* blind to his own feelings to believe what they were sharing at the time was just deep companionship.

Now that he had spent enough time with his husband to see through to his true nature, he could entertain other options. Not that Atticus was one of them. Or that he would *actually* take courtship seriously at his advanced age.

Even as he thought this, the ring glued to his chest felt like it was boring a hole through his skin. Cyril cringed.

I'm not doing *anything, for fuck's sake.*

"It seems I've finally bored you." Cyril realised Atticus was looking at him with some empathy, trying his best to decipher the lull in the conversation.

Cyril shook his head. "I can assure you that isn't the case."

Atticus flashed him a reassuring smile. "Still. I've stolen more than enough of your time. We've taken three full turns around the ballroom at this point."

He blinked. Had it really been that long?

"Besides, I have other guests I must speak to. I've been putting it off for some time, but eventually I'll have to face the brother-in-law." Cyril followed Atticus's gaze to the back of Eufrates's perfectly coiffed head. He had a glass of dark-coloured liquor in one hand that Cyril had *not* spotted on the refreshments tables. "Wish me luck. He's been glaring at me like he wants my head on a pike."

Cyril had not noticed this at all. "I'm sure he's protective of his sister."

Atticus let out a breath of laughter. "His sister! Yes, of course." Then, he *winked*. "I shall bid you goodnight, then, Laverre. But I hope to see you again soon."

Cyril felt the tug of a smile creep up on him even as the ring pulsated hot against his chest. He pointedly ignored it and curtsied. "Likewise, Atticus."

Once they were parted, Cyril saw Atticus bravely stride across the ballroom to Eufrates, who by then had only half a drink remaining in his grip. He made the rookie mistake of crossing eyes with the prince, and the look he gave him was so chilling he could feel the pinpricks of frost in his bones.

He could not *possibly* be jealous. If he were jealous, he would have intervened in the dance. If he were jealous, he would not have held Cyril up like a pinned specimen against the bark of a tree. If he were jealous, he would not have *let him go*.

Cyril turned sharply on his heel away from Eufrates and went about procuring his own drink, a glass of imported white wine, and a handful of hors d'oeuvres to ensure he did not become inebriated. Then, he sat at one of the emptier tables in a secluded corner of the room and let the rest of the party run its course, chewing on finger-sandwiches and fried savoury pastries.

All the while, he watched Tigris Margrave like a hawk. She was a wonder to behold. A natural social butterfly, fluttering from guest to guest with what Cyril knew was an encyclopaedic knowledge of their names, titles and claims to being here tonight. She smiled, she laughed, she curtsied, and everywhere she went the room felt brighter for it. She spent surprisingly little time with her future husband, but when they were together, they were picturesque. He supposed they both thought they would have many years ahead of them to get to know each other.

He wanted more than anything to go to her. Tigris was always such *fun* at parties. He couldn't remember the number of times she had gotten him outrageously drunk and made him hurl spells out a window onto unknowing courtiers (he'd turned one into a frog before Heléne intervened), or swept him up in a mockery of a dance that had them both stepping on every foot in the room, despite neither being particularly clumsy. He would even like it if they just sat and talked a while, traded gossip over stolen food and a bottle of sweet spirit. It had been so punishingly long since he'd *truly* spoken to her.

But if he approached her now, it was a guarantee that she would not seek him out later. And he *needed* her to find him once the night was over, or all his plotting would have been for naught.

So, whenever he saw her from across the room, getting dangerously close to coming to greet him, he stood up and took a dance partner, then another, then another, keeping himself busy until his feet hurt and the soles of his shoes were worn.

And when the dinner finally wound down, and all the royal retinue had either left or retired for the evening to their respective guest rooms, Cyril started to make his way over to the tower.

And Tigris followed.

SIX

"Cy!"

When she called out to him, it was all he could do not to sigh in relief. He would've had to find her otherwise, and as shown time and time again, he was a middling actor at best.

Still, he had practiced excuses under his breath all the same, testing out different ways to lure the princess to his quarters in the event she was recalcitrant to follow.

Cyril turned to greet her, and luckily for him his smile was quite genuine. "Tig? What is it?"

"What do you mean *'what is it?'* You've been avoiding me all evening!"

His brows rose. "It's your night. I hardly felt it appropriate to monopolise you."

"Is that why you danced *three songs* with my fiancé?" She stalked over to him and gracefully linked their arms together. "I've not seen you in a whole *month*! Did you not miss me? Have I done something wrong?"

Cyril's heart broke for her all over again. A month would have been like the beat of a hummingbird's wings compared to how long it had been since *he'd* last seen *her*.

He shook his head. "It's not that. I did not mean to offend, Tig."

"Well, you have. And now you're to spend some time with me, as your future queen."

Finally, he allowed himself a moment of levity. It came

easier than he'd expected. "As my queen? Shall I curtsy? I can walk two steps behind you if you'd like."

Tigris's face soured. "As my *friend*. You are *friends* with the future ruler of Farsala! Don't you feel lucky? You should *want* to rub elbows with me as much as possible!"

"I had thought tonight you would want to spend time with King Atticus."

Surprisingly, she rolled his eyes. "I'm about to spend the rest of my life with that man. He can spare an evening without the pleasure of my company."

"Do you not like him?" He had no idea how she *couldn't*. He had been so charming on that dance floor. And from what he could remember, he was a remarkably reliable man.

She waved her hand in front of her face in dismissal. "Oh, yes, I like him fine. He is very pretty, I suppose. He is kind to me, and the match is well suited."

"Don't you sound smitten."

She shoved his side. "Oh, I'm *sorry*. Not all of us can have *whirlwind childhood romances* with my brother."

Cyril felt his grimace so strongly he feared his teeth might shatter. He should've known this would be the first thing she'd ask about.

He was still going to *attempt* ignorance. "Mm. Sounds like gossip, which of the courtiers has her fluttering eyes set on our dear Eufie?"

"Oh, shut *up!*" She shoved him again. "Don't be shameless! Especially not after the way he danced with you tonight."

"Like he wanted to wring my neck?"

Tigris rolled her eyes. "Like he wanted to do *something* to you, certainly."

"Commit an atrocity..." he murmured.

Her brows knitted in concern. "Have you said something to upset him? Can I help?"

Cyril relaxed, shoulders slumping to be flush against hers, and sighed. "No, no, it's... we are having a disagreement. I can fix it."

"...I don't think he's truly mad at you," she said after a moment. "He thinks you hang the moon."

Maybe he used to.

Cyril let himself smile again. "You've done an expert job changing the subject from your own love life, my queen."

"Sto – p! Don't call me that, it gives me gooseflesh."

"Tigris..." he prodded.

"Well, what do you want me to say? He is wonderful, Cyril. His palace is beautiful, he speaks well, he carries himself nobly, he has curious interests, he keeps some game as pets, he likes the snow, he excels at mathematics, he is very handsome, he is older, but not a lecher. We will be happy and our kingdoms will prosper."

Cyril really took in the last sentence. Even if Tigris was saying it in jest, he would make sure it came true if it was the last thing he did.

"But?" he said.

"But... but nothing. That is it. He has no flaws that I can think of."

"So you *are* happy."

Her whole body sagged. "Can we go back to talking about *your* little spat?"

He was truly surprised. He hadn't expected Tigris's feelings on her fiancé to be so divided. But, in all fairness, he had never *asked*. The princess was such a shining beacon of light, and every time she talked about Atticus, she was effervescent, enthusiastic about the match.

But Tigris Margrave had a way of making *anything* sound exciting.

He patted her arm. "I do think you'll warm up to him. He was very kind to me tonight."

That got her attention. Her eyes lit up. "Truly? I told him you were fragile."

Cyril very nearly choked. "*Fragile*?"

"Not in a *bad* way! You're just... you're *our* Cyril." she reached up to card her hand through his hair, thoroughly ruining the styling. "But I just said if he upset you, he would not be worth my hand."

"Ah. I am the secret measure on which you choose a match."

She shrugged. "I trust you."

His heart caught in his throat.

After a beat, he shot her a mischievous grin and tugged on her arm. "Do you know what I think we should do?"

Tigris said nothing, but her chin lifted in curiosity.

"I know Tantie keeps a stocked liquor cabinet in the kitchen floor of the tower. We ought to throw you a bachelorette party."

Her face split into a *huge* childlike grin and she hung onto his arm to allow him to lead the way. "You always have the best ideas, Cy."

They snuck up to the fourth floor of the tower like a couple of children, despite Tigris having complete reign over everything within and outside of the palace. Tigris grabbed bottles of sweet, sugary liquors and bitter spirits and Cyril collected glasses in his arms, in all sizes, so they'd be able to mix absolutely foul concoctions more easily than swirling liquids from bottle to bottle.

"Is Auntie even able to drink any of this?" Tigris giggled as she tucked a bottle of absinthe (*absinthe*!) under her arm.

"I'm sure she does" – Cyril waved his fingers vaguely in front of his face – "something to the pattern so she doesn't poison herself."

"She'll outlive all of us if nobody stops her," Tigris joked, and Cyril did his best to laugh in a way that didn't betray a shakiness in his breath.

When they finally made it down to his quarters, he was a pile of nerves. He opened the door first and ushered in Tigris, who had already started on a stout vial of old whiskey. Either she was desperate to have some actual fun or she *truly* had doubts about the wedding. With some hope, Cyril would be able to assuage one of those, if temporarily.

He cast a surreptitious glance at the cage he had purchased earlier. It hit him about waist high, and was big enough to be conspicuous, but in the mess of his room, it was almost invisible. Just to be safe, though, he had blanketed it with an old sheet and, fearing the newly unpredictable whims of the creature within, wove a silencing spell into its threads.

Tigris, unawares, deposited all but the one bottle she was drinking from onto a desk. Cyril did the same with his collection of disparate glasses.

"Actually, should we go into your room?" she said. "I'll braid your hair for you, it'll be like we're kids again."

Cyril did not look her in the eyes as he scanned the living quarters for anything that would give him away for what seemed like the dozenth time.

He did manage to crack a thin smile. "Ah, yes, the alcoholism of my childhood."

"You know what I mean!" She was next to him now, and prodded a finger onto his back. "I will give you the *finest* advice on how to woo my brother."

"I am sure I don't know what *you* mean."

She ignored him outright. "He likes blondes."

"I *am* blonde, Tig."

"Then you already have a leg up over the competition!"

The truth was, during their sixth month of marriage, when Cyril had been going through a particularly jealous streak watching Eufrates charm foreign dignitaries day in and day out, his husband had almost shyly confessed to him that every single person he had courted in his youth had held some passing resemblance to Cyril himself, be it the colour of their hair, their build, the way they dressed. It had become such an object of distress for Eufrates that after a while he had sworn off courtship altogether, instead of settling for imitations of what he truly wanted.

The memory of it made Cyril shiver. They had been happy together, once.

But now he could not afford to think about Eufrates. He guided Tigris deeper into the room as she rambled on about her brother's likes and dislikes, as though Cyril didn't know the man inside and out.

"Further, he is a most embarrassing lover. I once saw him draft a three-page letter to a girl he was seeing –"

Hm. Mine were five pages.

" – only to discard it because it didn't '*feel* genuine enough'."

"I think you are avoiding talking about yourself again."

"I am *no–*"

Finally, she was where he wanted her, in the centre of the room, where Cyril had spent hours crafting that damned sigil. Her bare feet (she had discarded her shoes at the door claiming discomfort) sank into the ancient rug he'd used to cover it up and, as if picking apart a cat's cradle, he unwove it so the circles he'd drawn were visible. They began to glow in a bright, yellow-white light.

He caught her limp body before she could hit her head against a side table. Cyril had grossly overestimated his own strength because he did not manage to do this as smoothly as he'd expected to. He heaved with her weight, nearly being pinned down underneath her, but somehow, he managed to drag her over to a nearby empty sofa. Evidently, he was not the strong, sturdy knight who could easily support a damsel in his arms like Tigris deserved, but he would have to do.

From his studies in anatomy, he knew the inert human body was a true burden to carry, but he was not expecting even her *head* to weigh as much as a ton of bricks when he tried to make her comfortable against some fluffed pillows on the edge of the seat.

Nervously, Cyril checked her pulse, taking her wrist against his ear and listening in carefully. He breathed a sigh of relief upon finding there was none to be heard. That meant his spell had worked, and he had *not* simply rendered his dear friend and future queen unconscious for no reason.

It was, as far as plans go, *completely unhinged*, but it was the best he could come up with on such short notice. He had the means, the resources.

Tigris Margrave would not be able to die from a human illness if she were not human. And it just so happened that Cyril had the perfect empty vessel following him around and eating his leftovers at his disposal.

With a flourish as though revealing a parlour trick, he lifted the white cotton sheet covering the cage and examined the animal within.

Oh. She looked *quite* angry.

"Okay..." he murmured to himself. "Alright."

Slowly, he found the nucleus of the silencing pattern and plucked at its string, dismantling the entire spell. The result was immediately cacophonous.

Cyril had no idea cats could get this loud, but Tigris was really putting that Abyssinian throat to the test. She yowled and growled and hissed with reckless, indignant abandon, pawing furiously at the metal of the cage.

"Tig – Tigris, sh – Tig, Tig, *please.*" He put his hands up like a beggar, trying to soothe her enough to explain himself, but he was doing a very poor job of projecting confidence.

"Tantie will hear," he tried. This only incensed her more. Cyril groaned and dropped to his knees so he was at eye level with the cat.

Slowly, he approached the cage. "Tig, I'm *begging* you to let me expl–"

Slash!

Tigris had managed to thread Shoestring's skinny arm through the bars and figured out how to summon his claws. As though she'd practiced being a cat her entire life, she had swiped three ruby red lines clean across Cyril's forehead.

That shut them both up for a moment.

Cyril reached up to touch the hot flow of blood that was beginning to sting under his hairline. She had cut him quite deep. For her part, Tigris eyed him horrified, and retreated into her enclosure.

He saw this and even as a red line cut across his left eye, he drew closer. "No! No, it's – it's fine!"

Because he made no attempt to stop the bleeding, it began to drip onto his clothes and the circle on the hardwood in a way that shouldn't be so familiar to him. Cyril ignored this and prostrated himself before Tigris so far down he was now smearing blood on the floor as his forehead pressed against the cooling wood.

"I did not…" he said, quickly. "I was not joking, when I said what I said to you some weeks ago. Tigris, I am your humble servant. You may cut me however much you would like. I am desperate to keep you safe."

He sat back up on his thighs and now there was a bright red splotch on his head, circularly diffused like a setting sun. He was trying not to concentrate on how much it hurt.

Tigris cringed at the sight and let out an afflicted mewl. His eyes widened.

"Ah, right. I had meant to do this right away. My sincerest apologies, Tig." He reached out carefully with both hands for her. "May I?"

She hesitated but gave him a slight nod. Cyril threaded through both their patterns until he found the particular way he wished them linked. Suddenly, if she wished it, he could hear her thoughts.

"For fuck's sake, Cyril, cover up that wound!"

Well. That was as good a place to start as any.

"Would… you like to be let out first?"

"You're haemorrhaging on the floor!"

"Alright, alright. I was trying to be polite."

He stood up (swaying ever so slightly) and found something within his claustrophobia of a living space to fasten over the cuts so the bleeding would stop. Then, he cleaned himself up as best as he could.

"There. All done."

"You've turned me into a cat, *Cyril,"* she said.

"Well. Actually. Turning you *into* a cat would have been far easier. See, if I rearranged your pattern, I could transmutate your form into that of a cat, but what I've *actually* done–"

"Shut up! Get me out of here."

Cyril *did* shut up, so quickly his lips disappeared into a line on his face. "Yes, ma'am."

He opened the cage and stepped aside to give her space to stretch out and wander the room. Mercifully, she did not try to run away, though Cyril had a spell ready for that just in case.

"What have you done?" she said.

"See, that's what I've been trying to–"

"Is it a prank? A hazing? Did someone put you up to this? Are you evil *now? Do you not want me to marry? Are you secretly in love with me? Are you secretly in love with* Atticus?"

As Cyril heard her recite her laundry list of theories directly in his mind, his head began to hurt all over again. He tried to address at least *some* of her concerns.

"I am *not* evil and I am gay, now if you'll let me–"

"Wait." She looked down at herself. *"What happened to Shoestring?"*

"Shoestring is dead."

That silenced her like a slap to the face. It gave him time to lower himself to the ground and sit, cross-legged, in front of her. He realised just how *exhausted* he was when his shoulders sagged as if under bags of wet sand.

She approached him quietly. *"I... since when?"*

"Over a month ago."

"But... but that can't be! I saw *you two together! Just a few days ago."*

"That was nothing. That was..." He rubbed at his eyes as though he could scrape the weariness from them. "A ghost."

Even with the memory of Shoestring trailing alongside him, nothing like his actual familiar, he had not been able to accept his death until now, until he had offered up his body to Tigris. He was slowly coming to terms with the fact that he was still very sad over the loss.

Despite it having been decades and decades ago by now, he remembered the day Shoestring had come to him like it was imprinted in his mind.

It was actually within his first year of living in the palace. He was only a child, having just turned six, and the pressure of suddenly being a courtier was beginning to weigh on him. It was not as though he was not of noble blood, but there was a difference between being a lordling over a handful of small fields in the outskirts of Farsala and living in the palace, taking lessons alongside the prince and crown princess.

One day, bolstered by the stupidity of childhood, he decided to run away. He had done it quite properly, too, just like in picture books. He left a note (*"Dear Grand Mage Aunt Heléne, I have decided to quit magic and return home. I am sorry. Goodbye. Cyril"*) and tied a bindle to a stick, carrying only the essentials (a favourite toy, a loaf of bread and sleep clothes – he'd forgotten water), and set off into the woods he was barely familiar with, treading through that year's particularly harsh winter's snow that climbed halfway up his ankles. He wrapped himself in wools and thick cottons and donned very sturdy boots, but he could still feel the bite of frost against his nose and through his gloves to his fingertips.

There was no other choice, though. Aunt Heléne was too severe, and the court looked down on him. Tigris was kind, but boisterous. Intense to the point of frequently putting herself and others in danger for the sake of a thrill. Eufrates was... well, Eufrates was a mystery. The prince stared at Cyril endlessly, eyes boring into him like he was trying to make him combust with the power of thought alone. He did not say many words to him, but they were all curt and indecipherable. He seemed to hate it when Tigris brought Cyril along on their adventures, claiming he would easily get hurt. Cyril was convinced it was actually because he found him a nuisance at best and an interloper at worst.

He had not exactly been *showered* with love back in his hometown, but he missed its familiarity. He had no interest in being grand mage. He didn't even have a familiar!

In any case, it was a story with a startlingly predictable end. Cyril had gotten lost in unknown territory, he'd eaten up his bread right away instead of rationing it and by the time the sun set, there were tears frosting over on his cheeks.

He tried to make his way back to the palace, but the woods were too thick and he couldn't see the light of the windows that was the lead to getting him back home safe.

In the end, grim though it seemed in retrospect, Cyril, age six and a month, had well and truly resigned himself to his fate. He sat down on a bank of snow and tucked his knees into his chest, fighting to preserve at least some warmth. Though, he doubted he'd make it through the night.

That was when he heard the smallest, most strangled, most pathetic mewl imaginable, coming from under a tree to his left.

On shaky legs, he got up to investigate and found a browny-orange kitten curled around itself – very much like he was doing earlier – and shaking like a leaf.

Cyril wasn't sure what he was looking at, not at first. But he had an inexorable feeling deep in his chest that, somehow, if he died here, the cat would die with him.

He unbuttoned his heavy coat, just enough to be able to tuck the animal inside it and closed it back up again, warming it up with his own heat. Upon realising this wouldn't be enough, he remembered the very basics of his lessons with Aunt Heléne, stone-faced and inflexible, making him repeat himself over and over again until sweat beaded on his brow.

The first thing a mage tended to learn upon instruction was how to spark fire.

Cyril's hands were frozen solid, even despite the gloves. He breathed and breathed and rubbed them against one another until he felt the painful sting of motility returning to his fingertips.

He strummed through the pattern in clumsy, defrosted motions, until finally a flame ignited on a pile of leaves he'd prepared. He kept the fire going through magic just long enough to make sure the snow wouldn't put it out and dropped the spell with a heavy, huffing breath.

The flame endured – grew, even – and Cyril drew himself and the kitten nearer to it. It felt invigorating. It was the best warmth he'd ever experienced. The animal tucked against his chest gave an agreeable purr that Cyril somehow instantly understood as pride.

They were found very quickly, before dawn, because the entirety of the king's guard had set off to search for him. One knight spotted him dozing curled completely into himself, next to the enduring flame that seemingly never spread but never went out. A ring of thawed, premature spring had formed around Cyril as he slept, and when told of this, Heléne said he was a marvel.

The king and queen were waiting for him, which surprised him no end. Rohan kneeled down to his level and ruffled his hair and Micaela let out a sigh of relief that almost sounded like a sob. Next to them was Heléne Laverre herself, who, for years after, Cyril thought had looked intensely cross with him, before the wisdom of adulthood made him realise the knot in her brow was actually guilt. She gave him a week off from lessons and the very first thing she taught him once that was over was how to project a shower of starlight within the confines of a room, a dazzling endeavour for a child.

The Margrave siblings were loath to be seen without him. They became a true trio, though Tigris was still quite rough and Eufrates was still as mysterious as ever. They had both hugged him tightly when he returned, though, and he noticed (but he did not think deeply into it) that Eufrates's eyes were sleepless and red.

There wasn't any question on whether or not he was allowed to keep the cat. It was *his* cat. *His* familiar. And, in a lazy, Shoestring-like way, he had saved him from a premature death.

Cyril named him Shoestring because, despite the wealth of toys he tried to spoil the stupid thing with, his favourite plaything was the laces on his boots. Also, he named him Shoestring because he was six years old and did not have a particularly brilliant mind for names. The cat slept in or around his bed from the day he found him in the woods to the day he died in that cottage.

In the end, Cyril had not gotten very far in his homebound expedition, but he had gotten exactly what he wanted, which was not to be alone.

It was almost comical how, even decades later, Cyril's *second* attempt at suicidal ideation had happened for the self-same reason.

He was awakened from his reverie when a paw softly pressed against his thigh.

"I'm sorry, Cy."

Cyril shook his head. "It is no matter."

Tigris tilted her head to look at her own limp, lifeless human body laid out on the sofa, and he could practically *see* her stomach turn. He had never actually witnessed Shoestring cough up a hairball, but perhaps there was a first time for everything.

"Why on earth have you done this to me?" she croaked.

"It is a rather long story."

"I'm sure cats have nothing but time."

He regarded her for a moment before he finally steeled himself and told her everything he could recall. Starting with the most ridiculous thing.

"I am not actually the Cyril you know. I lost count a while ago, but I must be approaching fifty."

"Fifty what?"

"Fifty *years old*, Tig."

She stared at him with those great, big, cat eyes, but said nothing. It was as good an indication as any that he was meant to continue.

"I am from a future in which nearly everything–" He paused. "*Everything* has gone wrong. There is so much, I hardly know where to begin."

"*From the beginning, Cyril.*"

The way she spoke to him was so preposterous in its imperiousness that he felt as though he was finally getting a glimpse of the queen she was meant to be. He flashed her a wry smile and made himself comfortable.

"The summer after your wedding, you fell terribly ill. We all thought it a passing sickness at first, a more severe symptom of a particularly bad heat wave. I might have guessed your death a thousand ways – which, for the record, I *did not* – but no one predicted Tigris Margrave would be felled by a simple *pox*.

"We suspected foul play, of course. Me, your brother, your husband, the guard. I can assure you we left no stone unturned in our investigation. There was no particular reason why you should die of *disease*, but in the end, we could find nothing. It was a natural death. An unfortunate tragedy. A normal, *human* illness."

He saw her brow furrow then lift in slow realisation. Tigris did not get the credit she deserved. She may not have been the most *intelligent*, but she was *impossibly* clever.

Cyril merely nodded. "The physician never determined *exactly* what it was, but it was *definitely* not borne by wildlife. And I doubt even more that it would fester within a familiar's body."

He could feel she had questions, but all she said was, "*So then what happened?*"

Cyril sucked in air through his cheeks. Somehow, that had been the *easy* part. Tigris, who was nearly as devoted to her brother as he himself had been, was sure to find the rest of the story unbelievable.

"Naturally, Eufrates was crowned shortly after. He wasn't... prepared for it. Not even when you were bedbound. I truly believe he was convinced you would bounce back stronger than ever any day then."

Cyril held a deep contempt for his husband. Despised him, even. But he found he did not hate the man enough to rake him through the coals in front of his own sister, so that was all he said on that matter.

But *'unprepared'* was a gross understatement.

Eufrates Margrave had been *terrified* by sovereignty. Cyril had never seen him so brooding, so tense, so *awkward*. He thought he might have to hold his hand while they were putting the crown on his head, like a child being fed medicine. He would wake up nearly every morning hoping it had been a terrible dream.

The prince had never wanted power. He had received the exact same education as his sister, and at times he excelled at it, but he hadn't taken it *seriously*. The idea of him inheriting anything but a plot of land (preferably by the sea) where he could retire to become a playwright or an author was completely ludicrous. He was the *bard prince* and Tigris was to be queen, and he would very proudly cheer her on or offer brotherly advice if she *truly* wanted it, and that was the end of that.

Often, in the first years of their marriage, he would corner Cyril in some alcove between meetings and, half joking-half serious, ask him to run away. There were plenty of councillors in his ear dying to take his place, let them fight for it. Eufrates was going to whisk his lover to the other side of the world with a handful of coin and stolen horses. Over time, his fantasies had grown quite elaborate. They would become traveling performers, busking for a wage. They would steal from the coffers, a small amount, just enough to live off modestly for the rest of their days. They would return to Cyril's parents' home, take over the land there. He would learn husbandry and Cyril could manage their accounts. They would become pirates on the high seas. They would tour the world, aimless, but in love.

Eufrates's words were so nectarine that Cyril found himself falling for them each and every time, if only for a moment. But then he would look him in the eye and ask if he meant it, and every time, Eufrates shook his head and laughed. He was being silly. He was being indulgent.

Eufrates had been noble, once. Dutiful. Cyril would not rip that away from him.

"But you never did recover," he continued on, though he was starting to feel a hoarseness in his throat. "I – we all saw the coffin to prove it. We all said our eulogies. And he had to be king. There was no one else.

"Honestly, he took it on the chin, at first. Tried his very best. And we were married shortly after."

Tigris's round eyes grew wide as saucers. *"You what?"*

He frowned. "Really? This is where you interrupt me? Over ballroom gossip?"

"I am happy *for you, idiot!"*

"Well. Don't celebrate just yet."

He sighed and steeled himself to keep going. This truly *was* the hard part.

"A while later, Tantie died – nothing as dramatic as you. She went peacefully, in her sleep. I think it was the grief, which seems awfully unfair. *I* was grieving.

"And just like that, I had her job. Imagine that. The pair of us, running a kingdom." He did not mean for the words to taste quite so bitter on his tongue.

"Nobody really liked it, that we were married. The grand mage had too much sway in court. As you know, I'm not from a particularly noble family. There were more suitable options. I couldn't even give him children, though – I *am* the greatest wizard of my time. I'm sure I could've figured something out if I got creative." Cyril pursed his lips and swatted the idea away as though it were a fly. "Regardless. It never came up.

"He was never as aware of what was said about me – about *us* – among the courtiers and council, but I'm sure it reached him eventually. I think that's what started it. We were too young. He became self-conscious. He wanted to prove himself."

Tigris was watching him with the held breath of someone witnessing a chariot careening off a cliff. She looked as though she wanted to order him to stop talking and tell her another story, or fix the ending to this one so it wouldn't be quite so dire. He wished she would.

"I think Eufrates grew... paranoid. He started putting together an inner council, only his most trusted advisors–"

"That sounds sensible," she said immediately.

Cyril nodded. "I thought the same. I was *in* it, after all. I helped choose the members. Whatever he needed, I *helped*. But it wasn't enough. It escalated. He began to see cutthroats in his own shadow. Foreign assassins posing as diplomats. He'd lock the doors and windows to our room at night. One time, I cut myself on the dagger he kept under his pillow." He let out a strained laugh, as if remembering a fond mishap. "He mustered up the royal guard into something more. A proper army. His more loyal knights were training soldiers now. His old hunting mates became generals. He had me brew both poisons and antidotes, just in case. I wove a barrier around the palace. I surveyed the construction of the wall built around the capital. If I wanted light entertainment, I could watch a phalanx march right under our window. I should mention he hadn't touched his lute in years by then."

The atmosphere in his room, once festive, grew tense and heavy. He glanced briefly at the bottles of liquor lined up on his desk. Perhaps there might be some use for them tonight after all. He wondered if enchanted cats could drink.

"Anyway, while all this was happening, we still had frequent meetings with your widower Atticus. I didn't speak to him much, but... Eufrates liked him, in the beginning. He was a guiding hand. Another young king of a small territory he could look up to. They spent quite a bit of time together.

"Which is why I was thoroughly perplexed when one day my husband confided in me his plans to invade Cretea."

Cyril began speaking faster, not giving Tigris the chance to interrupt him.

"He didn't call it that. No – o, he called it something else entirely. The *annex*. They were allies anyway, there was no reason the two countries shouldn't be as one. He came to me with this like it was a logical solution to a problem we'd *always* had. And you know your brother. He has quite the way with words.

"He was convinced, he swore it on his life and mine, that if he didn't make the first move, Atticus would. That King Wulfsbane would take advantage of his youth, his naiveté. I don't even think he thought him an *evil* man. Just a sensible king who saw a good opportunity.

"The day after he proposed this plan to *me*, he pitched it to his war council – there was a war council now, by the way – and at that point no one would say no to the king."

"You would."

Cyril gave her a heartless, tired smile. "It was a clean takeover. Only took a few weeks. Minimal casualties, really. I think Atticus surrendered once he realised Eufrates wasn't in any mood to take prisoners. The Cretian Annex happened twelve years into King Eufrates's rule. So, you see, it was a gradual shift. The lobster doesn't realise it's in a pot until it's soft and tender for dinner.

"I didn't hear much about Atticus after his dethroning. I think he went into hiding, tried to rally up some kind of rebellion. Not that he was the first one. The *first* fool to try and start a revolution against Farsala's handsome new despot was *very* publicly beheaded."

"And you – you sat there *and did* nothing?"

"Don't be ridiculous. It's not one of my strengths, but I'm still a trained healer. I administered the anaesthesia."

Tigris stared at him for a long moment, slack-jawed, waiting for the punchline that wasn't going to come while he raked a hand over his hair, still slick with fresh blood.

"I loved him," he said.

"*...Keep going.*"

"Are you sure?" Cyril asked this as gently as soothing a babe.

"*Yes, Cyril. I am sure.*"

"Very well. You'll be happy to know we're almost at the end. Mostly because I left court just four years after the annex. I couldn't do it anymore."

"*What broke you?*"

"Cowardice."

She narrowed her eyes at him and repeated herself. "*What broke you?*"

Cyril let out a long sigh. "I don't know. I think... I–" By instinct, his fingers reached up to grip at his chest, where the ring hung. "He didn't love *me* anymore."

She was looking at him like something disgusting at the bottom of her shoe. He thought if she tried to scratch him again, he would gladly allow it.

"Anyway," he sighed. "Believe it or not, after the annex was when things *really* started going south. Before, all of this was politicking, with little to no effect on the common man, but then... well, rumour spread that King Eufrates somehow *cursed* the land. He was a bad king, the gods or the fates or nature or... *something* was coming to collect divine retribution. It's a shame it was at the cost of his people. Crops withered, plagues spread, cattle died. The landscape became so dull and grey you could barely grow a weed without it shrivelling away to nothing. *I* went to Farol – did Atticus ever take you there? It's beautiful for honeymoons. A must-see if you're in Cretea – which is a seaside town, so it took a while for the rot – that's what the locals started calling it – to spread, but it did. It reached everywhere your brother ruled. It even changed the seasons. One long winter, all year round. Red clouds in the horizon. Like a bad dream."

He had been trying to avoid remembering those bleak, bygone days that by now seemed a nightmare away. Recounting them like this opened up fresh wounds and seemed to drain him of vitality. He was sure that if he could spell his way into looking through Tigris's eyes, he would see himself as he was again, back bent, head down, old, withering, waiting to die.

"It got *so* bad the sky went dark. The *whole* sky. I was rationing candles like they were ingots of gold. And the food? Well, when there *was* any it was awful. You should raise the kitchen's wages when you're queen, by the way. They're the backbone of this entire palace."

"I'm not taking queenship advice from you."

Cyril raised his hands up in surrender. His tone and mannerisms had been light, defusing, but he instantly sobered up upon hearing the acid in Tigris's voice.

"That's... very fair. I am sorrier than I can ever be. I am *here* because I want to *fix* it."

"How are you here in the first place?"

"Ah! Yes, well. There's the end of the story so far, isn't it? After Shoestring died – don't worry about that. It's mage business – I realised *I* wasn't long for this world either.

"So I devised a bit of a... last resort. A spell so powerful it required the loss of life to rightfully balance. Took me the whole month to look into it, too. It's not like there's a surplus of mages willing to dabble into human sacrifice, but I'd taken most of my books and notes with me when I... left, so I was able to scrape something together.

"It was a coin flip. I didn't think it would truly work. More likely I was to die in Farol in a pool of my own blood surrounded by the scribblings of a desperate madman. But evidently *some* higher power took pity on me, because here I am.

"I am back, over twenty years in the past, and I had the chance to make things right."

"Had the chance?"

She was *too* clever, really.

"Well... my *first* plan failed."

Tigris said nothing, which meant he had no other out but to elaborate.

"I was going to kill him." He quickened his speech again so there could be no interruptions. "I was remarkably bad at it, but I did try."

"You tried to kill my brother!?"

"If you had *seen* what he'd become–"

"What did you become?"

She might as well have punched him in the gut. His throat felt dry and sandy.

"I know... I *know*. But I told you, I'm *trying* to–"

"Why couldn't you kill him?" She sounded hopeful, which is when he realised that he'd omitted the most important part.

"I know what you want to hear. It's because we are married, but not in the way you think. When we were wed, I... well. This is embarrassing, now that I've got to explain it out loud..."

"Cyril."

"Yes, alright. I wove a spell into the pattern between us. A *powerful* one, too. Vague though the wording was. The vows you say during the ceremony? I made sure they *stuck*." He pulled the threaded ring from his shirt to show her. "I put it all on this. We would share our burdens, we would never be apart, in sickness and in health, in... this life or the next."

Cyril spoke slowly now, as he let the words sink in. She would figure it out on her own without coddling, and he watched with no relish whatsoever as she did.

As an aside, he had never seen a cat go through the full range of human emotion before.

"He's here too."

"Indeed."

SEVEN

He explained to her the plan, then. How, after his failed assassination attempt and discovery that he'd brought the worst version of Eufrates from the bowels of hell, he had focused his attention on keeping her safe. He was going to take care of her body, preserve it somewhere no illness could touch, at least until the summer was over and there was no danger of contagion. She was not dead, he reassured her, her body would not decay, she would just be in a state of stasis for a little while. And as there was no evidence of her demise, Eufrates could not lawfully inherit the throne for himself.

Tigris was a surprisingly good sport about listening to it all, despite her obvious misgivings. Chief among them:

"You expect me to be a cat for six months?"

He nodded. "At least, yes."

"You're– you– that's– you could've at least let me get married *first."*

"I let you have the dinner, didn't I?"

"Cyril!"

Cyril raised his hands again. "I'm sorry. I *did* time it on purpose. There's less claim to an annex when there isn't an alliance between your and Atticus's kingdoms to begin with." He tried out a grin. "Think of it as being star-crossed."

"What makes you think Eufi– my brother won't... abuse his powers in the interim? He's still the prince."

99

His eyes lit for the first time that night. "So you do believe me!"

Tigris sauntered closer to him and gave him a facsimile of a cat's smile. *"Cy... I have known you for nearly twenty years. No offense, but you aren't this imaginative."*

He wanted to shake and cry with relief. He had been fully prepared to prostrate himself in front of her again until she at least gave him a *chance*.

"None taken! Absolutely none at all. And... there is not so much power in regency as there is in kingship. He would have checks and balances. Tantie would be there, for one."

He would not have noticed her come in if it weren't for the look of wide-eyed alarm on Tigris's face.

It was like he had summoned her. He was a penitent, and she was the apparition here to castigate him for his misdeeds.

Except Heléne was very real, quite solid and was standing at his doorway, which she had opened without knocking, as he'd learned any good parental figure was wont to do. Ganache was perched on her shoulder.

"Cyril, it's the middle of the night, Ganache says you won't stop chatter–"

"Hel–lo, Tantie!" He threw himself in front of Tigris (the cat) so she could not see her. "Great party, so exciting, I could barely sleep."

Belatedly, he realised he'd made two grave mistakes.

The first was he still had signs of a fresh wound dappling his forehead, despite the bandage he'd hurriedly applied as a stopgap.

The second, perhaps more obvious, mistake was that he should have attempted to cover up Tigris (the human) who was still currently inert on his sofa.

His gaze pivoted from Heléne, to Tigris (human), back to his aunt again.

"She's had *such* a rough night."

"Gods, you're terrible at this."

"You be quiet!" he hissed back at Tigris, who was unhelpfully peeking over his shoulder to see.

"What have you *done*?" Heléne said slowly, as though maybe if she had enough time to think, it would begin to make sense.

Cyril sat up to his full height, cross-legged with his hands on his knees, making himself big enough to obfuscate a cat roughly the size of a small lynx. "Tig's quite the lightweight. We were–"

"She's not *breathing*."

Ganache squawked her agreement, which Cyril didn't particularly think was any help.

"Oh," he said quietly. "You can tell from that far away?"

"*Cyril!*" his aunt snapped.

He had a sudden flash of unbidden memory. The very first time he ever met Heléne, he followed her around – rather like an imprinting baby duck – for lack of a better choice in their lonely mage tower. She had indulged him the first few days. He was starting to let his guard down around her. She was a round, kind-looking old woman with big, round spectacles and a flash of silver hair pinned into a tight bun.

One day, though, apparently seeing that her new ward had begun to warm to her, she caught his attention and said to him over a breakfast of porridge and fruit.

"Duckling. I do hope you are comfortable here, as you will be staying for some time. But if I ever hear you calling me Gramma, Nana, or anything of the sort, I will have Ganache pluck your eyeballs out of your head like smooth marbles and keep them in a jar for pickling."

He had never been more terrified of her in his life, until *this very moment*.

"I didn't kill her! I swear it!"

Ganache flew to Tigris's body, pressed her feathery head to her throat, and let out an alarmed little cluck.

"Then why does she not have a *pulse*?!"

"*Cy! Let me talk to her!*" Tigris was scratching at the back of his tunic. He refused to turn his head to face her.

"I'm not sure how that can *help*…"

"Oh, alright. I'll leave you to your *idea, then."*

Cyril bit the inside of his cheek so hard he tasted the copper of blood. As if he needed more head injuries that evening.

Slowly, *carefully*, with his hands up so as to not alarm Heléne, he stood up and revealed the cat behind him. His lips were pressed into an ill-fitting, contrarian smile.

"…Where is Shoestring? Who is that?" she said immediately.

He had been right to hide the animal shadowing him from his aunt all these weeks. She knew something was wrong immediately.

"Shoestring is… not here." He would unpack his lack of a soul with her later, perhaps over another cup of mediocre tea. "This is Tigris. If you'd like to confirm it, you can speak to her."

He palmed the air as if pulling back a curtain and revealing a trick, and Heléne furrowed her brow. To the layman, he had done little more than swat at nothing, but to her he had revealed the exact pattern he'd used to be able to communicate with Tigris. She could read it and replicate it, which she easily did.

"Tigris?" she called out.

"Hello, Auntie."

Heléne removed her spectacles to pinch the bridge of her nose. Her nails dug indents on her already prune-wrinkled skin.

"There are *better* ways to deal with cold feet before a wedding, girl."

"I'm not scared of getting married!" Tigris snapped immediately, and, in Cyril's opinion, much too quickly.

"Explain yourself, then."

"Me! You should ask your ward *what's going on."*

"Wh–" Cyril snapped his head back to look at Tigris. "I thought you wanted to talk to her."

"To tell her this is all… consensual." She paused. *"So far."*

"One of you will explain yourselves right this very moment or I will have you both hanging by your ears from my balcony."

Cyril again looked to Tigris for some semblance of support, but she merely nodded, waiting as patiently as Heléne was growing displeased.

So he sighed, threaded a hand through his hair (now beyond repair, save for a long, hot soak) and told the entire sordid tale again, from the beginning.

He made some edits, of course. It was impossible to repeat what he'd told Tigris word for word. And by now, his throat hurt from speaking and choking up and trying his level best not to scream, so it was an abridged version of the tale. If he forgot something important, Tigris reminded him. If Heléne needed clarification on something, he gave it.

He felt he was being exceedingly calm and well-adjusted, considering he was telling them the equivalent of the ramblings of a madman.

His aunt pointed out the very same thing.

"And I suppose you've no proof of this, then."

Cyril folded his arms in front of his chest. "Tig believes me."

"Tigris is barely out of diapers."

"I'm six-and-twenty!" she actually yowled this out at the same time as she thought it.

"That – that's right! And *I'm* nearly fifty, I should hope I've gained enough life experience to at least be *trustworthy*."

Heléne just stared at him, the very portrait of unimpressed. "Child–"

"I just *said*–"

"Child." She did not raise her voice, but it felt as though it carried throughout the entire building. "I am ninety-two years old." (Gods, he'd been close.) "But you could tell me you are as old as the Earth itself and you would *still* be a century too young to measure up to me. I have been placed in this tower to protect the kingdom. Now, do you have *any* proof of your ridiculous claims?"

"I–" Cyril hesitated. "I'm–" He patted himself down as if a solution would present itself upon his person. Upon his jester garb and colourful silks. When he reached his chest, though, he lurched to jam a hand inside his shirt and show her the ring.

"This!" He held it triumphantly. Though not very high up, as he could not remove it from his neck. "The ring! It's my wedding ring. Surely you can see the spell woven into it. Here, I will open up the pattern for you."

"That won't be necessary." She approached him and gestured for him to lean down to her level so she could examine the band. He expected to see her open up the magic around it, pluck and strum at the weave until she was satisfied, but she only *looked*.

"These are the same make as Rohan and Micaela's," she said.

Cyril shrugged. "Well, yes. It's tradition. Eufrates always liked the design. We didn't see the need to change–"

"It's timeworn. By quite some years." He might as well have been a fly on her shoulder. "Not magically, either. It's a deceptively simple spell to unravel."

Once she finished her inspection, she tucked the ring back into Cyril's shirt.

"Besides, I saw the prince wearing the same model when he took his gloves off to eat."

"Oh," he said. "Well. You could have... led with that."

"*So it* is *true...*" Tigris whispered.

Cyril whirled around to her with disbelief written boldly on his face. "I thought you believed me!"

She sniffed. "*It's good to have proof.*"

Heléne cleared her throat and the pair of them turned their attention back to her.

"Now, then. What would you have me do?"

"I..." He was truly speechless. "Keep it a secret, I suppose."

She clicked her tongue in disdain and Ganache flew back to her shoulder, casting Cyril a sour eye. "You have the grand mage of Farsala at your disposal and your only instruction is *not to gossip*? No wonder your kingdom fell to ruin."

Cyril opened and closed his mouth, over and over, trying to form words, but instead a bubble of manic, shrill laughter escaped his throat.

"That really hurts my feelings, Tantie."

"What exactly did you intend to do with this?"

Heléne, claiming the toll of the years weighed heavily upon her, had managed to shift Tigris's body so it was curled up into itself, and sat herself down next to it, completely unfazed. Now, she was patting the corpse on the side of her leg as though it was an inconvenient piece of luggage.

Cyril cleared his throat. "Well, I'm preserving it, of course. The spell is already in place. And then I intend to... hide it?" The inflection on his tone sounded less like a certainty and more like he was taking a middling grade oral exam.

Heléne tapped her nails against the arm of the sofa, clearly unimpressed. "Either I've taught you nothing of causality, or you need to clean your ears, boy. What happens if she catches the disease while in this state? You wouldn't know until it was far too late to do anything."

"She won't..."

"She might be *meant* to catch it."

Tigris bristled. *"So what? This is all for nothing?"*

Heléne waved a hand in her direction as if swatting her concerns away. "It may very well be, if you take sloppy half-measures the way you're doing now.

"Not to mention, if there was a plot to kill her, you've made her a sitting duck if..." she paused. *"Once* her body is discovered. Or do you think you can hide the *future queen* for very long? Perhaps in that trunk over there." She motioned to a large chest Cyril kept winter clothes in. "Or behind a screen. No one will find her then."

"There wasn't any plot to kill her," Cyril said.

She looked past him, directly at Tigris. "We are trusting the judgement of a love-blind twenty-something on this, then?"

"Now that you mention it..."

"I was *not* the only one looking into it!"

"Two love-blind twenty-somethings!" Heléne spat.

"Alright. Clearly *you* have this figured out." Cyril had been standing up still, but he slumped back onto an oversized pillow like a petulant child. Tigris joined him, batting at the tassels on the corner of it like she was beginning to get a bit too used to the idea of being a cat already. "What do you propose we do, Grand Mage Laverre?"

"We do nothing. *I* will take care of this, duckling. Hiding her body was a preposterous idea to begin with. You came up with it while flying by the seat of your pants, I'd wager."

Cyril went mum. He would neither confirm nor deny the accusations, but he did remember feeling particularly lightheaded throughout most of the planning phase of his hare-brained scheme.

"What are you going to do, then?" If Cyril wasn't going to say anything, Tigris might as well speak for him. She hopped off the pillow to stalk towards Heléne and the sofa currently housing her prone figure.

In way of answer, Heléne stood up on ancient, groaning joints and took a step back to look at the body, like a sculptor examining a block of marble.

"One of you – I suggest Tigris – will just have to keep her with you at all times."

"What, just carry a corpse on her back?" Cyril said.

"Stop calling it a corpse!"

Heléne had left the pair to argue as she approached Tigris (human) and drew long, pulling motions around the girl as if working a loom. As she threaded the pattern around her, braiding it with deceptively dexterous fingers that belied her age, the body began to vanish, yarning into itself like a ball of silk, glittering with magic in the candle and moonlight of Cyril's apartments. It shrunk, and bundled and condensed until it was the size of a playing marble and hung in the air, an iridescent multitude of all the colours that made up the princess of Farsala.

Cyril saw it flash the midnight of her hair, the tree bark of her eyes, the brown of her skin, the golden and yellow and red of her clothes, until it finally settled on a marvellous duochrome. Maroon to orange. A sunset gemstone.

Heléne caught it in her hand with the same ease as a throwing stone and held it between her thumb and forefinger to inspect her work.

"Surely it will be no trouble to carry this on your back, child," she said.

"Wh–" Cyril gaped at the gem, eyes so wide they might pop out of their sockets. "You can't just *do* something like that! The transmutation is too complex, you need a circle to keep the pattern contained!"

She was only half-listening as she rummaged through drawers in Cyril's room looking for something among his myriad accessories. Once she found what she was looking for – a plain choker – she strummed a quick weave to attach the gem to it, and made her way to Tigris.

Heléne knelt down and fastened it around Tigris's neck like a fanciful collar for a favourite pet.

"Once you break this, the gem will unfurl itself back to how it was and you will be flung back into your original body, so time it wisely."

"Further," Cyril continued. "There would need some time to prepare the circle, even if you only envisioned it, there's a ritualistic aspect of casting that you need to obs–" He jerked his entire body to face Heléne. "*And* you messed with *my* pattern on her?!"

Heléne walked towards her ward with avuncular serenity.

She reached up and mussed up his hair, stroking her hand through the tangle of wheat-coloured, blood-soaked locks. "I've said it before, Duckling. You've a hundred years of catching up to do."

He was again forcefully reminded of her in the past, exasperated, helping him dress for court functions and cleaning up after his childhood messes.

On the bright side, he'd never felt younger.

He nodded at her. "Thank you, Tantie."

She sniffed. "It is my job to guide your hand. I am well-worn to it."

Once she pulled away, she regarded Tigris once again. Ganache, who had been perched comfortably on the upholstery of Cyril's sofa as a spectator to the entire debacle so far, flew to her shoulder.

"You did not tell me what has happened to Shoestring," Heléne said.

"He's dead."

He braced for impact. For outrage, for a lecture, for horror, for disgust, for contempt. He did his best not to betray any emotion and he held her gaze with eyes made of stone. He could not bear to disappoint her, but he knew he had.

Heléne also regarded him and, for a moment, this is how they stood. Cyril was sure she noticed the rise in his shoulders. The way the hairs on the back of his neck stood on end. For a very long time, she said nothing at all, but her mouth was pressed tight into a thin, nearly invisible, line on her face. She looked directly into Cyril's eyes with an expression that was unknowable to him. Heléne Laverre kept her cards close to her chest and, perhaps, this was preferable to the alternative. He couldn't bear the thought of losing her if she really did now think him an abomination.

He was tense as a nocked bowstring.

"Well," she said, finally. "It is very late. And I am a very old woman. I must have my beauty sleep."

She turned away from Cyril with a nonchalance that startled him, and his entire body felt like melting into the floorboards. It wasn't absolution, but he would accept it gratefully.

"I suggest you two do the same. We will, all three of us, speak later," Heléne said from his doorway. She shut the door behind herself.

Both him and Tigris stood staring at the space she had occupied, before Tigris broke their silence.

"You say she died from grief?*"*

Cyril shrugged.

As much as he would have liked to immediately collapse on his bed and sleep like the dead for the next *minimum* eight hours, Cyril still looked a mess. He'd slept in kohl enough times to know it would not be a comfortable day ahead of him if he did not do at least a bare minimum to clean himself up.

Tigris watched, balancing on the edge of his sink, as he performed his ablutions. After soaking the front of his hair in hot, soapy water, he had pinned it back and was now lathering his face to scrub away the flakes of old makeup and crusted, dried blood. He applied a fresh linen patch over what he knew would be a permanent scar on his forehead. At least it could easily be covered up by his hair.

"I miss having hands," Tigris sighed as Cyril rubbed a soothing cream all over his face.

He cocked a brow at her. "You've been a cat for little over an hour."

"And it is not at all practical."

"It is *safe*." It was his turn to sigh.

Tigris let out a huff of a laugh. *"I never expected* you *to be keeping me safe."*

He turned to her, about to speak insulted words, and she caught herself.

"Not that you're not competent, Cy. I would have liked it very much if you were my mage. I still will. But do you know why I told Atticus you were fragile?"

Cyril was thoroughly unamused. "Because I'm half a head shorter than you, and you could toss me over your shoulder like a bag of flour."

"No – well. You were the one to say it, not I. I shall not tell you if you truly do not wish to know." She sounded nervous.

"Out with it, then."

He noticed that she was examining his toiletries, his sink and the open cabinet over it. The fogged mirror he had wiped clean to make sure he had scrubbed his face raw enough.

"Because, Cyril. Ever since that night you ran away, I've always had the feeling one day we would all wake up and you would make yourself disappear again."

He did not grasp her meaning until he realised what she was looking at. A razor, languishing in disuse from how infrequently his whiskers came in, a vial of sleeping drought he used on difficult evenings. Most damning: a tell-tale crack in his mirror, chalked up to carelessness, actually from when, in a moment of airless neurosis, he had slammed his head so hard against it he truly thought he might not survive.

Cyril's tongue tasted chalk.

"I would not…" His tone was level. "Would not do something so foolish."

"I know," she said primly. *"I do not suffer fools. But…"*

But.

"But you just… you remind me of the magic you talk about. The weave, the pattern, how they… how you can unravel *it. It feels like you are unravelling. Like you are a bundle of string, and no one can quite touch the whole of you."*

His laughter sounded tinny. "I'm not sure I want people *touching* me–"

"Oh, shut up."

He shut up.

Tigris mewled in frustration. A rare sound from her, unlike the original host of her new body, and jumped from one end of the sink to the other, where Cyril had paused towelling his face.

"I am not your damsel. I am not a pawn in a plan. I am helping you as much as you are helping me. Have I made myself clear?"

Cyril nodded, slowly. Almost afraid nodding was the wrong move.

"Yes, ma'am."

"Good. You ought to have come to me with all this to begin with. Idiot."

"I thought you did not suffer fools."

"Not the same."

"Mm."

He took a moment to brush his teeth and recentre himself as he spat remnants of a herbal paste into the running sink.

"Did he think the same? That I was string?"

"Who?"

Cyril narrowed his eyes at her. "You know who."

"Oh. Cyril, you don't dominate my brother's and my every conversation."

"Humour me."

"...He thinks – he thought he could weave you back into a real boy."

The mint on his lips took on a sudden, bitter aftertaste. He laughed and it came out wrong, throaty.

"Like a fairy tale."

"Let's get some rest, Cy."

Later, tossing and turning in his bed as Tigris slept beside him, cast in the milk light of the full moon, he thought about the events of the evening. They had all gone entirely wrong, wholly unpredictably, but he felt a sense of security bubble in his gut that he'd not felt in years.

Heléne, Tigris and him. *They* had hatched this foundation for a plan. *They* were all in on the secret. Ganache too, if he was feeling generous.

It was unfamiliar to him.

Cyril was suddenly overwhelmed by heady self-assuredness. He could see why Tigris thrived in her own confidence. It was intoxicating.

For once, sleep came to him very much bidden. He was exhausted, and he wasn't as afraid of what anxious night terrors might plague him as he usually was.

Cyril felt good. He felt optimistic.

This feeling would be fleeting.

Unsurprisingly, the queen-to-be's disappearance was the talk of all the palace within a single day after her wedding dinner. There were swaths of knights patrolling the palace and all its surroundings, in search of the missing princess.

For her part in their plotting, Heléne had seemingly started her own little homespun rumour mill, which she was enjoying a bit too much (so Tigris had told him). From the newest scullery maid to the most established duke, all knew of Tigris's sudden vanishing, but the chief theory behind it went from a roguish kidnapping to what the courtiers had begun to call "wedding jitters".

It would have been funny (it was, perhaps, a *little* funny, still) if it had not left the kingdom in arrears.

Cyril couldn't believe he ever thought he could hide Tigris's body. They did not suspect him of foul play, he was the *least* of their worries, but if the princess had indeed absconded from her duties by her own volition, who better than a trusted friend to conceal her? Within half a day after the dinner, there were guards and even a knight apologetically ransacking his quarters for any sign of the missing Tigris. All the while she lounged at the top of a bookshelf right under their noses.

Overall, while there was growing unrest over the entire sordid matter, somehow Cyril felt it could have been much worse. There was a certainty that hung in the air that, sooner or later, the princess would be found alive and hale as ever. He marvelled at what one bit of gossip mongering could do.

He only truly felt bad for Atticus.

The King of Cretea seemed utterly dejected. His bride-to-be had run away a mere week before their nuptials, and he was left with nil explanation as to where or why. Especially when she had been in such high spirits when he last saw her.

Cyril was sure the man felt he had caused this, somehow. He had chosen to stay in Farsala to help with the search, offering up his retinue in aid. Every time he passed him in the halls, he had dark rings under his eyes, and he looked positively *haggard*. Cyril wanted desperately to say something to him. Perhaps he could be something of an ally to his growing resistance against the doomed future that encroached ever closer, but even he was not so stupid as to think it would be *good* to share such an important secret with yet another person. Perhaps if Tigris herself wished for the help of her fiancé, he would personally take her to him and explain everything, but she had barely mentioned him at all since the dinner, save for an agreement that she, too, was regretful they were causing Atticus so much grief.

He had strongly urged her to stay in his chambers. Cyril without Shoestring would be of little notice in the midst of all the commotion in court, but Shoestring with a fancy, opulent new collar, while not completely unusual to the passing servant or courtier, would doubtless strike a chord of suspicion with Eufrates, who had all but openly declared he was observing Cyril's every move. It was, perhaps, an overzealous precaution over something that could easily be excused, but Tigris put up little fight. She complained frequently that the cat shape was uncomfortable (*"Like an ill-fitting dress, Cy. It's driving me mad."*), and so preferred to spend her time sleeping under a sunlit window in his bedroom.

As the days passed, he also made a valiant, incredible effort to avoid Eufrates at every turn and every corner.

He knew the sound of the prince's footfalls by heart, so he could always hear him coming from half a mile away if he kept himself on high alert (which he always did). Then he would pull a vanishing trick of his own, hiding in shadows or in corners. If there were others around, he would grasp an unwitting courtier by the arm and chatter on about the weather and the princess and King Atticus and fashion and whatever other gossip came to mind until Eufrates gave up his pursuit entirely.

He slipped up only once.

It was high evening and he became careless leaving his rooms in search of a fresh pitcher of cream for Tigris's delicate kitty-cat sensibilities. There was no cream in the tower kitchen, so he had to go into the palace.

When he reached the garden path leading to the back entrance of the palace, he felt a leathered hand grab him by the back of the neck as though a cub, and pin him against the nearest wall.

Cyril blinked rapidly, refocusing his vision to the dim evening light, and the haunting face of Eufrates Margrave became clear before him.

"What have you done with her?" he growled.

There was a sense of urgency here that Cyril had not heard yet from him. Before, Eufrates had been languid, teasing. A cat playing with its food. He called him pet names and made sure to humiliate him in every conceivable way, reminding him with every honeyed word that they had once been in love. Making a mockery of it, as though it had meant nothing to him but a way to pass the time.

Not this. This was an act of desperation. Eufrates had been hunting for him, and now he caught him, he had no intention of toying with him further.

Still, Cyril did not care to be prey.

"I can't imagine who you mean, Your Highness."

"*Cyril*," he said his name so forcefully it felt like a curse. "You know who I *am*. You have seen what I am capable of. I can *make* you talk."

The hand on his chest keeping him pinned slid its way up to his throat, wrapping dexterous fingers around a too-thin neck. It was all very familiar. Briefly, he thought Eufrates should diversify his methods of intimidation.

"I assure you I won't say a word if I am found here in the morrow, laid out on the grass, strangled."

Eufrates scrunched his entire face. He almost looked confused. Still, the grip on Cyril's neck may as well have been iron.

"I know you... you *did* something to her."

"I *still* don't–"

"*Tig!*" Surely he had not *meant* for the desperation in his voice to be quite so loud, but Cyril heard it. It nearly overpowered the anger, the venom he had been spewing moments before. But why would *he* care?

He should have made himself disappear again. He should have made *Eufrates* disappear. Sent him to the dungeons, or the middle of the woods. Somewhere he'd have a hard time crawling out of to ruin Cyril's life.

Instead, he relaxed his shoulders and murmured, "The princess is quite safe." After a moment he added, "I have heard."

To his great confusion, the hand wringing his neck slacked a bit.

"Just *tell me* what you've done, Cyril. I *know* you've got some new, imbecile plan. What are you even *attempting* at?" He sobered and pulled away. Not to give Cyril room, but to loom overhead. "I am to be regent. The court is discussing it now."

He did not *sound* happy, but, then again, Cyril had not heard his husband sound *truly* happy in many years. And he was a consummate performer.

"Congratulations." His affect was flat.

"You are not going to tell me, then?"

Cyril pursed his lips. "There is nothing to tell."

Eufrates regarded him for a long while, inscrutable, and his hand loosened altogether from his neck. It traced the centre of Cyril's chest until it found the ring beneath his tunic. The two bands were so close together now, it almost stung. He looked rueful.

As rough as he had been gentle a mere moment ago, Eufrates shoved Cyril against the wall and stalked away, turning his back to him.

"So be it, my love."

EIGHT

Cyril could feel that Tigris wanted to trust her brother. She would ask about him, sometimes, under the guise of making sure he was doing a good job keeping a secret. Or merely because she concerned herself on whether he was worried about her.

She swore she trusted everything Cyril had told him about the future, but the part of it where Eufrates had turned into a despot, a tyrant, a *monster*, she could not believe.

Cyril just hoped she would not have to *see* it for it to sink in.

Tigris would not dare come to him with the suggestion to reveal everything to her brother. Cyril wouldn't abide by it. They were fighting *against* each other. Their last encounter in the gardens had made this very clear (though he hadn't told a soul about what happened, not even after he arrived back at the tower frazzled and distinctly lacking any cream). But still, he saw how not being able to trust him was weighing on her.

He hoped, for her sake as well as his own, that these next few months passed quickly.

There was a two-week lull: a grace period where Farsala was being run by a council of talking heads and the fact that most of its people weren't too concerned about politics to care that there was no instated ruler. But as it became clearer that Tigris could not be found, neither would she reveal herself, anytime soon, the time eventually came for the court to turn to her handsome, well-spoken younger brother.

Just like Eufrates had promised, he was nominated temporary regent until the Tigris situation resolved itself (one way or another). The power vacuum could not sit out in the open much longer without causing some damage.

From what Cyril had heard through the courtier grapevine, Eufrates had been surprised at the proposition. Humbled, awkward, ill-at-ease with taking his beloved sister's place.

When he walked down the halls, he heard murmurs of how the palace dwellers found the new regent-incumbent *so* charming.

Cyril found him a son of a bitch.

One would think that, leading up to his own crowning, to the sole event that would forever change the course of his life, Eufrates would finally ease up on his newfound penchant for mage hunting. This could not be farther from the truth. Cyril felt himself stalked everywhere he went. Just now he was realising exactly how many watchful eyes Eufrates Margrave, with all the resources at his disposal, was able to set upon him. His saving grace was that it was easy to avoid the rest of the palace when one was so deeply ensconced within a mage's tower, protected by Heléne's reputation of aloofness.

What Cyril did not expect in these volatile times (though he was sure if Tigris could've bore witness to it, she would have scolded him endlessly on how he should've known better) was that, being the prince's ostensible *dearest friend*, he would soon be sought after, just as fervently as Eufrates himself.

The crescendo, which would culminate in the upcoming coronation, weighing on all of Farsala like a leaden anchor, had bolstered Cyril's modest popularity from "pleasant curio" to "much-procured cog". He made himself even more scarce as he travelled his own home, having on occasion to resort to spells of concealment or invisibility simply to wander out into town in search of an ingredient for Heléne (who, no matter how dire the situation surrounding them, made sure Cyril did not lack on his duties as the grand mage's ward).

It was the first time in this reality that when he overheard someone ask for "the mage" they meant him and not his aunt.

Still, given how recent the development, he did not think himself particularly rude if he chose to feign ignorance, just as two unsuspecting nobles were about to gesture in his direction.

"Laverre! Oh, Laverre!"

Cyril did not have the deepest friendship with any of the Farsalan courtiers. If anything, he got along better, felt more of a kinship, with the serving class, sharing in their warmth and commiserating against the more *difficult* nobles within the palace. After years of snubbing lordlings and ladies alike, as well as being snubbed in return, he thought he would not be bothered by any of them unless it was very important business.

Clearly, this was business, though there remained some doubt on how "very important" it could be classified as.

Cyril braced and plastered on his most patient smile. He never should have wandered outside the tower in the first place, even if Tigris *was* growing quite annoying in insisting he procure some of her books from within her chambers so she could while away her confinement. This had the makings of his cream incident all over again, though hopefully these particular nobles would not prove themselves so brutish.

"Yes?" he said in lieu of a proper greeting, because he truly could not remember the names of the two young men who had approached him. Especially not after twenty years and some change.

"So glad to have caught up with you!" one of the men said.

It was the second time he had been stopped just this morning. The first had been by a gaggle of baronesses (sisters, whose names he faintly recalled all began with the same letter) who giggled and batted their eyes and pleaded sweetly with Cyril to put in a good word for them with the prince, as they were such *good* friends. Cyril would have gladly done this if he thought it would help even minutely to get Eufrates off his back.

In another lifetime, the beseeching would have irked him for a much worse, more virulently jealous reason. Now, he pitied the girls who were so enthralled by his husband's performance.

Cyril squinted. These men did not seem the sort to be lovesick over their bard prince. He could not fathom what they wanted, and he would not find out and be on his merry way unless he *asked*.

"What can I do for you? Is my aunt indisposed?" he said, as this was the first way he tended to interact with nobility. Pretend they were in great need of his magical abilities.

"Oh, no. We've no business with her," the first noble, shorter of the two with a pencil moustache Cyril had once been rather jealous of when faced with his own smoothness, assured. By now, the two men were flanking him, one on each side, with a heavy wall behind Cyril's back. It meant he would have difficulty extricating himself from the interaction.

"We've been looking all over for her ward," said the second. This one was taller and had a strong jaw.

"That's me."

"That's you!" He nodded, pleased. "You've been quite difficult to track down."

Cyril raised a brow. "Is it very important?"

The first man – pencil moustache – waved a hand in front of his face. "Oh, no."

Mystery solved, then.

"What he means," Strongjaw re-joined before Cyril could make his daring escape. "Is that there is no *urgency*. But *I* happen to think it quite important, actually."

Pencil frowned, as though he'd been one-upped.

"See," Strongjaw continued. "We two found that, save for the prince and our dear missing princess, you tend to be very alone quite often."

Cyril made no move to speak, so Pencil continued. It was like they had practiced this.

"It feels a great folly on our part, to have overlooked you this long."

"I can assure you I've taken no offense—"

"But we have! How many times have you, Laverre, the ward of the grand mage, dined alone up in that tower, because the Margraves had been otherwise engaged? If you are introverted, it is because we have enabled your seclusion."

Cyril blinked, slowly. "Beg pardon. Who is 'we'?"

"All of us courtiers, of course." Strongjaw this time. "But only a select few were wise enough to realise the mistake. I, for one, aim to rectify this." He proffered a gloved hand. "It would delight me to have you as a friend from now on."

Cyril's eyes darted to Pencil, who nodded. They *had* practiced this.

He supposed it made some sense. If they had been unsuccessful this far getting into the future regent's good graces, his best friend was a decent consolation. He wanted to laugh.

"Oh, thank goodness," Cyril said jovially, letting Strongjaw clasp their hands together. "I had been wondering if the two of you *also* wanted me to put in a good word with Eufrates about your marital prospects."

Pencil gave Cyril a strange sort of look and huffed a breath of laughter. "Why bother? It's *you* he takes to bed, isn't it?"

"Come now, Laslo. There's a difference between wedding and *bedding*."

They had momentarily forgotten Cyril was there, laughing quite gaily at the shared and, apparently, not unexpected joke. Which was good because he needed the moment desperately to compose himself.

Slowly, he drew his hand away from Strongjaw (the one who *wasn't*, apparently, Laslo). "I... am not sure what you mean?" he lied.

Cyril knew of his own reputation. He had become cognisant of it at the tender (but slightly embarrassing) age of three-and-twenty, immediately after Eufrates's rushed first coronation, as Farsalan nobility vied for a chance to become the kingdom's next consort. The reasons it had taken him so long to puzzle this out were twofold. For one, he was very stupid. This stupidity had been strongly enabled.

Cyril was used to being spoiled and coddled and protected. By Heléne, by the king and queen, by Tigris and most especially by Eufrates. None would allow the kind of gossip that had been brewing between the two young lovebirds since he returned home from the Academy to reach his sensitive ears, and Cyril thought too little of himself to reach such an outlandish conclusion on his own.

By the time he caught hold of the flourishing grapevine entangled around Eufrates and himself, the two were already a week into their short engagement and, truly, it was hard to be offended by a rumour that ended up being true.

The second reason why Cyril was able to live in blissful ignorance for so long was because, in all his days in court, even after the wedding, even during all those balls and functions and galas and councils and state meetings, no one had *ever* had the gall to say something so brazen directly to his face.

Perhaps the title of king's consort earned him more respect than that of grand mage ever could. Perhaps everyone inherently knew if a single word was breathed publicly against the king's favourite pet, the accuser would find themselves suddenly missing a tongue. Either way, Cyril was ill-equipped for dealing with malice so brazenly spoken.

He was so taken aback, he wasn't even sure it *was* malicious.

"Please," Pencil drawled. "We're among friends. And court affairs, as I'm sure you know, can be an awful breeding ground for the most horrible gossip, but it is obvious to anyone with a decent pair of eyes to see our dear prince is taken with you."

Cyril thought very carefully on how he should play this. Firstly, he would have to start telling Tigris to run her own damn errands.

"If he is... *taken* with me, as you say, he has not made it known to *me*. I've not seen him since the ball."

Strongjaw spoke this time, giving him an incredulous look. "He asks after you at every gathering we have attended. It has actually started to grate."

"If he wants me, he can come and find me. My question is why do *you* want me?" A redirect, gods willing, would help his predicament.

"You are not so naive as that. The ear of the king is just as precious as the king himself."

Cyril flashed a thin smile. "The king is dead."

Pencil let out an exasperated sigh, running quickly out of goodwill. "We are trying to help you, Laverre. In plain, as you've proven incapable of grasping the subtleties of court, we are here with a deal that can prove mutually beneficial."

"Oh." Cyril made his eyes wide as saucers and hit a balled fist dramatically against his open palm. "My apologies. You should have said something sooner." Then, he slunk himself against the wall and made to escape. "I'm not interested."

Before he could successfully leave, Strongjaw caught him by the arm with deceptive forcefulness. It was at this point that Cyril had to keenly remind himself that attacking a member of the court with magic so close to an impending coronation, in a period of so much political instability, would not only be a horrendously bad idea, but it would also thrust him directly into Eufrates's arms to be "dealt with" accordingly.

Knowing this, Cyril breathed slowly through his nose and turned once again to look at the pair of nobles still dogged on his tail.

"I'm not sure you–"

"He won't marry you, you know?" Pencil said abruptly.

Cyril blinked. It was such an outlandish thing to say all he could do was let the man carry on.

"Perhaps as the second son the pair of you would make a lovely couple, but the future king can't just propose to the court mage just because he's got pretty eyes and an open pair of legs. Be reasonable."

Cyril scrunched his brow and inhaled sharply. "You think I've got pretty eyes?"

"*Laverre*," Pencil snapped.

"No," Cyril said. "You listen. I have entertained you long enough, I think. The *king* died at sea not even a month ago. There are plans, from what I've heard, to instate a temporary regent in the absence of our rightful queen, Tigris Margrave. Any talk on the contrary flirts with treason."

Strongjaw, seeming to be the more relaxed of the two, loosened his grip on Cyril's arm to wind it up to his shoulder, grabbing him just under the throat. It was too intimate and too threatening all at once. Cyril felt himself swallow convulsively, the muscles working against Strongjaw's palm.

"We understand you care for the princess," he said in a measured, appeasing tone. "But if you bothered to attend court as we feel you ought, you would know what is said within these halls. Someone who disappears like that, Laverre, either does not care to be found or will not be found alive."

He could think of nothing to say to this. It felt, in retrospect, like such a singularly stupid oversight, borne of his years of eschewing nobility for the comfort and familiarity of magic and a selective inner circle. Tigris would know how to quell these whisperings. *Eufrates* would know to put an end to this.

Neither of them were here.

"I..." He wet his suddenly chapped lips, nervous, and noticed how Pencil's eyes followed the motion. "I am admittedly unfamiliar with the workings of our court. My duty is to provide whoever sits the throne with magical aid under guidance of my aunt. I am not comfortable speculating on the order of succession."

"We are not asking you to do anything *untoward*," said Strongjaw. "Right now, the pendulum swings in favour of Prince Eufrates inheriting the crown. We know how... precious you are – you have been, always – to him and we think you deserve your seat upon the court, instead of sneaking around into his bed like a common courtesan."

No one had *ever* called him a courtesan to his face before. At this point, he was bracing for '*whore*'.

"A seat upon the court," Cyril repeated, stupid with the sudden heat of embarrassment.

"If it is amenable to you, you're welcome to marry one of us. The Laverres are petty nobility, are they not? Certainly not enough for a legitimate claim to be palace courtier. *I* am a baron." He motioned vaguely to Pencil, who seemed to have stepped even closer. "If you've greater ambitions and worse taste" – this earned him a playful shove on the ribs – "my friend here has claims to a duchy once his mother passes."

"You rise in rank," Pencil continued. "You'll be able to escape your aunt's shadow. The gods know how many more years that woman will serve the Margraves before she relinquishes power. Do you not tire of pretending to be content slumming it with scullery maids and cook staff?"

"This is," Cyril spoke very slowly, suddenly acutely aware that he *was* being flanked by two outranking nobles, who, by the looks of it, had a combined fifty kilos on him as well as a distinct lordlike inability to gracefully accept rejection. At the same time, the ring on his breast made itself known by flaring red hot against his skin. As though he was even *considering* either man. "A very unusual marriage proposal. I am not sure I am sufficiently flattered."

"If it helps." Strongjaw's thumb brushed against his skin where the collar of his shirt began. "You *do* have very pretty eyes."

"Doesn't he just?"

Years of gruelling, immersive experience meant that if Eufrates Margrave chose to make himself a commanding presence, he was able to do it as easily as taking a breath. Very like him, too, was the way he materialised around the corner of the hall, projecting his voice all the way down the corridor so three heads snapped in his direction immediately, like in a pantomime.

Pencil took a long step away from Cyril and, at the same time, Strongjaw took his hands off him as though his skin now seared on contact. Cyril, for his part, was torn between the gratitude of relief and deep resentment that he had once again been caught by a much worse predator than a pair of power-hungry young nobles.

When seconds passed without a word from any man, Eufrates walked towards them and gregariously held out his arms. "Lord Laslo. Lord Bayard. I did not realise you were so familiar with my Cyril. I have been looking everywhere for him."

Cyril cringed visibly, avoiding eye contact as soon as the words "*my Cyril*" left the prince's lips. Still, he made himself as pleasant and obsequious as polite company called for.

"Eufrates. I am allowed to have friends."

Eufrates raised a brow. After the first acknowledgement of Laslo and Bayard, it was as though they had melted into the walls. "Indeed. Are these friends the reason I've not seen you in days?"

Cyril flashed a small, ingenue smile. "I did not realise you were looking for me. My apologies."

Eufrates's expression darkened for a fraction of a second before he brazenly stepped into the triangle that had naturally been created by Cyril and the nobles, putting himself firmly as a barrier between them.

"Thank you for tracking him down," he said to Strongjaw (*Baron* Bayard, it seemed). "If you would give us a moment in private."

Laslo, of the thin moustache, shot Cyril a knowing glance instead of facing his prince directly. It seemed to carry with it the reminder that, whatever contempt Cyril felt for him or his friend, Eufrates held similar feelings towards Cyril himself.

It was part beseeching and part warning. It would have been impactful, had it not been entirely redundant. Cyril hardly needed a third party to know *exactly* how his husband felt about him.

Bayard, the bolder of the two, finally spoke. "Forgive me, Your Highness. We were not finished speaking. If you could wait but a moment."

Eufrates shifted his weight towards Cyril and threw an arm around his shoulder in a boyish display of possessiveness. Today at least, Cyril was not beating any rumours.

"Cyril isn't going anywhere! I am sure you can ambush him later. You know where to find him better than I do, that's for sure."

"But–"

"Leave." Cyril looked up and saw the rigid set of Eufrates's jaw, so unfamiliar in his youthful form it nearly made him shudder. And as Eufrates's shoulders relaxed, his grip on Cyril tightened, vicelike. "Consider it an order. Or am I not still your prince?"

Laslo was the first to step away, bowing deep as he retreated. "Of course, Your Highness."

Bayard left in very much the same frightened rush, until just the two of them remained. For lack of a better subject, Cyril took to staring directly at the tiled pattern on the floor.

"I ought to go." He broke the silence, just as Eufrates dug his nails into his shoulder and stopped him in his tracks.

"You were not content with stealing my sister's happiness? Now you expect proposals from my courtiers as well?" His tone was dripping revulsion and his countenance was so dark that Cyril feared, ring-bound or not, if he tried to escape now, he would be found dead in the morning, beaten senseless.

Despite this – or, perhaps, knowing Cyril's thoughts – Eufrates deigned to let go of his arm, and Cyril, in turn, did not run (yet).

"Stealing your sister's happiness," Cyril repeated, unsure what to make of it.

Eufrates groaned. "Atticus. Do not think I've not seen the connection between your very public flirtation at her dinner and her instant, mysterious disappearance. Isn't he a bit young for you, my love?"

"Gods." Cyril ran a hand through his hair. "You think I want her gone."

"I *know* you're behind her disappearance. This is the only reason I could think of for it happening in the first place. Well." He paused. "That and you wish to torment me."

"I don't recall obsessively stalking your every move through the halls of the palace," Cyril said.

"'Keep your enemies close' is a perfectly good adage."

"We are enemies, then." This was a stupid, senseless thing to say, and it somehow still hurt to verbalize.

"I don't know, Cyril. I am not the one who tried to lure you out into the woods to slit your throat."

"You have had me choking against a wall *twice*," he hissed, suddenly impatient. How many more times were they to have this confrontation?

Eufrates stepped towards him so Cyril's back hit the stonework. Cyril flinched when he raised a single gloved hand just at chest level. "If I recall correctly, you did not use to shy away from my touch."

"You did not use to be such a *prick*."

Full of surprises, Eufrates caught him by the chin to tilt his head up instead of grabbing at him roughly. Here, in one of the many public halls of Farsala's palace, in broad daylight, the implications were endless.

"They're right, you know? You do have the most striking eyes." He glanced down, peering at Cyril's body through his lashes. "The legs aren't bad either."

"You were *listening*," Cyril exclaimed, trying his very best to keep the violent flush on his cheeks at bay by concentrating on more important matters than the predatory way his husband leered at him.

"I wanted to see where it went. I did not expect a *proposal*. The courts have truly fallen on desperate times."

"Because marrying me is an act of desperation."

Something inscrutable shone in Eufrates's eyes, so quick it was gone in an instant.

"*You* are the desperate one if you think it wise to accept. Do you think any of those men care for you?"

"I don't think *any* man cares for me, but it would certainly help smother some *baseless* accusations I've just heard."

Eufrates showed him a mean smile. He was so close Cyril could feel his breath on his face. Knew Eufrates felt his quickening pulse on his fingers. "Baseless? Truly?"

"We are not married here. We never will be," Cyril managed to grit out.

"Ah. I don't recall them mentioning our happy betrothal."

Cyril scrunched his brows into a frown that dissolved to horror when he grasped Eufrates's meaning.

"You are not so much of a pig–" he started.

"I'm not. I am chivalrous and beloved. I would not aid such gossip, especially not once you've behaved and told me exactly what simpleminded, hare-brained plan you've concocted that requires Tigris's disappearance."

"You *know* I'm not going to do that. How many times must we have this conversation? You are like a *child*."

"Oh, there will not be many more chances for you to surrender to me, my love. I am giving you until tomorrow's coronation."

"Generous."

Eufrates pressed him suddenly against the flat of the wall, so close, a breath away, that for a maddening moment, Cyril thought he was about to be kissed. He felt heady and overwhelmed and his heart thrummed violently in his chest.

"I am done with *games*, Cyril. I am giving you a chance. I am trying to be civil."

"Yes," he croaked. "That's exactly what this feels li–"

"Shut *up*," Eufrates growled. "You are stupid, and you are reckless, and if I wish it, you are *alone* in this court. Left to your devices, cut off from your kingdom, your responsibilities, from *me*. It is, it seems, all you've ever worked for, so I am *baffled* as to why I am being tormented yet again.

"But it's clear to me I am, and I intend to pay you in kind. All your magic and scheming cannot keep me from you. I am trying to give you a chance to take the *reasonable* course of action here."

Cyril was acutely aware that his breathing was coming up short and laboured. That Eufrates could hear and feel the beating of his heart, see the sweat beading on his brow. It would be simple – if he were being honest with himself, it would be *good* – to admit defeat and throw himself at the mercy of his husband the way he had done for years and years, unfailing.

But he *wasn't* quite as alone as Eufrates thought. He had Heléne and he had Tigris and if he let either one of them down, he would've squandered this second life he poured so much blood and magic into carving out for himself.

So, instead of following instinct and leaning forward, closing the distance between them, collapsing into Eufrates's arms, he curled his lips into a thin smile while threading the first strands of a spell behind his back and said:

"I haven't been reasonable since I agreed to marry you."

Then, he receded into the wall, melting backwards against the stonework. The last thing he saw before coming out of the other side of the palace into a small, flowering bush, was the stormy look in Eufrates's dark eyes. Angry, outraged, and... hurt.

* * *

It would be impossible to escape attending Eufrates's coronation. Heléne was obligated to be there and, as her ward, so was he. Tigris could have stayed in the tower if she wished, but she wished this as fervently as wanting to take a pickaxe to the back of the head. She yowled and hissed and scratched up all of Cyril's nicer furniture until he relented and took her with them to the ceremony.

They stood in the back, grouped together with some minor nobles who had mercifully left Cyril well enough alone over the past week, while Heléne took her place on the left side of the throne. Atticus, who had not yet given up the search but who *had* briefly returned to his kingdom, fearful of leaving it unattended too long, was given a seat of honour somewhere in the middle-left of the hall when he came back for the coronation, set on congratulating the new regent. Cyril couldn't help watching his profile for any clues that he was still upset. He owed the man *such* an apology once this whole ordeal was over.

And Eufrates, sat upon the throne, looked *devastating*. His hair was meticulously styled to look easy and carefree. It hung in tight coils over his head until it faded down around his ears and the nape of his neck in an immaculate buzz. The curlicue would not let itself be tamed, but it lent him a boyish charm. He wore tailoring reminiscent of his father's, but better suited for his own build, broad and lean at once. It was also calculatingly casual in a way Rohan never had been. An asymmetrical collar, a couple of buttons done too low, higher boots. The bard prince in the flesh.

Cyril's only saving grace was Eufrates's beard. Neatly trimmed and rugged. It was his least favourite style on his husband, so he refused to be lovestruck. He folded his arms in front of his chest and watched, bracing.

Very evidently, Cyril had *not* heeded the prince's increasingly beseeching pleas – *threats* – to reveal what he had done with

Tigris, and what he had been planning altogether. Before the actual ceremony, he had been a bundle of nervous, frightened energy, awaiting from every shadow to be whisked away by newly appointed royal assassins and dealt slow, gruelling retribution for his lack of cooperation.

But Cyril had been left alone. For one final night, he was left to his own devices, blissful and free to roam around as he pleased with no one on his heels, no indication of stalking or the threat of being cornered, caught and tied to a chair or the walls of a disused dungeon.

Were he a stupider man, he would've relaxed. Knowing his husband, he had gooseflesh so intense he wanted to scratch all the way through his skin to the bloodied bones underneath. Every time he started picking at the pathetic nubs that used to be his fingernails, he felt Tigris nudge the side of his leg and stopped, opting instead to chew the inside of his cheek raw and metallic.

He waited, and waited, and *finally* the man of the hour deigned to sit upon his father's throne, gingerly as though he was lowering onto a child's bench, not an ancient stone-wrought seat.

Cyril felt as though he was witnessing high art. Eufrates Margrave was acting his heart out.

The man sat on that throne as though he'd never even seen a chair before. He was awkward and flustered and uncomfortable. When they put the crown on him, he *flinched* as though it were going to take a bite out of him.

He held his first (*First*, Cyril scoffed) court with a humbled grace that instantly ingratiated him to all present. It was no wonder he had managed to invade an entire foreign territory. He gave a brief, unsteady speech on how he was intent on doing right by his sister, and how although he missed her every day, he needed to do right by Farsala as well. Cyril wondered if he had written any of this down or if it was improvisational talent.

Once Cyril heard a baroness standing next to him *swoon*, he decided perhaps he didn't *actually* need to stay for the entire speech. If Eufrates had something planned for him, surely either the moment for action had passed or it would come later, in private, when he could once again be backed against some wall and pressured into capitulation.

But then Eufrates began speaking of the grand mage.

"I have spoken of this to my advisors, and..." He drew out a nervous chuckle. "After *quite* some needling, I managed to make them see my way of things.

"I am a new ruler. And, gods willing, an *exceptionally* brief one. I will need many steadying hands, which our esteemed court has pledged to offer as I steady myself upon this dais. However, from all this surrounding experience I have asked for but one single indulgence."

Cyril could not possibly predict where this was going, but his whole body tensed. It was not going anywhere he would like.

Eufrates stood, suddenly, and they locked eyes for barely a second. He knew instantly he was right. He wanted to dash out of the room, but it was like the soles of his shoes were pitched to the floor.

"Grand Mage Heléne has been a great friend of the family and servant to the crown for many, *many* years." He gestured to Heléne, whose face was stone but whose familiar was casting Eufrates a confused look. "I – *we* – are all in her debt.

"But I am sure the sands of time weigh heavy on her shoulders, and I cannot imagine how true a blow it was for her to lose both my parents, her dear friends, as well as Tigris so close together. I cannot ask any more of her. I can ask but one thing and it is to enjoy a well-deserved retirement."

Heléne's stone countenance was quite good, but not against *this*. She looked completely stunned. She opened her mouth to say something, but Eufrates did not give her the chance. He strode to her side and effusively took her hands in his.

"Dear Auntie, do not think I am casting you out! You may stay in the tower as long as you like. For the rest of your life, if it pleases you, but the world turns, and I have thought it best to select a new grand mage to accompany me. Someone who will grow *with* me."

Cyril's stomach lurched. He was going to throw up on the swooning baroness's expensive dress.

"Cy, what's going on?"

Tigris was craning her long neck to see the dais. She asked this of him as though he had any idea what went through the mind of the most Machiavellian man on earth.

"I don't know," he whispered. "It doesn't sound–"

"Cyril!"

He snapped his head up and realised all eyes were now on him. This was not only because his name had just been called, it was also because Eufrates was crossing the room (the crowd had parted easily for him), and was already halfway to him.

Cyril shot Tigris a look he hoped conveyed *'stay hidden'* as clearly as possible, and then he stepped forward, half of his own volition, half from being pushed on by the courtiers near him.

"Cyril…" Eufrates said again. They were mere feet apart now, and the new regent reached for him. For his hand.

His smile was saccharine, pleading, when he drew Cyril out of the crowd to stand close to him and traced his knuckles with his thumb in a gentle, soothing pattern.

Cyril thought he was meant to say something, but all he could manage was a blank stare.

"I would like you to be my mage… I do not know what my sister would have done, but you have been…" Eufrates spoke carefully, *shyly*. "…a *beloved* friend to the both of us for many years. I should like nothing more than to have you take your rightful place by my side, if you accept."

Cyril could feel rather than see the eyes upon them. Upon

their clasped hands. Upon the way Eufrates's gaze, heart-melting and pure with adoration, was meant for him alone. The word *'courtesan'* jumped to the forefront of his mind, followed immediately by something more insidious.

He wanted to laugh in his face. If he had less self-control than he was exerting right now, he might have. He felt unhinged.

"I..." he began.

Eufrates wasn't through with his impassioned plea. He wasn't through with *him*. He grabbed his other hand and pulled, the picture of feverish desperation.

"Cyril..." The way he was saying his name was much too casual. Held too much sentiment. "My friend, do not make me beg... I will get on my knees before the entire court if I need to."

"Of – of course!" Cyril blurted in a tight voice. Then, he added, "It is what I am here for, after all."

Eufrates's perfect face split into a troubled frown. "Do not speak like that."

Before he knew what was happening, Cyril was being tugged towards the throne. Eufrates stood him beside Heléne, who had managed to once again school her expression so it was illegible.

"I am aware it is tradition for the mage to take up the central tower," Eufrates said.

Oh, no.

"But these are... different times. The circumstances are dire. You are not just a servant to me, Cyril." He put his *hand* over his *heart*. "I *need* your help, and I would like you close.

"The palace... my chambers are in the east wing, and I hope I do not come across as forward, my friend, but there are empty rooms next to it you could occupy. I would *personally* make sure you are comfortable. Taken care of."

Cyril wished someone would *take care* of him by cleaving a dagger through his eye.

"The tower is…" he said, as though he could say no to Eufrates like this. His palms were slick with sweat. "The tower is perfectly fine, Your Highness."

Eufrates put a hand on his shoulder. On the crook of his neck, to be specific. Too intimate a gesture.

"I insist. And *please*, Cyril. Call me by my forename. We should not be so distant."

Cyril knew what was *happening*, but he could not, for the life of him, understand why Eufrates was playing the role of the stupid, lovesick fool in front of all and sundry like this.

That is, until he noticed he wasn't the only one of the two who seemed to have an interest in their captive audience. With a small flicker of his eyes, Eufrates revealed his own investment in the surrounding courtiers.

It hit him like a mallet to the skull that Eufrates Margrave was a *genius*.

The blow was twofold: first and most obviously, Eufrates was taking him away from his tower and placing him in a room only separated from his own by some stonework and paint. Cyril would be under his watch at all times. Pinned under his thumb like a rabbit caught in a bear trap. He would not be able to breathe without Eufrates being by his side to monitor the airflow from his lungs and count the beating of his heart. He would suffocate. Hiding Tigris as well would become a monumental task unless he left her with Heléne, which would raise suspicion of its own.

Second, though, and something he maybe hadn't immediately realised was happening because some part of him still didn't think Eufrates could sink this low, was that he, Cyril Laverre, was now the most hated and maligned man in the palace.

He could hear the threads of gossip echoing along the walls already. A minor noble, wizard or not, enchanting the regent with his wiles. He was being given preferential treatment. He was *clearly* adored by Eufrates. And 'adored' was a term used *very* generously. Hopeful suitors would despise him for ruining their chances with prince charming before they could even try. Greater nobles would sneer at the nerve of him to be elevated so above his station. Most *everyone* would think him a foolish choice for grand mage, with his youth and inexperience.

It all felt very familiar. He was once again Farsala's dancing monkey. Their precious, useless little jester. And he was Eufrates's favourite pet. His docile plaything to be paraded around, never needing the commitment of a band or a vow.

This time around, though, it felt true.

NINE

The grand mage had always been a nebulous position. They were a courtier, yes, but they were a separate entity altogether as well. They did not live with the other nobles, dine with them, partake in their daily lives. The fact that they were a servant to the palace as well had always led to a sort of pleasant kinship with the staff. Frankly, Cyril would rather spend his time watching knights in the sparring grounds or observing dinner preparations in the kitchens than attend any kind of formal ball.

Even the servants, who he had a better-than-average rapport with, seemed to turn on him. He was snubbed even as they helped him carry his essentials to the east wing. It really did sting. He had lived in these halls his entire life. He knew most these people on a forename basis, and now they would not look him in the eye.

There was some kind of poetic irony to how, just days ago, he was bolstered by the idea of connection, of working together to keep a shared secret, and now he was, as foretold, completely isolated. Cyril was beginning to *really* hate poetry.

Tigris had declared she would help him move out of the tower. Then, she had declared she had no hands to carry anything with, so she was lounging on his sofa pruning her claws on the upholstery.

"He wants to be close *to you! Explain to me again why that's so awful."*

138

"Predators want to be close to prey," he said curtly. He was not in the mood to humour her about her brother. Tigris had not been there in the garden at night, in the hallway with the nobles, in the woods by the creek. The brother she held in her heart was sweet and tender. He wasn't sure even twenty years witnessing his corruption would help her see differently.

"It's like you did not hear how he spoke to you! He is the same as he ever was, Cy! He is beside himself with love!"

"He is certainly beside himself."

Cyril was ordering and reordering his books. He was unsure if he wanted them alphabetically ordered by title or by author. And, also, if he tried to think about anything else, he would need powerful libations.

"Why can't you even entertain the idea that he might have changed?"

Because he had me by the throat five days ago, he wanted to say.

"Because he hasn't, Tig. Listen, I'm sorry, but your brother isn't the same person anymore. And he isn't coming back."

"He is trying to make amends! We should tell him about me."

"Do you truly think he would make so public a declaration to me? So *clumsily*? Your brother?"

"You don't realise how he is around you."

"Oh. My mistake, it seems *you* were the one married to him for over a score. How very unusual. Is that not frowned upon?"

"You are being cruel, now. You won't even give him a chance."

Cyril slammed the book he was mindlessly piling away onto his desk and ground his nails into the lacquered wood.

"Fine. *Fine*," he snapped. "He is your brother. You have your doubts. We shall give him a *chance*."

He left the books on the desk and stormed out of his rooms, pausing only to wait for the sound of paws clacking against stone floor to signify she was following him.

He had coddled her too much. She needed her eyes opened.

* * *

They made it to the east wing in the early evening, when the sun was dipped low on the horizon and the sky was the colour of blood. It felt appropriate. Cyril paused at the door to the room he had entered more times than he could count, looked down at his companion, who fixed her eyes on the brass knobs with a creased brow, and knocked.

"Enter," was the response from within. So he did as he was bid.

It was the first time in years that he had entered Eufrates's room again, and he was instantly awash with memories, very much against his will.

He had spent countless hours here in another life. It was a palladium for the aspiring artist. Bright and airy, with windows near as tall as the ceiling streaming light in all hours of the day. They allowed the inhabitants of the room to observe the romantic outside gardens to their hearts' content. Bookcases tall enough to need a rolling ladder flanked the walls on the half of the space *not* occupied by windows and they were overfilled with poetry, anthologies, novellas and epics alike. A reading nook took its place somewhere between those shelves, in a spot where Cyril knew the sunlight shone comfortably. There was shelving dedicated to instruments and another to writing, composition, draftsmanship.

Compared to how much room Eufrates dedicated to his hobbies, his actual living space seemed impoverished. There was a medium-sized armoire where he kept his leathers and silks (though Cyril knew if Eufrates was lacking in clothes, all he needed to do was have a new outfit commissioned as the town's finest tailor had his measurements memorised) and a double bed, sparsely made, where Cyril had sat endlessly and watched the prince debut a new idea for a play or a song or simply regale him with a melody. He had not felt so adored as he had in those moments, where Eufrates's hot gaze bore a hole through his chest and the silk in his words wrapped around his heart, so even if he had wished to (he had not), he could not give it away to anyone else.

He did not want to remember this. It pulled at his temples and beset him with a headache.

Eufrates was sitting at his desk, reading through one document or another on kingdom affairs. Again, completely unwanted, he remembered how the prince (the freshly crowned king) would whine and cling to him like a spoiled child that he did not *want* to know about state matters.

Bathed in this dusk light, though, the room looked more like a *lair*. It helped him centre himself.

Cyril cleared his throat in way of drawing attention. "You wished to see me."

Tigris was trailing two steps behind him. He had instructed her to make herself as unobtrusive as possible. To *observe*.

Eufrates turned and stood, and his smile *dripped* with sarcasm.

"The man of the hour! Everyone is talking about you, you know? Dare I say you've overshadowed my own coronation."

"*You've* overshadowed your own coronation," Cyril snapped. He was not here for them to dance around one another. "You *dismissed* Tantie!"

Eufrates's brow dipped in mock concern. "Aunt Heléne is to die within a year. You do not think she deserves the respite?"

"Do *not* pretend to care for her!" he fumed. For the first time since they had found themselves in this strange old life, Cyril was the one to approach Eufrates, taking quick steps towards him. He was furious.

Eufrates looked suddenly very tired. He flashed him a look as though struck, but it was wiped clean the very next second. Spotless as if it had never been.

He looked past Cyril, over his shoulder, and finally seemed to notice the third party.

"Why, I've not seen that cat in weeks. I was starting to wonder if you were afraid I might skin him."

Cyril betrayed nothing. He hoped Tigris would do the same.

"You asked for the grand mage. What is a mage without their familiar?"

"Mm..." He examined Shoestring's figure, standing very tensed. "I did miss Shoestring. He's always liked me quite a bit." This was, unfortunately, true.

"But I thought he despised accessories. You once tried to give him a collar and he nearly bit your finger clean off."

"Shoestring has mellowed out in his old age." The lie fell out of his tongue so smoothly he was almost proud of himself. "Did you summon me here to see my cat, Your Highness?"

"No." He shook his head and drew closer. Within touching distance, but Eufrates stayed his hand. "I am once again going to ask you what you are plotting, my love. I hope to hear an answer this time. You've little resources left at your disposal save that *charming* stubbornness."

The corners of Cyril's lips curved. "I am sorry to disappoint."

Eufrates clicked his tongue. "You've not realised the position you are in, then. I am all that you *have*. Now you've spirited my sister away and Auntie is relegated to the tower, you've no allies in this place. Nowhere left to *hide* now that I've wrenched you away from your precious tower."

"And yet, my lips are sealed."

A grimace. His husband was beginning to crack. "I'm not sure you understand the position you are in, Cyril. You are *reviled*. I have given you the worst black plague a courtier could catch: a *reputation*."

"I am used to isolation. You will need to try harder." Even as he said this, he took a step back. He did not wish for Tigris to see *violence* if it came to it. "What will you do next? Perhaps you will wed me again. *That* will really rile up the courts. All those suitors might riot."

Eufrates followed, step by step, stalking him like an animal. But he no longer looked frustrated. Instead, amusement bloomed in his features. He looked entertained, like he had the upper hand again.

Which, unfortunately, he did.

"*Marry* you? Oh, beloved, you are too narrow-minded. The protection a wedding would offer you, the *power*. Not to mention I am loath to make that same mistake again. No. I will keep you here, in the intimate confines of my wing, close to my room, and without ever needing to put a second ring upon your finger, the courts will rile *themselves* up."

Cyril was beginning to follow, and his bones were chilled. It was not as though he had not thought of this himself, had not been *warned* about it by the courtiers mere days ago. It was that, somehow, some way, he still did not expect Eufrates Margrave to sink so low as to tarnish the reputation of the man he'd once claimed to love.

It was quite the blow.

"What is keeping the regent's attention?" Eufrates continued. "Why is he not entertaining marriage? Even if it is temporary, it is natural for a sovereign to want to wed. It must be the boy he keeps at his heel. The fresh-faced enchanter who had no business rising up in favour like that. What else has he done to our dear Eufrates?"

Cyril felt as though he was speaking through a mouthful of tar. "You are making me your courtesan."

"Precisely! Very *clever*, Cyril!" *Now* Eufrates was upon him. He placed a hand on the crook of his neck and stroked upwards to his cheek, the caress of a lover. "What a good boy..."

Cyril was, at his core, very weak. He shuddered.

"*Cy,*" Tigris said into his head. He had truly forgotten she was even there. *"That's enough. We should go."*

He ignored her outright.

"*Why*?" he croaked.

"Because I am torturing you, my love. That is how information is withdrawn, is it not? I will get you to spill yourself onto me if it's the last thing I do." With his other hand, he traced lazy crosses over Cyril's heart. The intimacy was scalding. "If I have to carve it out of you with my bare hands..."

"I have said, Your Highness." Cyril's voice sounded so much like a whisper to him he wondered if he was hearing it only in his own head. "I've nothing to tell."

Eufrates pursed his lips into the mimicry of a pout. "Not to worry. It is only our first night together."

"Cyril!"

He decided Tigris had seen more than enough, once his fogged mind remembered she was there. He pushed Eufrates away in a frenzied, jerky motion and, remembering who he was and what he was capable of, tugged the edges of the pattern in Eufrates's room so it went completely dark.

"Good night, Your Highness."

As Eufrates was gathering his bearings, he turned on his heel and, quick as a phantom, scooped Tigris into his arms and ran out. It took him getting all the way down to the end of the hall to realise he was not being pursued.

He felt suddenly impossibly tired. He put the cat down and cast her a weary, pleading look.

"Satisfied?"

Tigris had nothing to say for herself, but she shook her head.

They walked together in silence for a while, wandering the empty halls of the palace before Cyril murmured, "I did not expect it to get that bad..."

Tigris stopped and looked up at him. *"You do not need to coddle me. I am his elder sister."*

"Well. He's actually–"

"Shut up, Cyril."

He shut up. A beat passed between them.

"...What will you do now?"

"Well. I don't have much of a choice, truly. I shall stay in my new room and make sure to keep you safe as promised."

"And Euf– Eufrates?"

Cyril thought on how to answer this. He wasn't going to start lying. Not about this. She had seen more than he had wanted her to. It was a depth of cruelty and mocking he had not expected his husband to resort to. But Eufrates was desperate to get him to talk, so Cyril wasn't sure how far he'd take it.

"He will attempt to break me. But I do not think he will go very far with it. He cannot. I think the rings prevent him from killing me outright."

"There is a long road between breaking and killing, Cy."

"…I also do believe he is desperate to see what has become of you. He would need me willing to talk."

"I don't want you doing this."

"You've no say, Tig."

"I do. I order you not to stay in those rooms. I am your queen, am I not? You are a humble servant?"

Cyril rubbed circles over his temples.

"What would you have me do, my queen?" he drawled.

"I… you should run. Hide somewhere."

"If I return to the tower he will know instantly. I have no excuses for doing so. If I ask Tantie for aid, she risks being cast out. I will not evict her from a home that is more hers than it ever was mine."

"No, I wasn't thinking Auntie. She's helped too much already."

For the first time that night, Cyril looked at her with genuine surprise. He had no more tricks up his sleeve. He couldn't fathom what secret way of escape was going through her head.

He leaned his head down, as if maybe then he could hear her better, even though everything she said echoed crystal in his mind.

"What *were* you thinking, then?"

"Not what. Who."

Cyril blinked in confusion, until the answer became apparent to him. His brow rose near to his hairline, vanishing within his fringe.

"Surely not."

"You're the one who sounded so keen on it. I thought you'd be happy."

"'Happy' isn't quite the word I'd describe."

"Are we going or not, Cy?"

"Wh– now?"

"Yes. Do you want to give my brother more opportunity to get you to betray me?"

"No, I just – I do not even know where he is staying."

"Near my quarters. Obviously. We are to be married."

TEN

Tigris happened to live a reasonable trek away, in the west wing – the other side of the palace. He had never understood why brother and sister had chosen to room so far apart from one another when they were otherwise glued at the hip in childhood, but Cyril had never had any siblings of his own. He *barely* had a family.

The far end of the west wing housed Tigris's opulent bedroom, which Cyril remembered as a love letter to bright colours, fashionable decor and a permanent state of disarray, no matter how many brave maids ventured inside. Guest rooms flanked the path to the princess's on either side. One of these in particular was where Tigris led Cyril in the dead of night, under cover of darkness like a cloak-and-dagger spy.

"What if he is not awake?" Cyril asked.

"We rouse him. What is wrong with you, Cy?"

They had discussed what they would say to Atticus on their way across the palace. To an onlooker, it would seem like Cyril was frantically whispering to himself. A madman. If there *had been* any spectators to their conversation, any nobles on a midnight stroll or guards on overnight duty, it would do no favours for Cyril's already languishing standing with the court.

"I simply do not know if I should be – be *dropping* all this on a man. A *grieving* man! It is too much to ask."

Tigris sniffed. *"It is the least he can do as my future husband."*

147

"Yes, see, that's exactly it! *You* are his fiancée. I am nothing to him–"

"You are my dear friend!"

"It would help, surely, if we told him about your situation!"

"Atticus is a generous man. He does not need to know all the details in order to help."

"Just – Tig, it would make this *so* much easier," he pleaded.

"I've said no. It is my secret to keep, and I do not wish to tell him. Perhaps in future, but right now my priority is getting you *out of here."*

Cyril grumbled under his breath, "I should have just knocked you unconscious and stuffed you in a closet…"

"Are you going to call for him, or shall I?"

With a disgruntled sigh, Cyril knocked on the door to the guest room. He waited an appropriate amount of time to knock again, confident the king would be fast asleep at this hour, but the courtesy was unnecessary. Within moments, he heard footfalls making their way to open the door.

Atticus looked *very* surprised to see him, which was a middling start. He could have been annoyed.

"Your Majesty," Cyril said, and bowed so low and so quickly that his hair cascaded over his shoulders in a mess of flax. "Forgive me for disturbing you at this time of night."

Instantly, he felt a solid, steadying hand on his shoulder. Cyril peeked up through his fringe to see that Atticus was looking down at him with concern.

"Laverre, please. I have told you to call me Atticus."

He was wearing thin, square reading glasses and had telltale ink stains on the tips of his fingers that indicated he'd been in the middle of writing something down. He also somehow looked the picture of propriety, despite being dressed only in silk sleeping trousers and a loosely done robe that exposed the better part of his chest. Cyril felt a flush and set his gaze back firmly on the floor.

"I am sorry. Atticus. I am… I seek aid."

Atticus lightly squeezed his shoulder to push him back to standing at full height. He doffed his glasses and stuck them to a pocket upon his breast. When he took a step back inside the guest room, Cyril was certain he was going to slam the door on his nose, but he merely stepped to the side and gestured inside.

"Friend, you look frightful. Please, come in."

Cyril glanced briefly at Tigris, who gave him a nod. They were ushered into the room.

The King of Cretea sat Cyril on a grand armchair that made him feel like a child and made him wait while he brewed what he had called a 'Wulfsbane specialty' with an assortment of cookery instruments laid out on a table. The drink turned out to be mostly melted dark chocolate, heated with cream and spiced with cinnamon, citrus zest and, curiously, crushed peppers. Atticus meticulously poured a layer of milk froth over it as though he was some sort of kindly tavern owner and not the ruler of a sovereign nation.

Cyril eyed it with suspicion, certain it would be much too heavy a beverage. He was wrong. Before he knew it, he had downed half a cup before Tigris hopped up onto his lap and shoved her head against his wrist, demanding to partake. He blew over the mug before sharing with her.

"Gods, I love this thing. It's worth marrying him for."

Cyril was inclined to agree.

Atticus cocked an eyebrow at the pair.

"Is he... safe to drink that?" he asked, sounding genuinely worried.

"Oh!" Cyril placed the cup on a nearby table and Tigris leapt up onto it to lap up the rest of the chocolate. "Oh, yes, he's not a *real* cat. Familiars do not suffer food poisoning, I don't think."

"Ah. How enviable. I myself am mildly allergic to tree nuts."

It took him a moment for Cyril to realise the king was making a *small talk*. He had delivered it with such a serious expression, but it was clearly meant as a distraction for Cyril's sake.

Cyril did manage a nervous giggle. "You must be having a hard time out here, then."

"Indeed. The south is known for its chestnut delicacies. I cannot partake, but they *smell* wonderful."

He felt another bubble of mirth erupt from his chest and, with it, the steadying of the hummingbird beat of his heart.

As he calmed down, he took in the guest room Atticus was settled in. He had been here for weeks now. Enough time that he had customized the space to show a glimpse of his personality.

There were books that did not seem to come from within the palace's library lined in no particular order on a small shelf. From the spines, they seemed to delve into the most eclectic of subjects. Potions, psychology, mathematics, a recent weather almanac and an astronomy chart. Regardless of the mix, it didn't seem as though Atticus held much love for fiction.

A table near the shelf held an assortment of equipment Cyril had just recently seen Atticus use. There was what looked to be a portable burner and a grill, a few pots, pans, beakers and vials. He had seen Atticus pull ingredients from a cabinet underneath the table, but he could not tell what exactly was within, other than bars of rich chocolate and jars of spices and candied fruit peels.

Next to that was a writing desk, which was clearly where Atticus had been before he had been interrupted. A quill dipped in fresh ink sat propped up against a paperweight, and it seemed the king had closed a journal over a letter he was writing. This was quite smart. Cyril did not *want* to snoop, but he was sure his eyes would wander if he neared the table, and he was sure it was merely the business affairs of a temporarily absent sovereign.

Most guest chambers were outfitted with comfortable plush blankets and upholstery, especially in the colder half of the year, but Atticus had clearly stripped his own room bare, save for a thin duvet and a couple of throw blankets for the sake of decor. He kept the blinds on the large windows pulled halfway down, and overall seemed to revel in cool shade.

Even the way he was dressed sent a shiver through Cyril. He could not imagine wandering shirtless this early in May.

"Oh, goodness," Atticus interrupted his scan of the room, sounding like he'd just remembered something. Then, he pulled the robe he wore tighter to his chest and knotted its belt. "I'm sorry, Laverre. I am quite indecent."

Cyril coloured all over again, and despite the cup being empty, he took it into his hands to have something to bring up to cover his face. "No! Do not worry yourself, I am the one who knocked at your door at such an unseemly hour."

"Why are you flustered? I thought you were married for over twenty years."

Cyril shot Tigris a glare and she sniffed and hopped back over to the arm of his chair.

Atticus watched them in polite curiosity and Cyril stiffened in his seat.

"Excuse my familiar. He has never been given to delicacy. I meant to chastise him for drinking so quickly."

"Not at all! Perhaps I should have made two mugs." He stepped closer. "Are you feeling any better now, though?"

"Ah…" As a matter of fact, he was. The drink and the light chatter had done wonders. "I am. Thank you."

Atticus nodded and his gaze turned serious. "So… what kind of aid am I to provide?"

"You do not have to agree to it, Atticus. You've not even heard what I have to say."

"I will always be happy to help a friend of Tigris's."

Cyril avoided looking at the cat at his side, who he knew was sure to be casting him a smug little smile.

"Well… it concerns Eufrates."

Atticus's brows rose. "The young regent? He is quite fond of you, is he not?"

He would have to do something about the colour this man drew from his cheeks. It was becoming untenable.

"He... I had thought so, yes."

"He was quite *passionate* when he named you the new grand mage."

"Oh, it's quite alright. He was a spectacle. I will not be offended if you say it."

Atticus hid a chuckle behind one hand. "It was not how *I* would have gone about it, no. But why have you come to me? Surely not for romantic advice, though I would gladly be willing to part with it."

Cyril shook his head. "No. I would not dare trouble you over something so trivial."

"It is not trivial–"

"Please," he interrupted. He had worked up quite a bit of nerve coming here, and Atticus's open generosity was making him lose it. He would feel endlessly guilty burdening this man. "Please, allow me."

Atticus was silent for a moment before he nodded and pulled a chair from where it was tucked under his writing desk. He placed it in front of Cyril and sat across from him, eye level. The way he looked at Cyril made him feel like a scared, lost creature.

"Forgive me. Do go on, Laverre."

"...Cyril is fine."

Atticus smiled warmly. "Cyril, then."

He was not the maestro his husband was, but he had run through this story enough times in his head on the way to the west wing that he had started to convince himself of its plausibility.

"I was happy, at first, when Eufrates asked to be closer to me. We have always gotten along. But when I went to see him earlier tonight, he... he is not himself."

"What do you mean? I am unfortunately not as familiar with the younger sibling."

"As I mentioned, we were good friends, but once we were finally alone, he acted strangely. He was not himself. I fear Eufrates has become insensible. He had never wanted any inheritance but for perhaps a plot of land of his own, so I am sure it has come as a great shock that he is now regent. As well, he worries about Tigris."

"As do I."

Cyril nodded. "Yes, of course, but... the way he has been affected. I know you are an outsider to our traditions, but it is highly unusual for the grand mage to leave the central tower. I genuinely thought he wanted my help, but I'm afraid it was more calculated than that. He is a phenomenal performer, after all. I think he believes I have something to do with his sister's disappearance, and he has vowed to torment it out of me."

It was much easier to twist a few truths than to conjure up an entire lie out of nothing. Cyril was telling Atticus what he needed him to know.

He did not, however, expect the king's expression to darken so immediately.

"*Did* you have some involvement in it?"

Cyril blinked. He was wholly unprepared to be scrutinised. Obviously, though, he had made a grave mistake. He came to Atticus expecting a kindly, generous mentor who was willing to help him, but he could be all these things and still not be a *fool*. It was a perfectly reasonable question to ask.

From behind him, Tigris hissed (at Atticus or at him, he wasn't quite sure), which snapped him out of his muteness.

"I – no, I assure you!" He was, perhaps, too impassioned, but he had waited too long to respond. "I loved Tigris as family, but if the rumours are true, I would not help her cause such uproar. You *must* believe me."

Atticus stared at him for a long while and then he let out a deep, exhausted sigh. Without a word of warning, he reached up to pat Cyril on the head, like he was soothing an animal.

"I'm sorry, Cyril. I am just as worried about my bride, so I cannot be too careful. I did not mean to scare you, though."

Cyril thought he might cry. He was this close to having *two* men trying to kill him over a girl. It was a situation so bizarre to him it made his head spin.

"You believe me?"

Atticus nodded. "I had my servants check your quarters, if you'll remember. You have not been concealing her and I do not believe you capable of foul play."

"...Thank you, Atticus." He could feel a sting of tears welling up that he blinked away. He did not expect this level of trust from a stranger. He hoped Tigris saw now how lucky she was.

Atticus removed the hand from his hair and leaned back in his seat. "This brings us back to the beginning, though. What *would* you have me do?"

This was it. This was where *Tigris*'s idea came in. He reached over almost absently to stroke her back.

"Asylum. I am seeking asylum from Cretea, at least until Eufrates has regained his senses."

Atticus looked stunned for a moment. "It is that dire a matter?"

"Yes. Removing me from the tower has put me at his mercy. I've no other choice but to flee the courts altogether. I thought... as Tigris's fiancé, you would be willing to help me." He swallowed convulsively. It was time to play the trump. "She had always said you were a kind man."

"Oh, good work, Cy."

He so wished she would stop making interruptions. He was going to lose focus.

Atticus's face softened even further, if possible, and he flashed him a small, reassuring smile.

"It would put me at odds with the current Regent of Farsala, as you know."

"Like I said, you are under no obliga–"

"Calm down, Cyril. I did not say I would not do it. I am trying to think of the best way about it."

He was agog. "You will help me?"

"Even if you were not well loved by Tigris, I could not stand here and do nothing after what you have confided." The smile crooked into a small, secretive grin. "I have always wanted to play the dashing hero."

Cyril laughed, his first genuine one of the evening. "I am not much of a damsel, I'm afraid."

"You do not give yourself enough credit. You look the very picture of someone worth saving."

Said by anyone else, Cyril would think it a cruel remark. Atticus made it sound like a genuine compliment.

Atticus extended a hand and Cyril took it, sheepish. They stood together and Atticus walked them over to the desk where he took out a fresh sheet of paper and a quill.

"Here is how we will do things."

ELEVEN

An hour later, Cyril and Tigris were in a carriage being snuck out of the palace by some Cretian valets in the dead of night. It was just as well that Atticus had such convenient means of egress on standby, as mages were known to teleport their way over long distances whenever –wherever, really – they pleased, but it required quite a clear visual familiarity with the intended destination and Cyril had never actually bothered to commit the neighbouring kingdom's royal palace to memory.

Also, he felt he desperately needed the time alone, secluded inside the plush upholstered carriage to soothe his nerves.

Tucked into his waistcoat pocket was the second of two letters that Atticus had given him after quickly scribbling them down and sealing them with the Wulfsbane crest. The first one he had parted with moments earlier, having given it to their coach driver along with a handful of coin, also from Atticus.

The letter held instructions to take Cyril Laverre and his familiar to Cretea's palace as soon as it was read, and to make sure he was comfortable and taken care of. Now, sitting in the comfortable interiors of the private coach with two valets on horseback flanking the vehicle, he was impressed with the efficiency of it all.

Atticus had developed his plan within record timing, the gears in his brain working overtime as he guided Cyril to his desk and explained exactly what they were to do.

When Cyril sought asylum, he did not exactly think much past it. He assumed he would get to Cretea one way or another, and from then, Eufrates would no longer be a threat. It was the same kind of scatter-brained thinking that got him caught in the middle of the night with an unconscious girl in his room by his own aunt.

Atticus was quick to point out that a sudden departure, clandestine at that, by the entirety of his retinue would not be taken kindly. If Eufrates himself did not take offense, his council certainly would. It was a promise of subterfuge, of a threadbare alliance falling apart. If he was going to leave Farsala, it would need to be public, during the daytime, and with significant fanfare and consent of their hosts. He would conjure up a reason to return, express regret that he could not further wait for the results of their search for his fiancée and set out the very next day, perhaps after breaking fast with the court.

Cyril did not need to tell him he would not be permitted to leave with the Cretian retinue. Atticus was one step ahead of him. He showed him the letters he had composed while explaining all this: identical, formally dated and signed, with the same wax seal branded upon the bottom right.

The other letter was addressed to the head butler of Cretea's palace. They were clear instructions to treat Cyril with the courtesy owed to an honoured guest and the delicacy owed to one seeking sanctuary. Atticus did not explain Cyril's exact situation in these letters, telling him if he wished to disclose more details, he was free to do so, but the choice was his. He assured Cyril that the head butler was an incredibly kind woman who would welcome him with open arms if she were given the letter. He would have rooms of his own and, if he should wish it, a place in court.

The riskier part of their plan was happening this very moment, with Cyril watching with a stab of longing the retreating figure of the mage tower in the distance as the carriage ventured north. Tigris, next to him, tried to sleep, but was kept awake by her own restlessness.

They were to be spirited away in the witching hour of night so as to pass completely unnoticed. It was not uncommon for Cyril to sleep in, to miss breakfast completely, and it would especially not be unusual for him to be sulking in his new bedchambers, resisting the call to leave and be treated poorly by most every Farsalan courtier in his home. The hope was that his escape would go unnoticed until at *least* after Atticus himself had left with the rest of his retinue and then there would be nothing Eufrates could do save giving Heléne her old post back.

"You will take my coachman and my carriage. It is a longer drive, but it is more comfortable," Atticus had said. "From here to my home with no breaks is a six-hour journey. I am sorry to make you travel so late in the evening."

Cyril then asked how Atticus himself would get back, which awarded him another one of those fond, dashing smiles.

"The *ride* back is a mere three hours. We are not such big territories, or as far apart, as that. By afternoon, I am sure I will have met up with you once more and we will both be out of the woods."

He could not believe this man he barely knew was willing to ride three hours on horseback for his sake. He hoped at least the saddle was comfortable.

"Do you think we will be caught?" Cyril asked, eyeing Tigris and then the palace out the back window nervously.

"At two in the morning? Doubtful."

She seemed a fair bit calmer than he was about this. Then again, it was not *she* who was being pursued by a madman.

"He is truly a very good man. I do not know how I will repay him."

Tigris spread her cat form over the seat opposite him in a lazy stretch. *"Technically, since you are doing all this on my behest, it will be me who repays him. I shall give him some islands to the east, perhaps."*

Cyril frowned. "You talk about your husband–"

"Fiancé."

"Yes, that. You talk about him so dispassionately. Were you not moved by his actions?"

"It is a bare minimum of decency. Anyone should have done it."

"He risks political conflict!"

"I would have done the same."

Cyril let out a breath of frustration. "Why must you needle the poor man? What has he done to you?"

"Nothing," she snapped.

There was a pause between them and, when Cyril said nothing, she continued, desperately trying to make sense of herself.

"He does not stir any greater feelings in me, Cy. When he courts me, it is 'nice'. When we dance, I feel 'good'. Even when he was showing off all that valour and charm by helping you all I could think was, 'Oh. Well, there's a great fellow!' It is driving me to madness! I think there must be something wrong with me!"

"Nothing is *wrong* with you, Tig…" He tried his best to sound comforting. "Perhaps you are simply not prone to great fits of passion."

Without a word of warning, she cartwheeled her small frame across the bench as though her body was made of molten sugar, boneless and aimless. She hit her head against a pillow on the dismount. All the while she did this, she screamed, inside Cyril's mind and out, letting out a steaming kettle's worth of frustration.

It startled him, so he pulled his legs up to his chest in case she began clawing at him again.

After some brief hesitation, he leaned in. "What is–"

"I want *passion, Cyril!"* she blurted. *"I have spent years watching my brother compose sonnets for you on the margins of his arithmetic notes. I should like something similar!"*

Cyril looked distressed. He had no earthly idea how to deal with this. Perhaps if he had had children or even *niblings* or *godchildren*, he'd have some inkling on how to handle her, but this felt like trying to reassure an adolescent in their romantic pursuits. He had spent a decade pining over one man and then he had been swept off his feet less like a damsel in a song and more like a sack of flour at a bakery for morning bread. He was out of his depth. In this, he was wholly an imbecile. Even being married, he had no real *advice* to give.

Still, he owed it to Tigris to try.

"...I think you would hate a sonnet. I think you would laugh at it."

She thought about this, and did not deny it. *"That's not the point, though! I would like to be in love!"*

"It is more trouble than it's worth."

"You are bitter. You make a horrible judge on these matters."

"And yet you wanted a love like mine?"

"Well!" she said. *"Not* all *of it!"*

Cyril slowly built up the courage to reach out and stroke the top of her head.

"Perhaps... an attachment born out of mutual trust is better than passionate love, Tig."

She rolled her eyes. *"An attachment. How depressing. I just wish I felt something."* Her gaze darted from out the window to his face. *"Honestly, it feels like you are more enamoured by him than I'll ever be."*

Cyril blustered, choking on nothing but an acute sense of shame. "I appreciate his *kindness*! You must understand, I've not experienced it in a while."

"I'm kind to you."

"You've given me a permanent scar."

Tigris pouted. *"Very well. Continue to moon over my fiancé's* kindness *all you wish. But dare I say he is a bit young for you."*

That cut quite deep. Cyril felt his fifty-odd years like a heavy weight over his back.

"You are so cruel," he whined.

"Should I call you Uncle Cyril?"

He clawed at a pillow next to him on the seat and screamed into it, his turn to resort to hysterics. They seemed to both be going through something that evening.

At least he had somewhat consoled Tigris. She was shaking with laughter when he looked up at her, no longer burdened with the oh-so-miserable idea of wedding a generous, handsome, gregarious king.

That is, until her head shot up from her boneless narrow shoulders.

"Auntie!" she cried.

"Well. I don't think that would quite work. *'Uncley'*, maybe? Actually, when I was a child, I was made to call my father's brothers 'tanton'."

"No, you dolt! We've not said a word about this to Auntie!"

Cyril's jaw fell in a small, panicked 'ah', but then he truly considered the wisdom of involving Heléne in his scatterbrain mess ever further than she already was. How shocked she looked when she was booted out of her post, used as a pawn in his husband's ridiculous crusade to destroy him. She had loved Eufrates too, once.

"...It may be for the best," he said slowly.

Tigris gave him such a look of singular betrayal it made him want to ask the carriage to be turned around right this instant.

"Wh– but, she will be worried!"

"She is highly intelligent. Tantie will know we're safe."

Cyril thought about his aunt. He had thought she had been on the path to recovery once he spoke to her the night of the king and queen's death. Perhaps she was not to die so soon after all, and he had reversed an injustice he didn't realise he could've saved.

But since their shared plan, aside from helping obfuscate the truth of Tigris's disappearance, Cyril had seen less and less of his aunt as the days went by. She had gone back to her isolationist ways, high up in her tower with Ganache, a handful of favourite liquors and provisions that would last a lifetime. He had been so absorbed in keeping Tigris secret and safe that he had not noticed the change until he truly looked back on it under a retrospective lens.

On one hand, letting her know might assuage some doubts about their whereabouts, but on the other...

"If she is implicated, Eufrates may press her for information," Cyril said. "And I know you want to think the best of your brother, but–"

"*Cyril, stop. I was in that room. I saw him as well as you did. I do not want him pestering Auntie.*"

Cyril nodded.

"I'm sorry. It must be horrible, speaking of him like that."

"*I'm not a fool, though you may think me one.*"

He balked at how suddenly and confidently this was said.

"What made you think–?"

"*Oh, I do not think it is malicious. You think me too stupid for queendom.*"

"I don't–"

"*And I think you too weak for grand magistry.*"

Cyril's mouth hung open like an unmanned puppet's. He had no idea how he was meant to respond to that, but it seemed he did not need to.

"*Which is why I think we will suit one another very well, when we inherit.*"

He stared at her a long while, then burst into manic, tearful laughter.

"*I am quite serious, Cyril,*" she said, very properly. "*It will be me, you, Tantie as a counsellor, perhaps Atticus if I am feeling generous.*"

"How nice a thought," he responded with a genuine smile, through dissipating giggles.

"*And we shall lock Eufie up in a dungeon where he will think about his crimes, and when he is good and normal again, we let him out!*"

Cyril wiped a tear from his eye and reached out again to stroke her head, heart so full he had not felt like this in years.

"I should like that very much, Tig..."

Tigris returned his smile in kind. "*Good. Then it will be so.*"

Cyril stifled another laugh and lay sideways on the carriage seat, propping his head against one hand and his elbow, like the subject of a languid old painting of a naked fae being hand fed grapes. It felt a bit like an abuse of Cretea's hospitality towards him, but he was feeling a bit childish at the moment. Especially after the comment on his age.

"You know, I had not thought of what to do after I defeated Eufrates. So much of my old life revolved entirely around him."

"Defeat?"

He swatted a hand over his face. "You know what I mean."

"You can do whatever you want. Do you think a lot will change for you?"

"Hm... I can't think of anything concrete." He frowned and grasped at the ring hanging at his chest. "I suppose I will die a virgin this time around."

"Cy–ril!"

She looked rattled, *mortified* by this new, unbidden information. The corners of Cyril's lips twitched. He did not realise he could inflict so much damage upon Tigris just by humiliating himself before she ever got her paws on his secrets. Shameless as he was in his *old age*, he would have to keep this new knowledge in mind for the future.

"You went to school abroad and you're trying to tell me you've only been with one person your entire sad little life?"

Or perhaps there was some humiliation to be had after all. Cyril ran a hand through his hair.

"I was focused on my *studies*, Tigris. And I have always been an... *awkward* youth."

She scoffed and, rather catlike, made herself into a neat loaf to rest easy on the bench.

"I'll bet you were too busy pining."

He would not fall into the trap of answering that. He pretended not to hear her and looked out the window, at the rush of trees and wildlife.

She was entirely correct, though.

In truth, Cyril did not *need* to attend the Academy of Arcane Arts. Not with a private tutor of Heléne Laverre's calibre at his disposal, grudging though she was to take on such a young pupil. Mages in general had a storied tradition of apprenticeships, especially those who specialised in a single discipline, taking one or two pupils under their wings and shaping them in their youth. The Academy, located in a conveniently neighbouring country, was a fairly recent addition to the annals of arcane history, and it was reserved for the very talented, the very wealthy or, in Cyril's case, the young mages whose masters thought it unhealthy that their only friends were a cat and a girl who'd shoved them off a swing.

Heléne had seen the lack in Cyril's life and tried to fix it as best as she could. It was less a failure on *her* part and more his complete unwillingness to mingle with his peers that made her valiant efforts such an utter waste of good intentions. A young Cyril Laverre spent his school days as a painfully shy, horribly obnoxious teacher's pet who holed himself up in his dorm studying until his mind felt numb, writing letters to a handsome prince and counting down the days to when he could be carted home again.

Admittedly, it would have helped if his aunt had been clearer with her intentions because Cyril, indulging in yet another one of his anxious little freaks, thought he had been shipped away to be *tested*. No other mage at the Academy had the burden of future grand mage weighing on their prepubescent shoulders. Cyril genuinely believed he was at the Academy to excel. To prove himself the best and brightest, to outshine any competition he might have, perceived or otherwise. And he soon came to learn there is little children like less in a classmate than a snivelling, antisocial show-off, cementing his wallflower status in something of a self-fulfilling prophecy.

He didn't entirely begrudge his Academy upbringing, though, despite the friction with his peers. He didn't really *need* friendship, not when he had one perfectly good friend at home and one boy whose heart he was desperately attempting to thaw and capture with every brain cell he had to spare that wasn't studying. Having a variety of different teachers proved enriching in a way Aunt Heléne, with her brutal, spartan ways, fell short of. They also taught him much in the way of magical etiquette, which was something his dear old aunt frequently thumbed her nose at as entirely frivolous. According to her, magic needed etiquette the same way fish needed fresh air (this was one of the *kinder* things she had said about this method of teaching). Cyril liked these guidelines, though. To him, they made sense. Mages were precious about their spells and snooping in on someone's pattern was akin to *cheating*, which in a school environment was akin to *manslaughter*.

And he realised the fact that he caught himself fondly reminiscing about the finer points of *magical contracts* and who his *favourite professors* were was exactly the problem. Maybe if he'd gone out of his way to make connections, he wouldn't be in a carriage relying on the goodwill of a foreign king he hardly knew. Maybe he'd have fallen for a nice, young wizard who attended his classes, and he would've given up the fantasy of a love far above his station. Cyril wondered if, given the chance to do it all over again, knowing what he knew now, he would've given up on Eufrates.

Perhaps without a cooperative, magically gifted spouse, King Eufrates Margrave would've had a harder time making a mess of Farsala. Cyril reminded himself of the hand to his throat, the grip on his waist, the dark, hateful eyes that speared through him like an arrow through the heart.

He told himself very firmly, very convincingly, that yes, of course, he would've given up. And then he forced himself to believe it in the same way a child is forced to take medicine.

* * *

Tigris was quiet for a while longer before she finally spoke again, both of them having dropped the pretence of ever falling asleep that night.

"I am sorry. I was being very selfish, regarding Atticus. He is a nice man. I should not be so harsh."

Cyril's head tilted. "I don't think it's selfish to want to be in love."

"Oh, yes it is. I am to be queen. You think I do not know this, but it has plagued me since my nursery days."

"You assume I think a lot of things about you, Tig."

"Hush."

She narrowed her eyes at him, suddenly sober and intense. She was taking the measure of him, but he did not know what for. Not until she began talking and he realised he was privy to a confessional.

"It feels as though I had made an unspoken pact with Papa and Mamã. I would be as wilful as I wished during my youth, but when it came time to inherit, there were to be no complaints, so I made the most of it. Did you know I pushed you off of that swing on purpose?"

Cyril blinked. The latter comment seemed such a non-sequitur he instantly honed in.

"Excuse me?"

"When you first came. I convinced you to let me push you on the swing set, because I thought it would be fun. That was my main motivation as a child: fun. But I thought you looked so very frail with your blonde hair and your big eyes, so when I saw you sitting on the edge of that seat, flying ever higher, looking quite afraid, I wondered what might happen if I pushed you off. So I did. It was not particularly satisfactory, I'll be honest. I expected more gore."

He stared at her because he could do little else. "You are trying to tell me you are not right in the head."

"What child is, Cy? I am trying to tell you that, until very recently, I did whatever I wanted. I pushed a child off a swing out of morbid curiosity, I went spelunking and nearly got my brother

killed, I decorated my room how I wanted, I did sword training drills with the guard, I won a jousting tournament, I wore obscene, flamboyant things to foreign events, I went on a tour through the continent on my eighteenth birthday. I was a spoiled, obstinate princess, and it suited me just fine. Nobody truly complained, because everyone knew when it was time to be serious, I would shut my mouth and do it.

"It is what I have been prepared for my entire life, after all. I cannot picture anything else. I have a sworn duty to my kingdom and, more importantly, to my family. I was, after all, to make sure my soft-hearted princeling of a brother never saw even a gram of power in all his days."

"That wasn't your fault, if this is what this is about."

"It's not. I know I can't change what happened to me... what happened to you. But marrying Atticus has been my very first taste of duty and... I am finding it difficult to swallow."

"Call it off, then," he said. "You are queen. You can do what you want."

"Oh, yes, I'm sure you did everything your heart desired during your tenure as grand mage."

Cyril glared at her. "I am sure Atticus would not be so offended."

"I've no reason to call it off aside from a feeling. *It would not be proper,"* she sighed and looked down at her paws. *"Mamã especially was so keen on the match."*

Ah, he thought. Tigris understood the look he gave her either way.

He did not want her thinking about their deaths. Especially not when he already felt so sick with guilt that he did not think to send himself back far enough to stop Rohan and Micaela from boarding that ship in the first place, so obsessed was he with foiling his husband at any cost.

Instead of continuing the thread of conversation, Cyril looked around himself and grabbed a pillow to prop under his elbow, which was beginning to sore.

"This is a bit like a sleepover, isn't it?"

Tigris smiled. *"Just like the old days! Oh, I do wish I could braid your hair. Did you keep it long in the future, too?"*

"Frightfully. Not many hairdressers *or* scissors to be had."

"I will never be used to not having hands. What day did you say I died again?"

"I didn't." He racked his brain for long-forgotten information. It had been so many years. He found, however, he could still remember the exact date of her death if he truly put some effort into it, like deep-cleaning a house. Unfortunately, it wasn't for a particularly *good* reason. Cyril cringed. "The eleventh of August."

Tigris looked actually *wounded*. He even heard one of her rare mewls. *"That's four days after my birthday! I will have to spend my twenty-seventh as a cat!?"*

"Afraid so."

"I don't want to!" she wailed, and he felt genuinely sorry for her. Especially when she was having such difficulty adapting, according to her incessant complaints about the body.

"I will personally throw you the grandest party once you are yourself again." He eyed her up and down. "Are you still having trouble being Shoestring?"

"I... well, Cy, I'm sure it's not your *cat in particular, but it just doesn't feel comfortable."*

Cyril's brow knit together, and he leaned in to take a closer look. "It is unusual for a transmutation to be so disturbing. Perhaps it is because it's a magical body."

"Whatever it is, it's awful. I feel like a parasite. It's like the body is trying to rid itself of me."

"How strange. It should be empty. It *is* empty, I've checked. Has it gotten worse?"

"...It ebbs and flows, I think. It's weird. Now, it's not so bad."

He sat up and tucked a knee into his chest, holding up his chin in one hand in rapt interest. "Curious. I shall have to examine it later."

"Gods, I wish you wouldn't sound so keen on it. Feels like you'll put me on a slab."

He coughed. "I... would never do that."

"Oh, yes, Cy, I feel perfectly safe with you around to look after me."

Cyril raised a hand as though taking an oath. "I swear on my life I will not examine you if you do not wish it." A pause. "But it *might* help."

Tigris hissed at him and hopped to sit diagonal, the farthest she could from where he was.

He raised his other hand, this time in surrender. "I am joking. Truly."

It was high time he steered the conversation yet again to somewhere where he wasn't risking a clawing with every word. Upon looking out the window and spotting one of the valets who was accompanying the coach, a man who seemed to be bored at having to keep up with such a glacial pace, he leaned against the small glass window to look more intently at the scenery.

"You lived in Cretea for some time, didn't you?" he asked her.

She cocked her head. *"So did you."*

It took him a while to realise what she meant. "Oh! Farol! Tig, Farol is a little seaside shipyard with a population to rival the turnaround of a small street performance. I mean the capital. The palace."

"Ah. Yes, that's right. When I was a princess, it was expected I would relocate there until it was time to inherit."

Cyril tried for a smile. "You will have to show me around. I have never been."

"It's quite beautiful. I hope we are allowed to go into town."

He leaned in, almost conspiratorial, and looked at her with a very serious countenance. "How is the food?"

Tigris burst into giggles. *"You will love it!"*

TWELVE

As most sleepovers with Tigris went, they did not sleep a wink that entire night. Normally, it was because she made a challenge out of it, keeping him, Eufrates and sometimes a brave courtier's child or two she had made friends with awake hours on end with cards, gossip, secrets and late-night excursions to the kitchens. She made her brother, eyes heavy with sleep, invent stories and entertain with song, and she made Cyril, who actually wasn't too bothered about being kept awake (the way he did it to himself night after night in fits of useless neurosis) conjure up as many magical delights as he could until his arms were spent from weaving so long and Tigris set her attention on another distraction.

Truly, everything had been very intense when it involved Tigris. It was like she was pursuing extreme, reckless sport in all aspects of life. After what she had confided in him, he supposed it made sense. She was wild and daring and she was to be confined into a pretty little cage, fit for a queen.

He felt even guiltier about turning her into a cat now he understood how frightened she was of getting her agency taken away. He was sure she would have loved nothing more than to confront Eufrates herself. Get him in a chokehold and throw him to the gallows with her brute strength. He was sure she could do it.

He could not risk it. He would continue to keep her close and stunted until it was safe not to, and if she wished to be mad about it later, he would gladly accept punishment.

170

Cyril had lived very long and had done very little. Tigris's life was a thousand times more precious than his had amounted to.

This time, though, it was not a sleepover by *choice*. They had both bravely attempted slumber throughout different times of night, in different positions, with different configurations of pillows. Cyril had even attempted to lie facing up on the floor of the carriage and breathe slowly in and out like an old physician had once taught him. The physician had been sent in after Cyril had a fit that left him gasping when he was eleven.

It did nothing to calm the war drum of his heart. He felt even the valets outside could hear it. It thrummed loud in his ears and, lying on the floor like this, the very vehicle seemed to shake with each erratic palpitation.

And if Cyril's poison was ravenous anxiety, he could tell by the way Tigris prowled around the same two feet of cushioning with raised shoulders that hers was adrenaline. She was wired, wracked with energy she could not expend save for haphazardly throwing herself around the seat. It did not feel like enough. Cyril thought she might curl into a ball and bounce herself off the walls, rattling the carriage and startling the poor coachman in the process. Instead, she stared out the window, eyes wide and pupils narrowed, with her ears perked up so high he thought they might detach from her head.

Occasionally, they would keep themselves distracted by chattering about trifling things, or playing traveling games like pointing out what one spied out the window. But for the most part, they sat in silence with their own personal ailments wreaking through their bodies.

So, in the end, they reached Cretea just before the dawn with nary a wink slept between them. Cyril could tell his eyes were blotched with the deep violet of insomnia. Not to mention he had not had time to remove his makeup, so it felt congealed on his face. He would not be making an excellent first impression with this head butler.

Bathed in the golden light of dawn, Cretea's capital and royal palace cut a beautiful silhouette out of the sky. It was opulent and regal in a way that surprised Cyril, who had lived in a palace himself most his life. But there was something about Cretea's architecture that conveyed a bit more refinement, if a little heavy-handed.

Where he was used to solid stone-brick walls there was now smoothed marble, carved into patterns that he could not imagine would weather the test of time, save for constant maintenance. High windows in wrought iron frames were replaced by stunning glasswork of many shades of blues and violets, their frame painted a sleek silver tone. While the palace in Farsala was built *up*, with its coppery rooftops for towers and high attics, the building he was about to step into spread *out* in seemingly endless expansion. At some point in the distant past, Atticus's ancestors had gained their lion's share of land, and they had used up every corner of it.

The ceilings, once he was ushered inside, were higher than he was used to. Dappled with pillars on either side that met in satisfying arches, equally carved out of that pristine marble, he felt as though he was looking at an interactive work of art. All the flooring of the palace was wooden as well, as opposed to only the main rooms, which he was sure would take a king's army to maintain, but that allowed for his heels to make satisfying *clicks* as he stepped. In Farsala, the floors were patterned stonework. Beautiful mosaics, the envy of any foreign dignitary, but quite cold to walk upon, especially on bare feet when making a late-night run somewhere.

Cyril was suddenly regretful he had not visited Cretea during the alliance. He had been too love blind to leave the palace.

He was finally led to an ornate grand foyer. He could have had Tigris follow behind him, but he insisted on carrying her in his arms like a babe. A sense of security in these foreign lands. It gave him something to do with his arms as well.

The head butler and caretaker of the palace was a woman of some years. She introduced herself as Maîtresse Miranda.

Miranda was one of the most stunning women he had ever seen, but he would not wager a single cent that her main employment was keeping care of a palace. Built like a watchtower: tall, solid, stalwart, she felt as though she'd be more at ease as a sell-sword in a far-off tavern or a huntress in the thick of the woods.

She had chestnut hair with streaks of grey, tied into a braid and pinned atop her head and she wore a conservative dress of all sepia, like a faded portrait. She towered over Cyril by at least a head and a half, and he was sure she could fit three of him in her width.

He set Tigris down and tried to get his fingers to stop trembling when he handed her the stamped letter. If she did not find it satisfactory, he had no doubt he would be secreted away to a dungeon cell by her strength alone.

"Is she not extraordinary!"

Cyril's nerves were temporarily broken by the trill of enthusiasm that rang loud in his head. He snapped his gaze over to Tigris and her eyes were aglow. He could not say anything, not in front of Miranda, without sounding like an untrustworthy loon, but he arched a brow at her.

"Oh, Cyril, I am sure you will like Maîtresse Miranda. I am so happy to see her again!"

A flash of realisation sparked into his mind as jolting as being electrocuted. He thought back, way back, to all his memories of Tigris. Specifically, of her many dalliances, all of which he had learned about completely against his will.

There was that stocky, young knight trainee with the premature beard. There was a baron from a kingdom up, up, up in the north, who entertained himself by seeing how many kegs of ale he could lift. There was Lady Aura, one of their hunting friends, who he once saw eat a fresh rabbit raw just to see if it would taste any good. There was the stable hand with powerful arms, who rode so well he could do jumping tricks off one horse to another.

He could go on, but the conclusion was the same. Tigris had a *type*, and it was not charming, kind, reasonable Atticus.

Tigris did not want to be *complemented* in her ferocity, she wanted to be *matched*. Which seemed odd to him, but at the same time so very like her. Formidable.

If she indeed broke off her engagement, he vowed to himself he would dedicate the rest of his life to scouring the ends of the earth for a more suitable match. He would look upon other planes of existence if that is what it took. It was what she deserved.

He noticed that, while he was staring intently at his cat, Maîtresse Miranda had said something to him. Several things. How fantastic it was that he had already behaved churlishly to his new hosts.

He rubbed sleep (and some flakes of kohl) from his eyes and looked up at her.

"Please, forgive me. The ride here was overtaxing, and I could not sleep. Would you mind repeating yourself?"

If she was insulted, she hid it very well behind the cultivated facade of stoicism.

"Of course." Her voice was deep, but it had a practiced soothe to its cadence. "Young Master Cyril, I had known of your arrival. I received a pigeon some hours ago from His Majesty, so the letter was a mere formality. It was in order to confirm your identity, which it has. I had inquired as to whether you would prefer to eat or bathe first. But perhaps you would rather sleep?"

He *was* starving. But there was a layer of grime upon his skin that felt like it bore through to his very bones.

"The bath, please. You are very kind to ask."

She nodded. "Think nothing of it. His Majesty should be back home by mid-afternoon. He will have matters to attend to, but you will be able to sup together if you wish."

"I would not monopolise his time."

"He has requested it."

"Oh," he said, intelligently.

He was led to his new chambers, which he had presumed to be in the servants' quarters. Atticus mentioned employing mages in passing, and even after being reassured this wasn't the case, he still had the feeling in his gut for no reason other than an excess of caution that he was to be treated like staff. But as they made their way through the halls and up a flight of stairs to the second and only other floor in the palace, it dawned on Cyril that he was being treated as an honoured guest, not an inconvenient refugee.

The room was sumptuous, just as lavish as any guest chambers in Farsala. There was a lush bed down the middle of it that looked remarkably inviting after a night of restlessness. To one side, by a large oaken writing desk, there was an unlit fireplace, ready to be stoked if the room's new southern occupant found the spring chill a bit too much for him. A wardrobe opposite it made Cyril realise he had left his home without any clothes or belongings of his own.

"I shall leave fresh linens and a change of clothes ready for you once you are done, young Master Cyril", Miranda said as though reading his mind.

"Thank you." He nodded in awkward assent, and soon was left alone with Tigris to explore the room in more depth. The air was fragrant, perfumed by candles and dried, scented flowers. He smelled a warm smell of vanilla and pinewood.

It was augmented even more when he finally set foot into the white tile of the ensuite. He shucked his clothes immediately (Tigris left him to his modesty, not as desperate for a bath when cats were so naturally well-groomed) and dunked his whole body into a perfectly tempered warm bath. Had it not been for the growl in his stomach, he would have been perfectly content soaking away the dirt of his travels until his fingers pruned, but given how ravenous he found himself, he towelled himself off as soon as he had scrubbed away a sufficient amount of grime to feel clean again.

The clothes they had lent him were plain, simple, but well-made. They would fit anyone's tastes in a desperate situation, but Cyril instantly missed the theatrics of his own everyday garb. The outfit was the same sepia tone Miranda wore, seemingly a staple colour in court, but while he found it complimented her complexion, on his own coppery skin it made him look a bit washed out. He was also devoid of any of his paints or kohl, so he would have to show up to the dining hall barefaced. There was a vulnerability he had not expected to feel being stripped of his costuming.

He pinned his hair back with a ribbon he found while perusing through the drawers and led by his gut and the smell of roasting meat, found his way to where he would be served his early luncheon.

It was technically a breakfast, but it was too late to be considered as such. Regardless of what it was, Cyril was very intent on having it. He was served a platter piled high with eggs, sausage, cuts of beef, a block of mild cheese, cooked greens and creamy mashed potatoes. It seemed they did not know what his dietary preferences were, so they were just giving him whatever was available.

Tigris was right. The food was *quite* good. It had a heartiness that Farsalan cuisine lacked, in favour of its temperate good weather and abundance of fresh produce that could easily be eaten raw.

For dessert, he was given fresh fruit – apples, grapes, berries – and the most exquisite pastries. He should have stopped after the first, but he felt compelled to try everything they served him. Farsala had a healthy tradition of cakes and sugary breads, egg-based golden with candied and dried fruits, but they were all very simple. Delicious, but not terribly good-looking.

He marvelled at the presentation of these Cretian pastries. He tasted lighter, more unusual flavours like almond, rosewater and anis seeds. They were often decorated with shavings of citrus or fresh cut fruit.

Beside him, Tigris was just as engrossed in her little feast. He wondered at how so much food could fit into such a skinny cat, but she was clearly making it work. He saw one of the maids give her a curious look and dabbed at his mouth with a napkin to intervene in any suspicion of animal cruelty.

"Don't worry," he said. "He's a familiar. Not real."

He thought he might need to offer up more explanation, but she parted her lips with an understanding 'ah' and nodded.

"We see many familiars in the palace. I have never seen one eat that much. Some I have not seen eat at all."

Of course. They must be used to mages. Cyril smiled at her. "They don't normally need to eat, no. Shoestring is quite the glutton."

This earned him a glare from Tigris, who was face deep into a bowl of mousse. He smiled very sweetly at her and forked another pastry onto his plate before she could get at them.

The lightly perfumed air lulled him to sleep and he was finally beginning to feel the build of exhaustion press down on his frame. Ill-advised though it was, Cyril collapsed onto his new bed as soon as he made it back to the room, immediately falling unconscious.

He had meant to wait for Atticus's arrival, but he was sure there were many hours still until he returned, and more still until it was time for supper. So he slept a peaceful, dreamless sleep.

When he awoke sometime later, Tigris was curled up on the pillow next to his like a great big dome of cat. He pretended Shoestring was back, only for a little while, before he roused himself properly and went to greet his saviour.

Tigris would have found a way to make him see stars if he dared exclude her from anything important, so he managed to drag her out of bed and with him through the halls.

It was a surprise how few servants he saw bustling about, despite the place being kept spotless. And the ones he did see were silent and overtly polite. He was used to the sneaking gossip of the Farsala staff. This palace, working as it did like a well-oiled machine, gave him just a hint of gooseflesh.

He supposed he would have to get used to it.

They were led through several doors to a smaller, more private dining hall than the one Cyril had taken his first meal in. The table fit six, perhaps eight people. Then, he was informed the king would be with them shortly. For whatever reason this made him terribly self-conscious. He snuck a look at one of the dessert spoons, reflecting his own face back at him, and spied to make sure he still looked half-decent even without his paints. He had not expected to dine with Atticus alone.

"What on earth are you doing?"

Tigris had positioned herself at the seat by his right side as though she had every reason in the world to also have a seat at the table. Upon being caught in his own vanity, Cyril's eyes went very wide, and he coloured.

"I am–"

He was excused from explaining himself by the sound of a great door being opened, and boot heels on wood floor.

From what he had heard, Atticus had arrived several hours prior, mid-afternoon, after a hard ride through the country. Cyril was sure the man needed to see to his affairs, catch up on his rule, decompress, but he was *dying* to know how his escape had gone over. It was eating him alive.

When Atticus entered the room, Cyril sat up ramrod straight and nodded, to show his respect.

Atticus behaved more casually when in his own territory. Gone were the overdressed, button-up suits, replaced with fine silk shirts under a loose jacket, decorated, but effortless. He did not look *slovenly*, not at all. But he looked *home*. Cyril could appreciate this.

He had been smiling when he entered the room, but as soon as he clapped eyes on Cyril they widened first, then shuttered in blank confusion for a moment.

Cyril shyly raised a hand in a short wave.

"Atticus. Did you have a nice journey back?"

His face seemed to split into a relieved smile, then furrowed in consternation immediately after.

"Oh, gods, Cyril! I almost didn't recognise you!"

Atticus crossed the room in a few steps and, rather than taking a seat at the head of the table as Cyril had expected, he took his left side, the space unoccupied by Tigris.

"Whatever happened to the little jester who charmed me so at that dinner?!" He laughed.

Cyril instantly felt his entire face burst into flames. To hide this self-inflicted immolation, he looked down very intently at his empty plate and spoke in a very small voice.

"I... we left in such a rush yesternight, I was not able to bring my paints with me."

To his mortification, when he glanced upwards, he found Atticus had leaned in to examine his naked face more closely. He had a pensive hand under his chin.

"Hm. I think it rather suits you. You look quite refreshing like this, Cyril. But if you would like, I can send someone into town tomorrow to get you whatever paints you request."

He snapped his head up. "Oh, no! That isn't necessary. If I find myself missing the makeup very dearly, I am sure I can venture out on my own."

Atticus furrowed his brow in consternation. "Still. I shall assign you an escort for day trips. It would be a waste of an escape plot if I could not keep you safe *now*."

"Cy, I am begging *you to stop flirting with my fiancé and just ask him if you are in any danger."*

He had relaxed enough that his complexion had evened but this coloured it once again. He resisted the urge to shoot Tigris a desperate, sour look, lest their host notice how strangely he was acting.

Cyril cleared his throat. "In any case, what happened after I left? Was there... did anyone notice? Did they trouble you? Did you have to escape as well?"

Atticus put a reassuring hand on his shoulder just as a couple of servants brought in cloches of food. He stiffened, once again sitting up very straight. The last thing he needed was *another* court thinking him some kind of sultry *enchanter* that ensorcelled powerful men.

"You do not need to worry yourself about me. I am a foreign dignitary and a king. Even if they suspected me of something, there would be no lawful reason to keep me. I was free to leave whenever I wanted."

"But..." Cyril urged, sensing there must be *some* sort of catch.

Atticus squeezed his shoulder and his eyes sparked with amusement. "There are no 'but's, dear Cyril! Everything was fine. When I left, they had not yet noticed your disappearance." He chuckled under his breath. "You've a very nervous temper, but I assure you everything is fine. You are free to stay in my palace as long as you wish."

"Did Euf– Did the regent not say anything, then?" He did not notice, but he had leaned close, hands gripping the linen of the tablecloth in rapt anticipation for news about Eufrates.

Atticus's smile split into an impish, conspiratorial grin and he leaned back in his own seat looking quite proud of himself.

"Oh, I am sure he felt some unrest, but I distracted him!" While he spoke, he lifted both their cloches to reveal a steamy plate of gratinated potatoes and a healthy serving of thinly sliced duck breast. He did not need to look at Tigris to know her eyes had bugged out on her face. "Shall I ask for another portion? Or will your familiar be sharing yours?"

Cyril eyed Tigris, who gave him a slight, desperate nod and he smiled back at Atticus. "I'm terribly sorry to inconvenience your staff, but Shoestring has found a taste for Cretian cuisine."

Once Tigris was finally served and they had begun eating (he could get used to the food here, he thought), Cyril not-too subtly tried to steer the conversation back into the burning need – he had to know what happened.

"You said you distracted Eufrates?"

Atticus's eyes lit up, clearly excited to talk about their shared subterfuge. "Oh, yes! I did not want him looking about for you, especially not if you were still on the road and not within my borders, so first thing in the morning I visited his chambers.

"He was quite groggy, so very easy to push around, so to speak. As a new regent, I *assured* him he would need my expert advice. I am sure I exhausted the man's ear talking to him of politics. I insisted it was *quite* urgent as I had received a report late last night that required my immediate attention back in Cretea this very day!

"I monopolised him all breakfast, most of the rest of the morning, and by the time I took leave I am sure his head was so swimming with needlessly convoluted matters of state that he didn't have a thought to spare for his beleaguered young mage."

While listening to this, Cyril's own smirk threatened to show upon his lips. Atticus had no way of knowing this, but he had not been dangling around a youthful, clueless new ruler who had gone just a bit mad after the disappearance of his sister. He had toyed with a man of some years, by now an expert in his own right in manipulation. He was sure Eufrates *needed* a lecture in politics as much as he needed a blow to the head, but he had humoured King Atticus out of what was sure to be a carefully constructed act to fool all around him. It gave Cyril no small amount of satisfaction that playing the innocent had backfired so strongly on his husband in this particular situation.

"I am sure you left him quite bereft," he said.

"Indeed. He would still be trying to remember all the names I assured him were crucial to memorise by the time I was halfway back here."

"I am sorry I took your carriage."

"Nonsense! I practically shoved you inside it. I'm sure the fresh air and sun did some good to my complexion, as well. I am much too pale."

"I think you look perfectly handsome." Cyril more heard the words escaping his lips than actually consciously said them. Immediately, he blanched. He did not *dare* look at Tigris.

Atticus, the gods bless him, did not overreact to this sudden compliment. He gave Cyril a look of pleased surprise and smiled warmly. "I am very glad you think so, Cyril."

THIRTEEN

"I don't like it."

They had returned to the room after supper with Atticus. The king had been a perfect host and gentleman. He assured Cyril once again that he was free to stay in the palace as long as needed, as a *guest* not a runaway. He would be cared and provided for, and Atticus vowed to keep him secreted in Cretea and safe if he were to be discovered. He would not be handed back over to Eufrates, even under threat of conflict.

Cyril thought he was being much too generous with his promises, but it left him starstruck all the same.

Now, he and Tigris were settling in for the evening. Despite sleeping away the better part of the day, he still felt a weariness that he could not yet shake. He was just finished changing into the cotton nightshirt a valet had provided for him when Tigris spoke.

Cyril turned to her, only mildly curious. Perhaps she was unsatisfied with the food.

"What do you not like, Tig?"

She had taken up one half of the bed entirely – despite being under half the size of an average human – and had crossed her paws over one another very properly as if she were about to lecture him on something.

"The way he is around you. It is too informal. I think he is courting you."

If he had a drink, Cyril would have spat it out. *"He?"*

"Oh, do not pretend ignorance. Atticus. I dislike how he speaks to you."

For a moment, he was speechless. He coloured, then paled. "Tig, I... I would not *dare* make advances on your–"

"I am not jealous, *Cy,"* she said. Cyril wasn't sure how much he believed her. *"I am missing and I am a cat. I do not expect him to be made of stone when we are not even married.*

"I just wish he had his sights set on anyone else."

"I do not think he has his *sights* set on me."

"Then you are stupid."

He opened his mouth to say something, shut it, then tried again. "That's–"

"He is much too old for you, for one thing."

Cyril balked. "I thought it was the other way round. Remember uncle Cyril?"

"He doesn't know that! He thinks you two-and-twenty and treats you as such. He called you a little jester! Like you are some child's bauble."

He made the decision not to share with her their dance at her wedding dinner, where he had been called both a Pierrot and a poppet, as well as silly. He did not mind it, truly. It did not feel malicious coming from Atticus.

"I was not offended, if it matters to you."

Tigris narrowed her eyes at him. *"Do* you *fancy him?"*

"I!– Tig, you *know* I would *never* dare–"

Tigris projected a noise into his brain that sounded very much like her impression of a babbling, whingey child, meant as mimicry of his own protests. It was quite rude.

"I did not ask if you would betray my sacred trust regarding my milquetoast affianced."

"I thought you liked him. Found him perfectly good-looking and nice."

"I do. You find my judgement of him unfair, which is why we are having this conversation. And you are still dodging my question."

He raised his hands in exasperation and threw himself on the bed beside her. "For fuck's sake, Tigris." He brought the same hands up to his face and dragged them up and through his hair. "Yes, I suppose I am a little taken."

"Ha!"

"A *little*," he hissed. "He is just... very *kind*. I am not used to it."

Tigris put a paw on his arm. *"I was not trying to torment you, Cy."* She frowned when he glared straight through her. *"Perhaps a little bit of torment. A healthy amount of hazing.*

"But it is good to be aware of your own feelings, I think. I had to watch my brother be in consummate denial for several years and it made him very, very dense and stupid."

Cyril finally relaxed and showed her a small, reassuring smile. "Fair enough."

He lay back on the plush, quilted bedding and propped his head under one arm. Then, he fished the string of a necklace from under his collar.

"I would not worry, though." Even in candlelight, even being old and weathered as it was, the ring glinted in his hand. "I am, after all, a married man."

Living in the Cretian palace felt very much like living in an ornate puzzle box. The legacy ones, passed down over generations, kept under lock and key. Not only did he get lost frequently and embarrassingly, there were also rooms and corners he knew even if he had the solution on how to enter, he could not. He was a guest.

In Farsala he was home. He walked freely and, within reason, could go where he wished. He knew every nook and cranny of the place he grew up in and the worst that would happen if he barged into a chamber he was not supposed to be in would be a mild sense of embarrassment. Or, when he was a youth, a scolding from Heléne.

Cyril realised that for all his proximity to power and nobility, not once had he ever been purely a *guest*. Even at the Academy, there had been strict rules and regulations to follow, on which he was instructed the very first day of orientation and he followed to the letter, to the annoyance of his more outgoing roommates who saw curfew as a suggestion rather than law. Here, he was told he had a great degree of nebulous freedom, and he was to make himself comfortable.

Not exactly knowing what either of those entailed, he chose to idle away his days devoting himself to very little.

He kept to a fairly monotonous path every day, from his room to the dining hall, to the gardens, sometimes to the library Atticus had shown him the second evening they dined together.

The library was small and interested him little. It held titles of a ludic nature, fiction and gossip, sensationalist pamphlets and fantastical novels. Cyril took a few with him back to the room, but he found himself too unsettled to truly concentrate on the words on the page. Also, Tigris insisted he read aloud to her, which, after a half hour, made his throat sore.

He was sure there was some sort of bigger, more expansive library tucked away in one of the corners of the palace he had not dared explore yet. Atticus was such a learned man: it was difficult to believe he didn't have an entire shelf somewhere dedicated to science theses and old treatises. Cyril was the studious sort. He would much rather be spending his time finding some way to improve his magic, his knowledge, his *usefulness* than to sit and putter, entertained by prosaic fluff.

The garden, though less stimulating, was at least a bit more noteworthy. He remembered when Tigris mentioned her husband-to-be kept game wandering around as pets. This was not true. They were familiars. Cyril couldn't tell right away, but after a closer look (and clarification by a very helpful butler) he figured out their true nature. Also, one of the animals was a whole, grown bear, and it was not attempting to eat or maim any of the smaller creatures wandering around the gardens.

Notable other familiars were a peacock, a snow-white fox and a tan-coloured hare that seemed to vanish from sight every time Cyril blinked.

"*Oh,*" Tigris said when he relayed this information to her. "*Well, that's quite a bit more fun. Maybe I've been too harsh on him.*"

Truly, he did not know why he expected any other reaction from her.

The menagerie indicated that, somewhere within the palace walls there were mages working for the king. Cyril would have done anything to meet them. Day in and day out, he interacted with a handful of servants, Atticus and Tigris and he was dying for variety. The thought of being surrounded by other mages made him miss his Academy days. There had been so much to learn. Cyril himself had specialised in a fair bit of everything, but the ones who dedicated themselves to one singular branch of the pattern always had him in wide-eyed awe. He liked surgeons the best. It had always been his worst subject, anatomy and medicine, and surgery was an even more refined form of *that*. Talking to them was fascinating. Seers and enchanters came a close second. Cyril was too much of a coward to delve into predicting the future, so he thought very highly of seers. And enchanters, with their easy words and effortless grace, were just always the most fascinating to hold a conversation with. They were very much like spiders, in a way. Nature's weavemasters, pulling on the threads of all around them.

He did not, however, find any of the mages. They did not dress like – as Atticus would so aptly put it – 'silly little clowns' and were thus indistinguishable from anyone else residing in the behemoth of a palace. He could, of course, go up to each and every person he saw on his way to eat and sleep and eat and ask if they happened to be a mage, but this might be regarded as very rude. He could also simply *pry*. Look into the pattern of the palace and its surroundings and search for any disturbances, held spells or more complex weaves. This, he was certain, *would* be regarded as *very* rude.

To stave off loneliness, he dined with Atticus every evening, doing his very best to avoid Tigris's scrutinizing eye as she lapped up a bowl of starchy, rich soup. He did not need her to tell him to keep the king at arm's length. No matter how tepid Tigris's feelings were for her fiancé, he had neither the intention nor the power – the wedding band was an ever-present reminder, after all – of stealing him away.

He had to admit, though. For lack of any other company (Tigris had at one point tried to selfishly make him spend time with Miranda to awkward, disastrous results), Atticus provided him with a comforting, soothing presence that he craved dearly at the end of each day. Just being close to the king undid decade-old knots on his spine that crept back into his body as soon as he stepped out of the dining hall. Atticus's attention and his need for some company that wasn't cat-shaped and demanding was a heady, powerful combination. *Almost* strong enough to get his mind off Eufrates.

But just almost.

He was told multiple times to try and relax, but he could not. There was a herd of ants crawling within him, just beneath the dermis, and he could not scratch them away. He felt like bouncing off the walls or melting into the floor in his uselessness.

In theory, all he really needed to do was wait out the worst blow to the kingdom – the crown princess's death. Eufrates had no right to inherit if his sister showed up on his doorstep, happy and healthy after a long period of mysterious absence. This was easier said than done when there was so much at stake.

Couched in all the luxury a king could provide for him, it was almost tempting to forget the future he crawled his way out of. But his mind made sure to supply him with enough night terrors of red skies, rundown shacks and barren beaches to keep him focused and just on edge enough to have the consequences of Eufrates's reign playing constantly at a low level in the back of his mind. With the *rot* at the end of a despot's war looming over him, it was difficult to sit idly by.

Perhaps he could find a way to bring time forward, all the way to the date of Tigris's death and then the two of them would go forth and win back their home. But he was fairly certain such a ritual would need preparation, and notes and a *circle* and he had none of these available.

So he spent these first few days wrought with agony. Until he asked, quite unceremoniously at dinner, if Atticus perhaps needed another mage in his retinue. Not a specialist, to be sure, but someone who could pick up odds and ends.

To his credit, Atticus did not immediately say no. He said no after a gregarious smile and a fond ruffle of his hair.

"My dear Cyril, I do not want you working for me."

Cyril frowned. Atticus didn't seem to quite understand. "No…" he said slowly. "But I would be glad to work for *you*."

He regarded him for a while with those understanding seafoam eyes and then sighed. "I am sure you would be wonderful. I have met your peers and I have heard great things. But if I take on Farsala's grand mage… it will have consequences."

Cyril's lunch turned in his gut. "Ah."

"Yes. I will have stolen you away. It would be lawful cause for conflict. The regent would demand satisfaction."

"But you did not steal–"

Atticus's lips twitched upwards. "Did I not?"

He had lost count of the number of times he felt heat creep up his cheeks when speaking to this man, but there it was again.

He said nothing, so Atticus spoke again, comforting. Laying a hand on his shoulder as he always did.

"Perhaps once the situation cools, if you still wish to stay, I will give you something to do. But for now, my only request for you, Cyril, is to unwind."

Cyril could do nothing but nod.

It was an almost impossibly difficult request for someone with his nature. He would fret and fidget over the smallest things. Relaxing under the threat of a declaration of *war* felt as ludicrous as if he had been asked to give the entire palace feet and make it dance the pavane (which, for the record, with enough time and resources, he *could* do).

And yet, over a couple more days, he did feel himself slowly lowering his guard. He was unravelling, but it did not feel like a bad thing. His daily walks about the palace became pleasant, almost dreamlike. If he forgot himself enough, he could even pretend like there were no problems at all. No deaths, no disease, no conflict, no war, no *Eufrates*. It was a state of blissful ignorance he rarely found himself experiencing. Even Tigris, who he was sure would have advised him in much the same way, found this change in behaviour unusual, but there was something about this new life, this sense of powerlessness, the fact that there were no expectations of him, that felt quite freeing.

After a while, he had even given up his search for other mages, for more knowledge. He stopped petitioning Atticus for a place among his servants. He had formed some half-wrought plan to ask *Miranda* for a cleaning job if his fidgeting became distressing enough, but even this he gave up as a senseless, childish endeavour. Better to do what he was told.

Through nervousness, and anxiety, and restlessness and finally this last dissociative state, one week and a day passed since he arrived at the doors of Cretea's palace that fateful dawn.

What he felt now, this gauzy, dreamlike *ghosting* through Cretea, its palace and its inhabitants was not entirely unwelcome. Cyril had grown from a trembling child to a fretful youth, to an *unbearably* anxious adult, but life in these courts, devoid of expectations, came every passing day with a new, rejuvenating sense of ease. He slept better, with fewer night terrors. He looked forward to whiling away the hours tasting local delicacies, reading all the fluff pieces Atticus allowed him access to in the library and to Atticus himself, jovial and entertaining. Understanding and uncomplicated.

He could not possibly be expected to retain loyalty for some conniving, brooding Machiavel who intended to keep him shut up in a room all hours of the day under his watchful eye. Regardless of how often he was reminded of that same man, every time the chill of well-preserved metal brushed against his breast, it was like a vexing warning not to stray too far into the comforts of these charming foreign courts.

It was difficult not to, though. And easier still to be secretly happy at how long he would have to be exiled. There were *months* until Tigris's day of death. And so far, not a move from Farsala in protest of his egress. Perhaps they were already much too preoccupied with *Tigris's* mysterious disappearance.

Perhaps Eufrates, thrust into this new realm where he had yet to muster up the full force of his influence, had deemed him too unimportant to seek out, despite what he had said otherwise.

Perhaps Eufrates did not care *that* much about him leaving, especially as this was technically the second time.

Cyril chose to try, to varying success, not to think about Eufrates at all.

He grew comfortable to the point where he had to tell *Tigris* to relax a bit. He had gotten into the habit of, when Atticus was unavailable, taking his meals in his room so he could chatter idly with her without being thought of as a madman. Overall, it was also going quite well. He had snuck a few more sweetmeats than he should've and was nibbling on one while he read the third chapter of a horror book on pirates to Tigris (he'd decided her commentary was worth spending his voice).

That same night, he heard a tapping at his window. Tigris reacted to it almost instantly, but his head felt so full of cotton and fluff that he had to shake it several times as though this would somehow help clear his ears.

It did not make any sense. Cyril was not staying on the ground floor and there were no trees or branches he could see outside. When the noise became recurring, he walked across the room, Tigris in tow, to investigate.

In the dead of night, with only the candelabra lighting his room, it was impossible to clearly see the source of the tapping, but he was fairly sure it was a bird. Cyril pressed his face against the window and a hard, grey beak and salt and peppered feathers slammed against him so suddenly that if it were not for the glass, he would now be short one eye.

He recoiled from the window with an undignified scream just as Tigris leapt onto the parapet. Her eyes grew huge, and she began to paw at the lock.

"Cyril! Open it!"

"Wh–what are you *doing*? It's trying to kill me!"

"Shut up. It's Ganache!"

Cyril blinked a few times, refocused on the view outside the glass and stepped forward for a closer look. It was, indeed, Ganache.

"Oh," he said.

Then, with a bit more urgency once Tigris shot him a sour glare, he rushed over to help her unhook the latch and open the window enough that the crow could pass through.

In such a grand room, it was doubtful anyone could hear them, but Cyril still lowered his voice to a whisper.

"Ganache! What are you doing here? Is Tantie alright?"

Ganache nodded and he realised she had to be. The bird would not look so hale and superior if she were somehow harmed. It flooded him with relief.

Before he could ask another question, the bird lifted up one of her talons to reveal a small, rolled-up paper tied to a string around it.

"Cyril, look!"

"Yes, I see it. It must be a message from Tantie."

Guilt burnt a fire through his belly once he realised he had not been nearly as worried as he should've been about his aunt. The past few days he hadn't even *thought* of her. He had gotten much too comfortable. With shaking fingers, Cyril undid the wrapping around the paper and unfurled it, careful not to rip. The lettering was small and tight, crammed to fit as much text as possible into such a small scrap.

It was not, in fact, a message from Tantie.

Cyril had not seen this handwriting in an age, but he recognised it instantly. Despite the limitations of the page, the calligraphy was beautiful. Immaculately clear and yet frivolous in all its flourishes. It deserved a frame and a placard. It was as much a work of art as any draftsman's etching, even before reading the words.

Cyril did not *want* to read the words, of course, but he forced himself regardless. The letter was addressed to him after all.

Dearest Cy,

As you know, you have always been my muse. My shining starlet. My endless beacon of inspiration.

I am sure, then, that it will bring you great joy to find out you have inspired me to invade the kingdom of the man you've chosen to shack up with a whole eight years ahead of our known schedule.

I did not believe you would sink so low as to run away from me a second time, even when you claim at every hour of the day to wish to foil me. I may have my foibles, my love, but I am not stupid. And I will not be kind.

I know exactly where you've gone, where you are and who is abetting you. You well knew that there was not a corner in this entire world you could try to hide from me where I could not find you. The only matter is whether I would leave you alone in your spinelessness or not. So, then, you have made your choice. You have dragged all who abet you down with

you in your cowardice, and I hope when I have managed to
take your life, your everything, we will meet again in hell so I
may do it all once more.
Return to Farsala only if you wish to fall upon my sword. There
is no calling off my decision. This is merely a formality.
I wished you to be the first to know.

All my love,
– E

If anything could snap him out of his stupor and remind him
of exactly what was at stake it was this. Cyril's blood turned
to ice, congealing him in place with the letter in his hand long
enough that he did not think to hide it away from Tigris. Once
he realised he needed to throw the scrap into the fire before
she ever read a single, horrible word, it was already much too
late.

"It is unprovoked! He will be the one to blame for the war!"

"That has not stopped him before," Cyril said, though his
throat felt desperately parched and the sweetmeats still on his
tongue took on an acrid aftertaste. "He is an artful orator. He
will spin it so he is right and his cause is good."

"We must go back!"

Upon hearing this (curious that Ganache was able to hear
her, but he did not have time to dwell upon it), the crow let
out an imperious caw, and a second, slightly damp piece of
paper fell from her beak.

This *was* Heléne's handwriting. He recognised the quasi-
illegibility immediately. The paper was folded four times over.
It was the same size as Eufrates's missive, but its contents were
much more concise.

DO NOT COME BACK.
KEEP HER SAFE.

Tigris saw this one as well, and looked on her way to mutiny until Cyril steeled his expression.

"She would not have written that if she were not right. I cannot take you back there, Tig. I will go alone."

"The fuck *you will!"* Her eyes narrowed into slits. She looked rabid.

Cyril flinched. He was not so good with a stern face as his aunt. But he held fast. "Then I will not go at all."

"We have to! We cannot let him—"

"Eufrates will find a way to start this insensible takeover one way or another. I do not matter to him aside from being a convenient excuse. The only *real* solution is to dethrone him."

"Then I will—"

Later, in retrospect, Cyril would have time to be proud of how fast he was. Faster even than a cat's nimble reflexes. He saw Tigris about to shatter her gemstone collar on the ground without a second thought and wove her to stop, plucking at the pattern around her until it looked as if she were caught in an invisible net.

While she struggled and cursed him to the hells, he carefully opened up Heléne's pattern on the gem (magnificent work, he might add) and added his own caveat to the spell. Tigris would no longer be able to break the collar on her own. The only one who could release her from the spell – well, now it was beginning to have all the makings of a curse – was Cyril himself.

He let her figure out what he'd done herself when he released her and she immediately tried to break the gem so hard and so vigorously she made a dent on the wood floor. Cyril would later cover that up with an expensive tapestry hanging on the wall.

"What did you do to me?" she hissed.

"I have *one* job, Tig. And it's to prevent your death."

"You are treating me like a child. *Worse than that: like an* object."

"I do not care what you think of me, Tigris Margrave. I will treat you like an exuberant crystal vase if that is what I must do."

"You are a coward."

"I have heard this one before, I'm afraid."

He saw the tears bead into the corners of her eyes and his heart felt like it was being squeezed by an invisible hand. He hated this. He did not wish to do this. He wanted no part in her suffering.

But, at the same time, he was no stranger to playing the villain. And he had committed much worse crimes than confining a princess to a gemstone indefinitely.

As if dragged by the weight of a thousand chains, he sank down to the floor to sit and be at her level, leaving himself defenceless against another scratching if she so wished. Mercifully, she did not take the bait.

"I am sorry, Tig. I wish I could just find a cure. Prevent the illness entirely instead of... of *this*. But I am frightened. I cannot lose you again."

She was crying now, and she did not raise her head to look at him.

"We will fix this together, in time," he pleaded. "It is only a few months now, and you will be queen once more, and there will be no war, and I will be your grand mage if you wish it, or... or I will rot in the dungeons if that is what you would prefer. But before that, we *will* fix this. I did not come all the way back here not to, and when we do it, we will do it as a *pair*.

"Queen Tigris and her mage. You said we suited one another, did you not?"

She sat in silence for a while, letting her tears dry, before she said something in a hushed, uncharacteristic voice.

"...I do not want you rotting away in a dungeon, Cyril."

"That is very kind of you. Exile, perhaps."

She tilted her head and gave him a wry smile. *"No. I do not hate you, Cy. I don't believe anyone alive hates you as much as you do."*

It caught him off guard, being laid bare so suddenly, but he tried for levity against all better judgement.

"Eufrates, perhaps."

"No." Her answer came so quick he wasn't even sure she had heard him. Surely, she hadn't. *"Not even Eufrates. I know it."*

Cyril sighed. "Alright. I... I will go back to Farsala and you will stay here, then?" There was a hopefulness in his tone that was wholly undeserved.

She shook her head, indignant again instead of upset. This was a much more manageable version of Tigris, at least.

"Absolutely not! You think I'll let your skinny little legs walk out there on your own? You'll be eaten alive before you get through the door."

"Might I remind you I am the greatest wizard of my time," he said, with no small amount of irritation.

"Meaningless if there is an arrow through your neck. You are not going."

"Then – then *neither* of us are going!"

She considered this. Chewed through it like a piece of sweetmeat. *"I am amenable to that."*

"A moment ago, you would have had my head."

"Quiet, you. I am formulating a plan."

Cyril's brows rose as far up as they could go.

"A... *plan*?"

"What? I can't make my own plans?"

"I didn't say that, I just–"

"I said quiet."

He quieted. It was an order from his queen, after all. While she paced around their room in circles, more a lioness than a cat, with her head down and tail swishing contemplatively, Cyril made his way back to the window.

He looked outside.

"Ganache... I don't suppose *you're* still around."

Without a shadow of a doubt meaning to scare him on purpose, Ganache descended from a high branch she had perched upon and cawed right in his face.

Cyril jumped. "Gods! That wasn't necessary at all, was it?"

The crow eyed him impatiently. Cyril pinched the bridge of his nose and took a deep, hopefully calming breath.

"You are to return to Tantie. I take it once you arrive, both she and Eufrates will know I've read their letters."

Ganache nodded as though this were quite obvious.

"Well, I... I would like it if you could buy us some time, that being the case."

She chirped and tilted her head to one side.

"Delay your return. I am sure it takes only a few hours to arrive back there. Give us a day, at least, to warn Atticus. It is his kingdom. He should not be caught unawares over a jilted lover."

She seemed to consider this.

"I know Tantie will know if you are in danger. If you are delayed and she feels nothing, it is of your own volition. We can keep you in here."

Ganache peered over Cyril's shoulder and looked at his opulent guest room with the same scorn one would gaze upon a hole in the ground. Cyril exhaled deeply.

"I will fetch you many, many raisins."

This earned him some attention at least. After some tortuous moments, Ganache finally hopped from the parapet of the window to a nightstand by the bed, where she perched territorially.

Cyril smiled genuinely at her. "You will have a king's breakfast, and then you can leave in the morrow if you like, but fly slowly," he said.

Ganache chirped her assent at the same time as Tigris snapped out of her own machinations. She jumped onto the bed to be closer to him.

"I've got it," she said.

Cyril folded his arms over his chest. "I am dying to hear it."

"Do not sound sarcastic before you even know what it is," she snapped, and continued before he could protest. "Atticus is protecting you at the moment, right?"

"I... yes. He is."

"Once you tell him about Eufrates – which I know you will – he might not want to anymore. It may be too much of a risk. We have to guarantee he wants to keep you safe."

"...You want me to tell him about you."

"No! Gods, you are very frustrating. This one's all on you, Cy."

"I'm afraid I don't grasp your meaning."

"You and he! You should court! Marry, perhaps."

He needed a second to pick his jaw up off the floor.

"...You think I should court your fiancé."

"Oh, I'm sure that ship has sailed. You like him so much more than I do! Ever since that wedding dinner! And I would like you to be happy."

"I thought this was a calculating ploy."

She shrugged. *"Two birds."*

Ganache crowed from her perch. Both he and Tigris chose to ignore it.

"I... Tig, I cannot *seduce* the king of Cretea."

Tigris shook her head and tutted as if speaking to a small child. *"Oh, Cyril. Oh, my dear, dense, stupid, idiot little Cyril."*

"Ey–"

"You already have."

Cyril flushed a deep red, threatening on violet. He felt as though all the blood had drained from the rest of his body up directly to his face and he must look like a vascular nightmare.

"'Ooh, Atticus, I am not a damsel'!" she crooned.

"I said that because I am *not*! I am a soulless old man!"

Tigris laughed. *"You are certainly shameless as well."*

"I am feeling a great deal of shame right now."

"Well, in any case, once you get over yourself you will see how beneficial this will be. Before, Eufrates's claim to war was that his mage had been stolen. Easy to spin as a noble cause. If you come out and declare yourself in love, he will seem cruel and a tyrant, getting in the way of a happy coupling by refusing to find a new mage."

Cyril leaned in, horrified and impressed all at once. "You've really thought this through."

"You may be very learned and intelligent, but I have been groomed for politics since birth. This is my *playing field."*

"Well. It all sounds quite solid, but there is one small issue."

Tigris cocked her head. *"If you say cold feet–"*

"No, no…"

He pulled his wedding ring from out of his nightshirt and brandished it at her like a holy symbol. Again, it glimmered and shone even in dim light, as if to remind everyone of its presence.

"Even if I were to form any kind of… *attachment* to Atticus, the ring would certainly prevent our marriage."

"You don't need to get married right away–"

"It," he choked. "It prevents other things, too."

Tigris gaped at him like he was the stupidest man on earth. Which, perhaps, he was.

"Why would you do that to yourself?"

"I was twenty-three!" he blurted. "I was in love!"

Tigris brought one paw up to her forehead and rubbed away a migraine. *"Is… there a way to undo it?"*

"Not that I know of. It's a powerful curse."

"Curses can be broken, can't they? I know that much about magic."

"Seeing as it's my own spell, I'm the one who ought to know how."

"You're very unreliable. Surely someone else could help."

Cyril glanced briefly at Ganache, but shook his head. "I cannot push my luck corresponding with Tantie. And it would not be something so simple that a few notes back and forth could suffice.

"I… think there is a library here somewhere. Or something of the sort. I see so many familiars in the garden, there must be wizards all over and they would need resources. I just have yet to see it."

"I will look for it!"

Cyril's face flooded with consternation. "On your own?"

"What will they do, arrest me? I am just a lost kitty-cat."

He chuckled. He did think her reasonably safe within palace walls. "Very well. You do that and get me once you've found it. What do *I* do?"

Tigris grinned. *"You've got a king to seduce!"*

"...Of course."

"Do not look so sour. You are only being bashful now because you have to do it on purpose."

Cyril sighed. There was perhaps some truth to what she was saying. He did not acknowledge it to himself, but it did feel good to speak to Atticus, to have his attention.

He imagined a life with the charming, gregarious king of Cretea. A good man who would treat him well. It would please him, he thought, if that was his fate.

And at the same time, a wave of nausea threatened to overwhelm him. The ring burned into his skin, but the pain was not what had his stomach tied up in knots. He had felt the sear of the ring. He had become used to it.

Cyril could not think of a future wedding day without remembering his first. The way he and his new husband danced all night, how he'd sang sweet, improvised tunes in his ear, how for years after he woke up every day in a state of lovesick euphoria because the man who owned his heart lay beside him.

He could not admit this to Tigris. It would make her immediately give up on her schemes. But he was, and would always be, desperately in love with his husband.

FOURTEEN

The first thing Cyril did upon waking was summon a maid and ask for a bowl of the biggest, sweetest raisins she could procure. Upon receiving these, he laid them out for Ganache like an offering to an old god, and watched the familiar eat ravenously before she decided she no longer enjoyed present company and hopped out the window to perch on a branch, making her molasses-slow return home to her master.

Tigris left him to his own devices shortly after declaring she would scour every nook and cranny of this palace until there was nothing left to see, so Cyril decided to seek out his mark.

It was mean to speak like that of Atticus, but that is what it felt like going to talk to him after he agreed to Tigris's plan. He had spent a great deal of his life hearing whispers of how he was a tempter, a wily fox looking to ensnare prey behind his back, he did not relish actually becoming one.

And he was not being modest when he told Tigris he really *was* very awkward. There was no way this could go but horribly sideways.

But he looked for the king anyway. At the very least he needed to tell him about Eufrates's threats. Warn him. He owed Atticus that much and more. If Atticus decided to thank him by fancying him just a bit, that would not be such a bad exchange.

Atticus happened to be unoccupied, bounding down the steps to the ground floor with a stack of scrolls tucked under one arm when Cyril found him. He was at the top of the staircase and called out, feeling suddenly very self-conscious of every little thing he or Atticus did.

Atticus explained he needed to get these scrolls back to one of his studies, but afterwards, if Cyril wished it, he would have his undivided attention. Cyril couldn't help but peek into the little writing he *could* make out inside the rolled-up pieces of parchment. They seemed to be old medical studies, which he found curious. He would not pry, though. Not when he was trying to get Atticus in a *good* mood.

Once his hands were freed and he had returned, Cyril worked up the courage to ask if he would like to breakfast together in the dining hall, since it seemed such a slow morning. Atticus flashed him one of his charmed smiles and said:

"I've a better idea."

A quarter hour later, they had ascended back upstairs, but in the opposite direction of the guest rooms. Cyril realised with some mortification that he was being led to Atticus's private quarters.

Cyril looked around, whirling his gaze in a slow windmill so he had to focus on anything but Atticus.

"I have never been to this side of the palace." He let out a nervous little laugh. "It feels as though I am not sure I am meant to be here."

"You are being invited by the king himself! It is a perfect excuse to explore."

Cyril nodded, palms taking on a sticky texture as he finally looked ahead at Atticus's broad back and neatly cropped blond hair. He knew he had the best of intentions, but Tigris had wormed herself so deeply in his head he would have been nervous if Atticus asked him to pass him a shaker of salt during a meal.

"Would it not be easier to take breakfast in one of the dining rooms?" he asked.

"Easier? Oh, yes. But this will be a fair deal more impressive."

Though he could see Atticus's smile even just by watching the back of his head, Cyril did not grasp his meaning until they arrived at the king's quarters.

It was not just one room. It was an entire living space, so grand Cyril could not even see a bed (he noted this with some relief). There were doors that led to other rooms in the quarters, one of them he assumed was where Atticus slept, but it resembled very much Cyril's own apartments in the tower, only on a much grander scale.

The room they had entered into was home to a few sofas for lounging, bookshelves stacked high with more literary fluff that Cyril could only assume was for entertainment, and a small table upon which one could take their morning meals or prop their feet up.

They bypassed this area entirely as Atticus led him down to a set of glass double doors through to an uncovered space. It was wonderful. A suspended patio – it was much too big to be a balcony – on the second floor of a palace, with its own modest gardens and benches and another table, this time wooden and bigger, that seemed to seat a party of perhaps ten visitors.

More impressive still was the covered alcove tucked to one side of the patio that contained cookware. A stovetop, a grill, an oven, cupboards with glass doors where he could see fine crockery inside.

He remembered, then, that Tigris had briefly mentioned this on their first encounter. He kept a grill in his chambers for game. It was such a reductive way of putting it when the man owned an entire private kitchen.

Atticus walked over to the alcove with childlike enthusiasm and began rolling up his sleeves.

"I thought it such a nice day, it would be a shame to eat indoors. It will have to be a simple meal, though, Cyril, I do not wish to make you wait an hour for some ridiculous confection."

Cyril stood, awestruck, before it struck him that the polite thing to do was take a seat at the wooden table.

"Tigris did mention you cooked... she did not say you were a chef."

Atticus laughed. "That is because I am not! I swear, it is a very easy hobby to pick up. Gives me something to do with my hands."

He cracked four eggs into a large pan one-handed, as well as adding thick-cut slabs of bacon. Into a mixing bowl, he began to whisk a combination of flour, milk and some other things Cyril had not been able to make out. Once the watery batter was done, he began doling out paper-thin circles of it into another, smaller pan, greased by a knob of fragrant, honeyed butter. It steamed and sizzled and smelled incredible.

Atticus laid out their meal in front of him like a proud artist. As usual, he sat himself beside Cyril instead of across from him, something he had grown used to enough not to jump when it happened anymore.

"This is delicious," he said between bites. "Truly. But it feels wrong, somehow, to be served by a king."

Atticus scoffed, not distastefully. "Then think you are being served by a friend, if that clears your conscience."

"You have been kind to me to an excess."

Atticus yet again laid a warm hand upon his shoulder, another thing Cyril had become accustomed to over the last few days spent in Cretea.

"I am happy you came to me. It shows trust and that is no small gift. But I had always wondered why you chose to come to me in the first place. Surely a relative would have been the obvious choice."

Cyril could not admit that he had not so much 'chosen' Atticus as been bullied into seeking him out by Tigris. Perhaps he was being too cynical, though. Perhaps he would have gone to him even if he'd been completely alone.

"I... am not very close to my family. Both my parents passed when I was quite young."

He braced for the pity that usually followed immediately after these kinds of statements. He did not feel he deserved it. His parents had shipped him off to Heléne when he was barely out of leading strings, and they did not even bother to visit very often. The guilt of it stung, made him feel monstrous, but he had not particularly mourned them. Condolences were a waste of good breath on him.

"Ah. We are very like, then."

Cyril blinked. He wasn't expecting that, and he wasn't quite sure he heard him correctly. When it finally sank in, he did the self-same thing he had been dreading almost immediately.

"I am sorry, Atticus."

Atticus gave him an amused look. "I doubt you killed them, if that is what you're sorry for. I have been king since the wise old age of sixteen. I am sure you were not capable enough to assassinate a royal couple all the way from the mage tower."

"They... were killed?"

"We've a few enemies in Cretea. It is why I was looking forward to allying myself with your own kingdom."

Cyril looked down at his plate, where the jam and butter on the stacked crêpes was melting together. "I am sorry about Tigris."

Atticus actually did laugh this time, instead of barely containing it.

"Again, Cyril! I do not think you were responsible for that either! Perhaps she simply did not care for me. I was actually desperate enough to ask for *Eufrates*'s hand in marriage, but I do not think we are on very good terms." He eyed Cyril up and down. "And I do not believe I am his type."

The guilt had him in such a strong, virulent chokehold he was having a hard time swallowing his bacon. He had given up his life to try and repair the future and yet here he was, making trouble for everyone around him. It was like he had chosen to be an active participant in his world's demise this time around instead of a lily-livered bystander.

This was the perfect moment to tell him about Eufrates and yet he was frozen in a swirl of emotions. Mercifully, Atticus seemed to take this as though he was not thoroughly enjoying his meal.

"Ah! You mustn't eat the crêpes like that. It is much better when they are warm and the butter is thoroughly melted."

Then, to Cyril's complete surprise, because he apparently was incapable of retaining basic information in his head, Atticus produced a small flame of magefire above the plate, warming up his food once more.

"Oh… I had forgotten…" he began.

"I am sure. Perhaps I just wanted to show off a bit. Though this is about the extent of what I can do. And it will hardly impress Cyril Laverre."

"No, no!" Cyril cried. "I am *very* impressed. Magic is difficult to learn, and you have so much to deal with already."

"Still. Fire is what you mages learn when you are barely out of diapers, am I right? From what I know of your abilities, they are much more varied. A jack of all trades, correct?"

Cyril nodded. "It is required for grand magistry. Though… I am not sure if I will ever fulfil that title now."

He was rubbish at this. It was insensible of Tigris to even conceive of him being some sort of seductor. He didn't know what to say, how to steal the conversation. Perhaps he could use magic, enchant the king. Bind them together in an invisible weave that would make Atticus see him as the most important man in the world, but the mere thought of it made bile rise up to his throat. He had never been much of an enchanter. He did not have the constitution for it.

Perhaps, instead, he could do what he had been doing all along, needling the king to covert annoyance.

"Atticus, are you sure there is nothing I can do in your court?"

"Cyril–"

"No, I... Listen, please. Yesternight, I... there was a letter from Eufrates. He seeks to challenge you for stealing his mage. But if we can convince the court, the populous, that I am here of my own free will, because I have sworn fealty to *your* crown, he will seem a madman. Unreasonable in his pursuit."

He had been putting off breaking the news so long and he finally blurted it out as though he had heaved the contents of his belly back onto the plate. He saw a glint in Atticus's eyes which he was sure must be horror.

"Do... did you keep the letter?"

Cyril blanched. "It was too painful. I was frightened. I burnt it, but you *must* believe me. He will make a move on Cretea and I do not want you caught unawares."

"It is a serious claim, but I have earned your trust so you shall have mine." The hand was there on his shoulder again, warm and reassuring.

"Please, let me help."

"You have helped more than enough. A surprise invasion would have been catastrophic."

"But this is *my* fault!"

"Do not say that, Cyril."

Desperation flared in his chest so wild and hot he might burst into flame despite the mild, beautiful weather. He had tried his best and still he was denied. He felt useless, powerless, like the cause of all the world's evils. It would have been better if he had died in the cottage, choking in a pool of his own thick blood. At the same time, he felt manic. Jittery with recklessness.

He leaned in, too quick to be stopped, and kissed Atticus on the lips.

He had not kissed or been kissed in a *very* long time. In an *embarrassingly* long time for a married man. It felt nice, comforting despite the frantic undertones.

Then the ring bore through his chest like molten metal. He felt like he was being stabbed with a hot iron, agonisingly slow.

Cyril ignored it. He held the kiss for a few seconds, enough for it to truly make an impact, then he pulled away as suddenly as he'd drawn in.

Atticus's expression was unreadable, but his brows were high on his forehead.

"I... please, forgive me, I–" Cyril blurted.

What Atticus said to him next was so incomprehensible at first Cyril thought he was barely parsing a long-forgotten dead tongue.

The king looked *regretful* as he carded a hand through his hair. "Cyril..."

"I'm–"

"No. Listen, Cyril, I did not... I do not want you to think I will not protect you unless I can get something out of you. I would be no better than scum.

"I am... charmed by you. I have said so a number of times, but you do not need to force yourself to seduce me just so you can guarantee a place in my court. If it is what you truly want, I will give it to you."

"I did not force myself," he lied in a very small voice.

Atticus flashed him a wane smile. "Truly? Your method of courtship is to kiss someone suddenly in the middle of a meal? I did not think you so brazen."

Cyril looked down at his now-empty plate. "No... it is not, but... I truly– I want–"

He felt the familiar squeeze on his shoulder. "I think you are frightened, and you do not want me to turn you in to Eufrates to prevent escalation. I promise you it is the farthest thing from my mind. He would have found a reason to turn on me sooner or later, I believe. He never seemed to like me."

This could not be farther from the truth. In the early days of his rule, Eufrates had looked to Atticus like a guiding hand, a reliable mentor. The relationship soured along the way, but there was a time when his husband cherished Atticus much more than Cyril ever did.

And now, looking into his eyes, being showered by his undivided attention, Cyril understood fully how easy it was to trust this man. To give himself entirely to him, as a friend, or a guide, or something deeper. Warmth fluttered in his chest.

Atticus stood up from his seat. "You are tired. I'll bet you barely slept since receiving the letter. I will let you rest, as I have preparations of my own to attend to now I've got a petulant new regent to deal with."

"Are you sure you don't need–?"

Atticus clicked his tongue and pulled Cyril up to standing alongside him. "I will grow tired of repeating myself. You've nothing to worry about."

Before he let go of Cyril's hand, he laced their fingers conspiratorially and smiled.

"And should you like to kiss me again when tensions are not so high, I would perhaps be amenable to it."

Against all odds. In defiance of some ancient covenant between the gods themselves, Tigris's plan had succeeded. Notorious wallflower and cripplingly awkward romantic Cyril Laverre had managed to get a man to fancy him on his wit and personality alone. This had only happened one time before, to catastrophic results.

He let himself hope that this time would be different. Atticus was not Tigris's type, but he was close to Cyril's. An attentive man who treated him like a precious gem despite how little he deserved it. It was a heady feeling, being wanted.

He had not felt a *spark* in that kiss. There was no burst of passion. His loins were not set ablaze like they're meant to be in novels and fairy tales, but he did not need whirlwind romance. He had experienced it already.

What had he said to Tigris? 'It is better to form a lasting

attachment based on mutual trust' or some such avuncular nonsense. He would believe his own advice this time. He was not in *love* with Atticus, but he liked him very much, and that was a brilliant place to start. An attachment.

His hand grasped at the ring that was proving to be the second worst bane of his existence. He just needed to deal with it first.

FIFTEEN

Cyril had not expected Tigris's excursion into the palace to be quite so fruitful, but the day was turning out full of surprises. It was midday when she returned.

"I've found it!"

She burst into the room, an embodiment of pride. He was sitting on a small armchair reading ahead on their little pirate horror romp. Half of the main cast had died by chapter five, and he was unsure the remaining characters could carry the story. Cyril put the book face down on the arm of the chair, so as to mark the page, and stood.

"What have you found?"

"You said there might be a library. I think I've found it! It is more of a warehouse, *really. Oh, Cyril, you will die once you see it."*

"A warehouse? I've seen nowhere in the palace with that kind of infrastructure. The ballroom and the main hall I've already visited."

"That's the thing! There is a basement!"

Cyril's eyes widened. He had not seen a single set of stairs leading down in his entire stay in the palace.

"Are you certain?"

"What? Yes, I'm certain! How can one hallucinate a whole basement? *And it is massive, spanning the area of the entire palace."*

"How did you even find it?"

"Well." She puffed up her chest. *"I am very smart, as you know."*

212

He nodded. "Indeed."

"So I went into the gardens and mingled with the other familiars a bit. I figured if there's a library for mages then there's bound to be mages *in there. I watched until one of them – the fidgety little hare I don't trust."*

"It is just a *hare*."

"Hush. It left the garden. And oh, it thinks it's so sneaky and clever, but I am the best hunter in court, so of course I did not lose its trail.

"I followed it all the way to a set of stairs by the servant's quarters leading down. I waited until it came back up and then I made my own descent and found your library. It is criminal *that Atticus has not shared it with you yet! You would thrive in it."*

"Well?" He felt a bubble of excitement in his chest, the need for a sense of purpose strong in the forefront of his mind. "Let us go!"

"Yes! There was no one in there when I found it. It's why I came rushing back. Oh, I am so relieved you were in the room."

"You would have found me."

"If you were not here, I would be afraid of interrupting a private moment."

They left at once. Cyril eager to do *something* in this palace other than read convoluted novels and gorge himself on local delicacies. He hurried to keep up with Tigris's feline gait. As they were making their way towards the servant's quarters Cyril nearly tripped over his own feet.

"How did that go, by the way?"

"It–" Colour rose to his cheeks. "I shall tell you later. It will have been useless if the library ends up being a dead end."

"Oh, so it went well! *What did you do? Did you play the ingenue again?"*

"*Again*?" he sputtered.

"Yes, you're right. That is just your personality. But I have been so bored here, Cyril, give me at least some of the juicy details."

"I said later!" He must be flushed as an overripe tomato. Tigris merely nodded.

"It is good that you are bashful. It means you truly like him."

Cyril chewed on his lower lip. "Perhaps…"

It was a long trek to the opposite end of the palace's ground floor where Tigris had seen the hidden staircase, but Cyril was so excited by the prospect he felt as though he had floated there. Ill-advised as it was to simply plunge into the depths of a darkened set of stairs, neither of them cared about danger or discovery when they began to climb.

"It is perfectly reasonable for one to have stumbled upon this place on their own," said Tigris.

He gave her a nod. "Quite right."

"If Atticus wanted to keep you away from somewhere, he would have set boundaries."

"Indeed."

"Besides, we are merely trying to help."

"And you did not see anyone else down in the basement?" As they made their way deeper into the hallways, he lowered his voice to a whisper.

"Not since last time I was here. And that was about a quarter hour ago!"

Bolstered by an unusual burst of confidence, Cyril wove himself a ball of magefire in his hand to light their way.

"How did you even see down here, Tig?"

"I'm a cat."

"Oh, yes. What was it *like*? The library, I mean."

"We–ll, I don't know the first thing about magic, but I was impressed. It was like Auntie's study, but bigger! And there were... tools and artefacts as well. And I believe ingredients for... um..."

"Alchemy?"

"That's the one! I saw an open book on the table. I jumped up there to try and read it, but I think it went over my head. Talked about... medicinal tools and something about being airborne. It honestly gave me gooseflesh, a bit. Felt like something from a lair."

"The book?"

"Yes, though... truly? All of it. You mages have a flair for the dramatic. The first time I set foot into Auntie's tower, I thought her an evil sorceress."

"Do not discard that theory just yet," Cyril said with a smirk.

Tigris led him down corridor after corridor of the high-ceilinged catacombic underground of Cretea's palace. There were some lit sconces here and there, but it was otherwise a frightfully dark place, with a draft coursing through it that chilled his exposed skin and made the hairs on his arms and the back of his neck stand on end.

It reminded Cyril of the dungeons in the lower ground of his own home, a place for cool stone, shadow and castigation that Cyril did not particularly like treading. He was, perhaps, being a bit harsh. An entire underground structure could hardly be made of wood and plush carpeting.

Finally, they stopped in front of an intricate iron door, finely decorated with sigils and runes. A curious piece of architecture. Cyril held the mageflame out in front of him to make out the runes and they were simple warding spells, easy for any mage worth their salt to disable. He was surprised Tigris got past, but he supposed she was a familiar now, immune to triggering traps set for mere mortals.

After plucking the wards undone, he pushed through the door. Tigris slotted her boneless body through the first breach available to walk ahead of him.

She was not exaggerating. It was breathtaking.

The library had been shrouded in darkness, and a single spark of flame would not be sufficient for how cavernous it was. Cyril went around looking for unlit candelabra and sconces and, one by one, conjured flames to bathe the room in light. It was palatial, the size of a grand ballroom, and its walls were crammed to bursting with books and studies and notes and texts.

A smattering of simple, practical wooden tables were scattered across the room. Some contained devices of alchemical import, others held open books and writing instruments: a quill and inks of different colours, from midnight black to apple red and a nub of a pencil that had seen many days of work plotting. Others, still, housed open star charts, maps, an astrolabe and compass.

Barrels and crates were filled with yet more treasures of the magical variety. Gemstones and herbs, ingredients used for spells, rolled up maps of every territory in the known world, vials of potion, some empty and others sizzling with promise.

He felt he could spend hours here. It irked him that he needed to sneak down like a common criminal.

"Are you enjoying your tour?"

Cyril was rudely snapped out of his reverie, and he looked to Tigris, who had scaled one of the rolling ladders attached to the shelves and was scanning through the books.

"If you're free, I'd love it if you could help me figure out how these are organised."

Cyril huffed and begrudgingly stalked towards her.

"You knew I'd get distracted! How could I not? Look at this place!"

"Yes, Cy, I've seen it. I'll admit, candlelight brings it to life, but doesn't it give you the chills? Just a bit?"

"It gives me the *thrills*!"

She made a face like she'd sucked on a lemon rind. *"Augh. Horrific. I hate that you've said that."*

Cyril chuckled and climbed up onto the ladder to help her out. She was right, of course. Tigris was usually right. But her bad feelings were surely because of the nasty draft that permeated the entire basement level. A *literal* chill that still had him goose fleshed.

From the vantage point atop the steps, looking down at the expanse of the library, there *was* something he couldn't quite pinpoint that gave it an eerie quality. He couldn't explain why, but he had an *incredibly* strong gut feeling that this place ought to be teeming with cobwebs, despite it being clearly frequently used and thus regularly cleaned. It just *felt* like somewhere household spiders would take hold.

But he was being mean. His own quarters looked like a war zone, he could hardly judge another man's place of study.

He turned, finally, to the books, reading out the titles. A few were in foreign languages he *didn't* speak (though he was sure Tigris, who had been schooled in every language under the sun since birth, could translate for him easily), but the gist of this particular shelf was clear.

"These are all on illusionism," he said.

"Well, I got that," she huffed. *"I can read. It's just I don't know where* curse breaking *falls in your pantheon of schools of magic."*

"It depends on the curse. The closest I can think of that the rings would be, perhaps… some form of prolonged enchantment. But it does not affect our *minds*. They are enchanted *items*, which is a subset all in itself."

"You've no idea where to start looking," she surmised.

"I have *some* idea."

He hopped down from the ladder and started making turns about the room, slowly, looking over each shelf to see if anything drew him in. It felt like a very erratic way of searching. They might need hours to scour the entire library and he did not know how much time he had.

"I am going to look for books on curses," Tigris announced.

He nodded. "Very well. I will… I will *look*."

Cyril spun his way around the myriad shelves, dizzying himself in the process. He could not figure out how they were arranged. Even the *Academy*, rife with unruly adolescents who couldn't put a thing back into its rightful place if they were *paid* to do so, had a better sorting system than this.

He thought about coming clean to Atticus. Asking for his help. But the thought of revealing, at once, that he was a fifty-year-old man and *also* already married discouraged him instantly.

Finally, he decided to just peruse the tables. The books and charts were wide open there, he could sample a piece of what the king's mages were working on and perhaps he would get lucky in the process. He was also just curious.

He walked to them slowly, one by one. The first table he looked at held a map of the two territories: Farsala and Cretea. Next to it, there was a quill still in its inkwell, as though the map were going to be scribbled upon soon.

The second table he found held a complex series of beakers and distilling contraptions. There was a large, upside-down glass vial filling with a gas emanating from a potion underneath it. Cyril was no expert alchemist, but he could probably figure out what was going on with a bit more context. For now, it seemed an interesting experiment.

Finally, table three stopped him dead in his tracks. There were more areas to peruse in the library, many more, but looking down at this one parched his throat and rendered him immobile. Open upon it was, likely, the book on alchemy Tigris had mentioned. She could not understand it, but it was a book about magic and Cyril read books about magic as a *job*.

Once, when he was but a small, waifish eight-year-old, a distracted servant in the palace, while attending to their cleaning duties – chiefly polishing the floor – had, in their rapt distraction, quite literally pulled a rug from underneath where he was standing. He did not weigh very much, so he was instantly sent flying in a graceless arc that finished with his face making direct impact on the floor. He broke his nose and Heléne had to reset it with magic through his shaking, overwhelmed tears.

He was experiencing this exact sensation again, down to the broken bone in his nose, but now it was all playing out in the theatre of the mind, where he was actor and spectator, chained to his seat. It was so visceral he could *smell* the tang of blood filling up his respiratory tracts and leaking into his throat.

"Ti–g," he called for her in a small, shrill voice.

To her credit, she was at his side immediately, ears perked on the highest of alerts.

"What? What's happened?"

Cyril took a deep breath and cleared the memory of the headache and the stench of drying blood from his mind. He pointed down at the book.

"I am going to explain to you what's in this, and what *I* think it implies," he said very slowly, chewing his words. "And you, in your infinite enthusiasm, are going to offer up an alternative, less incriminating explanation."

Tigris said nothing, but she nodded. He looked down at the pages he'd been staring at and flipping through for what seemed like hours now.

"So," he began. "This is, indeed, a book on alchemy. But it also draws quite a bit from medicinal magic and surgery. It speaks of poisons and their antidotes and, this particular page, has a full description of one of the rarer breeds of poisons an alchemist can make. It is undetectable within a person's pattern because it is indistinguishable from a... wasting disease." He paused to swallow convulsively.

"*However*, this brew *can* be spotted under autopsy. By examining the victim's blood system, the lining of their stomach, an experienced surgeon can pinpoint the cause of death, hidden though it was, as not being borne of natural disease.

"That is where *this book*." Cyril pointed at a smaller tome which had been closed, but he had leafed through ravenously, to the right of the alchemy book. It had the tell-tale stains of ink in its margins that indicated it was filled with notes. "Comes in.

"This is another alchemical piece, much more specific than this comprehensive list of potions. It is a guide on how to sublimate potions so they are... airborne. Ingested via inhalation. It makes them less potent: for example, the *wasting disease* would take hold in a few weeks, not days, but it *would* make it essentially indistinguishable from a real illness. The perfect concoction.

"...What do you make of this, Tigris?"

Tigris looked at him in silent contemplation for a long, excruciating while, and then she let out a small breath, like a disappointed tutor.

"Sounds like a couple of bumbling oafs failed to solve my murder."

"Gods *fucking* damn it, Tig."

She hopped up onto the table and looked at the books laid out, as though she could confirm it for herself.

"I knew *it! I did not like the man the moment I laid eyes on him."*

"Wh– you did not *know*!" he scoffed.

"I knew I did not trust him as far as I could throw him. My intuition is never wrong."

"You– you tried to *set me up* with him!"

"We have to go back now, do *we not?"* she said, ostensibly ignoring him.

"Back... to Farsala?"

"Yes! I do not want you around a killer!"

"To be fair, he has not done anything yet."

"Oh? You think this is his first *crime? The man with the dark evil lair?"*

"It could be... it could be one of his mages has gone rogue." Tigris gave him a look like he was insane. He *felt* insane for even entertaining the idea. It was ludicrous. He just hated to have been so *wrong.*

"Still... your brother still wants my head on a platter."

"We go to Auntie! Sneak into the tower, she will hide us. Gods, Cyril, you are so bad at thinking on your feet."

"I do feel I need to sit down..." he said faintly.

"I know where Atticus keeps his horses. We will escape immediately; he will not know we are gone till we're far beyond his borders."

"You think we can make it?"

"Of course! This palace is mostly empty, I'll bet we won't run into a single servant on our way to the stables."

Cyril nodded, feeling suddenly emboldened. "Then I shall... I shall put these back to how they were."

He started fussing around with the books, hands shaking in equal parts fear and adrenaline at the discovery.

Tigris, seeming to have remembered something important, cast him a rueful look.

"I'm sorry, Cyril."

He barely glanced at her, but raised a brow. "Sorry? Whatever for?"

"He... you really liked him, didn't you? I am not relishing this revelation. Well, I am a bit, but not because your *relationship has been ruined!"*

"There was no relationship. I... was taken by him, but that was the extent of it."

"Truly?"

"Yes, I am serious. I don't think I was ever in love with Atticus."

He did not hear the solid clicking of boots at the doorway until it was far too late. The voice that followed, measured and soothing as ever, though, he heard icy clear.

"Oh, Cyril. That really hurts my feelings."

SIXTEEN

Cyril's blood did not run cold, because he was sure it was not running at all. He had frozen, frightened to death. Any reaction he had to Atticus standing at the door to the library, leaning against the doorframe as though he had *not* just found his guest reading up on his private research, was being performed by his spectre, which was the only remnant of him left on earth after his entire being turned to dust.

He actually would have very much liked that, turning to dust. It would make for a smooth exit.

Instead, his hands trembled as he turned, *slowly*, to properly face Atticus and opened and closed his mouth like a fish out of water.

"Great work, Samson," was the next thing he said. This confused Cyril greatly until he realised Atticus was not speaking to *him*.

From behind his legs, a pair of tan, alert ears peeked out, followed right after by the snout and body of a hare. Atticus leaned down and scratched it on the top of the head before turning his attention back to Cyril.

"It's hardly fair, though, is it? Saying you didn't really love me *now*. Feels a bit like a cop out. I had expected at least a *bit* more mixed emotion." Atticus started to walk towards him, and Cyril felt like his legs were made of stone. "Or were you *actually* trying to manipulate me. I'm impressed. It hardly suits you, Cyril."

Cyril's gaze darted back to the hare. He had called him Samson. He had petted him. It did not take a great mind to work out the relationship.

"That's *your* familiar."

He was ignored outright.

"In any case, I wish you had not wandered down here on your own. What were you even *doing*? I do not believe you were trying to *unmask* me; you do not have the insight."

"You're a wizard," he croaked.

Atticus rolled his eyes. "It is taking you a while to catch up."

Suddenly, he could move again. He stepped back, back, until he had his spine pressed to the table and pointed at the alchemist's tools.

"*You* did all that? All this time you've just been down here… making *poisons*?"

Atticus stared at him a moment, then laughed so heartily it felt as though the room shook.

"An *alchemist*? You think I am an alchemist?" The laughter took on the edge of a sneer. "Alchemists are crones and madmen. Do not insult me after taking so many liberties within my own home."

"Then how?"

"I have *told* you how! Cyril, I've told you very few lies. I have mages who take care of the schools I am not so specialised in for me."

Cyril could not figure it out. It was driving him to madness. It was like a portion of his brain had been set aflame and he could not put it out. It was an itch he could not get at, buried deep. His head was swimming. His vision threatened to turn hazy.

In a moment of desperation, Cyril broke the one rule of propriety held in high esteem by all self-respecting mages. He would like it stated somewhere, for the record, that it was an unorthodox situation, and he would not have done something like this otherwise.

Cyril made a diamond with his fingers and held it over one eye, then he pulled it apart, the motion like looking through thick foliage into a clearing.

He looked into the pattern.

It was *oppressive*.

In the middle of this tall, gargantuan library there was a spiderweb of fine thread, branching in every direction, its nucleus the epicentre of the room. It covered every nook and corner of the ceiling and reached its silks out, out, to beyond this one room, beyond the basement and from there – who could tell?

It was intricate, delicately woven together thread by thread. Cyril judged that it must have been amassing for years. There were thick ropes of magic, dangling heavy on their own as well as thin strands, almost floating from how weightless they looked. They coiled and tied together in beautiful, horrible patterns. It was so much and so overwhelming. It was like a veil had been placed over the room, glowing a white, lifeless light.

He stared so hard and with such rapt intensity, his eyes began to hurt. When Cyril blinked away the tears, Atticus had moved within inches of him.

Cyril let out a startled gasp and bumped against the table.

"I did not give you leave to do that, but I cannot begrudge anyone from admiring my handiwork. It goes unnoticed so often," Atticus said.

"What are they…" It was a monumental effort for Cyril not to shake. "Who are they even *attached* to?"

"Have I not said I've many in my employ?"

And then, Cyril realised there was one strand, like a silver hair, that was not spreading out of the library. It was hanging down, towards him, *onto* him. It was attached to his shoulder.

"It is hard work," Atticus sighed. "It is *gruelling* work. It is *thankless* work, but I am proud of it."

"You should not be! What you call employment, it is – it is *enslavement*."

"I pay my mages a living wage."

Cyril felt like a trapped animal. There was nowhere else to run for him.

"You've ensorcelled them into a plot to kill your *wife*–"

"Fiancée."

"*Widow* if I've anything to say about it!"

"*Good one, Cy.*"

Tigris was so *very* clever, but sometimes... sometimes she was not.

Cyril, panicked that he had forgotten all about her, immediately swept his gaze all around the room until it fell upon Tigris. Atticus followed and his face split into the widest grin.

"That's her, is it not? The woman of the hour."

"*Go fuck yourself, Atticus.*"

He could not be bothered to tell her Atticus could not hear her. He didn't think it'd make a difference.

"I don't know what you mean. That is Shoestring."

"Oh, you are a *horrible* liar. Wear your heart on your sleeve. It's how I knew you'd be the perfect souvenir to bring back.

"I had suspected she asked you to stash her away somehow, but inside a *cat*! She must have *truly* despised me. Which suits me fine." Atticus cast a derisive glance back at the cat. "I never liked the stupid bitch. I would've been doing Farsala a favour getting rid of her, not that it matters *now*."

Cyril's hands balled into fists at his side, so hard his fingernails dug into soft skin. If he were the hero, the protector Tigris deserved, he would have thrown hands with the king of Cretea right then and there. But he was a coward, a clown who had messed up every step of the way, and he knew a fistfight between them would only end with his head under a boot.

His mind snagged on something, though.

"'*Now*'...?" he repeated.

"Ah, yes! Yes, yes, yes, well! I did not expect the brother to be so much easier to manipulate! Take away his prized little courtesan." Cyril heard Tigris hiss. "And he loses his head! He will be such a vicious king. A despot. A brutal invader, jilted over his runaway wizard. He shall do his damage and when the people are practically *crying* to unseat him, Cretea will rise again, and I shall save the day. Honestly, I had expected a longer timeline for the *actual* war to begin. You are a *wonder*, Cyril Laverre."

Atticus put a hand on his shoulder again. The same squeeze, the same pressure, but it was more intense this time, somehow. He felt dizzy. His brain felt swollen in his skull.

"I had planned on just adding you to my court as a mage, but if you are worth starting political conflict over, there may be something to that courtship."

The way Atticus said the word *courtship* sent a chill down Cyril's spine, but, immediately after, it was as though it was being doused with hot water. He could not think straight. Could not find it in himself to truly hate Atticus.

And still, the man *talked.*

"Worry not. You will be a jewel to my collection. The way you've constructed her body to function the same as a familiar's. I mean, the way she *eats*! It is a one-to-one replica."

"I am..." Cyril slurred. "I'm a very good mage."

"You *are*! That you are, pet," said Atticus.

Cyril could see out of the corner of his eye that the thread on Atticus's shoulder, once barely noticeable, was starting to become thick, snakelike. It coiled up from Atticus's fingers, tapping a pattern onto Cyril's very core, and hung around his neck like a choker. Like a *noose*. He could not breathe.

"Yes, I believe I pointed it out to you earlier today, even! You are... the ultimate playing card in my deck. A joker." Atticus's smile spread on his lips even as Cyril struggled to draw breath. Cyril nodded.

He should've given up by now. It would be easier. And yet, at the same time as his mind was going numb, there was a fire against his chest that threatened to burn straight through to his heart.

"You are a jack of all trades, Cyril. But I am a *master* of mine."

And there it was. The final squeeze. A chain around Cyril's neck that made him stupid and empty and *pliant*. He could not think of anything. He could not think of Tigris, or Heléne, or even Eufrates. He could *just about* think of Atticus and that was only because the man was stood in front of him, as pleased as an artist looking upon a masterpiece.

The only thing that *truly* grabbed his attention was that *damn* burning in his chest. It felt like it would engulf him in flames at any moment. It burned, but it did not sear. And it grew, and it grew.

And it grew.

Light bathed the two of them. Mageflame so bright and hot it burned blue at its core. It was like looking at a penitent on a pyre, but Cyril did not burn. Atticus did not burn. The only thing that caught fire, withered and turned to ash was the thread between them. Shocked and scared of being engulfed himself, Atticus drew back.

Cyril looked down when he heard a soft clinking of metal on a shirt button. The ring had weaselled its way out of his shirts, as though looking for credit for its gracious deed. It now hung over them, sparkling on his chest, still a bit incensed.

"What is *that*?" Atticus hissed.

"It… is not as much of a curse as I thought," he murmured to himself.

Atticus's face was that of the Undertaker incarnate. Everything about him spelled death. He lunged at Cyril, hands making to grab for his throat. It was difficult to tell if Atticus wanted the ring, or wanted to strangle him, but Cyril was cornered.

Cyril ducked and raised his arms up over his face in a pathetic mimicry of self-defence. He braced for the blow, but instead he heard a feral, angry yowl and the wet, sickly sound of tearing flesh. His eyes flew open.

He caught the tail end of a flurry of messy, shaggy orange fur overwhelming his assailant. Tigris had leapt up, thrown herself onto Atticus and had managed to successfully take out a chunk of his jaw with her claws, having just missed his throat. It was brutal to look at. The blood started flowing immediately, richly fragrant in its metallic tang.

Cyril would not be outdone by the very woman he had sworn to protect, so he did two things at once. The first was he clumsily kicked Atticus in the stomach, rendering him prone for at least long enough to give them time to abscond. The second was, with a pluck of the pattern behind him, he set the table with the alchemical books ablaze.

"Let's go, Cyril!" He heard coming from somewhere already far closer to the exit than he was in. He sidestepped Atticus, lost in the frenzy of stopping the bleeding and the pyre in his own home.

He passed the hare, Samson, as he ran. Cyril expected Samson to try and stop him, but he was obviously less important than the desecration of years of research and its master's grievous wound. Samson leapt past him like a bolt of lightning.

For good measure, as soon as he and Tigris were outside, he turned around and closed his palms into a hollow clap in front of the door. It disappeared into the very stone it had been slotted into. It would be some time before Atticus could get anyone to help with his entombment.

Enchanters were not very physical mages.

As they began their mad dash to the stables, Tigris apparently still had the energy to insult him.

"Augh! You have always been so slow! Release me back into human form and I will carry you."

"What? No!" He balked. "Absolutely not!"

"I will do it with as little humiliation as possible!"

"That is not the *point*, Tig." He was frazzled and stressed and in no mood to be gentle. "Use your *head*. He knows who you are. He will try to kill you on sight. No matter how good you are at *fighting*, you've no magic. Right now, your body is near indestructible. It is the safest you'll be until he is dealt with."

"And you intend to deal with him? Alone?"

"I... I will come up with, with..." His breath was coming up short. He was *also* not prone to physicality. "With something once I've had time to... to think. Tan... Tantie will help."

"Gods, Cyril, I'm going to drill you till your bones ache once this is all over."

He did not respond. He was conserving air. He had heard somewhere that in moments of great danger, the human body was capable of extraordinary feats. Clearly no one bothered to tell *his* body about this as he huffed and puffed and skidded his way into a halt in front of the stables outside the palace.

Tigris pointed out a horse she had ridden before and was quite fond of. Cyril may have been a bad athlete, a horrible seducer and an overall mess, but he was still a *courtier*. He knew how to ride.

It had been years since he'd last been on a mount, but it came flooding back to him as soon as he figured out the saddle. He gracelessly climbed up onto the horse's back – Tigris said her name was Titania and she was actually a mare – and willed her to speed off, far away from Cretea.

Once they had ridden on for about five minutes and no one came after them, Cyril let himself relax ever-so-slightly. He let out a deep, exhausted sigh and looked down at Tigris, who was cleaning dried blood from her claws.

"Thank you for that, by the way," he said.

"What happened back there? You froze."

"Atticus is... a wizard, as you might have surmised. Specifically, an enchanter."

"Those are the feelings mages?"

"Feelings, thoughts, ideas, personalities... *people*. Yes. Enchanters are the purveyors of the mind."

"You were being mind-controlled?"

"Yes. The ring... severed it. I am not sure why. Perhaps me belonging to someone else did not agree with it," he said with some degree of bitterness. "But mind-control is not... it is not the enchanter's bread and butter. Their art is that of subtle manipulation. Of influence. A good enchanter will never even have to reveal themselves, all the while controlling a person's very sense of self. It is a slow-acting poison, in its own way. Could be years until you'd see the effects."

Something snagged in his mind, then, when he said that. Like a loose thread caught in a nail and as he untangled it, it began to spell out a message.

Eufrates... the way Atticus spoke of his husband was *excited*, eager. He welcomed a war. He would like very much if his home was taken over. He had said it was happening *sooner* than he had planned and, oh, what else? That he would swoop in and fix everything.

I have always wanted to play the hero.

SEVENTEEN

Shit.

Cyril had all the clues. All the pieces, tiny but substantial, to this jigsaw puzzle, but he had not figured out how to slot them together until now. *Now* the picture before him was very clear, only, instead of a field of flowers or a portrait of a dear kitten, the picture formed by the puzzle was a grim heralding of his own death.

He might throw up on this horse. He was *sure* he would throw up on this horse.

"I am so, *so* stupid," he murmured.

Tigris tilted her head up. *"What? What is it?"*

"There was nothing wrong with him. *I* am the idiot. *I* am the fool who was played for *years.* I had one job, one *fucking* job in that court and I failed at it so miserably, and so–" The words became difficult to form around the lump swelling in his throat. "There is nothing *wrong* with him but *me.*"

"I... can think of many things wrong with Atticus."

"Not *Atticus*!" he screamed and the cold wind from the ride buffeted his words, muffled them as though he were speaking through a pillow. *"Eufrates!"*

Despite how she looked, desperate to ask more questions, Tigris let him continue.

"I told you about him, did I not? How he was not himself. How he became insensible. How he was *paranoid.* Diseases of the *mind.* He *wasn't* himself. Perhaps if I had not been so absorbed with being a *good* grand mage, a *proper* young prodigy, I would have taken a moment to look beyond my own selfish little nose and into the pattern and *seen* the entanglement. *Seen* the threads suffocating him."

Cyril thought of Eufrates. Young, grieving, struggling to understand the power that had been burdened upon him. He himself could not help, so self-absorbed was he in living up to a legacy, but *Atticus* – oh, Atticus Wulfsbane was a perfect mentor. A friendly face, a brother-in-law to replace the sister he had tragically lost.

Atticus, the master enchanter, had had free access to his tender, golden-hearted husband for *decades*.

And he had *ruined* him.

Cyril was having trouble breathing, or perhaps he was breathing too much, he could not decide.

"And *me*?" He let out a high, shrill laugh. "*I've* no excuse for abetting tyranny save for my own cowardice! I watched him be turned into – into a *monster*, a *ghoul* of his former self, and I sat there, and I *left him*! Tigris, I *left him* there *alone*! I had no threads of magic guiding me aside from my own blackened heart. It is no wonder I lost everything. It is no wonder I do not have a soul."

He thought of Eufrates, Eufrates, Eufrates. Eufrates struggling to grasp onto his own sanity, begging him to run away together. Eufrates with a darkened cowl that Cyril had just *assumed* was his hidden nature. Eufrates ordering an execution but flinching at the sight. Eufrates, alone, having to face the rot on his kingdom while having no idea what was causing it, thinking it just punishment for his deeds. Eufrates *here, now*, transported all the way back to the beginning and being forced by his own husband to live through the torment all over again.

He had tried, had he not? To reach out. He had asked Cyril, so many times, what he was doing. When he pulled him close, when he clawed and grasped at him. He had asked about Tigris. *He* had been the one to first suggest preventing her death.

Cyril felt the hot tears burn his eyes and dry on his cheeks against the rush of cold air. His shoulders shook and he sobbed, sobbed so loud he was sure any moment a creature from deep in the woods they were traversing would find him and tear out his guts with its teeth. If he were not so concerned about Tigris and the horse, he would seek the beast out himself.

It was a wonder he managed to stay upright on the mount.

Tigris watched him. She did not say a word. She did not reach to him with a paw, or touch her soft head to his chest, or do anything that would comfort him. She just *watched*. Cyril was eternally grateful. He did not deserve comfort. He did not deserve kindness. He had let her brother be driven to madness, and he should hang for it.

"Cyril..." she said, finally, after his sobs had calmed down into a quiet weeping, the salt of the tears crusting over his face and lashes and blotting his vision.

He nodded towards her, to indicate he was listening.

"If he... was under Atticus's control where you are from. Is it still happening now?"

Cyril shook his head. His voice came out cracked and hoarse. "I do not think so..."

"Then why...?"

"Tigris, if you had been poisoned for a score of your life, what do you think would happen?"

Tigris sniffed. *"I would develop an immunity to it."*

He did not think it possible, not for the rest of his life, but the small huff of a chuckle escaped his lips. How very like her.

"What about your brother?"

"...He would–" Her face fell in realisation. *"He would internalize it."*

He grimaced. "Just so."

She was quiet for a moment, then said with great urgency, *"We have to go to him!"*

"Yes."

"I am serious, Cyril, we have to–" She paused. *"Yes?"*

"Yes, Tigris. He needs to know."

Cyril yanked on the reins and urged the horse to ride faster, breakneck along the beaten path that led back to Farsala. The wind against his face turned from a cool gust to a constant sting. He had not dressed for travel, so his hands burned red, and his ears hurt so badly he wanted to slice them off.

No matter what, he would make it to Eufrates. He would find him and tell him everything. He would not beg forgiveness; he would only await judgement.

Cyril thought about the letter. He had memorised every line.

His husband had made him a promise.

They made it there with the sun cresting over a copse of pine to the west. It wouldn't be long until nightfall, when the palace would be engulfed in darkness.

If he were smart, he would wait until then to make his entrance. Under cover of shadows, like the rat he was. But, as had been already made abundantly clear, Cyril was *very* stupid.

It was decided they would scale up the window to Eufrates's chambers. They left Titania tied to a tree in a grove just outside the palace and Cyril cast a spell upon them that rendered them sight unseen, invisible to the eye unless one knew what they were looking for. This is how they arrived at the wall to the east wing, underneath the regent's lofty windows.

He let Tigris climb onto his back, digging her claws into his shoulders to get a good hold on him without a word of complaint. After dropping the first spell, he wove another to make them light as air, gliding up the rocky side of the wall with ease. It was the only way Cyril would ever be able to perform such a feat.

He reached the balcony outside the room, balancing precariously on the railing before he jumped down from it on silent, slippered feet – again, he had not dressed for travel – and he hesitated at the glass door.

It was one thing to be committed to doing something that would most certainly break your heart. It was another entirely to actually follow through with it. He needed a moment to brace himself, to breathe. He wiped the salty rheum from his eyes and slapped his cheeks for courage. The curtains were drawn, so he could not see inside, but the door was unlocked.

Slowly, he pushed in.

It was like looking into a crime scene.

The crime was suicide.

EIGHTEEN

Eufrates was not in his bedroom, but he had left a mark, indelible and clear.

The room had been trashed, turned upside-down and inside-out. Cyril did not think Eufrates, the man, was dead, but he had committed a sort of self-inflicted brutalisation upon Eufrates the bard prince.

Books of poetry and prose, some of them favourite works, but the overwhelming majority original compositions, were torn and shredded beyond recognition. Pots of ink had been spilled onto years of careful work without a thought to their value. Some looked to have been stomped on. There were broken quills on the ground and a nauseating smell of burning paper still lingered in the air.

His instruments, for Eufrates had many, did not escape a similar fate. A lute he had seen weeks earlier, looking ready for a serenade, lay broken in half, strings snapped askew across the bed. The harp Cyril had loved so much, because he could sit and watch for hours as Eufrates's calloused hands danced across the strings, so similar to magic he thought himself enchanted, was beaten beyond repair. There was a sword wrenched into a viol. Everything that could even remind someone of art was destroyed, in a frenzied, mad, hateful tirade.

Scattered throughout the hardwood, glittering pieces of a broken full-length mirror dotted where they walked, a few crusted in the deep maroon of dried blood.

There had been portraits hung about the room, decorating the walls. Every single one of them depicting some moment of companionship, or a cherished family member or friend. Every single one of them was smashed on the floor, the split wooden frames littered at their feet. The one exception was a painting of Eufrates himself, small and unobtrusive. A gift for his eighteenth year from a generous artist. That one had been slashed through with a knife, carved as though a cursed object.

Eufrates owned a single cameo of Cyril. Yes, of course, they had posed for portraits together, as he was a dear friend of the family, but Cyril had very few likenesses of himself alone. Eufrates had needed to beg him to sit for a proper portrait, and, unbeknownst to Cyril for some years, he had kept the small, palm-sized artists' sketch that preluded the full work for himself, in a pocket-frame protected by glass. Cyril knew he kept it in his writing desk, because that is where he had found it the first time and confronted him about it, impish and teasing. He walked over and opened the first-left drawer.

Perhaps Eufrates had just forgotten about it.

The cameo was intact.

"He is not well." Tigris broke the silence after some time perusing the carnage. Cyril thought this a bit of an obvious observation, but it would help no one to point it out.

"Where is he now?" she continued when he didn't respond.

"I don't know. He's your brother."

"He's your husband."

He realised she was right.

Eufrates had never wished to meld his kingship with his personal pursuits. It depressed him, doing state work and looking through accounts in his own quarters. In their first life together, he had found a room in one of the spires of the palace, reserved for guests but generally deemed too draughty and uncomfortable, that he had set up as a private study.

Without a word, Cyril crossed the room and made for the door. It had been locked. Sealed off, which was not a surprise. He artlessly broke into the pattern of the lock and pulled it apart, causing the doorknob to split in twain on each side of the door.

"Let's go," he said to Tigris.

It turned out that the entirety of the east wing had been sealed off, warded against anyone coming in and seeing their new regent's true nature. It made navigating the area quite easy, but Eufrates's study was *not* in the east wing.

He did not know he had the kind of confidence it took to stride into a corridor and completely disregard anyone in it until he did that self-same thing, marching through the palace with single-minded purpose, even as servants and staff tried to call out to him or stop him outright. He did not hurt anyone, he would not dare, but he was powerful enough to keep them at bay.

He only truly met a worthy obstacle in front of the very doors that led up to the spire.

Tomás was one of the younger members of the royal guard who was training to be knighted. He was only a centimetre taller than Cyril, which amused the both of them to no end, and Cyril got along with him fine, as Tomás had been one of the few guards to be somewhat learned in things other than combat drills. He liked Tomás.

Currently, Tomás was the thorn ripping open his side.

"Let me through, please," he said curtly.

Tomás was looking at him very wide-eyed. Like he was seeing a ghost.

"Young Master Cyril!" he gasped, then steeled his expression. He had a lance held in both hands that he had at a diagonal to prevent passage. "You are... you are not welcome within these walls."

"I am here to speak to Eufrates."

"He does not wish to–"

"I did not ask you what he wishes."

Tomás, with his great big lance, started to push Cyril back. Cyril humoured this, but his temper was boiling over. He did not *like* using magic on *people*.

"Master Cyril, I do not know how you got here, but you cannot – I have orders to apprehend you."

"Not before I see him."

"That's not how it works, sir. I'm trying to help, I don't want to have to – you know."

"Let me *through*, Tomás." His volume rose.

"I can't!"

"I am *going* to speak to him. I demand it." Cyril balled his hands into fists at his side and tried to move past him. "Arrest me later."

Tomás grabbed his arm. "I really can't let you do that. You don't have an audience or the grounds–"

He didn't think he ever spoke this loudly and this infuriated to anyone in his life. "I don't *need* an audience and my *grounds* is that he is my *husband* and I can see him whenever I *wish*."

Tomás blinked. "I – well, that's not true."

"I am the greatest wizard of my time, *boy*." Cyril twisted his arm in Tomás's easy grasp so he could break free. "You've no idea what I'm capable of."

Then, just as impatient, Tigris took over the reins and jumped directly onto the guard's face, making him spin madly out of control as Cyril stepped around him and climbed the short spiral steps of the tower leading to Eufrates's study. He did not bother to knock, or even to turn the doorknob. He blew the doors open and stomped his way inside.

"Eufrates, it's me!"

"I know," Eufrates said. "I could hear you from up here."

At his worst, Cyril had looked like an abyssal creature. Haunting, nightmarish, but withering, brittle and ugly. He had looked like a child's monster, or a deep-sea animal. A rotten corpse of a man.

Eufrates, though. Eufrates had hit rock bottom with a grace granted only to the very blessed. He stood at a writing desk, palms spread atop it as if he'd just risen from his seat, and, even bathed in the red light of dusk, seeing the whole of him took Cyril's breath away.

He was dishevelled, unkempt, frayed at the edges. There was a frenzy in his eyes, but he looked like a fallen, vengeful god. His face was still perfect (nothing would ever change that). The aquiline line of his nose, the high, noble cheekbones, the rich skin. Even marred by a darkness under his eyes, an unshaved jaw (Cyril guessed he had not bothered with it since the night they last spoke), unruly hair, he still stunned. There was a preternatural allure to Eufrates, even like this, that made him devastating to look at. That made Cyril's heart stop as though Eufrates himself had reached out and grabbed it. Inhuman, but not a *creature*. A *deity*. He would always be superior to Atticus. Perhaps to *any* mage, because he did not need any magic to enchant.

It was hardly fair.

"Did you read my letter, Cyril? Or did you see who it was from and burn it, coward that you are."

"I…" He had so many things to say. He did not know where to start but now, seeing Eufrates again, like this, he was completely speechless. He could not imagine how much suffering he had put him through.

"Perhaps I am right." Eufrates rounded the desk until he was in front of it, and now they were face to face, a single room apart. He was not in full armour, but he was dressed as though, if there was a battle, he would win. There was a sword at his hip. "If you had read it, you would not have returned."

"I did," Cyril blurted, his voice coming in in short bursts. "I read it. Eufrates, I–"

"Aha!" he barked. "You have come, then, to lay your head upon the block. How generous. It is not like you, my love."

"Please…"

"I will not be merciful, regardless of our shared history. Not when you have insisted on becoming my *personal* tormentor."

"Eufrates, listen–" Cyril could not get his voice loud enough. His nerve had all been wasted on that guard.

"I was happy to leave you in that *thing* you called a cottage. You decided to abandon me, burden my shoulders alone with a kingdom while you get to play the innocent, that is your choice.

"But to drag me back here, to dangle a second opportunity in front of my face and then – and then–" Eufrates carded a hand through his hair, distressing it even more. He was not often at a loss for words. "You are making me relive it. What for? Some sadistic pleasure? A *test*? Would I become the tyrant you fell out of love with all over again if I did not have you? The answer is *yes*, Cyril!"

"No!" he shouted.

Eufrates paused. Recentred himself, schooled his features. "No?" He had been looking at the floor before. At a point just over Cyril's shoulder. Now, he was looking straight at him, and it felt like being immolated with disdain.

"The answer is *no*, you have *never*–"

He unsheathed his sword. "You could not even give me *time* with my dying sister. You took her away from me! A week after you made me bury the empty caskets of my parents! Why are you doing this to me? Was I such a *terrible* husband? I am a cruel man, Cyril, but you are a demon."

"*Please*, listen to me–"

The way they advanced on each other could have been choreographed. They were pulled together, like puppets on a string. They spoke over each other. Cyril pleading, stuttering, cowering. Eufrates, angry and demanding satisfaction. Neither could make themselves be heard in the cacophony they were creating.

"There is nothing evil about you, Eufrates! You have always been *good!*"

"I don't understand what you are trying to do coming in here."

"You are the bard prince!"

"And you have made me into a tragedian."

"I – yes, but–"

"You are punishing me!"

"No!"

"You *are*. You could not kill me by that stream so now you have sworn to make me miserable. You have won!"

"I'm sorry! Eufrates, I'm so sorry–"

"Enough *tricks*. I will cut you down and I will know peace again."

"None of it was your fault."

"Shut *up!*"

"Please…"

"I *tried* to reason with you before, Cyril, I really–"

"I know."

"You just kept running away."

"I know."

"You've taken everything from me."

"I know."

"You *left* me alone!"

"I *know.*"

"Death is too good for you."

Cyril was about to repeat himself. *I know, I know, I know* over and over until Eufrates finally saw that he was well and truly ready to prostrate himself before him in penitence. He would bare his neck to the blade like a caught animal, genuflect on the chopping block, if only Eufrates would let him explain how horribly he'd ruined everything.

Before he could do this, though, he felt a sharp sting on his side, low under where his heart would have been, if he believed he was still in possession of such a thing.

He did not look down. He touched where it hurt. It felt warm and wet, sticky. He was surprised, in all his years, that he had never felt this before. It was not as bad as a broken arm, he thought, in a fit of mania.

"Cyril..." Eufrates said in a soft, incredulous voice. Oh, how he missed that voice. They had not been this close since the dance. Cyril wanted to collapse into his arms. Perhaps Tigris could tell her brother about what they had discovered. His first death had been such a disaster, he did not want to waste this second one, which seemed perfect and correct.

Eufrates did not pull the sword from his stomach, which felt fair. The quicker he bled out, the quicker he would die and that would be too merciful. His hands were shaking. One still held onto the hilt, the other was now on Cyril's waist, like he wanted to keep him upright. When Cyril looked up, he saw that his husband looked horrified.

Cyril's brow knit together. But, of course, his true, noble husband would feel no joy from a murder, not even of a creature such as he. He needed to tell him it was alright.

He tried to speak again, but a bubble of thick bloody phlegm swelled inside his throat, and he choked and coughed an orchid of red all over Eufrates's cuirass. Eufrates flinched as if stung. He was right to. That was disgusting. And Cyril had cheapened the bronze.

"You– you are right," he finally managed. "You have been right all along. I am a flighty, empty-headed fool. And I am sorry. Eufrates, I am so sorry."

"Do not speak," Eufrates said in a very strained voice.

"No, please. I would like your ear once more, as I used to have. You have never been cruel. You are not a tyrant. If I had been able to see it, I would not have gotten you into such a horrible mess. Tig – Tigris, she will... she will explain everything to you–"

"*Tigris?*"

"Shh. Yes, ask Tantie and she will make it so – so you can speak to her. Eufrates, I should not have stolen her away from you." He tasted another wave of copper on his tongue. This time, he forced himself to swallow it back in, choked as a sob, so it would not tarnish Eufrates again.

"Do *not* speak," he said louder, more commanding.

"Let me *finish*. You will not forgive me, but I am sorry." Eufrates's hand was on his back now, cradling him. Cyril ventured to bring his own palms, bloodied as they were, up to Eufrates's chest. Like this, from a distance, they were lovers again.

"You are not making sense." There was a tense, pleading note to Eufrates's tone that Cyril didn't understand.

"I am sorry. Ah – I've said that. How can I say it more? Perhaps you should have stabbed somewhere less fatal. Made it last."

"It is not fatal!" Pleading turned to a strange, desperate anger, but it did not seem directed at him. Eufrates was trembling. "Cyril, I had not meant to–"

Cyril smiled and reached up to stroke through Eufrates's hair. "I know. But for what it's worth, I would not have had it any other way."

"Stop it! Stop *talking*! Shut up!" The hand that was on the sword finally let go of it to palm at the wound, as though a stopgap. "Gods, you have always been so *dramatic*!"

When he bucked forward to laugh – a huff of air that instantly turned into another cough – his head collapsed with Eufrates's shoulder. Perhaps he was right. It was time to shut up. He felt pathetic like this, making Eufrates worry over killing him when it was all he had wanted but an hour ago. He closed his eyes and breathed deep in through his nose, inhaling as much of his scent as he could.

Then, because he could not possibly have a peaceful, quiet death, he felt a scorching in his chest, an overwhelming heat that threatened to engulf him spread all the way to the wound like a cauterizing fire.

Cyril gritted his teeth and bore it. He only opened his eyes when he heard Eufrates scream.

There was a pained expression on his face, scrunched tight and sweat beading on his handsome brow. He gasped and pushed Cyril away as they both collapsed to the floor in front of each other.

Cyril was used to this feeling of being burned alive, so he took it better than Eufrates, who shuddered on the floor, convulsing with his arms over his stomach as though he himself had been stabbed. He wanted to reach out to him, but any movement made him feel faint and dizzy.

As though he were experiencing it second-hand, he vaguely noticed the sword plunged into his side was sliding out of him, still slick with blood. He blinked a few times, and when the pain, the heat subsided, he looked down at the wound.

It was not gone, but it had transformed. Cyril lifted up his shirt to show a soft, toneless midriff and, near his ribs, a flash of deep, white scar tissue, starbursting out of him.

He looked up and noticed Eufrates was looking at the scar too. Eufrates opened his mouth to speak, then closed it again, stunning himself back to silence.

Just then, a cat padded in, claws clicking against neat flooring. Cyril turned to look at her, then pointed.

"Oh. There is Tigris," he said to Eufrates.

Then, he collapsed.

NINETEEN

Cyril found out later that he slept for a mere hour. After all, it was not as though he had any wounds to render him bedbound. The shock of the day had just triggered a fainting spell, which mortified him no end.

In that hour, he had been transported from the study all the way back to his chambers in the tower, and his blood-soaked clothes had been traded for a clean nightshirt. When he woke up and looked to his left, he also found a fresh outfit he'd be able to change into when he was ready.

To his right was Eufrates, sitting on a chair, arms folded over his chest, watching him with a furrowed brow. He had not shaved – thank the gods – but he did seem to have washed his face and donned lighter clothes.

"I am alive," Cyril said, stupidly.

Eufrates did not humour him. "Tigris told me everything. About Atticus and the enchanting business and the plot for her murder. She did a much better job than you, considering you have been parading her around as your pet and do not even let her speak."

Ah.

This was how things were to be, then. Of course, Eufrates was angry at him. Maybe even furious. He had prepared for his own death and maybe, in a delusional corner of his brain, he had prepared for a reconciliation, but he had not prepared to live in the same world as him and be nothing more than embittered strangers.

It frosted his heart over.

"You managed to speak to her," he said conversationally and sat up on the bed.

"Auntie allowed us to communicate."

"I am glad."

Cyril undid the better part of the buttons of his nightshirt while Eufrates pretended to look around the room at his hoard of baubles. He stopped when he reached the new scar. He touched it and it felt rugged and strange, but not painful.

"I have never had a scar."

Eufrates scoffed under his breath.

"Did Tantie look at this?"

"Yes. She says it's your curse." He paused. "Well. *Our* curse."

Cyril tilted his head. "What made her say that?"

In way of answer, Eufrates tugged the hem of his undershirt up. He *did* have a few scars. He had been accident-prone as a youth, and he was much more physical than Cyril. Cyril thought he knew every mark on his body, but there was a new one.

A starburst, faded as if it had always been there, on his side under his heart.

Cyril's eyes widened and his hand flew to the ring. "I'm sorry..."

"Save it. I knew there was risk in trying to kill you, but I stabbed you anyway."

"You said you hadn't meant to–"

"I lied," Eufrates said. "I thought I was doing a kindness to a dying old man."

"Oh."

They were quiet for a moment. Cyril fiddled with the edge of his comforter, twisting it and tying it up in knots in his fingers. Finally, because he could not stand it anymore, he spoke.

"Where is Tig?"

"Upstairs. She is trying to convince Auntie to change her back."

Cyril let out a breath through his nose. "She cannot. Only I can release her."

"And will you?"

"With that madman of a king on the loose? Over my dead body."

"Of course. You always know best for everyone."

"What does *that* mean?"

"Nothing."

Cyril yanked the comforter off himself and stood up, steadying his legs as he paced around the room. The first thing he did was grab the clothes that had been laid out for him.

"I am going to get dressed. You can stay and watch if you'd like."

He did not have Eufrates's heart, but he still knew it well and he knew the man's chivalry would make him leave the room as if in a cursed catacomb.

Just as he thought, Eufrates also got to his feet and tucked his shirt back into his trousers. Once he made it to the doorway, he said, "I will be with my sister."

Cyril should not have dawdled while getting ready. Not when there was so much looming over all their heads, but he needed a moment to himself where he *wasn't* completely unconscious.

He sat at his vanity once he was fully dressed and began working on his paints, elongating his lashes and rouging his cheeks. It was a calming ritual for him, and it helped him think.

Eufrates hated him. That was nothing new. The only thing that changed was now he was being despised for exactly the right reasons. Cyril pulled the ring from its hanging place again, examining it carefully for the first time in weeks. He could barely comprehend how so much magic was able to fit into such a tiny circlet of gold. It had spared him twice by now, saved his life in its own horrible, immolating way. He could no longer call it a curse. Selfishly, he did not truly want it removed anymore.

But he would. He would find a way. Because *Eufrates* had called it a curse. *Their* curse. He had spat the words, as though the fact that it bound them together was worse than any physical pain it caused.

Cyril was going to dispel it even if it meant going into the pattern and tearing it apart, severing the strings with his bare hands like a clumsy fledgling of a mage. Cutting up a pattern was disastrous – the damage could be as little as a spark in the earthly atmosphere or a horrible explosion – but it seemed worth it to finally be rid of their link.

He looked into the mirror and saw himself again. It had been a week since he had been given drab, earth-coloured clothes and essentially told to blend in as seamlessly as possible with the Cretian court. He did not *hate* how he looked now, dressed down like this, but there was a wrongness to it. He was a clown. A little harlequin tasked with serving Farsala's higher power. The paints and the costuming spoke of tradition. He was going to perform his duties whether he was wanted or not.

Once he was finished, he climbed up the steps of the tower. He had expected all three of them – Tigris, Eufrates and Heléne – to be in the same room, at the very top. However, he found the Margraves alone in the kitchen floor, sharing a platter of preserves, sweetmeats and a jug of what looked like wine someone had scavenged from somewhere within.

"Cy!" Tigris's head shot up when she saw him. *"I am so glad you are alright! Please, come sit!"*

Cyril looked from her to Eufrates, who was pointedly not looking at him at all.

"I am sorry I kept Tigris from you."

He snapped his head up and scowled deeply.

"I am sick to death of your apologies, Cyril. Sit down."

This really was how it would be between them, then. That was fine. It was no less than what he deserved. Now he'd had a moment to think about it, he decided he would not let the barbs make it under his skin, no matter how much they tore at the dermis.

Cyril sat across from Eufrates and took a sweetmeat from the platter. He was starving, now that he thought about it.

"Where is Tantie?" he asked.

"Upstairs."

"She said she was working on something and did not have time to watch us argue."

"Is Shoestring truly dead?" Eufrates asked.

Cyril blinked. He had not expected that.

"Yes," he said.

"A shame. He was the only good part of you."

Ouch.

Cyril turned to Tigris. "So what have you been arguing about?"

"Strategy."

"'Storming into Cretea and laying waste to its sovereign isn't a *strategy*, Tigris. It is barely an *idea*."

"It's better than what you've come up with which is, um, absolutely nothing."

"No plan is better than a bad plan!"

"Gods, I can't believe they ever let you be king."

He did not realise how much he missed seeing them together like this until it was right in front of him. He could not believe he had kept them apart so long.

"I take it." Cyril cleared his throat. "You've not been planning for *long*."

"No. I had to pick Eufie's melancholy arse off the floor and explain everything to him because you *fainted."*

"What is... everything?" he asked with a touch of embarrassment.

"I mean, I'm not a genius with magic, but I think I did alright. He knows he was being enchanted, he knows about the poison. He knows Atticus should die, essentially. I told him while Auntie was taking care of you."

"Wait, Tantie doesn't know?"

"She didn't question it when Eufie carried you over to the tower."

Eufrates stiffened and focused on a spot of dirt on the wood of the table.

"Oh, we should *tell her, though, right? See if she's got any insight."*

Cyril cringed. "Ohh... no, I don't think so."

"What? Why not?"

He made himself very small in his chair. "...She will be very cross with me."

Eufrates scoffed, finally speaking up. "I cannot believe I was so besotted by you."

The morsel he had been chewing suddenly tasted like chalk. He swallowed it down anyway. A spark of irritation pulsed in his blood. Eufrates was allowed to hate him, but he was not allowed to be unproductive when it was his sister's life on the line.

Cyril steepled his fingers and smiled, saccharine. "You were taken by my ingenue charm. That's not on me."

Eufrates flinched, but scowled deeply at him. "It has taken you *decades* to become self-aware. You should get stabbed more often."

"Boys, please!" Tigris chided them in the same tone she used when they had all been children, but she had been, ostensibly, the *oldest* child. *"Are there any other reasons not to tell Auntie other than that you fear being lectured?"*

"She will not *lecture* me, Tig, she will hang me by my ear–" He quickly silenced himself when he saw her unamused stare. "No. There are none."

"Good. Then we call her down."

He poured himself a glass of the wine.

Cyril was wrong. Heléne had not come for his ears. Instead, when she heard the whole, sordid story, the first thing she did was smack him across the head so hard he felt his brain rattling in his skull. Even Tigris and Eufrates flinched.

"You did not look at the pattern?" she said, sounding beside herself. "You let another wizard play you for a fool for over twenty years because you did not bother to *look into the pattern*?!"

"Tantie!" he whined and rubbed the sore spot on the side of his head. "I – I couldn't!"

"Why on earth not, child?"

"It's in the rules! It is – it's the fifth rule of magic. Do not look into another mage's pattern unless you are given permission."

"Where did you learn something like that?"

"The – the Academy! They drill all the rules into you, do you want to hear the others–"

"No, I don't want to hear the *others*. They are sure to be just as asinine!"

Heléne massaged her temples, staving off an oncoming migraine. She looked like she might try and stab Cyril herself if he let his guard down.

"I thought sending you to that school would help you make *friends*, not scramble your brains to mush. I should have never let you leave here."

"If it helps, I did not make that many friends."

"Cyril, I don't think it helps," Tigris chimed from her corner of the table, where she sat at a very healthy distance from Heléne.

"The first opportunity I get, I will march over there myself and ohh, I will give that headmistress of yours an earful. The entire staff will hear."

Cyril blanched. "Oh, please don't do that, Tantie. I am a grown man."

"Who thinks like an obedient *child*! Always check the *pattern*, Cyril. How do you think I lived this long?"

"But – but then why would it be in the *rules*?!"

"It is propriety *nonsense*. They are training you for court politics, not real danger. You will not have the luxury as grand mage."

"I just think it *is* quite rude – oh, gods, Tantie, please not the face –"

"Anyway." Eufrates sat up in his chair and smacked a hand on the table to distract Heléne's attention away from her ward, who she was about to hit again, harder, just to make sure he understood the lecture. "Now we know Atticus is a wizard. What do we do about it?"

"An enchanter," Cyril added in a small voice, because it did matter.

Heléne considered this. Her eyes looked stern and pensive through the round spectacles balanced on her nose.

"The way you'd defeat any other wizard, I suppose," she finally said. "You kill him."

All three of them stared at her. Cyril openly gaped. This was the smartest and wisest person they knew. The one remnant of the old guard. He had, perhaps, expected something a bit more elaborate.

"*I'll drink to that,*" said Tigris. And she did. It was actually quite funny to see a cat lapping at a goblet of wine.

"What? No. Tantie, you cannot be serious." Cyril turned from Tigris to look at Heléne.

"Why not? Wizards are just mortal men. *Enchanters,* especially. They are lily-livered milksops. I've not met a single enchanter who I couldn't take in a fight, and I have arthritis. He is not trained in any combat magic. He cannot wield the elements or the physical world. What will he do? Whisper at you to stop?"

"*He is trained in actual combat, if you all must know,*" said Tigris.

"Of course he is!" said Eufrates. "He's a king, he would not be able to leave the house without knowing how to swing a sword."

"You're all afraid of swords now?" Heléne raised a brow at the Margraves.

"*I didn't say that.*" Tigris sniffed.

"The *swords* are not the problem, Tantie." Cyril downed a swig of his wine. He did not think having allies would make things *more* cumbersome. "He is an enchanter, he has cultivated his weave for years. I am sure he will have powerful mages under his control."

Heléne made a disgusted face. "Eugh. I did always hate those slimy little vermin. Enchanting should be banned."

"Very helpful," Cyril drawled, and helped himself to more libation.

"Well, do you have any idea what his pattern is like *this* time?"

"Yes." He nodded. "I saw it."

"Oh, well, good. Destroy it."

Cyril very nearly choked. "Tantie, you did not see how big it was! It would take hours to untangle, and I don't believe I'd have that kind of leisure."

"I did not say to *untangle* it, boy." She made a scissoring gesture with her fore and middle finger. "Destroy it. There is your problem solved."

"It was – it was the size of a *ballroom*. I have no idea what it would–"

Eufrates cleared his throat. He was on his second glass of wine, and he looked from Heléne to Cyril.

"Would anyone do the kindness of enlightening us unlearned masses?" He pointed at himself and at his sister. "We *are* the royal family, after all."

"Your lover is being a coward," Heléne said.

Eufrates said they were not lovers at the same time as Cyril exclaimed he was not being a coward.

"Both of you are terrible liars."

"I too could use an explanation. What happens when you destroy a pattern?" Tigris interjected.

"We don't know. No one knows until it happens. It is why it's such a *foolhardy* –" Cyril shot his aunt a sour look "– idea. It restructures the very material plane. It could cause an explosion. An avalanche. A torrent. It could rupture the earth itself."

"Oh, yes, I am very worried about preserving the beauty of Cretea's royal palace." Heléne looked ready to hit him again.

"*We* would be in the palace."

"It's worth it," Tigris said. *"It is, isn't it, Auntie? You wouldn't suggest it otherwise."*

The witch's expression softened. "It is not 'worth it', child. It is the only way. You would be outnumbered if you allowed the pattern to continue to fester."

"Right, because... he has all those mages."

"Yes. You want to get to his core? You will need to destroy his advantages."

Tigris nodded. *"Cyril, can you destroy the pattern?"*

Cyril huffed. "Anyone who can see a pattern can *destroy* it. It is an artless thing to do. You just..." He mimed tearing through an invisible web with his fingers. "Do it."

Heléne finally smacked him again. It was at least a lighter hand this time. Warning. "I did not teach you to be *smug* about magic, boy."

"You are being so horrible to me today!" he moaned.

"We've got a plan, though! We go in there, mess up his... pattern, or whatever it is, then we take Atticus to task while he is powerless."

Eufrates had his hands pressed against his forehead. He groaned. "Again, Tig, that is not a *plan*."

"What?"

"A plan should not have that many holes. What you've come up with is not a chart, it's a *net*."

"Oh, you've become quite comfortable on the throne, haven't you, brother?"

"I am nearly twice your age. I have acquired some experience."

"On what?" She laughed. *"Being suckered?"*

"I am trying to *tell you* that I have been 'suckered' enough to know we are running right into his waiting trap."

"Then explain it to me properly."

Eufrates looked at her exasperated, "We have no grounds to attack him! Before, I at least had a *hint* of an excuse, but Cyril is back in Farsala, so now I am just power hungry. And that is fine with me, but I will not let it be our entire *kingdom's* legacy. Not when you are to rule."

"Is his plot to kill me not reason enough for you, Eufie?"

"It would be the *perfect* reason if *someone* had not burned down the *evidence*." Eufrates glared directly through Cyril, piercing him yet again.

Cyril raised his hands up in surrender. "I panicked!"

"What about how he mind-controlled you?"

"As much as I would love to pin that on him, it was in another lifetime entirely."

"And you do not think he is the perpetrator of other crimes?"

"It is not our right to punish him for it. It is Cretea's and anyone else he has harmed."

"You just keep shooting things down! Why don't you try coming up with something, then, old man?"

Out of the corner of his eye, Cyril saw his aunt balk at the insult. He poured her her own glass of wine. They would be here a while, it seemed.

"Tig, I'm not trying to be contrary–"

"The hell you're not! You've been insufferable since we got here. You are sullen and mean-spirited."

Eufrates ran a hand through his hair. "I am sorry to disappoint, Tig. I don't know what you expected."

"I expected my brother!"

"I *am* your brother. You are mad at me because I am no longer entertaining your ridiculous ideas! Tigris, you are in *danger*."

"He's right, Tig," Cyril said.

"And *you*–" Eufrates turned to him with so much rancour in his eyes Cyril thought *he* might have a go at slapping him too. "We would not be embroiled in this mess were it not for you. So, I suggest you grow a *spine* for once in your life and take your aunt's advice. She is clearly the better mage."

"Aha!" Cyril sat up in his chair. "And *you* have offered so much help and insight!"

"My *insight* is that you should never think or have ideas again for the rest of your days."

"Fine! I will sit here and drink my wine, and you will perform for us the tale of how you are going to protect your sister and save the kingdom from ruin."

"He's not going to do any of that because he's never had a strategic thought since birth. Did you know he copied off me for government essays?" Tigris interjected.

Cyril's brows shot up. *"Really?"*

"Enough!"

All three of them ceased their bickering to look at Heléne, who was fuming. It could not be good for her frail old heart, feeling emotions this strong.

She jabbed a finger at the Margraves. "I did not sit for over thirty years through your *parents'* political squabbles over cold food and too much alcohol to have to do it again *now*, at my advanced age, with the three of you halfwits. I have given my insight on the wizard. I do not have any thoughts on the *king*.

"I am not a lover of government. I barely know the names of any of your courtiers. It is getting late. I will retire to my chambers. Send for me *only* if someone else gets run through."

With that, Heléne ascended the stairs to her tower and left the three halfwits alone to discuss among themselves. Cyril was first to break the silence.

"Has she seemed more reclusive to you?"

He expected Tigris to say something, but the answer came from Eufrates, who had temporarily dulled his tongue.

"I thought the same. She has barely left the tower. I did not know what to make of it." He paused. "Honestly, I did not know what to do other than let her be."

"I... I thought I'd saved her, somehow. That this time around I wouldn't find her body in a year's time."

Eufrates scoffed, but it did not have the sting of its predecessors. "Optimism. How very unlike you."

"You do not need to be so–"

"Oh."

Both their heads snapped to Tigris, who sounded as though she'd just uncovered the secrets of the universe. After Heléne left, she had been sitting in an uncharacteristically contemplative silence, brow furrowed so hard it might put wrinkles on a cat's face.

"I have thought of something," she said.

Eufrates looked unamused, but Cyril knew better by now. Every time Tigris had some sort of epiphany it ended up being something so brilliant he wished he'd thought of it himself. She had saved him from his own meandering, frayed mind so many times already.

"What is it?" he pressed.

She turned to Eufrates. *"You say Atticus has not committed any crimes against us. You are wrong."*

"Again, Tigris, attempted murder will not be enough–"

"No, Eufie!" Now that the euphoria of discovery was fading, she suddenly looked very troubled and a little enraged. *"Our parents!"*

Eufrates looked at her like she had lost a screw during their discussion. He leaned in and spoke in a softer voice.

"Tig... our parents died at sea."

"So? I died of a wasting disease.*"*

Cyril swallowed convulsively. "Tigris, what are you trying to say?"

"Cyril!" She turned to him with a fierce determination. *"Can mages control the weather?"*

"I – some specialists yes, quite easily."

"Rain?"

"Sure."

"Storms?"

"Oh, certainly."

"Eufie." It was Eufrates's turn to be scrutinized. *"What were you doing the day of their death?"*

"Gods, Tig, that was decades ago."

She tilted her head at him. *"You've forgotten?"*

"…No. I was… I had been hunting for a couple days with some friends. We were in pursuit of a beast one of them swore up and down to have seen in the woods. I did not even see them off when they boarded the ship."

"And what did you find at the end of your hunt?"

Eufrates did not get a chance to answer because Cyril did it for him, after he picked his jaw off the floor.

"A hare."

Tigris nodded. *"But just to be sure. What colour was it, Eufie?"*

"I… it was tan. Does it matter?"

Tigris's brain was working so fast it did not have time to answer. Cyril could see the gears turning behind her wide eyes.

"As for me, I had tired of Cretian delights about a week before I actually returned home. But my darling fiancé insisted I stay a while longer."

"…Tig." He was about to say something, but it looked as though she desperately wanted to continue.

"When we were in his room in this very palace, he had some peculiar almanacs, recording weather patterns from a month or so ago. In the library, I found a chart of the seas between Farsala and the ship's final destination."

Eufrates finally interjected, "I do not know what you are implying, but Mamã and Papa were not *alone* on that voyage. They had courtiers with them. They had *Cretian* courtiers. They had offered to share the journey. Would Atticus just sacrifice his own retinue?"

"Yes," Cyril answered immediately.

"Definitely."

"This is all conjecture, though," Eufrates said.

Tigris frowned. *"What is the matter with you? Are you defending him?"*

"No – no!"

"Cy did say you two got quite close, but he is evil, *Eufie."*

"I know that!"

"He had our family murdered!"

"That I do not know."

"What?"

"You've no proof."

"What?" she repeated, completely incredulous.

Cyril saw the tremor in Eufrates's hands. He looked like he was about to burst, to disappear in a cloud of smoke. Against better judgement, he began to reach out to touch his arm, but Eufrates exploded before he could make contact.

"It cannot be that simple, because then I am the one who failed to prevent it!" he roared.

Tigris blinked. *"We both failed to prevent it."*

"No! You were *abroad*. I was camping in the woods on a *leisure hunt.*"

"You could not have known about the storm," Cyril said softly.

"Shut *up*!"

Cyril flinched. There was a smoked ring of violet around Eufrates's eyes that made him seem haunted. He looked at Cyril like a wild animal, caught and lashing out.

Cyril struck him across the face.

"Get a *hold* of yourself," he hissed.

It could not possibly have hurt that badly. Cyril had air and magic where muscle should be. But by the look Eufrates gave him, you would have thought he had been hit with a mallet.

It did not deter Cyril one bit.

"You *cannot* blame yourself for a murder plot on *open sea*. That is *insensible*. And if you are responsible for it, I am even worse because as I have been told multiple times already, I should have just *checked the pattern*. In fact, I should have set a specific date to when I sent myself back in time and made it specifically *before* their death, should I not? But instead, I left it to fate, I made you bury them again and now I will go to my own grave knowing that blood was not a freakish accident. It is on my hands."

"Cyril–" He knew exactly what Tigris was going to say and he did not let her. He would drown her out with his own words.

"I am the mastermind of all your tragedies. I am perhaps the worst thing that's ever happened to the Margraves, but there is one left that I will *not* let die on my watch." He pointed at Tigris. "So I could play this blame game with you all night, *darling*, and I would win every time, but I have more important things to do."

He was breathless when he finished. Red-faced with frustration. A pregnant pause hung over the kitchen for what felt like hours before Tigris stood on her four legs and hopped off the table.

"Auntie was right," she said. *"It is getting late, and we are getting nowhere. I am going to sleep."*

She left the kitchen without another word, heading downstairs to Cyril's bedroom.

Cyril raked a hand over his hair. "She is right. It's best to continue this in the morning. At the very least we know what we are to do."

He was talking more for his own benefit than Eufrates's, who was still looking into the middle-distance with a stunned expression. Cyril got up and busied himself with putting away the platter of food and the wine and, much to his surprise, Eufrates followed suit.

Something occurred to Cyril.

"Where have you been sleeping?"

His rooms were destroyed. The entire east wing was sealed off.

Eufrates finally turned to him with those dark, red-rimmed eyes.

"I have not."

"Ah." It took Cyril a while to figure out how to respond to this. He could not show he cared overmuch, or Eufrates would just say something to tear at his heart. "Well. You should take my bed. You will have to share with Tig, but it is big enough. I will sleep on the sofa outside the bedroom."

"I don't need you to–"

"Your chivalry is wasted on me, Eufrates." He took an emptied glass of wine from him into his own stack he had been collecting and suddenly they were very close. Cyril held his breath. "I'm sure you would agree."

Eufrates grimaced. "You think me very weak."

Cyril didn't answer. It was a trap, set to careen them back into an argument and he was too tired to indulge. Instead, against better judgement, he reached up with his free hand to hover it over Eufrates's cheek.

"I did not hit you too hard, did I?"

Eufrates let out a huff through his nose. "It was an open-handed strike. I barely felt it."

"Good. It means I can hit harder next time."

He started to withdraw his hand, but Eufrates suddenly closed a fist around his wrist to hold it there. Cyril's heart began to beat so loud he was sure even Tigris could hear.

Eufrates encroached on him like a hunter on prey, nearly closing the distance between them. Heat pooled in his stomach from the proximity. His insides were on fire again, but this time it had nothing to do with the rings or any spell.

They stared at each other, unblinking, for an eternity. Eufrates opened his mouth to speak, but, seeming to think better of it, closed it and finally withdrew from Cyril, giving him leave of his senses back.

"Do not stay up too late," he said and followed in Tigris's footsteps out of the room.

Cyril had to steady himself against a chair from how jellied his knees had become. He decided he would clean up their feast in the morning. So he would not cross paths with anyone, he waited an appropriate amount of time to make his own exit and made his way to the sofa he was to sleep in, collapsing onto it like a spent, old ragdoll.

TWENTY

Though the body was willing, the mind was far from the realm of sleep. Cyril was still feeling the effects of the fainting spell and his thoughts were racing, caught on a loop. He closed his eyes and images of the pattern he would have to destroy flashed behind his eyelids, arachnid and sprawling. He could not imagine the damage it would cause.

When he kept his eyes open, laid out on the hard crook of the sofa in an inert, comatose state, it was not any better. For whatever reason, his brain began forcing him to remember his wedding day, putting him through the torture of juxtaposing a tender kiss upon an altar with how he had been run through with Eufrates's blade. He would start crying again if he thought too hard on it, so he just let the thoughts play out without dwelling on them.

He wanted his husband back, which was a request so ridiculous in its selfishness it would be hysterical to anyone else.

There was no use ruminating on it, but it felt like there was a spark of electricity bouncing off the inside of his skull. He forced himself to count sheep, begging the sandman to come take him away. He was about to crawl off of the sofa to find his trusted bottle of sleeping draught, at the early hour of five in the morning, when he heard frantic banging on his door.

Tigris was in the room before he could even muster the strength to lift himself up.

"Do you hear that?"

Cyril rubbed his eyes and finally sat up.

"Yes… yes, who could it be at this hour? Servants hardly come up to the tower."

"Open it, Cy! Might I remind you of my lack of hands."

"Alright…"

Despite not having slept a wink, his mind on high alert, his body felt groggy and out of sorts. It took him three tries to successfully unlatch the lock that kept his door shut. All the while, the banging grew louder and more desperate.

As soon as the door opened, a flushed, plump maid stumbled in so brusquely Cyril thought she might fall into his arms and topple them both over. He vaguely recognized her. Her name started with an 'L', and she had a cutesy affect that often grinded on him.

She also looked *horrible*. The stench of bile and rot lingered in the air around her and her eyes were bloodshot and sickly. She held a kerchief over her mouth and nose so tightly Cyril feared she might suffocate herself.

Before he could even ask, she blurted, "I was told His Highness the regent was staying here!" Then, her big eyes finally fell upon Cyril and she gasped, "Oh! Young Master Cyril, you are back!"

"I… yes. I should not have left."

"Focus, Cyril! Ask her what she wants!"

Cyril inched closer to provide some sort of comfort, but she snatched herself away. "Do not come any closer! Oh, I must speak to His Highness!"

"He is–"

"I'm right here."

Eufrates stood at the doorway to his room with the look of someone who had gotten dressed too quickly. The buttons on his shirt were one hole off.

"Oh, thank goodness!" she exclaimed. "Your Highness, there is a plague."

"What?"

"What?" Eufrates repeated.

"A… a *plague*! It is spreading throughout the lower floors. It began in the dungeons, I believe, but now it has spread out to the servants' quarters. It is – it is like a smog!"

Cyril blinked. "You can *see* it?"

"Yes! It is horrible! I do not even have all the symptoms!"

Cyril could see how the malaise was affecting her. She was struggling to even draw breath between words.

"It is so quick, Your Highness! A few of the older servants have died from it already."

"When did it start?" Eufrates was pale.

"I don't know! Perhaps not even an hour ago! There are not many in the underground, no one noticed it. Oh, what should we *do*?"

Eufrates looked at her like he did not know why she was asking *him*. At the same time, Tigris had gone to the window. Though dawn's first light was not optimal illumination, Cyril still saw her eyes widen at the sight.

He followed her to the parapet.

What they were looking at was a plume of miasma, spreading outwards from the centre of the palace in an acrid yellow-green cloud. It just about smacked Cyril in the face with how unsubtle it was.

From his vantage point of the bird's eye view, he spotted victims of the 'plague'. A stable hand, dead on her way to her morning duties, pockmarked by pustules and so pallid she did not look human. A gardener, heaving over his blooms and sweating profusely. A courtier on an early-morning stroll, bent over on the ground, shaking with exertion.

Cyril did not *need* to look into the pattern to know this reeked of magic, but since he had been chastised so brutally for not doing it before, he tugged on the corners of the material plane and looked.

The threads of an alchemist were all over the palace, branching out of it like worm's silk. Cyril remembered the book he had found in that library, a manual on how to sublimate an ingestible poison, transforming it into a gas. When he squinted, he could see the weave combined with some elements of transfiguration.

It hit him then that if it was this easy for Atticus Wulfsbane to conjure up a plague on such short notice, to control the elements and cause a shipwreck, he would have had more than enough resources at his disposal to send a whole kingdom, bit by agonizing bit, into dark-skied ruin. Into *rot*. He'd suspected, but the confirmation was such a relief it nearly threw him off kilter. That no matter what happened, no matter which of them survived this ordeal, if they could only deal with Atticus, at least Farsala would be spared a horrible fate.

"*He is desperate,*" Tigris said.

Cyril shook his head. "No. He's finally playing his cards. He is ruthless."

"*What? No, Cyril, he has openly attacked us! There is no way he can spin his way out of the consequences, even if we are all dead. Who will believe this to be a natural disease?*"

"He is an *enchanter*, Tig. He can spin flax into gold with a household bobbin if he wishes it.

"*Atticus has grown tired of subterfuge.*"

"Will the two of you stop debating what he will do once all of us are *dead*?" Eufrates snapped at them. He had guided the maid to a chair and was giving her water.

"*Oh, poor Larissa.*"

Larissa! That was her name. He should have known Tigris would know everything about everyone in the palace. He mourned that she never got to be queen all over again.

"Call for Tantie," Cyril told Tigris. "Wake her up. She will not be so angry if it is you."

Eufrates shot him a look like he wanted to call him a coward again, but he was busy tending to the sickly woman on his chair. A smattering of angry, red blotches had begun to mar her skin.

* * *

Heléne looked very unimpressive, having just been roused out of bed at the crack of dawn. She had not made up her face, and her hair was wrapped in a bonnet. She wore a knitted shawl around her shoulders that made her look like someone's kindly grandmother.

The way she moved, though, in such striking precision, one could have mistaken her for being half her age. She examined the maid, holding her eyes open and looking into her mouth, despite the protests that she should not be touched.

"Nonsense, child. It is not contagious. It only spreads to those who breathe in the miasma." She turned to her ward. "Cyril, did you look at this pattern?"

"Yes, ma'am," he said very quickly.

She sighed. "Better late than never, I suppose. What do you make of it?"

"I–" He felt like he was being quizzed, and there was little time for that, but then he realised Heléne truly wanted his opinion. "It is complex, but it can be unwoven, for lack of a proper antidote. If we can manage it, the disease will fade."

She hummed to herself, pensive.

"We do not have the time…"

"Tantie, if you suggest we destroy the weave again–"

"No! Do not be foolish, Duckling. It would only make things worse. We need a stopgap."

Tigris jumped up onto a vanity to make herself heard. *"What we* need *is to get to Atticus! Cut the problem off by the root!"*

"No, that will not–" Heléne shook her head.

At the same time, Cyril said, "Yes… yes! He will keep sending mages to attack us if we do not. Tigris, you are a familiar. You are immune to the poison. I can create a similar immunity for myself and Eufrates. We will ride out and confront him."

"And return to an empty, pestilent palace?" Eufrates snapped.

"No! No, it is like Tantie said... we need a stopgap. Perhaps if we *froze*..."

Heléne finished the thought for him. "Frost staves off disease. I will cast it over the grounds, and it will give me time while the three of you deal with that enchanter."

"I had expected when we marched upon his palace we would have some kind of an army."

"The barracks are on the ground floor, Tig. I don't believe we have the luxury anymore," said Cyril.

Just then, Larissa burst into a fit of coughs, culminating in her emptying whatever was left in her stomach on Cyril's nice, embroidered carpets.

The silver lining of her drawing their attention to the floor, though, is that they noticed that once more the miasma was beginning to rise. Slow and steady, to fill Cyril's living quarters.

"Alright!" he said in a panic. "We've got a semblance of a plan. Tantie, head upstairs and get started on the spell."

Heléne nodded and climbed up to the topmost level of her tower.

"Eufrates, come here."

To his credit, Eufrates did not hesitate to get close to him. He allowed Cyril to put a bubble over his head that would keep the miasma from penetrating.

"Larissa." Cyril turned to the maid. "Has the plague affected any of the animals?"

"Oh..." She struggled through her words, but she answered regardless. "No... I guess it hasn't."

Cyril nodded and wove a bubble over his own head. He could not help Larissa, but he told her to stay very still and move as little as possible. Any exertion would quicken the effects.

"Good. We will return to Titania, then."

"Titania?" Eufrates asked.

"One of Atticus's horses. She's very fast."

Eufrates frowned but did not complain any further. They moved as one down the stairs, past the sick green of the miasma and the plagued denizens of Farsala's palace.

As they were passing by all these people, Cyril noticed something. Heléne had begun her spell. He could see the white frosting the corridors and the people within them, but... it was not enough.

He grinded to a halt, skidding on his feet in front of a butler who was nearly all frozen solid, but the ice around their fingers, their face, was beginning to thaw. Cyril dropped to his haunches to feel their forehead, unconcerned with his own well-being. Their fever was climbing higher to combat the frost. Whatever this plague was, it was nasty and powerful, and he had grossly underestimated it.

Tigris stopped behind him, impatient. *"What are you doing? Let's go!"*

"It's not working." He turned back and cast a desperate look at the Margraves. "Her spell isn't working. It will not be enough."

"What?" Eufrates's tone was cautious. Like he knew what Cyril would say next and he was trying to make him not say it at all.

"I have to go up there. I need to help!"

"You will be trapped in here with everyone."

"No! No, I will not. I will find a way to get to you, I swear it."

"You want us to go on without you?"

He swallowed convulsively. "Yes."

Eufrates still tried to reason with him. "Auntie is an accomplished witch. She will figure something out."

"I am not running the risk."

"You do not trust her?" This was meant as bait. A challenge with a clear right answer. Cyril chose to disregard it.

"I trust her with my *life*, Eufrates. I love her more than any excuse for a parent I've ever had. I am going up there and I am making sure she gets through this."

Eufrates stepped closer, he grabbed Cyril's arm with a gentleness Cyril didn't think him capable of anymore. Not towards him. "Please don't do this. It is a *ridiculous* idea."

"Eufrates." Cyril schooled his features into a wry, teasing smile. "Do not make the mistake of having me believe you still care for me."

Eufrates let go of him immediately, his jaw was set into an unreadable scowl. "Fine. As you wish."

"You promise you will meet us?"

"*Yes*, Tigris, I would not let you two fight him alone. I swear it on my grave."

"That means very little."

"I swear it on *your* grave."

"Better."

As soon as she nodded, Cyril turned on his heel and sprinted back to the tower. He was out of breath by the time he reached the seventh storey, having climbed the spiral staircases leading up two steps at a time.

Heléne stood in the middle of the room, eyes screwed shut and brow furrowed in concentration. Only Ganache saw him and let out an agitated caw.

Her chambers had changed since he'd last been up here. She was clearly working on something. There were fresh notes and sketches of magic circles strewn about several surfaces. Research books piled high on her desk. He stifled his curiosity and marched his way towards her, taking her hands in his, but not disturbing her spell, instead helping her weave. Her eyes flew open, and he made sure to speak before she could raise her voice to scold him.

"It is not working, Tantie. They are thawing," he said.

"You should not have come back here. I don't need a fledgling mage's help."

"I will give it anyway."

She shook her head. "No, boy. Your place is not here. I know exactly what I am doing."

"And yet outside, your weave fails you."

"I am building it up. The youth is so impatient." Her voice held a note of annoyance, which Cyril expected. What he did not expect was the undertone of resignation, very like someone about to deliver crucial and, more importantly, *parting* advice. "But since you are here." She glanced a second at her desk, at her mess of notes and papers. "Lend me your ear a bit, Cyril."

Cyril chewed his lip, wanting to say no just so he did not enable these sudden whims of hers. In the end, curiosity got the better of him. He nodded.

"I have never had children of my own, you know. I did not care to have them. The opportunity did not come up. But, Cyril, you are *mine*."

He heard the emotion climb up her voice. Never had she spoken to him like this.

"Tantie..."

"Sh. You are my child, Cyril, as humiliating as that may be for the both of us. A twenty-something and an old woman. Family. The only family we've got, as far as I'm concerned. And as my child, it was my duty to raise you. More than grand magistry, my only goal was to mould you into someone you were proud of.

"So, when you came to me and told me you'd lost Shoestring, I knew I'd failed."

Cyril listened, so enraptured he surprised himself when he choked back a small sob.

She blamed herself. His own guardian, the woman he loved the most and had made suffer through his own foibles and horrible temperament. "Tantie, it was never your fault–"

"Let me finish. Duckling, I have been looking for a way to bring him back. Your familiar. Your heart. I have not discovered it yet, but I feel I am close, and I know you will be able to interpret my findings."

His eyes went wide. He had a feeling this was coming, braced for it, but a part of him did not believe Heléne to be this sentimental.

"You are talking as though you are saying goodbye," he murmured.

"It is a precaution, Ducky. The ice I will imprison us all in, I am not sure I will be able to withstand it without becoming feverish myself. And there is only so much a woman of my age can bear."

He could not believe what she was saying to him. Heléne had slapped him across the head so hard he was still seeing stars not even a full twelve hours ago and now she was giving him an entire speech on self-sacrifice. He would not allow it. Tenderness and grief roared into a sudden, bubbling outrage.

"Bring my damned familiar back yourself, if you're so worked up about it!" said Cyril.

"I have slowed the hands of time for myself far too many times. It is catching up with me."

Cyril let go of her and looked around, desperate for some kind of way to prevent this. He could grab her. Stop her spell midway. But this would only spell the deaths of the people in the palace, and she would never forgive him.

The hands of time… slowing the hands of time. Cyril blinked, then looked around the room. It was a mage's paradise. Perhaps he could do it. He had dabbled in time magic before, and that had been much more substantial.

But it had also taken him a month of preparation. He could not possibly draw a circle so big and so complex. By the time he was done with it, everyone would already be dead, even if he knew exactly what he was drawing – he did – and etched it out with unmatched agility.

Then he remembered Heléne. That night, when she had so effortlessly woven Tigris's body into a delicate little bauble. She had told him she did not need circles. And perhaps, Cyril didn't either. He had trained under her all these years, after all.

He closed his eyes, scrunched them shut and pictured the spell in his mind. A different kind of freeze. Not physical, but *temporal*. He would stop time on the palace grounds until he could return to take care of the pattern. And he *would* return.

He was going to save his aunt's life. He was going to save *everyone's* life, even if this spell had him spent and frayed and dying slowly by the end. He would not let himself perish until he did what he promised he had come back here to do.

And that was fix everything.

When he opened his eyes, he instantly felt dizzy and weak. The bubble around his head popped, exposing him to the stench of rot coming from the floors below.

But he had done it.

Heléne was immobile. Ganache, too, stood like a statue on her perch, mid-flap of her wings. He looked out the window and saw the servants had also entered some kind of stasis. Everyone had.

Except for the moving dot cutting through the woods, the Margraves, who had managed to clear the grounds in time.

Cyril breathed a sigh of relief.

Now all he needed to do was fulfil his promise.

He doubled back to the door out of the palace and instantly realised his predicament when he saw the cloud of poison wafting upwards to him, promising contagion. He had no way out. He had spent his magic on one singular powerful spell and even if he could recreate the bubble again, he would not be able to sustain it for long enough to run outside.

Cyril backed up against the balcony of the window and looked out. He could see Titania, moving at a glacial gallop as though waiting for him. The miasma had spread to immediate grounds, but it did not move upwards unless it had structure to engulf. He was so tired he *certainly* didn't have the energy or focus required to teleport even such a short, visible distance away. He swallowed convulsively. There really was only one way out.

From all the way across the room, on shaking legs, Cyril sprinted to the window and took off in a running leap.

TWENTY-ONE

It was a long way to go to the horse and the Margraves. About fifty metres. Had he been an ordinary human, his body would already have splattered onto the garden below instead of following the graceful, hovering arc it needed to do.

Cyril was far from ordinary.

It felt like swimming laps in an icy lake with absolutely no training. He would come up for a breath, a respite from tugging desperately at the threads keeping him floating, and then a second later he would go under again. It was laying down tracks while inside the moving cart.

He was flying – literally – by the seat of his pants, but what else was new?

Cyril kicked his legs as though he were running underwater, in slow, grand movements, navigating the space that separated him from his goal. When Titania was no longer a speck in the distance, Cyril took a deep breath and shouted.

"Incoming!"

He shut his eyes tight to brace for the impact as he collided with the horse. He hoped it did not injure the creature. In retrospect, this was a horrendous idea. But, at the same time, he was committed to it. He knew it would work. All his other stupid ideas so far had worked.

He felt a solid, steadying hand on his waist, grabbing his shirt and drawing him in. The hand snaked around his middle and held him in place, pulling Cyril into an awkward embrace.

Cyril opened his eyes, and he was being held sideways, face centimetres away from Eufrates's jaw. Tigris was inside a satchel Eufrates had fashioned and attached to the saddle on Titania. She looked like a swaddled babe.

"What the *fuck* was that?!" Eufrates yelled directly into his already delicate eardrums.

Not even he could dampen how much of a colossal triumph that had been. Cyril burst into a fit of laughter and threw his arms around the prince.

"You are *unhinged*. Did you have your *eyes closed*?"

Cyril smiled so wide his jaw hurt from the strain of it. "I knew you would catch me!"

Eufrates's face took on an intense ruddiness.

"Is Auntie well? What happened in there?" Tigris asked. There was a glint of fascination in her eye that felt inappropriate for such a serious question. He could not judge her. This was the most fun thing she had ever seen him do.

"Tantie will be fine, I made sure of it." He felt the dip in Eufrates's chest as he breathed a sigh of relief, warm against his hair. "I was having trouble with the bubble, and time was of the essence!"

"And you could not have made, I – I don't know! A slightly less dangerous exit?"

"If I was having trouble with a *bubble*, there is no way I would have been able to weave anything to get me out of there *safely*."

"What was the trouble?" Eufrates's brow furrowed. "Are you hurt?"

"Did you get sick?"

Cyril waved a hand dismissively, though he still clung to Eufrates instead of righting himself on the horse. He would take the intimacy where he could get it, and Eufrates had not yet made a move to push him away.

"Oh, no. I have never felt better! I thought my back would split in half for sure at my old age of fifty, but–"

"*Fifty?*" Eufrates raised a brow.

"Yes? You know how old I truly am."

"Cyril, *I* am fifty. You are *forty-seven*."

Cyril's eyes grew huge. "Oh, Eufrates! That is just about the greatest gift you've ever given me!"

He pretended, very politely, not to notice how his husband's face coloured again as his brows knit in mute protest.

They rode on for a grand total of five minutes before Tigris became restless. Inaction did not agree with her and neither did patience. She looked out into the woods.

"*Can't this horse move any faster?*"

"It's a horse, Tigris. There is only so much it can do." But Eufrates urged it to gallop on anyway, clearly just as anxious.

She turned her head to Cyril, who was still, all these minutes later, catching his breath.

"*What about* you?"

"I am not a better rider than your brother, Tig."

"*No, idiot!*" she huffed. "*Are you not the greatest wizard of your time?!*"

Cyril blinked, repeatedly.

"Oh," he said. "Yes, I am."

He should not have been able to do what he did. Not through the exhaustion that soaked through his bones. He didn't think he had anything left to give, not for a *while*, but that was wrong.

Cyril was filled with a manic energy that burned inside him as hot as the sun. He had saved his aunt. He had jumped off a building. He felt unstoppable. Something was fuelling him, something good and unconditional and endless and unknown, and it was making him the marvel he had pretended to be for so many years.

He finally untangled himself from Eufrates's embrace, shifting so he was in front of him on the saddle, riding between his thighs.

Were he not so laser focused on the task at hand, he would have flinched at the sudden heat at his back. A warmth that made him wonder if Eufrates had somehow contracted the plague while he hadn't been looking.

Eufrates still had his arms around him, awkwardly leading the horse, and Cyril placed his hands on his to guide them.

"Excuse me, darling," he said on instinct, before he could even think about the words.

Since arriving in this timeline, Cyril had felt himself slowly regressing to his youth, buoyed by an agile body and the way he was seen and treated by his peers and, more often, his betters. Now, though, sharing a saddle with his long-estranged husband, addressing him as he used to, his true age caught up with him, not in its usual weary manner, but in a much more hopeful way.

He could not guess at how *Eufrates* felt, but the heat on his back was volcanic.

"Eufie, you look about ready to pass out."

Eufrates grunted something unintelligible in response. Cyril laughed, a true and genuine laugh and yanked on the pattern of the reins.

The horse, Titania, took flight. One gallop was now crossing dozens of metres of land and she was running fierce and light as air. They soared over the beaten path with unparalleled grace. Cyril was instantly buffeted by the wind on his face, scattering hair over his eyes and into his mouth and freezing over the tip of his ears, but he still hooted like a madman.

Now they were *riding*.

Tigris matched his cheers, eyes rapt with delight as she watched tree after tree pass beside her in a flash of greenery. She reached up a paw to pat him on the thigh.

"That's my grand mage!" she yelled.

"He is *my* mage, actually," Eufrates murmured under his breath.

Tigris scowled. *"Not anymore! We have developed a rapport!"*

"Unless you've *married* him, I don't want to hear about it."

"He likes me better!"

"Children, please," Cyril called from the front of the horse. "I love you both equally."

"Shut up, Cyril!" both Margraves snapped in unison.

They made it back to Cretea in half the time and were heralded by a grey sky bloated with rainwater, tell-tale of the oncoming storm. An omen if he had ever seen one, but Tigris was emboldened by it.

"They will not see us coming. It is a blessing."

Cyril looked up at the clouds. "Let us hope you're right."

They dismounted the horse a short distance away from the palace and Cyril, still high on adrenaline and a warm buzzing in his veins, wove a spell over the trio that allowed them to easily sneak inside.

Tigris took the reins of the operation immediately.

"We take out the pattern first, then we take out the man."

"There will be mages waiting for us. Atticus himself, perhaps. If he finds we are coming, he will protect his web," Cyril warned.

"Can you handle the mages?"

"I…" He looked at his own hands, at the sparks at his fingertips. "Yes. Yes, I believe so. I do not wish to kill them, and I am not trained in combat magic, but I can get creative. But…"

"But?"

"But Atticus himself. I do not know if I can take him. He overpowered me very easily last time. He is a duellist. I will have a hard time weaving if my hands are disabled, and I am sure he knows this."

"He doesn't expect us… perhaps he is not even in the library."

"If he is alerted to it, he will find a way there. A weave that big, it is his *oeuvre*."

"Then… a distraction."

"I will do it."

Cyril and Tigris both turned to Eufrates, who was following them a few steps behind and had not said a word since they dismounted.

"Eufie?"

"You are wrong, Tig. Even if he does not know you are coming now, he is certain you *will*. He is waiting for you, and he is waiting for Cyril. He is not waiting for me.

"For all he knows, I am still a madman. An imbecile easy to ply. If I show up in his palace alone with a sword in my hand, he will think I have well and truly lost it. Perhaps he might even try to get me on his side. I can keep him busy while the two of you get to the pattern. I am, after all, a consummate performer."

Cyril shook his head. "You cannot go in there alone."

"I can. I have two legs and a newfound recovery of my senses." Eufrates tapped the blade at his hip. "Besides, I have been wanting to duel him since that ball."

They had been walking enough that now they were in the belly of the beast. Though Cyril's spell obscured their words and actions, it was still nerve-wracking to wander the palace's deserted corridors.

Eufrates spotted something in a decorative suit of armour and wandered off to it. The other two followed.

He pulled a slim, bronze sword from a metal scabbard and fastened it to Cyril's hip before he could even begin to protest.

"I know you are not much of a fighter, Cyril, but be sensible. There is a pointed end and a blunt one. You aim with the point."

"You cannot be serious about this."

"You will not convince me otherwise."

"Take – take Tigris with you, then!"

Eufrates looked at Tigris. "If you try to follow me and leave our waifish little mage to venture alone in a basement, I will kill you myself once you are back in your body," he said.

Tigris frowned. *"Like I'd ever choose you over him."*

"Good."

Before Cyril could protest further, Eufrates closed the distance between them, lightning quick, and snaked an arm around his waist. He pulled him so close they would meld into one, dipped him back and kissed him so hungrily, with so much desperation that Cyril felt like he was being lit on fire from within.

This was the spark, he realised. He could not believe he tried recreating this with anyone else in the world.

He melted into the kiss, candlewax against the hard edges of Eufrates's frame, and reached up to tug at his shirt and make sure they would never break apart. He was a million different things. He was jelly, he was a flower in full bloom, he was butter on hot bread, he was a warm summer breeze, he was the nascent flush of first love.

He was Eufrates's.

If it were up to him, he would stop time again. But eventually, the both of them needed to come up for air. Cyril pried himself away begrudgingly, hot and panting and flushed. He must look a mess and his husband only looked more beautiful than ever.

He was dazed for only a second before realisation hit him, and he grabbed Eufrates's arm to prevent him from escaping.

"That was a goodbye kiss! You are saying goodbye!"

"Cyril–"

"No! I will not allow you to go!"

Eufrates kissed him again, if possible harder this time.

"Gods, you are always *so* dramatic. It is a *promise*." He held fast onto Cyril's waist and when he nodded their foreheads came together. "We will continue this *later*." He almost growled this last part.

Cyril looked up at him, eyes wide and just about to well with tears that he managed to blink back.

"Oh…"

"Yes." He placed one final kiss on the corner of his eye and then let go of him entirely. "If I was going to be saying goodbye to you, I would have had you against that wall."

"Okay, disgusting! Inappropriate!" Tigris wailed. Cyril *had* briefly wondered how much longer she was going to stand for this. *"Get out of here, Eufrates!"*

He did. Without a second glance back at them, he dashed the other way into the depths of the palace, away from their protective weave.

Cyril balled his hands into a fist and began walking to the library.

"Cyril..." she called after a moment.

He glanced down at her. "Yes?"

"I never want to see that again."

Cyril let out a huff of laughter.

TWENTY-TWO

They came across their first obstacle once they got to the staircase leading underground.

During his week in Cretea, Cyril had not laid eyes on a single mage, but now it seemed the entrance to the basement was teeming with them, going in and out in their drab, sepia clothing with scrolls and familiars under their arms. Cyril was confident he could take on a *few* mages, but not a full platoon of them.

"We are being stealthy, then?" Tigris said, more a polite command than an actual question.

Cyril nodded. "I'm just not sure how. If even a single one of those mages looks into the weave, they will spot us. Is there another way in?"

Tigris thought very hard about this. *"It is a basement level, but there must be some sort of ventilation. In fact, I am sure I spotted some kind of iron grate while we were there."*

"You want to sneak in through a *vent*?"

"Unless it does not agree with your delicate sensibilities."

Cyril sucked in the air through his cheeks. It didn't. It *really* didn't. But he had no other choice.

It was surprisingly easy to find ingress through one of the openings to the palace's ventilation on the upper level, and Cyril quickly strung together a compass that would lead them in the direction of the library, using the most concentrated source of magic – Atticus's web – as an anchor. The only thing left to do was make the gruelling journey there on his hands and knees.

Tigris strolled ahead of him. Despite her large size for a cat, she still could fit perfectly into the network of tunnels and seemed to resent him for his human limitations.

"Hey, Cy," she said after a while.

"If this is about your brother again – my *husband*, by the way, so I am allowed to–"

"I was actually trying very hard not to think about that."

"Oh. Well, what is it then?"

Perhaps he was the one who was thinking too much about Eufrates, but he had been sick with worry from the moment the man left his line of vision. They needed to take care of the weave as soon as possible to reunite with him.

"Everyone... I mean, all you mages. They keep saying I'm a familiar, and that's a good thing."

"Well, that is an oversimplification. You are not *really* a familiar. You are not the manifestation of my soul, as far as I'm aware, but you possess all the qualities of one, being in a body that is tied to mine."

"What does that mean?"

"It means you will not die."

"I'm indestructible, right. You've been saying that. Poison, curses. They won't affect me."

"And neither will physical damage, to be honest. You might get scuffed up, but as long as *I* am hale, it will not end in your death. And even if I die, it will just undo the spell keeping you trapped in that body. It is why this is the most secure form for you," Cyril said this last part with a bit of impatience. He had grown used to her pleas for him to turn her back.

Tigris looked back at him and rolled her eyes. *"I've given up begging for my body back, Cy. I know you are stubborn as a mule on this."*

"And I am correct."

She sighed. Another beat passed between them until she finally said, *"I am worried about him too."*

"...Yes."

They seemed to move faster through the vents after that, Cyril's knees bruising and scraping against the solid rock and metal lining. It was a blessing when they finally made it to the library.

The aperture they ended up in was several metres above ground level, and Cyril could *sense* the pattern, in all its foreboding silks and woven casting. He could *also* see about half a dozen mages parading around the room, doing research or simply idling by.

He was in luck. Six was exactly the number he set in his head of how many mages he could take on.

"I cannot wait to get at those freaks. When I am human again, I would like it if you could fashion claws for me. I will miss having them dearly."

Cyril shot her a look. "Remember, we are not trying to *kill* anyone here."

"But if we must…"

He swallowed convulsively. "You are the one who is queen. You make the call." He looked up at the ceiling. "I could just tear at the pattern now… but I would be vulnerable to attacks."

"I am a wonderful distraction if you need one, but… Cy, I have been wondering."

"Mm?"

"You said destroying a pattern would cause a disaster. What do you intend to do when that happens?"

"I… thought I might figure it out along the way."

To her credit, Tigris said nothing, but she looked very pensive.

He was not good at thinking on his feet, this was historically true, but with his and, more importantly, *Tigris's* life on the line, he was compelled to come up with something. Perhaps he could give himself some kind of shield if he could weave it in time.

There were so many risk factors to take into consideration. For one, Tigris's survival was tied to his. She could distract the mages on the ground as well as she could, but if even a single one of them was trained enough to strike him down from the *precarious* webbing of Atticus's spell while he was tearing it apart, both their lives would be forfeit.

It was stupid to go in there without some kind of well-defined plan. And not even the *good* kind of stupid, like jumping off a seven-storey building into the arms of a man he currently had a complicated relationship with. This did not fill him with a warm, heady feeling of determination. This made his heart thunder in his chest.

He looked from one mage to the next, trying to identify any weaknesses, but he could not distinguish their specialised talents from this far away and with so little to go on. There had to be *one* alchemist in there, as that seemed to be Atticus's *modus operandi* for anything that wasn't manipulation, but they were all dressed so alike he could not make out any distinguishing traits. Especially not from a grate five metres up a rock wall.

And, most humiliating of all, he could not think straight, because he could not stop worrying about Eufrates. Every other moment he had to force a wave of nausea back down his throat because, even if by some twist of fate he had been lied to again and the prince *was* just humouring him with that kiss, using it as a quick way to get him to shut up. Even if after all this he was just as hated as he'd been before, the thought of Eufrates run through and pooled in blood made him want to tear himself inside out.

He could not possibly continue to dwell. He had to take action, for better or worse. Cyril leaned forward to push open the grate to the library and he felt a paw on his hand.

"Wait."

Cyril glanced down at Tigris, stunned at the sudden interruption. "What... what is it?"

"Cyril, I think we are doing this backwards."

He tilted his head towards her. "How do you mean?"

"You said before… in the tower, when you were explaining it to me. You said anyone could destroy a pattern as long as they can see it."

"I… yes. It would not take an experienced mage. A child could do it."

"But you did not say a mage."

"Well, mages are the ones who can see pattern, generally."

"Generally?"

"…What are you trying to say?"

"Can familiars see the pattern?"

Cyril's eyes widened. "I… with the amount of judgement Shoestring has levelled at me throughout the years, I would guess they can."

Tigris stiffened, suddenly very alert and stared out into the room, scanning it. *"Help me see it! What does it look like?"*

"Tig, what are you doing?"

"We have been thinking about this all wrong, Cy! I'm not going to distract those mages! You are!"

"You want to go up there?"

"I am a cat. Cats destroy things by nature. Further, I am an indestructible *cat."*

His instinct was to tell her no. That getting that close to a pattern was dangerous, suicidal, even, but that was exactly what *he* had been just about to do. And she was so much stronger and, frankly, leaps and bounds more athletic than him. In retrospect, if he had tried to hang onto that web, he might have just fallen off to his early demise anyway.

It was worth a shot.

Cyril pointed Tigris towards the centre of Atticus's weave. "See there? It looks like a spider's web. The strings on it are a dull white and shining. Can you picture it in your head? Are your eyes adjusting?"

He had no idea how familiars saw magic. He just assumed they *did*, being magical creatures themselves. Maybe the next time he saw one he would try and make time to ask, despite not really knowing exactly how he would manage to communicate with it.

"I... it's a bit faint. I can't make it out." She tried rubbing her eyes with her paws, but it didn't seem to help.

Cyril leaned in closer to her so he was at the same eye level. "Let me try something."

He made the same diamond shape with his hands, thumbs and forefingers closing against one another, as the one he had made the *first* time he looked into the pattern, pried the material world apart to look at its inner workings. This time, though, he did it in front of Tigris's eyes. They narrowed, then went wide as saucers. Her pupils dilated until her entire irises were black as night.

"Oh. That is very impressive."

"You see it?!"

She nodded. *"I don't think I'd want to work in here, personally. It'd be very uncomfortable."*

"I think that's the point..."

Tigris blinked, over and over again. She rubbed her eyes with her paws and shook her head, all to make sure the weave wasn't a vanishing afterimage. Once she was positive it would not vanish while she was clawing at the damned thing, she prepared to leap at it.

"I just need to tear it apart, right? I can get up there from here easily!"

He nodded. "Yes. Give me some time to deal with the mages first, though."

"Of course. Cyril, I want you to be very far away from this entire basement level when I start hacking up that thing."

Cyril blinked. "What?"

"You said you'd no idea how you were going to protect yourself from the blast. Well, there is your solution. You are going to run from it."

"...We will be separated."

"Aw, Cy. It's okay, I don't want to be apart from you either."

"That's not my–"

"If you try to feed me any more of your nonsense about needing to protect delicate flower Tigris Margrave, I will scratch you again, and I will do it somewhere much more visible."

He immediately shielded his face. "I – Tig–"

"I will be fine. I trusted you to be right behind us when we ran from this palace, now you need to trust me." She put a paw on his chest. *"Will you do that? Please?"*

Cyril's shoulders slumped. They would be arguing for hours if he did not concede. And had she not proven to be his better multiple times over by this point? He did not say anything, but he let out a beleaguered sigh and nodded. A courtier indulging his queen.

"That's my wizard." She paused and her expression turned serious. *"Besides... I know you want to get to him as soon as possible."*

He gave her a wry smile. "You think I'm pathetic, don't you?"

"I do! But it's because you can't lift a simple sword without your arm trembling, not because of that."

"That's more than fair." He gave her one last smile, broader this time, and opened the grate to make his descent down the wall of the library.

"Knock them dead out there, Cy."

He used magic to slow his fall, and landed just behind a shelf densely packed with pickled ingredients for poultices. The stench of preserved insect and reptilian filled his nose, and he had to clap a hand over his mouth not to make a sound.

For all his talk of being able to take on an imaginary, random number of mages, Cyril had actually never been in a fight. One time, in his third year at the Academy, a girl in his class cursed him to have warts growing all over his skin and he immediately turned her into a frog. They were both sent to the headmistress and his aunt was called. She scared him so thoroughly away from picking stupid fights that for the remaining years of his academic career, he was ghosting the halls from how little he interacted with other students.

He had never excelled in combat. Not as a mage and *especially* not as a *person*. He was sure he did not have any muscle within his body, despite having enough anatomy lessons drilled into him to know this wasn't physically possible. And magical combat relied on two things that did not come easy to him: good reaction time, and an ability to think fast. He did not have the kind of skill it took to disarm a mage, to bend the weave around them so that their hands would be bound, and they could not perform themselves. The spell itself was simple, childishly so, but it was like throwing a punch. If you were not trained in it, the only injured party would end up being yourself.

There was also the fact that he had to make sure these mages would not be left in the library to *die*. He wasn't sure how many of them were ensorcelled and how many were here out of their own sick volition, but he was not comfortable taking that kind of risk with other peoples' lives. Not after the miserable existence he led as grand mage to a corrupted Eufrates, aid and accessory to needless cullings and executions.

Out of the corner of his eye, he saw one of the mages get up from where they were seated to look for a book. Cyril panicked and hid further into the shelf, really breathing in the toxins of the preserving liquids. His face was near flush with a vial of beetles. Next to it, a great, big jar of...

Oh.

Cyril thought about that horrible little witch who had cursed him all those years ago. How easily transformation magic came to him. And, as he stared deep into the antennae of a jellied cockroach, how some creatures could survive almost anything.

Cyril darted to and fro in the library, hiding under shelves and desks wherever he saw them. It was all very theatrical, and he was sure if Tigris was watching him from up on that vent, she was laughing at him. But he would rather this than alert every single person in the room to his presence by just standing up and casting a spell.

The first three mages went down easy. They did not even see him. He hid in the shadows and shot his magic like a cutthroat wielding throwing knives (if said cutthroat was dressed to attend a harlequinade immediately afterwards). Each of his successes was indicated by the skittering of insect feet on stone floor.

He had to admit he could've handled the fourth mage onwards a bit more delicately. He realised he'd been spotted after he narrowly dodged being hit with a vial of some sort of acidic concoction that burned away a lock of his hair. Luckily, the mage who had seen him seemed to be a physician of some sort, so no expert in physical spellcasting. She *did*, however, very physically manage to hit Cyril in the side with a wooden chair before he managed to shift her successfully.

Number five, hearing the commotion, actually had the presence of mind to grab a knife and lunge at him. They made a very valiant effort, and it surely would have succeeded if Cyril wasn't a coward who bobbed and weaved behind tables and chairs, and if transformation spells couldn't be cast at a two-metre distance.

The sixth and final mage threw him for a loop completely. Not due to any particularly proficient fighting skills or magic, but because she was a small, round old woman with thick-rimmed glasses who reminded him very much of his aunt. Cyril blinked.

We're entrapping old ladies now, Atticus?

She looked at him like she had no idea what to do. Cyril was sure she was somehow also enmeshed in Atticus's weave, but it had not given her the desire to be particularly hostile. Honestly, he retracted his earlier thought. She *didn't* remind him of Heléne. Heléne would have already stuck a sword in his vena cava.

He hesitated. He truly did not want to *curse* this woman minding her business and doing her job, but it was a necessary evil. He cringed as he hurled the spell at her and watched her scuttle into a secluded corner of the room.

He had put a timer on the spell. It would last twelve hours, then unfurl itself on its own. He did not enjoy the thought of having to search through the wreckage of a library for six roaches himself.

It was only after the final mage was well and truly hidden away that he realised he'd done it. His eyes grew wide with wonder, and he looked down at his hands, watching them spark and crackle with lingering magic.

It was only when he heard a low yowl from up on the vents that he realised he had become much too absorbed in self-adulation.

Cyril turned and looked at the orange blotch of colour contrasted against grey stone walls that he knew to be Tigris. He motioned to her that she could enter the room, and she immediately motioned back for him to *leave*.

Ah, right.

He ran out into the halls of the underground, cloaking himself in threads so fine they made him appear near invisible to the eye as he passed and ducked by one or two straggler servants and mages who were still around. The library was massive. He was sure whatever happened in there would take enough time to spread that anyone alerted to the sound would know to run away.

And, by now, he was feeling overtaxed.

His joints strained and his muscles ached, as if he'd performed some great feat of athleticism. He had never had to weave together this much magic – powerful magic at that – at once. The only thing keeping him together was a strong sense of duty and a shot of adrenaline that coursed unbidden through his veins, making him jitter and crackle with yet-unspent determination.

Cyril had not been alone with his thoughts for some time. He instantly missed the peppy, unafraid wit of Tigris echoing in his head and egging him on into increasingly more insane acts of heroism. He could not imagine returning to a world without her.

He could not imagine returning to where he came from at *all*. Not when he had come this far. Not when he had turned himself and everything he knew upside-down, solved all the mysteries that had haunted him for years, *decades*, and prevented the worst tragedies in his life. He had saved Tigris and he had saved Heléne.

For the *coup-de-grace*, he would save his husband.

All he had to do now was *find him*.

Cyril reached the top of the staircase to the ground level, slightly pink in the face and out of breath. Perhaps he would take Tigris up on her offer to train him. The sword at his side felt like it weighed a tonne, despite him knowing it was one of the slimmer models anyone could possibly find save for a rapier. Eufrates gave him far too much credit in thinking he would be able to wield it. He wanted to get rid of it., but at the same time, he knew that was a horrible idea.

He pressed his back against a wall, half-hidden within an alcove, and looked around, trying to suss out where he was meant to be going. Outside, he could hear the light patter of rain against marble, heralding worse yet to come.

Cyril reached into his shirt and tugged out his wedding band. He stared at it a while, brow furrowed in concentration.

If you'd like to prove to me that you're not a curse, now would be the time.

He squeezed the ring so hard he thought he might dent the metal.

Somehow, that worked.

The ring glowed in his hand, a delicate sheen of golden, pulsating light. And almost as if it were trying to escape from Cyril's brutalising hand, it began to pull away from him, hovering in the air until the string that held it to his neck stopped it from moving any further.

When Cyril took a step forward, to right it again, the ring simply floated on. Like a guide.

As a guide.

Cyril moved furtively through the halls, following his beacon as though he had blinders on, not even realising where it was taking him until he felt the droplets of rain hit his nose.

He was outside, in the garden. Eufrates and Atticus were fighting somewhere in here and he was going to find them and disarm the king of his charms. As soon as he stepped fully into the paved rock path, though, something distracted him from the purpose at hand.

There was a rumbling coming from somewhere to his left. Somewhere several metres away, but still within the palace. It made the foundation of the building itself shake and shudder, but it was only a prelude. Tigris had finally gotten her paws onto that weave.

The corners of Cyril's mouth began to curl upwards, imagining her tangling with it like a cat with a fresh ball of yarn. But only a second later, when he heard a strange noise coming from ahead of him and snapped his gaze forward, the smile died on his lips.

He had found Eufrates. The ring had done his bidding and now rested, snug and contented, on his breast.

Eufrates, however, was not snug and he was *not* content. He lay sprawled over a patch of grass and wildflowers left for dead, with his sword a few steps away from him, bloodied, but disarmed. A pool of red bloomed around him and dyed the soil a thick, sludgy maroon as it mixed with the rainwater.

He looked like a master's painting, laid out like this amidst the flowers and trees, but Cyril was at his side, dropped to his haunches next to him to disturb the scene immediately.

TWENTY-THREE

"Eufrates!" he called.

The prince had his eyes closed, but he opened them partway when he heard his name.

Cyril looked over the length of his body, searching for the wound. He had a shallow one on his outer left thigh, the fabric of his trousers sliced to reveal an open gash that stained the material. This was not the trouble. Eufrates's disabling wound was up on his chest, where a plume of crimson spread across his shirt and a thick, knitted vest he had put on as *some* form of cover as he was dashing out of that tower.

Cyril thought about the cuirass he had bled upon, how it had been wasted on fighting *him*. If only Eufrates had had time to put it on here.

Quickly, he tore open the front of the shirt to assess the damage. He hoped the cool drizzle of rain was at least soothing on the wound.

"Cyril...?" Eufrates blinked a few times against the light, eyes dull and dreamy.

The thundering in his chest amplified when he realised Eufrates was conscious enough to sleep. He would keep him awake.

"What happened?" he asked. He tore a piece of fabric from his tunic and used it to push down on the open wound, stopping the blood flow.

Eufrates shut his eyes for a moment and when he opened them again, they were in focus, gazing up at Cyril's face.

He chuckled, which was not at all what Cyril was expecting.

"This isn't helping my case at all..." he murmured under his breath.

Cyril knit his brow in confusion. "What? What *case*?"

Eufrates hissed when he felt Cyril press harder on the wound. "*Ah...* never mind. You asked what happened? Clearly, I lost a duel. I do not think I am the weaker fighter. I gave him enough trouble that he has fled to lick his wounds, tail tucked between his legs, but he did not play fair."

Cyril couldn't help the snort that escaped him. "You didn't think Atticus would play fair? He is *evil*."

"*I* am evil, Cy."

"No, you're–"

"Oh, shut up." Eufrates looked up into his eyes, but he was not quite angered. He was frustrated. Annoyed. He reached up, weak as he was, to grab Cyril's hand. "I suppose if I am not to make it out of here, I may as well ask for a moment of your time."

"You're not going to *die*. Now who's dramatic?" But there was a note of desperation in Cyril's tone, like he was trying to convince himself more than Eufrates.

He should have been going after Atticus. Putting an end to the monster once and for all if it meant having to wield a proper sword for the first time in his life, but he was rooted to the ground. Atticus could escape into the safety of political asylum for all he cared.

And if Eufrates wanted to wax prose at him in what he thought were his dying moments, Cyril would do something useful with his time. He was not an expert physician. He had *barely* passed surgery at the Academy, but he knelt down next to Eufrates's chest and began to thread the wound.

"You should not be wasting your time," Eufrates said.

"You shouldn't have let yourself be hurt this badly," Cyril sniffed.

Eufrates grimaced. "And that is the crux of it, no? I am weak and you are my caretaker."

Cyril looked up from his work for a long moment. He was about to ask what on *earth* he was talking about, but Eufrates continued, in a high, cloying voice that did not suit him.

"'Poor Eufie, meek little Eufie, taken in by the plotting of a malicious sorcerer. It saddens me so that I did not prevent it. It is my fault he is evil'," he said.

"Where… is this going?"

"Cyril, I thought the worst thing you had ever done to me was leave. Regard me with suspicion and disdain. Abandon our marriage because I disgusted you so deeply you could not stand to share a *home* anymore, let alone the same bed. You had your reasons, but I did not take it kindly. I did not handle it… *well.*"

"But I was *wrong*! I've asked forgiveness–"

"I do not *need* your apologies!" Eufrates roared, and the hole in his chest pulsed with new blood that Cyril desperately tried to weave over. "Listen to me, please. If I die here and the last image you have of me is the one you've concocted in that frayed brain of yours, I will not be able to forgive *myself.*"

Cyril was silent. He waited.

"It does not *matter* that I was enchanted. I am glad to know it, I am sure it would have changed things, had I not been influenced, but we cannot know that. I will never be king in this lifetime, and that is a *good* thing. That is a *wonderful* thing.

"The truth, Cyril, is that were it my sister being ensorcelled by a mage, it would not have taken hold. A seed needs water to grow. It needs fresh air and rich soil. Tigris's mind is a barren wasteland of insecurities. I am a garden.

"I do not think he even needed to go through the trouble of using *magic*. I think he could have just said the right things to me, and I would have made the self-same mistakes, over and over. I did not care about government. I did not care about being *king*. But I needed the respect, because there was one thing I cared about above all else."

Eufrates reached up to stroke his cheek. His hand, stained red, left marks on Cyril's hair and dappled his face in blood. Cyril did not care one bit, but Eufrates flinched at the sight and pulled away.

He looked up at the sky for this next part, avoiding his gaze. "Since our wedding, I had advisors and courtiers alike needling me about my mistake. How I was besotted and inexperienced. How you were unsuitable, irregular and... well, worse things. And I was fresh, a princeling. Easy to push around, so it seemed. I did not have the respect I needed to assert myself. And I *especially* did not have the respect I needed to protect *you*."

Eufrates looked up and to the side, suddenly swept away by some self-consciousness that prevented him from looking directly at Cyril. "I was always acutely aware of how you were seen in court. How I *made* you be seen in court. If it were up to me, you never would've known about it, because I would've sent each and every slick-tongued gossipmonger to the gallows. Unfortunately, even being king didn't allow me such a direct approach, not at first.

"But respect is so difficult, time-consuming to cultivate. Fear, a strict iron grasp on the throne, is much easier."

Cyril finally spoke, voice crackling with emotion and the strain of magic. "I don't need your protection."

Eufrates let out a huff of laughter from his chest. He rolled his eyes. "And I don't need *yours*. Do you see the predicament we are in, my love? You think me soft, tender. A sweet man who was suckered by a smarter, better wizard. Cyril, that is the picture you have started painting in your head and I would rather die than pose for it. I was tricked, yes. But I was also lucid. My mind was hazy, but it was my own. I have done things I thought I'd never do, that I was not strong enough to resist, but these are *my* failures. You will let me own them or I will perish in humiliation. I would rather die than see pity in your eyes whenever you look at me."

Cyril was impressed by how much the man could talk while having an open wound in his chest being stitched back together. He grunted and shook through the process, making Cyril just narrowly avoid missing a stitch a couple of times, but he kept a hand on his chest, as firm as he could manage, and continued on with his work. It was difficult to see through the rain, and through the tears misting his eyes as he listened to Eufrates and saw his bloodied, battered chest at the same time, but when he was done, his shoulders nearly shook with relief. It was not a replacement for proper treatment, but it would keep the wound closed and Eufrates alive for the foreseeable future.

When he was finished, he finally looked down at Eufrates's face and fresh tears beaded from his eyes down to his breast. Cyril wanted to tell him he would be alright. That he had managed to stop the bleeding. Something pragmatic and useful, a promise that they would perhaps continue this conversation later.

Instead, he blurted, "You still love me?"

Eufrates regarded him a long while, utterly baffled by the question. Like he had not heard right, or Cyril had started speaking in a foreign tongue. Then, once it truly sunk in, he laid his head back against the soft, wet grass and breathed out a sigh that almost sounded like a laugh.

"I have never *stopped* loving you. Vexing though it may be, there is not a thing you could say or do that would make my world stop revolving around your light. I am your adoring, your begrudging, your eternal satellite, my love. Whether you want me or not."

Cyril's chest felt like it was going to burst apart from the buzzing inside it. He dipped his head to plant a kiss on Eufrates's forehead, then another, soft and tender, on his lips. He tasted blood, but he also tasted honey and nectar and love. Eufrates reached up to wrap his arms around him and he sank into the embrace.

"It is a shame, but I love you too," he said, quiet, mirthful, against Eufrates's lips.

They only broke apart when they felt the earth shake and rumble beneath them, as though being pried apart. Despite knowing what it was, Cyril still startled at the jolt.

"What is *that*?" said Eufrates, looking wide-eyed around them as though he could find the source in the garden.

Cyril beamed. "Tig is almost done, I think."

Eufrates blinked, grasping his meaning. He returned the smile. "Can you believe we tried to run a country without her?"

"I cannot!"

He could perish like this. Cradling his husband in his arms, so full of saccharine his teeth ached. He needed to make sure they made it out safe, of course. But this might be the best his life was going to get.

But Eufrates's expression had changed. It fixated not on Cyril, but on a point behind his shoulder and his lips parted to say something. A wordless shout, and he bodily shoved Cyril into the grass and the wildflowers as he shot up, pushing himself on his uninjured leg with his right arm outstretched to deflect something.

Cyril watched, sprawled and helpless, as Eufrates's hand was run through by a blade, pierced all the way like a threaded needle. And he watched as Atticus, disappointed, yanked the blade back and Eufrates fell to his knees in agony.

"I came back to finish you off," Atticus spat down at Eufrates. "And what do I find instead? *Two* lovebirds to stone instead of one."

Atticus did not look on the verge of death, but he did not look well. Like Eufrates, magic or not, there was only so much healing a mage could do in so little time. Sweat beaded at his brow and he was ghostly pale. His breath was laboured, like he needed to be concentrating on when to breathe in order to carry on without bursting into an airless fit. The rainwater had glossed his ruddy hair over his forehead, and he was bleeding from a cut above his brow that made him hold one eye semi-closed. Eufrates had given as good as he got, even though he ended up losing the fight. Atticus had had the benefit of magic and trickery and better armour. Eufrates had gone into a fight knowing he was bound to lose, and Cyril would give him an earful for it *later*.

The king of Cretea turned to Cyril.

"Did you get bored with me so easily? I suppose your type is…" He glanced down at Eufrates, clutching his hand to his chest. "Well. See for yourself. Really, Cyril, you should have stayed with me."

"It was never an option," Cyril said through gritted teeth. He got to his feet and held his hands out at his side, going through the overwhelming list of spells that lived in his mind. He truly wasn't very good at reacting.

Atticus sneered at him. "Big talk for someone who's failed to undo my pattern. You are here, and I can still feel it in my blood."

Cyril took a step back and Atticus advanced on him. This was good. It was getting him away from Eufrates, bit by bit. "I am not destroying anything, Atticus. I would have a word with your fiancée."

Atticus blanched. The violet rings around his eyes grew darker. *He* understood the situation immediately. He lunged at Cyril just as Cyril began to weave a spell, *any* spell, to push him back, but Cyril was not a trained duellist, and Atticus was.

He did not strike Cyril with the sword, though. Instead, he had a spell of his own. It must have been the only offensive spell the king knew, but it was the only one he needed. He could not reach Cyril at the distance they were standing, not in time, not physically, but he could cast.

Cyril's hands seized and cramped up, balling painfully into fists against his will. It felt like they were wrapped in gauze, layers and layers of it, he could not flex or contract his fingers. He could not weave.

That was when Atticus unsheathed his sword again, ready to have Cyril at the other end. But that is also when the constant rumble underground came to a crescendo, building faster and faster to a peak.

The garden shook around them. The earth cracked, soil was displaced, trees were felled. It had been a massive pattern, and it would have massive consequences. But it was far enough away that they did not have to run from it.

Yet.

Atticus screamed. It was a grotesque, angry scream, inhuman and feral like a wounded beast. Immediately, he lunged for Cyril again, but Eufrates stepped in front of him, sword out this time, and even with his hand as mutilated as it was, he managed to parry the blow before his legs buckled and he fell to one knee.

"You think you will get away with what you've done?" Atticus roared. "I will kill the both of you. You, Eufrates, the crazed tyrant, poisoned by weakness, and your powerless little *pet* will be reunited only by the Undertaker."

He held his sword up like an executioner ready to behead, frenzied and convulsive. Cyril had no magic to fix this. He would have no magic to salvage it if it came to pass. For a moment, time stopped.

They kept putting themselves in front of each other. Self-sacrificing in the name of love, in the name of family. That is what he was about to do. He was about to let Atticus tear out his throat with his blade if it meant Eufrates got to live, but his blood was boiling. He was angry and afraid and desperately determined.

He did not want that. He did not want to fall on the sword for Eufrates, but he did not want him dead either. He wanted them *both* to live.

It was a wild, foreign feeling, but it had been building up within him ever since he woke up in that clearing again, bleary, confused and *hopeful*. Setting things right didn't *have* to mean self-sacrifice. It just had to mean he would do anything within his power to get exactly what he wanted. What they *all* wanted. This sudden, brazen selfishness was the driving force that made him push his husband away and lumber towards Atticus himself.

He had promised he would save everyone. *Everyone* he had failed to save the first go around. He could do it. The thrumming in his chest, the overwhelming sensation that filled and fuelled him, be it mania or courage, had him convinced he could.

He was going to save *everyone* he held dear.

Including himself.

TWENTY-FOUR

Cyril had never thrown a punch before.

Surprising, yes, but the occasion never came up. He knew the basics of it, though. He had seen it done. He understood the theory behind it, the *gist* of the movement. And his hands had been balled into fists for him, so he did not even have to worry about that part.

Cyril threw his weight forward, between Eufrates and Atticus. He had not used any magic, because he couldn't, but it still felt as though time slowed to a snail's crawl. He could feel somewhere in his body that he was doing this wrong. It was going to end up in injury.

But it was not going to end up in *death*.

Before Atticus could even begin to pull the momentum to swing his sword, Cyril's fist was flying towards his face. He felt his shoulder snap strangely as the blow connected, hitting Atticus hard and square in the jaw. He was sure some of his fingers had broken against the bone. He had put so much force into the blow, it sent Atticus reeling back, sword useless at his side as he fell backwards into the mud. Cyril only didn't fall himself because Eufrates held him back by his shirt, preventing him from landing on their assailant.

Belatedly, as he steadied his feet into the wet soil, he realised he had been screaming the entire time.

Atticus looked at him like he was gazing upon something unknowable. At least for a second, before he spat out a bloodied tooth – a front one, Cyril remarked with some pride – and shot him an incredulous, wicked snarl.

"I see. You've bought yourself some ti–"

He was interrupted – *all* of them were interrupted, really, by a flash of golden light, as though the sun itself had manifested within the garden and exploded into glimmering, blinding particles. Cyril could have sworn it stopped raining in that moment, too, but he could not be sure. He shut his eyes tight as soon as the light became too much to bear and shielded his face with both arms, as though he would be buffeted back by some invisible force.

A second or two passed. Cyril heard footsteps stirring the grass and felt a hand on his waist, reassuring, but impatient. It took the unused sword fastened at his hip from him with practiced ease.

"Oh, what? This one's so *light*! What am I meant to do with this?"

Cyril opened his eyes immediately, because it was *her*. She was standing next to him, in front of him, her full half-a-head-taller height towering over Cyril's frame. She was looking back at her brother with the sword brandished in one hand.

Eufrates gaped for a moment before he finally said, "I had to give him something he could *use*, Tig."

Tigris examined the blade, held it up to look down its handle as though appraising fine jewellery. She held it out to Atticus with a contented smile. It would do.

"Did you miss me?" she purred.

She was in her gown from that wedding dinner, still. It was soaked through with rainwater and clung to her body, wrapping around it. She looked ridiculous, but not even a hat made of fine, garish feathers could stop Tigris from cutting the most intimidating image he'd ever seen at that moment.

The sky had begun falling upon them again. The rain formed a halo around her head that made her look divine. She advanced on Atticus when she did not hear an answer.

Atticus, regaining his senses, got to his feet and drew his sword, pointing it at her with the same fervour as if he were trying to banish an evil spirit.

"It was a mistake for you to return to that form. I had planned to kill you quietly, but now I can rip you apart alongside your pathetic retinue."

"You know what I've always hated about you, Atticus?" She sliced a diagonal across his breast that he just barely parried away. "You talk too much."

"Airheaded *bitch*," he spat.

"Snivelling rat."

It was like she had trained to fight in a wet evening gown, in a field of flowers during an oncoming storm. Any disadvantage she might have had being trapped inside the body of a cat for so long was cancelled out by her vim and vigour in the face of Atticus's failing health and frayed sanity. She cut and flourished at him like a predator playing with its food. It was not a matter of *if* she would manage to best him, but *when* and *how*.

Cyril watched their one-sided duel, hands still glued into those pathetic little fists, his left one now tinted with blood from Atticus's jaw. He could not believe he was, just a moment ago, fully intent on going to try and fight, but he was elated he had bought time until a true dashing hero arrived.

The fight did not last any longer than two minutes. Atticus did not have the stamina and Tigris looked like she was growing bored of the uneven match. She disarmed him. Then, without a single word of goodbye to the man she had been about to marry, for the *coup-de-grâce* she stuck him through the throat with Cyril's sword.

He collapsed onto his back with a dull, wet sound, spasming, fighting to pluck the weapon from himself. His hands trembled, his whole body shook. Cyril watched his mouth open and close, gurgling horribly and noiselessly through the sound of rainfall until it stopped.

When he was dead, on the ground in a pool of his own blood and the sword still pinning his neck, she turned to the two of them, Cyril and Eufrates, staring wide-eyed back at her.

"That wasn't quite the tone I wanted to set for my first day as queen, but I don't dislike it," she said.

Cyril ran to her. He wrapped his arms around her shoulders in an embrace and she picked him up and swung him a full turn before she let him down again.

"Oh, I have been wanting to do that for *days*!" Tigris beamed.

"Tig!" he said, and stepped back to truly look at her. "I am so happy to see you!"

Tigris wrapped a fond arm around his shoulders and drew them together, pressing her forehead to his.

She murmured, "Cy, that was the worst fucking punch I've ever seen in my life."

Cyril let out a bubble of laughter that nearly had him doubled over.

She went to her brother next, who was still kneeling on the ground, frozen as though he still had no idea if any of this were real or if his head had truly been lopped off in combat and he was in the middle of delusions of victory. As if to prove him wrong she hugged him so tight that Cyril could see him try to push her away after a few moments.

Tigris helped him to his feet and Cyril ran after her to help. They each took one of Eufrates's arms and hoisted him up. The wound on his chest, the most dangerous one, still held fast to its makeshift stitching, so he was no longer in danger of bleeding out. But when he stood up, he wobbled on unsteady legs and his eyes screwed shut, fighting off a dizzy spell.

Tigris ripped off a section of her dress to wrap it around the hole in his hand while Cyril held him upright.

"Can you walk?" he asked, looking down at the wound on Eufrates's thigh.

Eufrates nodded. "It is not a deep wound. I am only lightheaded from the bloodletting, but I will recover in a moment."

Cyril was about to lead him further into the garden, to sit under a copse of trees and rest, but Tigris grabbed both their arms and pulled him towards the palace gates instead.

"Oh, no," she said. "We need to get out of here."

Cyril tilted his head at her. "Why?"

She opened her mouth to answer, but she did not need to. The rumbling of the earth they had experienced before returned anew. This time, though, it opened cracks in the soil, and churned it so badly Cyril's feet began to sink into the mud.

Under Tigris's guidance, they took off running.

TWENTY-FIVE

The entire palace was crumbling around them. The earth quaked, causing pillars to strain overhead. Wooden floor splintered into slats and fragmented chips, the ceiling cracked ominously over their heads and they were just barely staying ahead of it.

All but one of them.

Eufrates lingered behind, failing to disguise his limp and an inability to run at full speed through his injuries. Even Cyril, who on a good day ran as fast as a courtier on a leisurely stroll, was outpacing him.

"Eufrates!"

He was about to double back, help Eufrates out under threat of both of them being crushed by debris, but a rush of golden-orange and dark brown hues flew past him. Before he knew what was happening, Tigris had thrown her brother over her shoulder and was running back to him, keeping with his pace. Eufrates was half a head taller than her, but she carried him like she would a sack of barley.

"I have always wanted to do this," she said brightly.

Cyril merely blinked at her, trying to conserve breath as they ran.

"Granted, I thought the one I would be picking up was you," she added.

Eufrates grumbled from her shoulder. "Tig, if you tell anyone about this–"

"Who will I *not* tell?!"

As they made it to the great hall of the palace, Cyril wheezing with exertion, he began to feel confident enough that they would make it out of this alive and unsplattered that he could speak.

"Tig, I... what *happened*? How are you...?"

He had not released her spell, though he had every intention of doing so once she was out of range of the web (he had not entirely thought of how on earth he would time this out, but, at the time, as far as he was concerned, a Shoestringed Tigris was still much safer than a vulnerable human one). Tigris had apparently somehow managed to get herself out of it on her own. He was eternally grateful for the stroke of luck, but curiosity burned a hole in his gut.

Then, he blinked, suddenly hit by a stroke of insight. "Did you destroy my *pattern*?" He balked.

Any gratitude he held for her cooled in a blaze of alarm. Certainly, it was not as grandiose as Atticus's web, but the combination of both his and Heléne's spells had the deadly potential to backfire so stupendously he was agog over the fact that Tigris still had all her limbs accounted for.

Tigris, seeing the shock bloom on his face, vehemently shook her head to dispel his theory. "What? No! Though, I'll admit, I did *try* it."

"*Tig*," he said urgently.

"What?" Eufrates, who looked a fright balancing precariously on his sister's broad shoulders, helplessly craned his neck to partake in their exchange. "What's happened? What's she done?"

"Nothing!" Tigris protested.

"At *best* you could be missing an eye!" Cyril said, then turned to Eufrates. "Your *sister* is playing fast and loose with the most dangerous manipulations of magic."

"I *said*," Tigris snapped, scowling deeply. "That I *tried* to destroy the pattern. I was not given the chance. Frankly, I thought *you* had done it, Cy."

Cyril shook his head, slowly, despite the punishing pace at which they ran. "I couldn't. My hands were bound."

"Is *that* why you resorted to pugilism?"

"Yes, yes, this will be a very good and very funny story to tell once we *make it out of here.*"

"Well." Tigris sniffed, almost petulant over not having been believed. "I didn't break the spell. And you know I'm telling the truth, because I'd be boasting about it otherwise."

That *did* make sense. Tigris was not a humble woman. If she had managed to outweave – in the *loosest* of ways – the self-proclaimed 'greatest mage of his generation', she would be screaming it from rooftops for years to come.

"Then... what was it?" Cyril couldn't help but ask, even though his lungs felt like they'd catch fire.

Tigris pursed her lips, in true and genuine search of a satisfactory answer that wasn't 'I don't know'. Finally, she said, "You'll remember whenever you asked me how it felt to be in that body."

He nodded. "Uncomfortable. It was a mystery to me as well, if I'll be honest. I wish I could have done something."

"Not just *uncomfortable*. Well, perhaps at first, yes. It was *just* discomfort. And sometimes, when we were in Cretea, or when you'd gone to see Eufie, it was even tolerable.

"But there were moments when – oh, I can't think of a better way to describe it. I was being *rejected*. Like I was some virulent thing that had no business being inside Shoestring. And not only that but it also felt like I was being *pushed* out. Like there was something that was meant to take my place, but couldn't, because I had made myself at home. Truly, it was one of the worst things I'd ever felt. Like being trapped inside an ever-shrinking cage, waiting to be spat out in one piece or multiple."

Cyril had slowed his pace to listen to her speak. Both of them had slowed, really, being well enough out of danger. And though the strain of contorting himself was too much for Eufrates's current condition, it was clear he was listening just as intently.

It would be too much to hope. Too big an ask.

Tigris continued. "At the very end, when I was running and running and running towards you, when I saw you defencelessly run into a man's sword, I wished very hard that there were *anything* I could do to prevent it.

"But there wasn't. You hobbled –" ("*hobbled?*") "– your way directly into Atticus's face with your fist and it was *so* stupid, but it wasn't..." Here, she hesitated. Suddenly at a loss for words, breathing shallowly as she jogged through the palace's pebbled entryway.

"It wasn't surrender," Eufrates said.

Both Cyril and Tigris turned to him. He had settled precariously on Tigris's shoulders as though this wasn't highly humiliating. Neither one would mock him with how serious he looked.

Ironically, Cyril thought he appeared very regal.

"Cyril." Eufrates looked at him. "I've seen you throw yourself recklessly into danger. My spies in Farol told me, days before I was transported back, that you had been drawing circles on the ground with your own blood. You *ran into my sword*. Do not think any of us forget the day you went into the woods, a *child*, with the sole purpose of dying quietly like an aging dog.

"That was different. Had Tigris not shown up to save us all, you looked like you would have thrown inadequate punch after punch until you had bought enough time to escape."

"I wanted you to live," Cyril said in a very small, very self-conscious voice.

"You wanted *you* to live."

Tigris clapped him on the shoulder, light, but firm, like she'd done a thousand times before in their youth. "You wanted all of us to live."

"I cannot think of a more soulful thing than the absolute zest for life," Eufrates finished his thought.

It was too much, all at once, to be laid so bare by his friends. By his *love*. He did not know whether to feel proud or mortified. He would surely have to return to Farsala immediately to share with his aunt the happy news that perhaps he *wasn't* a shambling, empty ghoul personified.

Yet, it did not entirely make sense. Tigris had escaped her prison, true. She had returned to her rightful body.

He looked around, as though he had just missed him. As though if he squinted very hard, he would find he had been stalking them all along, dashing through pillars and jumping off debris.

"Shoestring?"

Cyril had meant to make a full sentence out of it, but his breath was already coming up short from his overtaxed lungs. Tigris's face fell.

"I... that is the other thing. I told you I'd felt like a parasite sometimes, in that body. As though it were trying to get me to leave it. Those last few moments the feeling got so bad I *had* to escape. It was like it was trying to *expel* me. I did not realise it was because it was going to disappear."

He was silent a moment. Stinging pricked at the corners of his eyes, but he blinked it back. He felt a warm hand on his face and was surprised to see it wasn't Tigris, but Eufrates, who had reached for him as they were running alongside each other.

Cyril looked at both Margraves and smiled. "It is alright. I am lucky I had that stupid cat as long as I did."

He would miss Shoestring. He would miss him as anyone would miss a part of their soul, even if that wasn't what the animal was anymore. But he wasn't alone. He was not desperate for connection, as he was in that cottage, and mad and suicidal. Shoestring had served his purpose for him. He was a crutch Cyril had carried for years, giving him an excuse to stay alive despite his uneasy temperament. He did not need an excuse anymore. He *wanted* this life, very desperately.

It felt right that he was being made to let Shoestring go. Perhaps losing a familiar did not necessarily mean losing one's essence. Perhaps, sometimes, it meant outgrowing who you were.

The stables were mercifully unaffected by the earthquake by the time they got there. Titania would not be enough for the three of them and, besides, Tigris wanted to set all the horses free.

She took another mare for herself, who she declared to be her second favourite after Titania and, as she did not know this one's name, she started calling it Shoestring. Cyril wasn't sure if the noble steed was very content with its new name, but he appreciated the gesture anyway.

Tigris took the newly named Shoestring, a tawny mount with a silvery white mane, and she helped Cyril and her brother onto their trusty Titania. Cyril held the reins, despite Eufrates's meek protests that he was perfectly hale to ride. After some discussion, the prince grudgingly wrapped his arms around Cyril's waist and let him steer.

Cyril was exhausted. He did not have it in him to perform the same miracle that had made their horse fly its way to their destination mere hours ago, so they rode fast, but not paranormally. The full brunt of the storm that had threatened them before finally thundered around them and at least Cyril still had the magic to shield them from that.

Despite the weariness, he still needed to keep vigilant. Eufrates was behind him, burning up from his injuries, and he would not let the man fall asleep. He had never before been grateful for the insomnia that had plagued him most his life, but now, red-eyed and alert, he thanked it every time he felt Eufrates loosen his grip on his waist or slump into his back. They had come this far together; he would not let the man's demise be by falling off a moving horse.

They did not speak as it would've worn them out far too much, but Cyril hummed to him to keep his attention. It was one of Eufrates's own compositions. A favourite of his, that he had written before they were even engaged. It was esoteric. About a dandelion that grew inside a stone tower and lit up every corner of the drab, frightening place as though it emitted a light of its own. The singer wanted to pluck it and keep it for themselves, but they knew it was not their place.

In retrospect, Eufrates had been very brazen with this one, and Cyril had been very oblivious not to understand.

He heard Eufrates croak a couple of lines from the song alongside the melody in his rough, unpolished baritone. Then, he felt him lean his face against his hair.

"I will die a million deaths before I let go of you again," he murmured against Cyril's ear.

Cyril's heart beat faster in his chest and he missed a note in the song. It did not matter. He urged the horse to move faster and smiled.

"No one is dying today, darling."

Once again, they returned to Farsala at dusk, rain-soaked and weary from the journey. Cyril could not believe it had been a mere twenty-four hours since he broke into Eufrates's study and walked into the end of his sword. It felt as though the events of the day had happened over the span of *weeks*, not a few precious moments of daylight followed by pouring skies.

It was at least a small blessing that, as they were riding closer to the palace, the weather changed from heavy and ominous to gently overcast, with pink skies and orange clouds hovering overhead. The wind from the journey that had whipped at their hands and faces had also managed to dry them out sufficiently that they were not dripping water onto the frozen courtyard of the palace grounds.

Cyril wanted more than anything to crawl into his bed and collapse from exertion, but there was work to be done. He gave Eufrates over to Tigris for safekeeping and had them stand aside as he delved into the bowels of the palace dungeons in search of the miasmic weave cloistering his home.

He found his answer in an emptied cell. The miasma had been delivered by an invasive species of rat, known for their diminutive size and nimble bodies, found just on the border between the two kingdoms. The rats seemed to have died as soon as their grim work was done. The dungeons had not held proper captives in some time – there were jailhouses in the city for that effect – but there were still guards and servants who maintained its upkeep and he'd needed to sidestep their pockmarked bodies in his search. Cyril was not a particularly religious man, but he hoped the casualties of the day found peace wherever they were meant to go. He did not dare get close to the corpses, did not want to disturb their eternal sleep, but he knew Tigris would make sure everyone who deserved them would receive the proper burial rites.

It weighed him down all over again, seeing the destruction wreaked by Atticus, but he persevered. He reached up to touch the strands, untangling them one by one. He was at it for at least an hour, handling the pattern so delicately he felt like he was sitting at a loom. Instead of putting together a fine tapestry, though, he was tearing it apart, string by microscopic string. Dismantling the portrait of destruction etched upon it.

When he was done, he went upstairs, all the way up, to the topmost tower, where Heléne still stood stock still in the middle of her cast. Very gently, Cyril dispelled his own magic upon her and the palace, and guided her hands so she could put a stop to hers.

He told her, briefly and breathlessly, that they had succeeded. More importantly, though, he told her about Eufrates. Heléne was not a physician by trade, but she was superior to him by far, and she did not have all the magic in her body sapped over the course of a full, arduous day. She would be able to right him as he could not.

He would tell her of Shoestring later, when his lungs and his throat hurt just a little less, but he was eager to do so, beaming with pride that he had not turned out to be her misery after all.

As though reading his thoughts, Heléne brought a hand to his cheek, tender and parental, and kissed him on his brow. It was an expression of love so rare and so unconditional that, had Cyril not sworn off reckless ideation, he would think that he could die right then, completely content.

Then, she ordered him to retire to his room.

Cyril did as he was told, with no desire or energy to change into sleeping clothes or wash himself. As soon as his head hit the pillow, he was gone.

TWENTY-SIX

Later, he was told he slept for seven days and seven nights. He did not doubt it at all. He felt very much like a princess in a storybook, if the princess had blood on her clothes and had not washed her hair in days.

When he woke up, though, someone had cleaned and dressed him. A small mercy.

A greater mercy, still, was that Eufrates was by him. It seemed he had managed to find enough space on Cyril's horribly cluttered floor to fit a bedroll, which Cyril spotted out of the corner of his eye. It was light out, though, and Eufrates was awake, sitting in a chair waiting patiently for him to wake up.

Cyril had not dreamt at all those last few unconscious days, but if he had, he was sure his dreams would be plagued by worry over what became of his husband.

To see him again was a great relief. Eufrates did not look the picture of health. He had bruises all over the exposed skin on his arms and collarbone, and there was a cut above his brow that Cyril had not noticed before, along with the heavily bandaged hand, but he was *fine*. He was recovering. He was clean and freshened up and his eyes no longer weighed heavy with sleeplessness. When Cyril opened his eyes, his beautiful lips split into a genuine smile.

"Welcome back, my love."

Cyril sat up so quickly he saw stars behind his eyelids. He

steadied himself with his hands on his thighs just as Eufrates braced to catch him if he swooned.

"Eufrates... oh, it is so good to see you."

"Your aunt told me you were unharmed. The overexertion had drained you and you needed rest. But I needed to make sure you did not pass away in your sleep." Eufrates's smile melted into a sheepish grin.

"Tantie... she is alright? She took care of you?"

Eufrates nodded. "Aunt Heléne will outlive all of us if we are not careful. And I have not felt better in some time."

Cyril had been so worried about Eufrates, it was only very belatedly that he noticed something about him had changed.

"Oh, no," he said. His hands flew up to his own jaw and he was genuinely dismayed. "You've shaved!"

Eufrates blinked at him. "Pardon?"

"Oh, darling, it is such a shame! You looked so much more dashing!"

"*Dashing*!" Eufrates brought his own hand up to stroke at his shaved chin. "Where is this coming from? You'd liked my beard trimmed, hadn't you?"

Embarrassed by the outburst, Cyril brought his knees up to his chest and hid his face behind them. "We had just started courtship... I did not want to offend." He paused. "But oh, I am sorry, Eufrates, I did always prefer the rugged look."

Eufrates regarded him for a long while before he burst into laughter, clutching at his stomach.

"That is so like you, I cannot possibly be offended *now*!"

"You do not *have* to—"

Eufrates waved a hand in front of him. "It is no trouble. It has always been a great hassle to maintain this shorter style. And now that I no longer have to keep up appearances..."

Cyril tilted his head. "How do you mean?"

"Ah, yes. You've been comatose."

"Because I saved your life, mind you—"

"I know, my love." Eufrates got up from the chair. He took the two steps required to close the distance between them and sat next to him on the bed. Then, he took Cyril's hand and kissed his knuckles. "Thank you."

Cyril flushed a deep pink. "You are... distracting me."

Eufrates rolled his eyes. "You make me sound so calculating." He sighed. "I have abdicated from royalty."

Cyril froze. He could not have heard that right. He did not believe it was even possible for him to *do* that. "You've...?"

"I asked Tigris if I could spend some quality time in the dungeons instead, as penitence for my horrendous stint as regent, but she denied my request so instead, well... I am no longer prince. I am barely a courtier, come to think of it."

"What... what does that mean?"

"It means I no longer have any claim to the Margrave wealth and privileges and, more importantly, it means I cannot inherit the throne. Even if my sister passed away childless, the title would go to a distant relative. I am unfit to rule."

Cyril understood his decision. He truly did. It was the kind of thing he expected Eufrates would do, if he knew it was an option, but that did not stop him from feeling melancholy for him. He was sure it was not an easy choice.

"...What will you do?"

"Well..."

Eufrates raised his right hand, the one that was not holding Cyril's, and he saw, finally, how it trembled just from the effort of keeping the fingers outstretched. Even after a week, the limb was still heavily bandaged.

"Auntie has said that it is nerve damage. It will heal with time, with practice, but it may never be the same."

Cyril looked at the way Eufrates's fingers jerked when he tried to wave them about.

"That is..."

"It's my dominant hand, yes. Silly to try and stop a sword with the other one."

He was crestfallen on Eufrates's behalf. So devastated his shoulders shook and he squeezed Eufrates's other hand tight, throat swelling with emotion. "What will you do? How will you write? *Play*?"

Eufrates gave him a fond smile. He kissed his brow and when he spoke there was an optimism in his voice that Cyril had not heard in years. "Cyril, my love, I have two hands. And I have an inordinate amount of time at my disposal from now on, after my disgraceful exit from politics. I shall have to learn my craft once more."

He was still unconvinced. "Do you – do you at least want me to – I could fix your room!"

Eufrates silenced him with another kiss, on his lips this time. He really did miss the beard. "It is not my room. I no longer live here, though I have been graciously allowed to stay until I can find a new home."

"Your instruments–"

"Cyril!" Eufrates was laughing – *laughing*! – at him. "Fine. If you insist, I believe I should be able to learn the fiddle quickest with my left hand. Fix it for me, please."

"I will fix all of them," Cyril huffed.

"I will not have learned much of a lesson that way."

"The fiddle and the lute and the viol and… and the harp. That is my favourite. And I will help heal your hand."

"Mm? How shall you do that?"

"There must be a way. I will ask a physician."

Eufrates's lips spread into a grin. "Are you to be my private attendant, Cyril?" He leaned in close to plant kisses down from his jaw, slowly, to his neck.

Cyril was easily lost to the touch. He melted under Eufrates's tenderness, and threw his arms around him to pull him closer, wrapping them together in an embrace that made his skin catch fire. He had not felt like this in so long: he could not believe he had ever given it up.

"Is he finally awake?!"

Tigris was at the door, braced against its hinges like she had just grinded to a halt from a dead sprint.

"I heard voices!" she said and entered the room without leave to sit on the other side of Cyril's bed. In the meantime, Eufrates had put some distance between them, much to his chagrin.

"She has come here every two to three hours since your collapse," Eufrates murmured in his ear. "It's like she doesn't have any duties."

Tigris, who had heard every word, shot her brother a scowl and pulled Cyril by the arm to her own side of the bed, so she could properly fuss over him.

"I am a new queen! It has been a very fraught transition; I am allowed to take breaks!"

Cyril's eyes lit up. "You've been crowned?"

"Oh, yes." She grinned. "Almost immediately. Oh, Cy, it has been such a mess! I shall tell you all about it once you are better rested and sworn in."

He blinked. "Sworn? In?"

"As grand mage! Auntie has been filling in for you, but she is so mean! And how she criticises! I think she is getting too old for the job."

"I... Tig, I cannot possibly. Eufrates has resigned, I believe I should also–"

"Perhaps!" she cut him off. "Perhaps both of you should leave me alone with the weight of a kingdom on my girlish, delicate shoulders!"

Cyril glanced at her shoulders, which were neither girlish nor delicate.

"Tig..." he said.

"But!" She grinned devilishly at him and patted his cheek. "Eufrates was just a common prince..."

"Still here, Tig," Eufrates said from his half of the bed. She waved him away as though he were a fly.

"You, however, are the greatest wizard of your time! I would be a fool to allow you to retire, even if it's how you've decided to self-flagellate. You are an asset too valuable to lose."

"You will not give me a choice?" Even as he said this, a smile threatened to tug at his lips.

"If you start any kind of descent into nihilism, I will personally smack you upside the head, how does that sound?"

"It sounds like I have to obey my queen."

"A quick study! Very good!"

Eufrates cleared his throat. "Will I get *any* time with my husband, dear sister?"

Tigris sniffed at him and wrapped an arm around Cyril's shoulder. "Perhaps if you had decided to stay in the palace. Besides, as far as the law is concerned, you two are not married. It is improper for a commoner to be so close to my mage."

Cyril gave her a wry look. "You are being so mean to your brother."

"Am I? Is he even my *brother* anymore?"

"Oh, don't *sulk*, Tigris. It's unbecoming," said Eufrates.

"Children, please," Cyril chided. "I love you both equally."

"That had better not be true," Eufrates murmured close to his ear, just as Tigris shot him a wild grin.

Cyril let out a theatrical sigh. "Very well. I love you both," he said, making sure to emphasise the retraction.

"She will get over it once she realises it means she will be able to get out of the palace every so often to visit me," said Eufrates.

Tigris perked up, just slightly, but she said nothing as she leaned her cheek upon Cyril's shoulder.

"Speaking of marriage, Tig," he continued, breaking into a Cheshire grin. "How has it been going with *all* your new suitors?"

Tigris blanched. "You are so right, Eufie. I am a very busy woman."

She planted a quick kiss on Cyril's cheek and absconded like a ghost, bidding them a curt goodbye from the door. Cyril gave Eufrates a confused look.

Eufrates shrugged. "It turns out, even if you murder your fiancée, a foreign king, with your bare hands, if you are Queen Tigris Margrave, you are still in very high demand. She has had to beat the suitors off with a stick. Says they give her nightmares."

"Has she soured on the idea of marriage, then?"

"Ha. I do not think she wants to think about it for quite some time. Besides, do you remember the Cretian butler?"

Cyril's brows rose well into his forehead. "Miranda?"

"Mm. Unfortunately for Tig, she was not the guileless accessory to King Atticus's schemes that my sister secretly hoped for. I have heard it is difficult to pine for a war prisoner."

He had to pretend *very* hard not to be delighted by this piece of gossip. "What *war*?" he said. "At worst, it was conspiracy."

Eufrates cocked his head to one side and seemed to truly consider this. "You've got a point."

Cyril laughed, holding a hand up to his lips, and shifted next to Eufrates on the bed. He let the warm, comfortable silence fill any spaces between them before he spoke again, making his tone overly casual even as he traced the band under his nightshirt with his thumb.

"Do you think *we* ought to? Get married again?"

"Mm…" Eufrates thought about it. Or, perhaps, pretended to think about it. "I don't know. It's such a hassle."

It seemed the unspoken agreement was to be very cavalier.

"It is! And we are so *old*!" Cyril said.

"Very old," Eufrates chuckled.

The door to his room burst open again with an ear-shattering bang. Tigris was back. Tigris, most likely, had not left. He hoped she had heard every word of their conversation and that her ears burned scarlet.

"If the pair of you imbeciles don't get married again, I am going to make unwed public affection *illegal*! I will lock you in prison! I will throw away the key!"

"Would we be sharing a cell?" Cyril asked.

"*No!*"

Cyril looked at Eufrates, who was returning his gaze. They held the stare for a long moment before the two of them burst into hysterics.

The next few days were ones reserved for Cyril to play a game of catch-up with the court. Despite Tigris's fervent insistence, she made sure he was well-rested and sound of mind when he told her he was ready to take on responsibilities as her mage. He only truly inherited Heléne's title after a gauntlet of proving to her he was ready and eager for the job.

He did not, however, inherit her tower. The top floor felt isolating and, frankly, a bit intimidating. He liked his quarters just fine, and he would have access to Heléne's vast studies whenever he wished. Besides, what kind of monster would displace an old woman from her home?

Once he was settled with his position, Tigris finally let him into the workings of their court. He had been dying with curiosity over why they were not under siege at this very moment by a handful of Cretea's allies and, as it turned out, once she had destroyed the pattern that held that kingdom together (the better part of it a series of enchantments captivating most of the region's magical talent), a bevy of mages had come forward before a grand court to testify against the wicked, conniving King Atticus.

Tigris herself had managed to spin the tale so she was a damseled fiancée who had stumbled upon her husband-to-be's plans and fought to put a stop to them. Cyril did not know what kind of damsel trounced her affianced so humiliatingly in combat, but he would not contradict her story even under knifepoint.

They were using Farsalan funds to help rebuild Cretea's palace and restore their government to some sort of order, which seemed to be appeasing to all. Cyril wondered why there were a lot more inhabitants wandering the halls of the palace, too, until he was finally told any displaced stragglers who presented themselves to Tigris would receive asylum within her walls.

Cyril thought this very generous, for a first decree. But with so many new mages wandering about, he checked every nook and cranny of the pattern every single day to an overzealous degree. He would make the rounds of the palace grounds and by the time he was finished, half the day had been spent in diligent surveillance.

It meant he did not get to see Eufrates nearly as much as he would have liked, which vexed him very much. But not nearly as much as it vexed Eufrates himself, who scheduled a most embarrassing audience with the queen to demand Cyril get at least one day off a week (though could it truly be considered a day off when he went seamlessly from being monopolised by one Margrave sibling to the other?).

He had been in the great hall when it happened, and Cyril heard the entire thing. He had to, mortified, with his hands covering his face, watch the Margraves squabble over custody of his time.

For his part, Eufrates took whatever he could salvage from his room and found a guest chamber to stay in until he had a more permanent place to stay. Cyril insisted if he wanted to see him so badly, he should simply stay in *his* apartments in the tower.

"If you let me into your rooms, I will make sure you never leave them," Eufrates had said to him, looking as pleased with himself as a well-fed cat.

Cyril, red-faced and flustered, told him he was much too old to be talking like that.

Despite all their put-upon, grousing insistence that they were already bound together and there really was no need for any kind of ceremony, Tigris did manage to drag him and Eufrates to the altar, in the end. Their first wedding had been bombastic. A state affair. A royal wedding fit for a king, but it was not what either of them had truly wanted.

Cyril and Eufrates were married in a quiet ceremony, with a handful of trusted palace-dwellers present and their family: Heléne and Tigris.

It turned out to be the happiest day of Cyril's life, and not just because he could finally get that damned ring off his neck and onto his finger where it belonged.

Eufrates, who had never taken his off, watched in amusement as Cyril struggled with the string around his neck, sure at any moment it would strangle him even as it offered no resistance. In retrospect, the fact that *Eufrates* had never removed his wedding band should have been the dead giveaway Cyril needed to know that no ridiculous, lovesick spell would bind them more tightly in adoration than what they already held for each other.

As a wedding gift, Tigris offered them an indiscriminate plot of land. She did not specify where, and Eufrates was immediately paralysed by choice, despite his grand musings of a cabin by the sea. But for once, Cyril's eyes lit up with the rare certainty that he knew exactly what to do.

On a sunny, summer morning, a day after they had returned from their honeymoon in Farol (which was much more vibrant and picturesque when it was not horribly cursed), Cyril led Eufrates out into the woods, past a copse of trees, a babbling brook with three rocks to cross it and into a clearing dappled by sunlight and wildflowers. With them, they carried barrels of salt, as it was impossible to draw upon grass with chalk and blood would be very inappropriate for the occasion.

Eufrates watched, practicing his left-handed fiddle as Cyril meticulously salted the soil with a circular design. It took him an hour to get it right, which was good. He had cut down his time quite significantly since the last magic circle he'd drawn.

Then, he ran to Eufrates's side and held him by the arm, urging him to watch as he set the spell alight and the ground rumbled and shook.

From the ground, sprung a small, fully formed, idyllic cottage, with a curved, chimneyed rooftop and an attached second storey that took up half the building and rounded off into a point. Its own miniature tower.

He had given it three rooms. One for the newlyweds, one for Eufrates's artistic pursuits (Cyril had a whole tower in the palace to himself, it was only fair) and another for… well. He did not know what it was for. It could be for anything, really. A guest room. Perhaps something more permanent. He thought himself silly, imagining himself a parent at his advanced age, but they were in a new world, and this was a new start. He felt younger every day.

One of the doors inside the cottage, that seemingly led to nowhere but a back wall, connected to Cyril's own study in the palace. He told this to Eufrates, who seemed instantly keen on abusing this privilege. Perhaps Cyril would look into fitting it with a key. Later. In the future.

Outside, there were the fixings for a garden, should they like to plant one. Cyril thought he would go into town on his day off and procure some tomato seeds. See if he could get the girth right this time. He did need a hobby now that he was not the right hand and lapdog of a horrible tyrant. (Yet. He would keep an eye out on Tigris.)

It was not the seaside cabin Eufrates had dreamed of and described to him an entire lifetime ago, but Eufrates had quickly and mercilessly discarded the idea as soon as it was made clear to him that he would need to stay close to the palace if he wanted to see his husband, the grand mage, every day. And he very much *did*. Cyril promised him many vacations to the beachside in return.

They had all the time in the world.

EPILOGUE

Just a month later, the pair of them had headed out into the woods. Cyril, in all his manias and stresses, had found that gardening soothed him and had gotten just a bit too into husbandry. He wanted to go out foraging, looking for wild mushrooms for potions and recipes. Eufrates had come along to make sure he did not step into a ditch and perish searching for a redcap in the wrong part of the forest.

Tigris's birthday was coming up, and they were debating what she would like more: a jewelled dagger or a pair of mother-of-pearl earrings. Both sides of the debate were Cyril, because his useless, unhelpful husband thought that she was the queen and she had enough material goods (and because he had written her a song like he did every single year).

Cyril did not think this was fair. They were a unit now, the least Eufrates could do was say the song was from *both* of them so he did not feel like a fool when he was outshone.

Eufrates was just on the verge of using his golden tongue to convince him that if he showed up to court with a basket of homegrown vegetables, Tigris would genuinely adore it. This was a ludicrous effort to undermine his authority with her and to get Cyril dismissed from his post and finally all to Eufrates.

He was about to point out the dastardly nature of this plan when he heard it.

It was faint and when Cyril asked Eufrates – who had a keen musician's ear – about it, he said he had not noticed it at all. But it did make sense. The sound was meant for *Cyril*. He knew it intimately and unmistakably.

Cyril shoved his wicker basket into his confused husband's arms and ran towards the noise. As it grew louder, he was more and more certain of what it was, because he had heard it so many times before. A grin, tentative and hopeful, pulled at his lips.

He was right, though. When he got close enough that even Eufrates could hear it, he knew what was waiting for him.

Cyril was hearing the smallest, most strangled and pathetic mewl imaginable.

ACKNOWLEDGEMENTS

I didn't think I was going to finish this book when I started it, let alone publish it. I've been writing and drawing comics for as long as I can remember, but there's something uniquely mortifying about prose. About how your words alone need to carry the whole work and not a part of it. Still, I wanted to give it a shot. When I started writing *Shoestring Theory*, all I had in mind was a low-commitment, deeply self-indulgent project I could pick up and put down without being beholden to any publishers or employers or, the horrors, an online audience.

The thing is, though, I love attention more than anyone I know. I think that might be one of the baseline requirements for being any sort of creative. I've never met an artist who says they create only for their own satisfaction and truly, wholeheartedly means it. So when I started flagging on the novel, when I started losing motivation, because there was no one behind me to pat me on the head and tell me I was making something worthwhile, I flogged the first ten chapters or so onto a handful of friends.

Novels are really difficult to read! Much more so than comics. They're a commitment, especially ones that haven't gone through any sort of editorial or pruning and that have ostensibly been written for the most part on an overheated iPhone in bed. My best friend was the only person to read those first chapters and to this day I think she did it out of pity, but something wonderful happened then.

She really liked it.

She told me it was worthwhile and she wanted to read more. So I wrote more and she kept up her end of the bargain. I fed Shoestring to her slowly, chapter break by chapter break, until one day I ran out of things for Cyril and Tigris and Eufrates to do. And I'd finished my first novel and I couldn't believe it.

Of course, immediately after I set it off to the side to work on my day job and didn't think about it for months until I realised it might be worth publishing. Then, I gave up on self-publishing, because it looked... really hard! And I love immediate results almost as much as I love attention.

Many rejected agent inquiries and several months later, you've consumed the product of one extremely bored evening at the international departures terminal of the LAX airport and I hope you had as much fun reading it as I did writing (and if you did, let me know!).

Shoestring Theory would not be possible without my agent, the very wonderful Christabel, who took that first chance on me. I'm equally indebted to the team at Angry Robot. To Eleanor and Des and Caroline and Amy, who feel more like a large group of friends I've greased my way into than a publishing house. It wouldn't be possible without Liz, Bev, Marty, Harriet and Emma, my dear friends who let me talk endlessly about my characters at them with what I hope was only mild irritation.

And, obviously, thank you to my patient zero and love of my life. I'm not exaggerating when I say Cyril's story would've been a faint twinkle in the back of a metaphorical drawer (I do my writing in Docs, I haven't touched a pen in years) had it not been for her. Thank you, Sloan.

Finally, thank YOU, if you've read this far. Whether you bought this book, borrowed it, found it in the gutter, or an old, mysterious hag shoved it into your hands when you passed her on the street, I am grateful to you from the bottom of my heart.

Talk to you soon,
Mariana